HUMAN STOCK

Vaughan Whitlock

Publisher: Inspiring Publishers,
P.O. Box 159, Calwell, ACT Australia 2905
Email: publishaspg@gmail.com
http://www.inspiringpublishers.com

A catalogue record for this
book is available from the
National Library of Australia

National Library of Australia The Prepublication Data Service

Author: Vaughan Whitlock
Title: Human Stock
Genre: Fiction
ISBN: 978-1-922618-85-6

Editor's Note

During the editing process of *Human Stock*, I revisited a book written by Suzette Haden-Elgin, *Native Tongue*, published by The Feminist Press, The City University of New York 1985. Where *Native Tongue* reinforces the idea of male domination and female suppression or, more accurately, a scientification of Victorian values and society, *Human Stock* visualises a world dominated by women, where men are the oppressed masses. A reversal of roles book? No; more an honest observation of trends within a selected society, the society created for this book. *Human Stock* is not sexist in the way Elgin portrays her future, nor is it a male backlash against the suggestions found in *Native Tongue*. *Human Stock* is more an exploration of an idea based on a combination of social ideas that have been with us since the birth of Science Fiction. Vaughan Whitlock has created a world where the outcome can only be the ruination of accepted social behaviour. There is horror, sex, adventure, love, hate, loss, discovery and failure in *Human Stock* but simmering beneath all this are deeper social observations. These include our inhumanity to man, our lust for power, lust for control and our inability to forgive one another for our failures.

Human Stock delivers a powerful story and one, I am sure, that will keep you thinking well past the last word.

Robert N Stephenson
February 2001

Prologue

Eight years into the third millennium, the Australian Government, increasingly alarmed by recent escalations in world conflict, had not yet conceded there was any real danger to itself or Darwin - a self-sufficient, but relatively small city with a population of just over one hundred thousand. Darwin was geographically closer to the action than the rest of Australia, but the city's isolation contributed to the feeling it was an insignificant target.

Four years ago, the Federal Government had vacillated in its reaction to aggressive warnings from Mushud Ahmed, a new Middle Eastern Islamic leader who blamed Western-aligned nations for creating the circumstances of war. Backed by nuclear, chemical and biological capability, as well as the latest conventional weapons, the threat to world peace became a harsh reality. In a resurgence of hostilities, a dramatic nuclear exchange occurred between Iran and Iraq. The Australian Federal Government - the Federals - was finally motivated into conceiving a contingency plan against world war, the Nuclear Survival Program (NSP). They called for expressions of interest for the establishment of subterranean communities that would survive if the threat became a reality.

An engineering conglomerate, having just patented three technological innovations relevant to such a project, worked around the clock to formulate a plan, enlisting its opposition as additional expertise. Together they were awarded the project and formed a joint venture, Eness Outcomes.

Sites were quickly identified throughout Australia and feasibility studies carried out. The Federal Reserve transferred a large financial package to Eness with the tacit understanding that priority would be for the major politically and commercially important cities of the southeast. But it did not eventuate that way.

The political machinery of the states bogged down in internal rivalries and confrontation with minority interest groups. The Northern Territory Administration watched the confusion mounting and swiftly prepared a scheme of its own. At the opportune moment, it presented a completed strategy that resolved all the logistical, environmental and land rights issues to do with its site, and was ready to proceed.

With a little reverse manipulation on the Federal Government, the Territory claimed the allotted funds and Eness set up on the outskirts of Darwin. The Federals' threats of legal action were futile. With finance secured, the powerful Eness, supported by a determined and committed administration, channelled all its resources to Darwin. The massive rock formations in the Northern Territory made it a favoured site geologically. Work commenced immediately.

People reacted in different ways. Superficially, the Darwin population was delighted to have the project on its doorstep. Local businesses enjoyed extra custom from an influx of workers, the electronically and technologically inclined took advantage of hi-tech expertise they could use themselves, and Eness was popular because it employed many Darwinians. Then there was the triumph the project represented in defiance of the Federal Government.

But not everyone was happy. Some remained scornful of the need for the project. Others protested about what they saw as the administration's roughshod treatment in overriding planning objections and its favouritism in the selection process as it recruited participants in the NSP. Demonstrations by protest groups were a regular feature in town and at the site. Eness and the administration ignored them. Construction was completed in three years.

Preparations for occupation intensified as the possibility of Darwin being targeted increased with the worsening world conflict.

PART 1
SURVIVING STOCK
Year 2008

Chapter 1

"Cyberspace is in front of you, not across the room, Benjamin!" the teacher said caustically. "Or perhaps your knowledge is enhanced by other interests."

She was middle-aged, plain in looks, but experienced in controlling her students. Her eyes switched to where Benjamin's attention had been diverted.

Kelly returned her look innocently, but fully aware of the reason for it. Whether she or Benjamin was caught first was a matter of chance. A ripple of amusement passed through the class of ten year-olds at the not unwelcome distraction. Benjamin and Kelly were inseparable. They had recently been shifted to desks further apart in an effort to improve their concentration.

With a frown, the teacher turned her attention on the whole class.

"There are better examples to follow than Benjamin's," she admonished. "Attend to your screens."

She returned to her own screen. Kelly stole a furtive look at Benjamin. Her mischievous smile was spontaneous and pale blue eyes captivating, warming his heart as always. He grinned, savouring a victory over boredom. Getting away with it this time, they returned to their work.

The reaction of other students was indicative of the popularity Benjamin and Kelly enjoyed. Benjamin's good looks, dark wavy hair and athletic build put him to the fore, particularly in sports. His manner was open and uncomplicated. He was academically bright as well - when his mind was focussed. Kelly, dedicated to her convictions, did well in class. She was a quiet, reserved girl, attractive, with curly blonde hair encircling a pretty face and fair complexion.

The next question came through and the soft staccato of clicking keyboards once more broke the silence. Having missed the last question, Benjamin was determined to score highly this time. Inspiration with a moment of steadying reason worked again and his fingers danced confidently over the keyboard. Better than his other muddled answers this morning. When his score came through, it was a good one, as it always was when he applied himself. But this was hard to maintain. Too many distractions on the other side of the room. And in the changes that had taken place in teaching methods, impersonal keyboard interaction lacked the stimulation of a voice or videophone. Preoccupation with the circumstances affecting Darwin was also a factor.

While the teacher was not looking, Benjamin had an opportunity to reward himself. He pressed a button at the top left of his desk, sliding the lid to one side, then transferred a coffee-flavoured lozenge from a packet in the tray to his mouth. He pressed the button again to close the lid. The lozenge nestled into one cheek, undetectable by the teacher if he was careful.

The next question was coming through. It stopped in mid-sentence. Everyone looked up. The teacher had broken off input and was standing, acknowledging the School Principal as he entered the classroom. He climbed the two steps to the platform and murmured a few words to her. He was holding a printout, which he referred to briefly, then turned to address the class.

"Please excuse the interruption," he began apologetically.

He came from an older generation, good-natured and well mannered, if somewhat pedantic. He adjusted his glasses and paused to assess the mood of the class. Upturned faces watched him in attentive silence. A personal appearance by the Principal meant this was big news.

"The time has come for those who will leave us. Participants in the NSP are to return home immediately. You have been well prepared for this and you know what to do. We have all been expecting it. The rest of us will continue as before, and we look forward to re-uniting safely at the end of the designated period. Those pre-selected for this moment, please stand."

Three responded - Kelly, Benjamin and a boy near the windows. An awkward quiet pervaded the classroom. The Principal glanced at the printout again, gave a quick nod then scrutinised each student standing.

"Please be sure to clear your desks of personal belongings and exit your screens before you leave."

Satisfied, he spoke briefly to the teacher, who responded with a half-smile. He descended the platform and departed. Kelly shot a quick look at Benjamin, winking playfully. If the teacher noticed this time, she didn't show it.

Benjamin accessed the tray in his desk again, scooped up the lozenges and dropped them into a cloth bag. He exited the screen, which slid down through a narrow slot to disappear into the desk.

He took a final look around the classroom, prepared never to see it again. Beyond Kelly, a rectangular screen filled most of the pale yellow wall. Their scores had not yet been updated, but yesterday's tally was still there. The name Benjamin Neale was just above the middle of the list. Kelly Winters was four places higher. Benjamin smiled to himself, knowing he could do better, but deep down he was proud of Kelly.

He looked to his left through the laminated double-plate windows. Outside, two classrooms were visible across a short stretch of open lawn. Several students were hurrying past, heading for the car park.

Tucking his bag under one arm, Benjamin followed the other two leaving the classroom. Despite what they faced, he felt positive, preferring it to the waiting mode that was the fate of his classmates, who generously wished them farewell and good luck. In the corridor, Kelly waited for him and they walked to the bike racks together, secure in each other's company.

"See who gets there first," Kelly goaded playfully.

Benjamin grinned. "You will. My bike is fast, but your father's car is faster. Just."

He dropped his bag into the basket on his bike and headed for the road. Kelly continued to the car park adjacent as her father pulled in. Benjamin waved and set off. Students from other schools were on the road as well. It was late morning, a hot, humid day with barely a cloud in the sky. He was wet through with perspiration, despite the easy ride. Electric cars passed regularly, looking like hooded birds-of-prey with their large solar roof panels. They glided stealth-like, sounding a thin, high-pitched whine. Since the decision to scrap vehicles dependent on fossil fuel, electric cars had become the only vehicular transport available. Most were of the same make, imported from China within the last three years.

Some older cars from the United States were still operating, but the Chinese model had been more readily available in quantity, more efficient in methanol-to-hydrogen fuel conversion and in solar battery recharge for the backup system. Difference in colour was all that alleviated their sameness. Front and back registration plates, an old system, had been modified to include a computer strip for scanner identification. Benjamin remained alert as he peddled along. The cars were not fast but numerous, and their electronic accident preventers did not preclude collisions with never altering bikes. He approached a Voader. It was barely moving. The road repairer cleaned the road then simultaneously melted and re-formed the bitumen beneath with infusion of new bitumen from a holding tank above. A smooth new surface, blending with the old, emerged ready for use. Benjamin swung out to pass, glancing at the operator, who was studying a computer screen in front of him and speaking into a videophone.

Benjamin passed the local Ditelbuy, with its colourful array of life-size digital television screens displaying products and services. Enclosed within a double-plate glass tunnel, shoppers slid past on a slow-moving platform or stood in front of the screens working their remote handsets, speaking by voicemail to product promoters and watching demonstrations. Processing and automatic deduction from the shopper's account was instantaneous upon ordering. Personal attention or reality viewing inside the building added a fifty per cent premium. Purchases were collected at the end of the tunnel. One of Benjamin's favourite places. He wondered if he would see it again.

Today, nothing appeared any different on the surface. But the underlying tension was there. Benjamin, an only child, had unusual maturity for his age. His father, a doctor, was a caring, sensitive man, at times vulnerable to the realities of life. Benjamin's mother was the quiet strength, dedicated to their well-being. Benjamin had been well loved and instructed, developing a precocious interest in human and world events through his father, who regularly cut out newspaper clippings and discussed them with him. Confidence in his ability to analyse had instilled a keen sense of justice in Benjamin. He tended to follow his own instincts.

So many children on the road provided evidence of the NSP call-up. He felt satisfied with his own fate. At last the day had come. He passed the hospital, where his father had worked till recently, then veered left. Nearly home. A neighbour greeted him as he swung round the back of an Eness Outcomes security vehicle and coasted into his front yard. An Eness officer was waiting to take over security of their home and contents. They were permitted to take only a few possessions with them.

"Hi, Mum, hi Dad!" Benjamin dismounted.

"Hello." George, at their car checking their bags, was wet with sweat. A thickset man with a slightly receding hairline, he looked older than he was. Years of hard work in Australia and overseas had taken its toll.

"How were the others at school, Benjamin?" his mother asked, as she approached. "Did they give you a good send-off? Give your bike to your father then come inside."

"Good, yes," Benjamin said quickly. His mother smiled.

Belying the urgency in her voice, Gloria was keeping calm. A diminutive woman, her contentment with life, centred on husband and son, transcended her features, making her seem more beautiful than she was. She brushed strands of sticky hair from her face.

Benjamin left his father fixing the bike to the back of the car and went into the house.

"If there's anything else you want to bring, get it now," Gloria told him.

He looked at his mother's face and saw a hint of the anxiety she was trying to hide.

He collected some personal items, a handset, a computer game and a photo of Kelly. They were ready to depart. George handed the house keys to the security officer, along with the two pagers belonging to Eness, which they no longer needed. They said goodbye to their home, as George backed the car out of the driveway.

Several streets away, another car, towing a packed trailer, was already on the way. Kelly was sitting in the back seat, her cheerful nature today not yet disturbed by her parents. But she was watchful. Lately they had been arguing more than usual.

Marcia had been an attractive woman. Her well-formed facial features, flowing red hair and a compact figure remained. However, her expression was a permanent picture of pessimism, character frailties already lining her face in early ageing. She sat fidgeting in the front passenger seat, her fingers tightly intertwined. She glanced at her husband, Alec, her thin lips pursed, eyes scrutinising.

"I hope when we get there you'll treat me with respect in front of the other women." She looked away from him as she spoke. An insecure woman prone to self-pity, she was always seeking a reason other than herself to blame for the way she felt.

Alec drove impassively, concentrating on the road ahead. He was a practical man, well suited to his profession of mechanical engineer. He looked the part; powerfully built, strong jawline and rugged, handsome features.

"That depends on you," he said softly. "I'm sure you'll find whatever you're looking for."

In the early years of their relationship, part of his attraction to her had been in complementing her insecurity. After marriage and over time, however, exasperation with her negative view of life caused his respect to dwindle steadily. Now, he was often offhand, although he kept a certain tolerance for the sake of his daughter, whom he adored.

His wife absorbed the comment and fed on it. "I know you don't care what people think of me. But we'll be living more closely with others from now on, so you can at least pretend to care."

Alec shrugged his shoulders and said nothing more. They fell into a tense silence. Marcia swung round to face her daughter, reaching over to clasp Kelly's hand. A familiar pattern. Kelly squeezed her hand in response. She had quickly learned how to perform the stabilising role.

Kelly thought of Benjamin, as she always did when pressured by her mother. She loved her father, but Benjamin was her main support. His understanding made up for the role reversal with her mother, saving her from becoming lost in an emotional wilderness. They had done everything together since starting school in the same class of five-year-olds. Each an only child, they found fulfilment in each other. Through them, their parents had met, the two families becoming attached.

Taking their place in a line of cars, the Winters family reached the turn-off just beyond the outskirts of town. Alec followed a red car. Soon the sealed side road dipped. They drove slowly down a steep cutting between high rock faces, the whistling of vehicles rising and echoing in eerie discord. They approached a high vertical rock face with an opening that was swallowing cars. The road levelled as they drove between a long, sleek transporter on one side and a concrete door on the other. An attendant directed them to a parking spot.

Alec and Marcia gathered their bags, placed them on a three-wheeled cart and joined the line of people boarding the transporter. The operation was running smoothly in an atmosphere of expectant co-operation. All knew what to do. After the psychological assessment and selection phase, months of orientation lectures and briefings had armed them with a mountain of information. Apart from a few people with direct involvement in construction and preparation, however, this was their first sight of the underground environment. Most reacted with awe at the sheer size of the space hewn out of the rock.

Inside the transporter, a light flashed and three warning beeps sounded through the cabin. The doors closed with a hiss and the driver pulled away from the parking bay. Kelly peered through the large window, looking for Benjamin and his family.

The Neales arrived as the transporter was leaving. While his parents were occupied with the bags, Benjamin drifted away from them. The cars and trailers took up only a small part of the massive space. Drums of methanol, tall stacks of batteries, a bulldozer, front loader, backhoe and crane stood to one side. Further on, he could see large covered machinery, generators, compressors, tools and appliances, dismantled windmills, lights, equipment for water treatment and methanol production. There were spare parts for everything.

"Wow!" Benjamin exclaimed, taking in the ambience of the cavern itself.

Laser sheets covered the rock surfaces in a transparent, red-tinged hue that glowed in the artificial light. Fixed by porous tubes, which collected moisture and channelled it away, the sheets kept the rock surfaces warm and dry. Batteries supplied the small amount of power needed to operate the simple but innovative system. An Eness patent. Benjamin knew about it through Kelly's father, who had been one of the privileged few NSP participants involved in the cavern's construction.

He wandered further into the rows of equipment. The full extent of the cavern was still not clear. More stockpiles, even bigger ones; bagged cement, sand, soils and fertilisers, water pipes, plumbing and electrical cable, glass, laminated plastics and building products. Benjamin stood looking up at a towering stack of boxes; a limitless supply of light bulbs.

His amazement grew. Even Kelly's father's description on top of the briefings had not prepared him for this. He headed for a pile of plastic sheet-covered furniture.

"You shouldn't be here, sonny," a man said, grabbing him lightly by the arm. The attendant led him back to the check-in point.

"Benjamin, where have you been?" his mother scolded. "The transporter is about to leave. Without you, if you don't stop day dreaming." She could not help a glint of amusement, having become used to his inquisitive tendencies.

Benjamin took a final look around. He stared agog at another Eness patent, the laser vehicles that had excavated the cavern. They were years ahead of other rock removal equipment, which still relied mainly on drilling and blasting.

"Look at them!" Benjamin again broke from the gathering group. He began circling one of the excavators. It was a simple car design modified to a short, narrow wheel-base. Perched on top was an operator's console. The main feature was a thin steel barrel, which protruded from generator-driven apparatus and could swivel to any position within a semi-circle and between the horizontal and vertical.

George followed Benjamin around the vehicle. "Maybe one day you'll see one operate, son. They're fast and precise. Up to ten were used to excavate all this. Come on now, we must hurry."

They joined the group of people, easing along beside the concrete entrance door to board the transporter. Soon it pulled away, climbing then turning onto the main road. As the transporter reached another side road, it slowed almost to a stop, hampered by a cluster of mostly young protesters wielding placards. Benjamin slid the window across and poked his head out to gain a better view.

The protesters were hurling taunts at the transporter. Police officers were restraining them. A familiar scene. But there was extra fervour amongst this lot, here to farewell the NSP group.

A scantily clad young woman thrust forward a placard: NSP DISCRIMINATES, LET GOD DECIDE. Her other arm was outstretched, pointing at a grubby-looking youth with a shock of blonde hair a few metres away. He was holding his own sign above his head: NSP DISCRIMINATES, CHOOSE ME.

Other banners read: DOWN WITH NSP, ONE FOR ALL, TOO SMALL NSP, WHAT ABOUT US?

George glanced at his wife. "They might appear antagonistic towards the program, but how many resent not being considered for it themselves?"

The transporter turned down the side road and descended a sharp decline, stopping in front of another opening in a high vertical rock face. Above the opening was a sign: NUCLEAR SURVIVAL PROGRAM Residents Only. The passengers disembarked and entered.

Benjamin and his parents presented their Australian IDs for scanning at a temporary checkpoint and joined the new underground community. People were milling about, waiting for the next stage in their new life underground. Benjamin looked for Kelly, who was hovering near the entrance. They quickly gravitated together.

"You're here at last. What took you so long?" Kelly grabbed his hand.

"I said you'd get here first." Benjamin was relieved to find her. "Where are your parents?"

"They're over there, talking with your mum and dad." Kelly pointed. "They argued again on the way over. I wish my mother could handle things better. She blames my father for feeling bad, but it's not his fault." Her eyes searched Benjamin's for comfort.

Benjamin felt for her. "Your father is strong and determined. Maybe one day things will be better."

They stood together, watching the action. Three-wheeled carts were bringing the bags in from the transporter, scooting around the perimeter of the cavern to deliver each bag to sticker-designated locations. In the centre of the arrival area was a media circus, television crews setting up lights, interviewers, cameramen, reporters and digital interactive operators on the prowl for news and any kind of intrigue or scandal. Jangling electronic music emitted from a black box at the end of a low platform adjacent to the checkpoint. An attendant spoke into the voicephone and the music instantly changed to the National Anthem, announcing the arrival of VIPs.

Fifteen dignitaries walked through the entrance, including several politicians in neatly suited attire. All eyes watched, no one spoke. The officious group climbed the platform with solemn authority and sat in simple chairs set in a line across the back. After a brief wait, the President arrived escorted by four armed soldiers in full military dress. A media scrum erupted briefly as reporters and cameramen shoved through and competed for front positions. When the Anthem was over, the President, a short, bald, bespectacled man, stepped up to the microphone. He was ill at ease, embroiled in the heated politics surrounding the NSP.

"Ladies and gentlemen, young people, families all. Welcome to Bunkertown. Thank you for your participation in the Nuclear Survival Program. You have all been through extensive selection and briefing procedures to prepare you for the time ahead. They were not always easy or comfortable. But this makes you the special people needed to fulfil the purpose for which Bunkertown was created.

"Australia is distanced from the rest of the world. We have forged our own culture from European origins and by integration with our eastern neighbours. Darwin is perhaps the finest example of the cosmopolitan life for which Australia can be truly proud. In the main, this has worked to our advantage. However, conflict is spreading throughout the world. And since the war turned nuclear last month, things do not look good for an easy end to hostilities. Only time will tell how extensive this will be. As a consequence, conventional warfare has intensified, and we all know about the use of chemical weapons against the Chinese last week. There is nowhere in the world that is safe. Except perhaps here and other places like Bunkertown.

"To its credit, the Federal Government anticipated this world crisis and undertook the Nuclear Survival Program when conflict in the Middle East first threatened world peace four years ago. We stand here today surrounded by the culmination of that undertaking. I congratulate Eness Outcomes for its accomplishment in constructing, supplying and preparing Bunkertown for occupancy. I thank the Northern Territory Administration for its part, including recruitment and briefing of the one thousand of you gathered here. Finally, I pay tribute to your courage and selflessness in accepting the conditions of the NSP and embracing the task at hand.

"No-one can know what will happen. You, here today, are the ones chosen to survive and start life above ground again should the worst happen. We all pray this will not eventuate and you will re-join us in peace at the end of one year.

"People of Australia, welcome to your temporary life in Bunkertown and good luck for the future."

A diplomatic speech. The President was careful to omit any reference to the political wrangling still stifling other NSP efforts throughout Australia. At appropriate points, he turned to acknowledge the Federal MP, the Managing Director of Eness Outcomes and the Chief Territory Minister.

The Federal MP, sent as a show of harmony given the funds sunk into NSP, spoke next. A senior figure, he had recently lost the race for President. With little room to digress, his speech echoed the President's, except for a twist at the end.

"And so," he concluded pompously, "I understand the position of those selected for this heroic task, and the disappointment for those who were not. Circumstances are often decided by factors out of our control."

He glanced at the President and stepped back. The Chief Minister followed, then the Territory Minister responsible for Capital Works, who finished with a slant of his own.

"Much as I would like to be with you, that honour is bestowed on others. I trust you will meld together as a co-operative community under those selected to administer your interests."

Frowning slightly, he pointedly ignored two of his colleagues who had been appointed by the Territory Parliament to lead the Committee of Ten that would manage the Bunkertown community. They and the eight other members, elected by a vote of fellow Bunkertown residents at a briefing session, sat quietly, relishing their positions.

A spritely, grey-haired University professor spoke about the effects on land and atmosphere of nuclear, chemical and biological contaminants. With unabashed enthusiasm for his chosen field, he declared that the worst of known chemical and biological agents would become benign within two years. Under the nuclear scenario, however, survival would be difficult with the loss of many lives. Travel to an uncontaminated part of the country would be necessary. Intended as a morale-booster, his presentation seemed only to confirm survival as part of a war game and gave no comfort to anyone.

The speeches done, it was over to media questions. The MPs handled most with expediency and well-practised rhetoric. One reporter, in a senior position with the leading television operator and having earlier spent time with the placard-wielding demonstrators, tackled the pompous Federal MP with an oblique reference to his final comment.

"What do you say, sir, to those denied the chance to reside in Bunkertown? With your experience, what advice can you give them for their future survival?"

The MP blinked, glancing at the President again as he stepped forward. "Perhaps you should advise them. It might become a full-time job for you. I understand you have enough contacts among the demonstrators."

No more questions were accepted. The official group left the platform. The media converged on the Committee of Ten, ignoring the others now leaving. Interviews resumed. People moved around sparingly, gravitating into small groups according to established familiarity. An uncertain, sombre mood prevailed, strangely at odds with the calibre of people chosen for their expertise and suitability to enhance a self-sufficient, well-rounded community.

"All my relatives are still up there. They're glad it was me chosen and not them," a woman said despondently.

"I'm with you, Martha," her friend replied.

A third woman, unknown to them, entered the conversation with surprising vigour. "All this talk about disaster. I don't see any disaster. These bombs going off, it's all on the other side of the world, anyway."

A man standing nearby overheard her. "Excuse me," he offered in a kindly tone. "Tokyo was hit yesterday. That's not the other side of the world, love. It could happen here with only an hour or two advance warning."

She snapped back. "You men cause all the problems. If women were running governments, none of this would be happening."

"Now, Jean dear, let's not start here." Her husband shifted his feet nervously.

But a television interviewer had overheard.

"Do you think the Committee of Ten is well-balanced with four women and six men?" the reporter asked, thrusting a microphone in her face.

Her husband, seizing the chance to assert himself, stepped in front of her. But he was too late.

"Ha, some men!" she replied sharply. "With a spineless gibbering idiot leading, how good can the other five be?"

"We don't want to talk to you. Come on, Jean." Her husband took her arm, his eyes darting between the interviewer and cameraman.

The interviewer let them go, flashing a smile at his colleague, who nodded and mouthed, "Got it!"

The Neales and Winters had observed the exchanges.

"That's one of the social workers and his wife," George said, unimpressed. "How did she slip through the psychological net?"

"Yeah. Maybe he's taking her for his first session now," Alec suggested.

They laughed.

George had been exposed to a wider view of the conflict than most in his profession while overseas with the Australian Medical

Corps. On return home a few months ago from his final assignment, withdrawn and troubled by the signs of rapidly worsening conflict, instead of returning to the hospital he had joined the team in the final stages of preparing Bunkertown. He and Alec had grown closer then. Both wives were accepting of the roles they would play. Only in the last few weeks had Marcia's feelings of inadequacy started to escalate. Alec and Marcia had kept a lid on it, in case they were dropped from the program.

Marcia stood apart from the others, unable to draw the attention of her daughter, who was engrossed in the occasion with Benjamin.

Technicians dismantled and carried out the platform and checkpoint. An attendant wheeled out the music black box. The public address system gave five short beeps and everyone stopped to listen with bated breath. A voice sounded, loud and impersonal.

"Attention all. Life support systems have been initiated. The entrance door will begin closing in half an hour. Thank you."

The media packed their equipment and were ushered out by security personnel. With the departure of the security staff, only the chosen Bunkertown residents remained.

"Attention. Five minutes to door closure."

All watched as a technician strode to the concrete door and opened a security box fixed to the back of it. The minutes ticked by.

"Bunkertown fully operational. Closure commencing."

A motor started, settling into a low hum as it drove a system of mechanical arms and levers. The door began to swing closed. The system, without computer dependency, was failsafe, even convertible to manual operation in the event of motor failure. Everyone's eyes were riveted on the door as it reached full closure and sealed against the square steel portal, snuffing out the last rays of sunlight. A breathtaking moment. The NSP participants were entombed inside. They hoped for one year, but knew it could be much longer.

Chapter 2

The outside world could have no influence over Bunkertown. It was an impressive achievement. Excavated surfaces were smooth and precise in line and level, the hard, non-fractured rock needing no structural support, even for a wide ceiling span. Red-tinged laser sheets cast their glow and blended with the lighting, which was softer than sunlight and without glare. The effects added depth to life-size murals on the walls depicting scenes of feasting and merriment.

"Looks like this is the Food Cavern," a man quipped.

The cavern was a large rectangle. At each end, high up, a row of digital screens displayed the above-ground temperature, humidity and wind in bold yellow numbers, as well as the weather forecast for Darwin. Beneath, a second row of three screens advised radiation, chemical and biological pollution. Currently these screens were solid white. Beside each was a scale denoting levels of change from white through yellow, orange, red, and then purple for the highest.

Wooden-framed face clocks with ornate hands provided a touch of old-style character among the electronics. Next to each set of screens was a four-year calendar, with current day and date highlighted in glowing orange. Throughout the cavern, palms and potted plants added a sense of a calm, relaxed atmosphere. Equally spaced down one side of the cavern were openings to the male dormitories, toilets and bathrooms.

Benjamin, Kelly and their parents followed others through one of four openings opposite, to the Rest Cavern, where chairs, lounges and coffee tables were arranged for comfort. Timber panels of diverse shades and textures displayed paintings, tapestries and indigenous works. Tinted spotlights shone down on each work of art. Clocks, calendars and sets of readouts were located at each end of this cavern as well. The female dormitories, toilets and bathrooms were off the far side of the Rest Cavern.

"Two caverns between us," George commented to his wife. "At least my snoring won't keep you awake."

"Yes, but I can't help what the other men might do to you," she replied, laughing.

One of the end walls captured Benjamin's attention. "Look, Kelly. It's glass, not rock!"

He took Kelly's hand and they pushed their way through the people clustered in front of a laboratory. Visible through the reinforced plate glass wall were three orange-suited technicians attending an array of electronic monitoring equipment.

"They told us about this, remember? It's the only major computer system allowed, to test for changes outside."

The briefings had emphasised a non-computerised way of life, training people to perform tasks manually, in case their initiative would be needed to survive in a hostile environment after leaving Bunkertown.

"Yes, so we can see what it's like back home," Kelly added enthusiastically.

"The news, too." Benjamin started towards a digital noticeboard scrolling the latest news, current affairs and sports results.

The public address system came to life. "Your attention. Please settle into your dormitories. Dining facilities will be ready in one hour and dinner will be served."

"Benjamin, don't wander off," Gloria called to him, arresting his progress.

Women began separating from men. A mass of bodies shuffling to opposite destinations, mostly in good humour. Every person held a card showing dormitory and bed allocation. Gloria, Marcia and Kelly departed for L4.

On the male side, boys were in a separate dormitory from the men, under the night-time care of two wardens. Benjamin's card was marked B-L12T. He reached row twelve and climbed to the top bed of a double bunk, left side. His bag was there. He unpacked a few items, arranged them along the shelf that ran the full length of the wall then sat, enjoying murals depicting mostly sports. Cricket, football, and hockey, his and Kelly's favourite game. He jumped down from the bunk and found himself next to his classmate.

"Hi, Omar! Where are you sleeping?"

Omar pointed to the bottom bed of row eleven and said nothing. Short in stature, with a dark complexion and straight, close-cropped black hair, he was naturally reserved. He and Benjamin had not been on good terms since they recently fought in the playground over Kelly, but Benjamin could see no reason to continue the feud.

"How about the pictures? Which one do you like best?"

"That one," Omar finally responded, indicating a scene exploding with kung-fu action surrounded by a firestorm.

"Wow, pretty lively!"

"If you say so." Omar walked away, obviously not interested in talking further.

Benjamin returned to the Food Cavern and was soon sitting beside Kelly with their parents at a table, exchanging notes about murals and nearby bed companions.

The cavern was filling rapidly, people hungry for their first meal in Bunkertown. Friends or those with some familiarity were sharing tables and starting to relax. They discussed the choice of menu, which was limited but interesting. Good acoustics kept the rising noise level muted. A cheer went up when waiters appeared, wheeling long, narrow, box trolleys between tables, supplying meals airlines style. The servings were small, but fortified and filling.

"Looks like we won't starve," George said. "Good, healthy food."

"Meat and vegetables," Marcia commented, poking at hers. "Hope there'll be variety."

"Stir fry and rice were on the menu," Alec could not help remarking.

Eating in silence, they could overhear the conversation at the next table.

"I reckon I can handle this for a year," a man said. "Everything laid on. How easy can life be? Right, Fred?"

"Yeah right, apart from our rostered duties. And not everything can be laid on anymore." Fred laughed.

His wife ignored him and his crude reference to the requirement for celibacy.

Committee of Ten members had spread themselves randomly amongst the tables. The Head, Joshua, a tall thin man with receding forehead, was in a perfectly pressed suit befitting someone conscious of his appearance. He was intent on presenting an air of control, to which his quiet, plain wife had apparently long since succumbed. He tried to be informal as he rose and went to a dais against the end wall to give his first speech.

"Greetings, everyone. I can see you're all enjoying your first dinner in Bunkertown. Our stay will be a comfortable one. The laboratory will keep us in touch with life above ground. The news and information screens will operate twenty-four hours a day. How do you like the old railway station clocks we were able to relocate?" He gestured proudly at them. "Please take advantage of the orientation tours tomorrow. Have a good night!"

Dining over, people moved to the Rest Cavern. Upon entering, they gazed upwards in wonder at a replica of the night sky above Darwin; a myriad of stars, Sirius, an even brighter Venus, the Southern Cross, the moon in its current phase. Light music was playing.

The parents settled into lounges, while Benjamin and Kelly went exploring. They checked out the laboratory again then ventured up a darkened passage past a bonsai forest with bridge across. They came to a door that would not open.

"They think we'll get lost," Benjamin remarked, disappointed.

They crossed the bridge to another door, which he opened. "Oh!" Kelly cried as light and heat burst forth. Benjamin chuckled. In front of them were rows and rows of hydroponics from floor to ceiling. With nothing more to see, they returned to the Rest Cavern.

The first night was strange for everyone as they settled down to sleep. In the boys' dormitory, some were restless, others chatted excitedly. A four year-old began crying. Using a buzzer system, a warden called his father who soon soothed the young boy to sleep.

Benjamin lay listening to it all, his mind active. Omar remained uncommunicative.

In M4, George and Alec shared a double bunk. Neither knew well the men in neighbouring bunks.

"No sex for a year," one started up. "How do I handle that, Brad?"

A groan sounded from the bed above him. "Same way as all of us, Jack. But not too vigorous. I don't want to get seasick up here."

Others laughed.

George sighed. "There's one in every crowd, Alec. Now I know why I'll miss Gloria."

"This is peace for me," Alec replied contentedly. "Now I won't have to listen to Marcia's sobbing."

At the recruitment stage, all couples had agreed to celibacy. In close communal living, lack of privacy made intimacy impractical. And in a community reliant on efficient use of resources, women getting pregnant and having babies would make circumstances untenable. The selection preference had been for childless couples, although the greater need for specific expertise meant couples with one child were common; there were even a few with more than one. Children totalled about two hundred, but none was younger than four years old. To maximise future population replenishment under the worst-case scenario, no woman was older than thirty-five years.

* * *

In the morning, Benjamin, Kelly and their mothers joined an orientation tour. Their guide, a portly man from the Education Centre, led the group to the laundry. Rows of non-computerised washing machines and driers lined the walls. Martha was there with her friend.

"Back to the old manuals," she commented.

"At least we won't catch something from other people," her friend noted, pointing to a dispenser with antiseptic-charged washing powder.

A bridge across a water display led to the Water Treatment room. An engineer greeted them.

"The water in Bunkertown will be the most potable you have ever drunk."

"Where does it come from?" a man's voice called out. "What if it gets contaminated outside?"

"The water source is an inland underground river, deep enough to escape contamination."

"And what if there's no supply above ground when we get out of here?"

"As you can see, the supply conduit in the far corner divides into two. One branch is for Bunkertown, the other runs into town and is currently closed off. If we need to re-establish life above ground, we'll close the valve into Bunkertown and open the other one for a continuous safe water supply."

The guide herded the group into the Waste Disposal Centre, which collected all Bunkertown waste, mulched it and processed it to methanol. A technician demonstrated the procedure.

"When you're rostered on, you'll know where to bring the rubbish. Extractors channel fumes here from every room. It all contributes."

The Control Centre drew great interest. It housed the machinery that created and sustained the artificial living conditions of Bunkertown. Three hundred air scrubbers, two hundred of them backups, recycled air and carbon dioxide to create constant atmospheric pressure and a comfortable temperature. Methanol-fuelled generators supplied power, heating and lighting. Reticulation networks delivered services throughout Bunkertown in a maze of covered ducts and channels excavated below floor level.

At the Maintenance Centre, Kelly whispered to another girl, "That's my dad!" as Alec explained how the centre ensured continuous operation of Bunkertown systems.

The Medical Centre made Benjamin feel proud as he listened to his father's talk.

"The centre contains enough supplies to last our community almost indefinitely," George assured them.

After the Child Care and Education Centres, the tour guide led the group past storage rooms of food, fuel, perishables and re-useables to the Computer Centre. The computers, for general use, the electronic-library and library held more interest for Benjamin and Kelly.

"They're with keyboards," Benjamin noted, fingering one wistfully.

"Yes," the guide responded. "They are good for basic tasks and that's all we need."

Brief stops followed at Counselling and Spiritual Guidance, the minigolf course, squash court and the Fitness Centre, then the Recreation Centre with tables and chairs laid out for social interaction. Access to a well-stocked bar was severely limited by ration card insertion to a machine.

"At least these restrictions aren't total," Brad commented.

"No wonder your wife was happy to come here," Jack ribbed him. "You might be a starter for that counselling service."

The group arrived at the Entertainment Centre.

"Here's where I leave you," the guide said. "Have fun."

Benjamin nudged Kelly as they passed through the colonnaded entrance into a huge cavern. A round ornate ceiling glowed with soft lighting that changed colour through the spectrum. Ground and mezzanine floors, the latter fronted by filigree iron balustrades, contained continuous tables and seating in tiered half moon curves. At the focus was a stage, backed by a giant floor-to-ceiling cinema screen. On each side, vertical ladders ascended to a high-flying trapeze.

A young attendant interrupted their murmurings of surprise. "Spectacular, isn't it? Note the individual pop-up screen with handset in front of each seat. For satellite entertainment, Bunkertown stored specials or Darwin television.

"The electronic wall schedule or any terminal will give you the full range of what's available. For live or screen shows on stage, use the voggles for zoom and dimension viewing and to vary sound. This room can seat everyone in the community. Any further questions, I'm here to help you." She smiled, knowing she was selling the best product in Bunkertown.

Marcia was studying the wall schedule. "They've got mechallops!" she exclaimed with rare enthusiasm. "I thought I'd have to give it up!"

At home, she never tired of wagering and watching on screen the mechanical jockeys whipping their horses past the post. Her husband used to complain about their bank account, but he would not have that worry here, where gambling was virtual.

"Oh no!" Kelly whispered. "I hope she doesn't expect me to sit with her for hours watching it."

"Let's have a look around here." Benjamin moved towards a section marked Games.

Great, they had his favourite! Asterflick used the Hubble No.3 telescope in the early detection of asteroids. The player deflected the asteroids with missiles, reaching the end of the game when an asteroid inevitably struck Earth. In Mars Exploration, a participant entered a simulator putting him virtually on foot or in a Mars Buggy called the Mockroach. Points were awarded for negotiating rugged terrain, discovery of water and minerals and length of survival time.

Benjamin played a few games then looked for Kelly. He found her at a table hockey match and watched till she and her companion finished a vigorous competition.

"This is my game!" The boy grinned as he brandished his handset in victory. "I play it at school."

"Yes, and he's good at it," Kelly said, looking relieved the game was over as Benjamin came up beside her. "This is Eric."

"I want to see." A little girl was tugging Eric's hand.

Eric lifted his sister till her chin was above the table. "Always wants to know what's going on," he said in an older brother tone.

Omar joined them. He quickly struck up a game with Eric. Kelly and Benjamin moved away.

Lunch passed without incident and orientation day wore on. After dinner, there was a play at the theatre, then all retired to bed.

* * *

With another breakfast over, the community began to settle into routines they would follow for the duration of their stay. The children resumed school. Many adults, without specific duties unless rostered on, pursued personal chores such as laundry, or sought leisure activities at the Entertainment and other recreational centres.

Daily briefings leading up to the habitation of Bunkertown had focussed greatly on the psychological impact of confinement and sudden change. Experts had given countless talks, scribbled or sketched networks on a whiteboard to demonstrate behavioural patterns, orchestrating potential scenarios played out in small groups to simulate environmental alienation.

Reality was different, however. Many residents wandered around the Rest Cavern aimlessly, too restless to sit and unwilling to be out of sight of the screens. Others hovered as near to the laboratory as possible. Only select personnel were allowed inside, including the Committee of Ten. The ten tried to remain inconspicuous until a problem arose, preferring the community to develop by itself. The community was largely self-policing, with everyone of equal status under common conditions and restrictions. Two small rooms attached to the Counselling Centre were available for detention if anyone became excessively difficult. And so the society developed in its own way; unchecked.

Gloria and Marcia sat near the laboratory amongst other women. The screens showed fine, sunny conditions in Darwin.

"Look at the beautiful day up there," a plump, ashen-faced woman blurted out, her thin lips twitching with indignation. "This would be my day off from the farm. I should be playing golf. What am I doing down here?"

"I'm usually at my sister's now," Martha responded. "We go to the Ditelbuy then back home to compare prices on the Ditelnet."

"What can we do here?" a woman with wispy, sandy-coloured hair complained. "Only a few computers, and they're next to useless. No net connections, no e-biz. Nothing."

Marcia had been watching the clock. The time was approaching 11.00am.

"Mechallops are starting," she said to Gloria.

Gloria smiled. "You go ahead. I'll stay here for a while longer."

Marcia departed for the Entertainment Centre. Gloria chatted with two women till lunchtime, when George and Alec returned from the Medical and Maintenance Centres. Marcia returned from mechallops, looking disgruntled. The children came home from school. Benjamin had enjoyed their first morning.

"It's better without computers. We talk about things," Benjamin said excitedly.

Kelly was more reserved in the face of change. "It's hard to know what the teacher wants us to do."

They went with their fathers to a noticeboard. The latest news was of nuclear hits on the Indian sub-continent, intensive bombing and chemical weapons across Northern Asia. The war was coming no closer to Australia. Reports from the USA and Middle East were examples of the fierce rhetorical battle raging. The screens portrayed normality in Darwin, a temperature of 32 degrees and high humidity.

That night in L4, Kelly lay awake listening to some of the women. The segregated confines of the dormitory provided an ideal forum away from the men.

"My husband never cared about the house," one woman said nastily. "He's in his element here. Now he doesn't have to do anything for me, so it's fair I don't give him anything either."

Her friend, Jocelyn, was in the next bed. "I agree. What we can't do here suits me. Fred can't be an animal in this place."

"They're all animals," another declared spitefully. "Mine's the same. The shame is having to bury myself down here to get out of his clutches every night."

A few others murmured their support, giving the impression of common disenchantment with their husbands before entering Bunkertown. Was it an attitude of convenience? Or had this type of person been easiest to recruit for the celibate lifestyle?

A fourth woman quickly expanded the anti-male feelings to a broader horizon.

"If it wasn't for men," she claimed, "we wouldn't be here. We wouldn't need a Bunkertown at all. Men have messed up the world."

"That's right, Jean," Cynthia, who had befriended her, agreed. "If women were in control, there'd be no war. We must be more assertive, demand more say in decision-making."

Jean was encouraged. "It's been happening, but not fast enough. Men still dominate positions of power. They seek more power incessantly, riding their roller-coaster ego trips. No wonder there's war."

"Exactly. And what's the result? We're down here in a tomb. It's not the quality of life I expected. If an opportunity comes to run things our way, we should take it."

Again, others sounded their support. Kelly felt uncomfortable, the sentiments foreign to her own experience. She was unsure how her mother, who remained quiet throughout, was regarding it. Gloria was careful not to get involved, finding the trend in attitudes disturbing. She looked forward to seeing her husband and Benjamin at breakfast.

Breakfast was enjoyable. It was a chance for Benjamin to listen to his parents talking. He was learning more about how people interacted. Alec often joined in, leaving out Marcia who was usually preoccupied with another personal grievance. Kelly hovered, emotionally as well as physically, between her mother and Benjamin.

The pattern of life was established. Day turned into night, night into day. Timed to coincide with above ground, the only way of knowing was by a clock, softer lighting in the evening until dimming from 11.00pm, and dawn simulation from 6.00am.

Chapter 3

People quickly became set in their new ways. With communal living allowing little time in private for couples, established groups strengthened and more formed. Segregation between groups created its own form of substitute privacy. Community spirits fluctuated as news updates varied. The spread of war, while not yet engulfing Australia, continued. Disturbingly, fresh reports were becoming less frequent. The read-out screens changed little from day to day, frustrating some people with their depiction of Darwin's easy way of life.

Gloria found a comfortable rapport with several women, and they routinely lounged near the laboratory till lunchtime. Often, she spent time on a computer, keeping stimulated from the electronic-library. To her surprise, Marcia lost interest in mechallops after just a few days. Without real betting, it lacked the element of self-pity when she lost, making it a sterile exercise. She stayed with Gloria and the others then, struggling to maintain self-esteem.

One morning outside the laboratory, the sandy-haired woman in a group near Gloria and Marcia's, spoke out.

"Look at the screens. Nothing's happening. Who says the war will destroy us? Everyone's enjoying life up there, and we're hiding away down here."

"Another day of shopping gone to waste," Martha commented, in the same group with her friend and the plump woman.

In a group next to them, Jean overheard. "Excuse me," she interrupted, leaning across to address the sandy-haired woman. "We're only here because men have forced us to be."

The sandy-haired woman swivelled round. Their eyes met in mutual respect for a similar point of view. They quickly engaged in lively conversation, and soon the two groups merged. They moved to a private part of the Rest Cavern. Gloria watched, concerned at the signs. They reminded her of the scorn in much of the Darwin population, but inflamed now by idleness and confinement with no justification yet apparent. Marcia took it all in, impressed by their self-confidence.

That afternoon, the news reported a breakthrough in war rhetoric. Political propaganda at last gave way to acknowledgement of what all sides were doing to the world. A moratorium on further use of nuclear weapons was agreed. World leaders began urgent talks. In the Middle East, Mushud Ahmed was strident in his demands, particularly of the United States.

The Bunkertown community held its collective breath, hoping for a premature end to their entombment. It did not come. The days passed, drifting into weeks then months. Frustration deepened in some as no evidence of change came through. Jean's expanded group was an obvious focus of unrest.

Three months had passed when one day, Jean's group was congregating near the laboratory as people were returning from afternoon entertainment. Some of the group were intoxicated with the sharing of resentments. Cynthia, a tall woman with short hair and a determined look, expounded a view that was crystallising amongst them.

"We should exercise our rights to go back above ground. Everyone should exercise that right if they want to."

"Yes," the sandy-haired woman agreed. "We can't influence anything here. The news updates get fewer every day. They don't care about us."

Jean stood, her face set grimly. "Where's that Committee Head? I'm going to tell Joshua what I think."

People in the vicinity reacted uncertainly, confused. Benjamin and Kelly, just returned from school, stood with their mothers watching and listening. A stuntman from the entertainment sector stepped forward.

"No!" he asserted forcefully. "We're here for a purpose. We'll have to replenish the population if everyone above ground gets wiped out. We must be prepared."

Jean pushed towards him. "Who says that will happen? It's because of you men and your failings that we have to be here, so why should we listen to you? Anyway, you and anyone else can stay if you wish."

Another man, a town planner, spoke. "We'll need a proper community for rebuilding if the worst happens. It wouldn't be possible if too many leave indiscriminately. I don't think we can take a chance on that."

More people gathered as the arguing intensified.

"I agree with him," a woman shouted, pointing at the town planner. "Many preparations have gone into this. We can't just change the plans now."

Alerted, the Committee of Ten emerged from their room and forced a way through the crowd. Joshua raised his arms, expecting his presence to be respected.

"Please, everyone. We must keep calm and be rational."

Jean confronted him. "Some of us want to go back. Return above ground. You have no right forcing us to stay against our will!"

Joshua was taken aback, challenged by the hard edge to her voice. The arguing died away and everyone focussed on him. His standing was at stake. Grasping for control, he gestured towards the other members flanking him.

"Do you accept the authority of this Committee?"

Jean glared at him coldly and said nothing. The crowd buzzed. The Committee, eight members elected by the people, enjoyed natural acceptance, although people did not regard highly the Head, an MP who had been appointed not elected.

"My Committee will preserve the interests of everyone in Bunkertown," Joshua assured them, detecting a swing in his favour. "We think we understand how all sides feel. We will consider the issue and make a decision."

No one seemed inclined to escalate the crisis further. Jean remained silent, realising her group was outnumbered if it came to disputing the Committee's role. The Committee left to deliberate over the problem. Half an hour later, they returned. Joshua addressed the community over the public address system.

"Thank you for your patience. For those unaware of it, the Committee has considered a request from some to return above ground. We have decided, by majority vote of seven to three, to remain as we are. Our stay here is just three months old, and it is far too early to make drastic alterations. In order to satisfy all sides, we will review the situation monthly. Thank you."

A subdued acceptance ensued and the crisis was averted.

Life in Bunkertown settled again, although an undercurrent of resentment persisted. Jean's group was gaining momentum. The Committee members, six men and four women, all refused to disclose which side they had voted on. The vote, seven to three, was food for much speculation. The women wanted to know who the traitor was.

The screens and noticeboards continued to be focal points. The waiting for something to happen, the uncertain reasons for being entombed, the vision and information unchanging from one day to another, yet the ominous lessening in frequency of fresh news reports from overseas, all played on their minds. The pressure was fundamental, more than the numerous activities and amusements could fully alleviate.

Lunch was a welcome relief each day. Benjamin looked forward to it, a chance for him and Kelly to check for any changes or news. Gloria was happier after she, Marcia and Kelly swapped dormitories with Martha, her friend and another woman in L3, who were as keen to be near Jean and her friends as Gloria was to be away from them.

George became increasingly preoccupied with the noticeboard, his checks coinciding with an ever-greater scarcity of new information. Early one morning, a sketchy update indicated a resumption of nuclear strikes, with Beijing and Johannesburg wiped out. And there was a disturbing spread of conventional and chemical warfare from North to South East Asia. With Benjamin beside him, George slowly scrolled to the end, and was about to turn away when a late-breaking item appeared. A large headline read: NUCLEAR STRIKES DESTROY CANBERRA AND SYDNEY. AUSTRALIA IS AT WAR!

The community soon knew about it. Tension throughout the caverns was on a knife-edge as people huddled in small groups, some crying in grief, many agitated.

News updates completely dried up after that. The community mood became increasingly sombre.

Three mornings later, Benjamin had a good view of the screens as they sat for breakfast. He noticed the change instantly.

"That screen just changed!"

Kelly followed his gaze and the others swivelled round to look up at the screens.

"So it did," George noted, his face pale with concern as he eyed the chemical pollution indicator.

The colour had turned yellow. Even as they watched, the colour shimmered between yellow and orange. Others around them noticed, and soon everyone had stopped eating to stare at the screens. The drone of conversation cut to silence, then a low murmur resumed as a reaction set in.

"It must be drifting here on the wind," Alec suggested.

"Perhaps chemical bombing has spread further south since the last report a few days ago," George added, as he continued to stare at the screen.

By the time breakfast was over, the colour had stabilised on orange. The two other indicators had not changed. The weather forecast screen was blank, as it had been for several days. The only information being received was through monitoring by the laboratory equipment connected to above ground sensors.

People glanced furtively at each other as the tension heightened. Joshua immersed himself in discussions with one of the environmental experts. They and the Committee soon left, heading for the laboratory. The meal over, people began drifting away.

At lunchtime, George and Alec checked the noticeboard.

"Still no information coming through," George muttered. "That's serious."

"When will we know?" Alec pondered.

The strain was obvious in people as they took their places for lunch, talking, pointing at the screens. Then suddenly, another screen changed. For the first time, the biological indicator was active! From a shimmering white, it moved steadily through yellow to orange. A collective gasp sounded. No one was interested in lunch, all eyes fixed upwards. Minutes ticked by. The chemical indicator moved again. Red. But already the biological colour was flickering on red then moved to purple.

The public address system came to life. Joshua was on the dais.

"Can I have your attention. We can see how the screens are changing. I appeal to you all to maintain calm. Above ground air quality and the detection of foreign bodies in the atmosphere have reached dangerous…"

A piercing scream drowned his voice. A woman was charging towards the entrance door, arms flailing as she crashed between tables, distraught.

"Open the door! My sister and family, I have to save them. Ple-e-e-ease!"

Her irrational hysteria sent shockwaves around the cavern, stinging others into action. A few moved towards the woman. One man swiftly intercepted her and spun her around by the arm.

"No! We can't," he yelled. "There's nothing we can do."

She beat her fists at him. The man stumbled; she pulled away. She staggered to the door mechanism, grabbing one of the levers. When it failed to budge, she targeted the security box, ripping at the locked cover.

"There's no time! I must find them!"

The man recovered and rushed to her side. He gripped her arms. "Wait! You can't…"

His words were cut off as a faint rumble reverberated around the cavern. Instantaneously, the top row of screens went wild in a blur of unreadable yellow numbers. Another faint rumble sounded and the cavern vibrated. People froze in their seats, shocked, their worst fears being realised.

The pattern repeated itself again and again, eight times in total. At last, the rumbling and vibrating subsided, replaced by an eerie calm. No one moved. Kelly was clutching Benjamin's arm. George and Gloria held each other. Alec was standing, frozen in mid-action. Marcia shook in her seat.

Slowly a few people started shuffling about. Several women and men began crying. The woman who had grabbed the door lever was slumped on the floor, face in her hands. Joshua stepped from the dais, his face drained of colour. He headed for the Rest Cavern. Others followed, then everyone was moving after him.

Inside the laboratory, Joshua spoke to the orange-suited attendants. One of them gesticulated at the equipment and shook his head. Contact with life on the outside was no more. A morbid melancholy spread rapidly over the crowd.

Joshua stepped from the laboratory and made to address the crowd.

"What's happened?" someone called out.

Face ashen, Joshua cleared his throat, then spoke. "We have just felt the effects of conventional, perhaps blanket bombing. Apart from the pollution sensors, the laboratory is no longer operational. We believe Sarin gas has been used. High levels have been detected in the atmosphere."

A shocked murmur rippled through the crowd.

"How bad is Sarin…"

"Bad," someone quickly answered.

"What's more," Joshua said softly, "the lab has picked up traces of Anthrax."

"Anthrax," a roar erupted. Many voices filled the cavern with panicked chatter.

"Bastards!" someone yelled over the din.

"Who would do that!" another shouted.

Joshua stood shaking his head, helpless.

* * *

The community was slow to settle again. Many were traumatised, disoriented, unable to comprehend what had happened. George and the medical staff hastily went about treating people for shock. The counselling facility was quickly overloaded. The circumstances drew Benjamin closer to his parents. Sensitive to the emotions in people, he began to mature in his understanding of the way of things, the workings of people's minds and their feelings. Kelly's own dependence on him was increasingly vital to her in counter-balancing the erratic thinking of her mother.

A technician switched off the screens, removing the distressing evidence. The black frames, where bright numbers and colours used to be, epitomised a common view of community prospects. An expert in weapons technology gave a talk, more poignant in the face of reality this time than previous talks. He tried to appear assured, pointing out there was no radiation fallout detected at this time. The evidence of chemical and biological weapon use was of major concern, dictating that a further two years of entombment was essential. This went unquestioned. Ironically, the loss of much of the laboratory's capability was almost a blessing. The black screens were unable to have influence or sponsor depression by displaying the doom they all felt.

A gloomy pessimism enshrouded Bunkertown as people returned to their routines. Everyone had friends or relatives in Darwin and around Australia. With no outside contact, no way of knowing the destruction in all certainty, they were unable to grieve properly for them.

As time marched on, a different type of social interaction gradually developed in the community. The tendency to form segregated groups began shifting away from couples and families toward gender-based factions. The strict requirement for celibacy had an insidious effect, even though more pertinent now than ever. Suspicion of couples breaking the rules grew, and the tension was deep. An aura of distance developed. Relationships became strained as the chance to gain comfort through intimacy was unavailable. Emotional needs, greater than before, had to find satisfaction another way, at times promoting aggression. The formation of factions was like a slow-building cancer, as more and more people cared less and less about each other. The community was developing into an unhealthy society.

Jean's group was well placed in this seething society, growing stronger, although now the women were not as openly aggressive as before. The group often talked to other women outside of their movement, in attempts to win over more supporters. Some evenings, the group huddled in private at one corner of the Rest Cavern, engaged in intense discussions.

One evening, as Benjamin, Kelly and their parents enjoyed after-dinner beverages before moving to the Entertainment Centre, Gloria indicated the group sitting not far away.

"One of those women tried to impress me this morning."

George was intrigued. "What did she say?"

"She wanted me to join them in a group discussion, as they call it."

Marcia suddenly changed from her sullen mood. "Oh, yes. I was talking to one of them, too. I said I might join them next time. It sounds interesting."

Kelly felt uncomfortable, knowing what was coming next. Sure enough, her mother turned to her. "You can come, too."

Gloria was uneasy, brushing a strand of hair from her face. "I think Kelly's too young," she advised firmly. "I don't think it's a group suitable for her."

George raised his eyebrows at the unusually negative reaction from his wife. He rubbed the top of his forehead with two fingers, following the receded hairline. "What do they talk about?" he asked her, suspicious.

"Well, I was concerned at the woman's approach. She talked about their intentions when we leave Bunkertown. They blame what's happened on men with big egos and visions of power. They want a future government to be run solely by women. They see themselves as the beginnings of that. It scared me, I must say."

"That is scary," George agreed, perplexed. "There'll be trouble if they push those attitudes too far."

Marcia responded, testy at being contradicted. "I don't think it's like that. The woman I spoke to was very friendly, not like most people here."

Alec had been listening quietly. He glanced with disdain at his wife, then turned to the others and spoke with dismissive sarcasm.

"People are good if they talk nicely to her."

His wife's temporary confidence was deflated. As her sullen mood returned, she leaned towards Kelly, who squeezed her mother's hand dutifully.

"What do you think, Benjamin?" Kelly asked, uncertain.

"I don't know," he replied honestly. "It's up to our parents to decide."

Kelly smiled, shifting closer to him. She put her hand on his. "Yes, I agree."

George looked at his wife. "How do they expect to achieve this?"

Gloria hesitated before replying. "They believe they can easily hold power over men. The woman suggested the way we live here without sex holds the key to controlling men. How does that sound to you?"

Trying to make light of it, she playfully tantalised her husband with the prospect. George was startled for a moment then broke into a relieving smile.

"As long as they don't expect all of us to follow suit."

Marcia and Alec remained quiet, feeling uncomfortable without the same sort of close bond between them.

Amusements and entertainment were crucial in maintaining sanity. Factional groups strengthened as people increasingly sought solace with others of like mind. Marcia was attracted to Jean's group. It irritated Alec immensely, particularly since she insisted Kelly go with her. It became a regular cause of friction between them.

Despite the many relieving outlets and psychological safety nets, violence regularly broke out, someone going crazy in the confining environment or attempting to openly break with the celibacy law. More often than not, over the ensuing months, the two detention rooms were filled.

The first year's celebration was a sombre affair. People cried for loved ones while others waited for the latest batch of tests to come through. There were still detectable levels of contamination above ground and quickly a rumour spread that a mutated form of Ebola had been detected. Violent crimes against each other grew. Jean's group swelled with dissatisfied women, including those who had been victims of men's lurid remarks and approaches. Life in Bunkertown was becoming feudal, man against woman, family against family. Joshua and his flunkies had failed to keep reasonable order and were seen less and less over the following year.

* * *

"It's been clear up there for two weeks, now," one of the scientists said as she exited the lab.

Joshua nodded soberly then turned to the restless community. He drew a deep breath before speaking. "We can go outside."

With a roar that tried to lift the roof from the cavern, the people of Bunkertown screamed, danced and hugged. Two years, four months and three days; their tomb would at last be opened. Breakfast was a party. The men drank and laughed, the women grouped, cried and reassured each other.

The afternoon pulsated with activity as people made preparations for the next morning. Technicians unpacked thick glass plates and fixed them in place around the entrance door to form an airlock. Joshua fended off arguments about who should be the first to leave. Though the news of pending release pleased the inhabitants, things were still tense and that night violence was at a community high. A man had raped his wife then hung himself in the entertainment cavern. The crime was disturbing, but more disturbing was that no one cared. Jean's group won over a new member.

When morning dawned, the community was ready to leave Bunkertown. The day of Re-emergence had arrived.

Chapter 4

"Quick, Kelly! Hurry!" Benjamin cried, as he took Kelly's hand and forced a passage through the crowd around the airlock. "Let's get closer!"

The crowd was massing in an eager throng, compressing ever tighter as people closed in on their common focus. A man blocked the way but Benjamin squeezed past.

"Not so fast, young fellow. We all want out."

The man's wife was clutching his arm, lifting herself on tiptoes and craning her neck. Others bustled forward. The crowd buzzed with expectation as all awaited the first signs revealing the fate of their previous world. Many were apprehensive. An expert making confident predictions in his talk the previous day had failed to convince them of what they would see.

Benjamin and Kelly ducked and bustled until they reached the front of the human mass. They were as close as the Committee of Ten were allowing anyone. Joshua was supervising final procedures. Two men, wearing life-support protective suits, breathing apparatus and armed with equipment for testing the environment, entered the airlock. A technician closed the door. One of the men opened the security box. Soon the motor settled into a low hum as it worked the mechanism, and the concrete entrance door slowly opened. Breathlessly, all watched as the first rays of natural light broke through to greet them.

With the door only part way open, the motor was cut. The two men exited, but before the second had disappeared, he abruptly stopped. Both backed up, returning inside. People in the cavern gasped in consternation as the door closed again, extinguishing the brief glimpse of outside light. When the technician had stabilised the airlock, the two men re-entered the cavern. The leading man removed his headgear. He was shaken, his face gone white.

"There are skeletons against the door." His voice choked.

A low murmur started and soon gathered momentum as others realised the problem.

"How many?" Joshua asked.

"Hard to tell, maybe half a dozen." The man looked around at the sea of staring faces. "I think it's best to remove them before we all head out."

"Can you do it?"

The man nodded grimly, bracing himself for the task. "We'll need bags."

Someone fetched a wheeled trolley with large tray carrying a bundle of plastic bags. The two men donned their headgear again and repeated exit procedure. This time both exited.

In the cavern, the setback quickly triggered outbursts from people whose pent-up fear and uncertainty could no longer be suppressed. A woman confronted Joshua.

"You were always in that laboratory," she accused him venomously. "You must have known about this. We could have saved these people. My family was up there. It's your fault they're dead!"

She glared at him, her voice hardening as she finished. Her radical stance acted as a release for the emotions in others. Cynthia stepped forward.

"I agree with her. You men always think you know what to do. Now look what we're left with!"

Joshua was bewildered as the groundswell gained force, the decision-making power of his committee becoming irrelevant. For the first time, he had nothing to say. In that instant, he seemed to lose control over the people. The crowd, mumbling angrily, slowly drifted away, leaving him and his committee alone by the airlock.

At last, the two men returned. They were strangely quiet; reluctant to reveal what they had seen. They announced only that the air was breathable and ground contamination not a problem, but advised all to put on warm clothing. The big moment was upon them! Technicians removed one wall of the airlock and fully opened the entrance door.

Benjamin and Kelly emerged with their parents, elated as two years of confinement gave way to natural light and air. Almost immediately, a sense of foreboding replaced the elation. Marcia was the first to comment.

"It's cold. Darwin's never cold." She hugged herself against the chill in the air.

George rubbed his arms in discomfort. "Yes, the temperature must be single figures. Where's the heat and humidity?"

The high rock faces towered above them. Slowly they climbed the steep incline. Other changes were evident before they reached the top of the cutting.

"The air smells funny," a woman commented. "Musty, like in a room with no ventilation."

"Look at the sky," Kelly observed. "It's red and hazy."

Benjamin had noticed it as well. He pointed skywards. "What about the sun over there! Like it's covered with a blanket. I can look at it without hurting my eyes."

"We've got a nuclear winter," Alec concluded. "Dust from the Earth is diffusing the sunlight and blanketing the sky. No wonder it's cold."

All around was still. A deathly silence hung in the air. The people of Bunkertown fell into uneasy conformity with it, realising they were entering a strange, alien environment. The slope levelled out, leading to an expansive view as they slowly reached the main road. Like sleepwalkers, they began making their way into town.

It was a scene of devastation. Everything in sight had been levelled. A vast sea of debris lay scattered before them. Not a single building or even a tree was left standing, just low mounds of grey rubble.

In a collective trance, the people picked a path down the broken, buckled road. A long train heading for the centre of town. Soon they were spreading out as many identified a location, using the roads as landmarks. They peeled off to seek out personal property and find the moment to grieve.

"Look how warped the roads are," George commented.

"From extreme heat," Alec noted.

"What about the ground over there," Benjamin observed.

Wherever the ground showed, it was scorched.

The further in they walked, the more decimated the town was; pulverised masonry, twisted steel, burnt-out collapsed buildings, car bodies mangled to unrecognisable shapes. But no signs of life, no birds, animals or any remains to show that life had ever been here. It was a wasteland. The world that used to sustain them had been obliterated, wiped from the map all held in their minds. Undisturbed for over two years by any visitor, the scene depicted finality, conjuring a picture of wider catastrophe. Had life been snuffed out everywhere?

Horror-stricken, some broke down and wept, many were traumatised when coming to where their homes had been or those of friends and relatives. Everyone was sobered by the enormity of it. Brad stood at a road intersection, staring at a set of ruins.

"That's the pub," he said to Jack, downcast.

"I'll miss Barbie," Jack said. "She pulled a good beer."

Benjamin stood between his mother and father as they surveyed what was left of their home.

"Where does it start and finish?" George wondered grimly.

Benjamin pointed at the corner of a concrete slab protruding from beneath rubble. "That's the garage."

They found their way to Kelly's home.

"Even the tree's gone," Marcia observed mournfully, clutching her daughter's hand. They stared at the jagged stump that remained just above ground level.

As the day drew to a close, the ruddy sky gradually lost its colour as the sun lowered. Everyone returned to Bunkertown, many waiting outside long enough to witness the sky turning pitch black once the sun had disappeared. The cold deepened. No one talked as a cloud of gloom hung over the community.

An environmental expert presented his assessment, offering encouragement for the prospects of living above ground, but stressing the need to seek shelter should there be any threat of rain, which could deliver acid rains and other contaminants. The dry, barren landscape had at least shown rain to be a rarity.

George had a difficult night treating people for shock, at the same time struggling to control his own feelings. The circumstances drew George and Alec's families closer, although Alec was distant from his emotionally depleted wife. But he was protective of his daughter, reinforcing Benjamin's regard for him as his second father. They were fortunate compared to many suffering the loss of loved ones.

* * *

A reticent mood dawned with the day. A mass of lost souls returned above ground, reluctantly, to start the process of reconciling what had happened. They opened the second bunker. Warmth and dryness maintained by the laser sheets had preserved the contents. Mechanics set to work resuscitating electric cars and heavy vehicles after two years of inertia. The bulldozer soon whined to life, the front loader shortly after. Both crawled up the steep incline, operators sitting on top having to re-familiarise hurriedly. Like the cars, manual control had replaced the computer.

The machines started clearing the road of debris. Encouraged by the action, people began working ahead, sifting through the ruins in search of human remains. The dearth of evidence was upsetting, a damning judgement. By close of the second day, skeletal remains had been found at random locations, but not the numbers expected. Again they slept in Bunkertown, feeling safe in its belly, safe away from the horrors of their new world.

At first light, two cars left to travel the road south and seek any signs of life further inland. They took short wave radios to pick up any signals coming from isolated groups. The others continued the pattern of search throughout the day, with the same result. By late afternoon, the bulldozer and loader had reached beyond the town centre to the end of the main road. They'd cleared enough space each side to encourage thoughts of new buildings. Unhindered by bureaucracy, the positive-minded operators were revelling in their self-appointed role, the only leadership in evidence. They began on a road looping away from the main road.

Tiring of stumbling through ruins, people stood around watching, trying to keep warm, unsure how to help. The Committee of Ten meandered about, doing little more than approve of the work done so far. Joshua typified a lack of direction, his character failing in the transition from mandated authority to practical initiative. With communication not a community strength, many drifted off in small groups or sat looking at the sky.

Just before nightfall, the two cars returned from their reconnaissance south. The drivers reported no signs of life, no radio signals, just a sparse, arid, tussocky terrain. Settlements they encountered were without the same material destruction, however, and were littered with human remains. It was as if a pervasive force had swept all before it. The community congregated to observe a solemn silence.

The morning dawned on a directionless, uncommunicative community. The lack of meaningful leadership, other than individual, was beginning to stunt progress. People gravitated to the centre of town. Benjamin wandered to the end of the main road with Kelly. They skirted debris and headed for the beach. Climbing a small rise, they stood overlooking the beach and ocean beyond.

"Empty. No ships," Kelly said in a subdued tone.

Benjamin scanned the wide sweep of sea stretching to the horizon, and the foreshore of the harbour to where the decrepit remains of the wharf were as lifeless as the town. "Not even an upturned hull or the skeleton of a crane."

Holding hands, they retraced their steps in silence, re-joining Alec, Gloria and Marcia. George had remained at Bunkertown, where the Medical Centre was still busy. They mingled with a group coalescing at the loop road junction, people who felt their expertise was relevant. A burly man, an experienced building tradesman, spoke in a gruff voice.

"We need to build immediate accommodation along the road, here. Let's get on with it."

The town planner stepped forward. "It needs to be properly organised," he asserted. "We need a plan."

The builder peered at him stonily, then the corner of his mouth curled with scorn. "What sort of plan do we need? There's only two roads."

A few chuckles sounded. The town planner bristled, indignant at the scant regard given his skills. He was about to reply, but another man, a concrete technician, cut in.

"We have materials in the bunker. We need to find a bulk substance, like gravel, to mix with the cement and make building blocks."

"I know a good place," a man, a geologist, offered. "I'll take the plant operators there when they've finished clearing."

The builder grunted his approval, switching attention from the forlorn-looking town planner.

"We should set up a depot," Alec suggested, "where we can deliver goods from the bunker, a place to launch our operations from. Back up the road would be best, beyond where construction of the last buildings will reach."

A large circle was forming as more people appreciated the signs of action. Several sounded their agreement as Alec finished speaking. Benjamin was looking forward to helping him, knowing the skills of Kelly's father would play a prominent role.

The town planner saw another opportunity. "The projections for building will depend on the demographic parameters of our community," he declared, pleased with himself.

The burly builder glanced at him and snorted. "That stuff went out with the computers, mate. We'll start here and build out to the depot."

A woman spoke. "What sort of accommodation are we going to have?"

"Whatever is quickest to build," the builder replied. "Single room apartments. In blocks of ten."

Several women from Jean's group were there. Cynthia pushed to the front.

"We need better class houses too. Not everyone will be suited to apartments."

Silence followed as most were unsure what she meant.

"We'll build what we can," the builder said softly.

"In time we can work on better housing," someone said from the gathered crowd. Cynthia and Jean made no response.

"A new Medical Centre is necessary," another woman called out. "That's a priority, so we're not returning to Bunkertown all the time for treatment."

"Yes. Past the end of the road, where it overlooks the beach, is a good place," one of the doctors offered. He pointed towards the sea.

"We need enough area for a main building and small rooms adjacent so patients can receive private care. We must re-establish the water supply. Also waste disposal and electricity."

The water engineer came forward. "The water main laid through Bunkertown is buried off the edge of the road, on that side." With a sweep of his arm, he indicated from beyond town to where the doctor had been pointing. "I'll organise the treatment plant if a building can be done as another priority. Near the main, opposite the construction depot, so treatment will be before first usage."

The waste disposal engineer joined in. "The terrain is low lying beyond the loop road. Waste pipes from every building can drain effluent there by gravity. I'll set up a processing plant for methanol production. That means more clearing and another building. I'll need two helpers to re-assemble the plant."

Both engineers looked at the builder as they spoke, seeing him as the most positive figure for construction requirements. An electrical technician took his turn.

"We should erect the windmills where the ground is highest," he stated, pointing to where the natural topography rose gently on the other side of the road. "Over there."

With a willing exchange of ideas at last flowing, an unusual spirit of togetherness began to assert itself. Everyone's priority was the same: a new start to life. A common purpose filled the leadership void as people thought of tasks that needed to be addressed.

"What about food?" a woman called out. "We can't rely on stored supplies forever. We must establish food production on a renewable basis."

"The low lying area is best. Where the soil will be richest for crops," a man who had once been a farmer said.

"And more likely to be contaminated," someone interjected. He was one of the laboratory technicians.

Jean pushed forward beside Cynthia, intent on challenging him. "Before we came out, those two experts said ground contamination was no problem. One man says something, another says the opposite. Typical."

The man who had given a talk on the environment was there. "The ground is safe," he assured her.

"How do you know?" Jean retorted. "Did you test it?"

"We've done further tests and analysis since the first day. We estimate that, because of the cold and low evaporation, rain has fallen on very few occasions, if at all. No radioactive fallout has come to earth here. Other contamination has dissipated, although to be certain, we should remove the top layer of soil and dump it. The soil stored in the bunker can be spread in its place."

All seemed satisfied, a course of action now clear. With nothing further offered, the crowd began to disperse, taking directions from each of the technical people. The builder moved across the intersection and picked a spot equidistant from the two roads. He glanced down the loop road at the bulldozer and loader busily clearing, then turned to stare up the main road into the distance.

"We'll start the first block here," he declared, planting the heel of his boot into the ground.

By late afternoon, cars and trailers were ferrying goods from the bunker in a steady stream, delivering them to an area cleared by the bulldozer for the construction depot. A crude building was started there.

* * *

With activity, the days went by quickly. Weeks passed as Bunkertown built a new town. Everyone found something to do. Construction of single room apartments progressed rapidly once methods became familiar. Anyone without specific skills contributed to the labour force, many to make building blocks at the depot; a vital, relentless chore. The loader kept a convoy of trailers busy supplying a gravelly earth from a location in the country identified by the geologist. Mixed with the cement from the bunker, it formed a grey earth-cement that was barely strong enough for simple construction purposes. With this limitation and the absence of steel reinforcement, only single-storey buildings were possible. Repairs were done to road surfaces using the same mixture.

With the depot operating smoothly, Alec became involved in organising and installing plumbing, waste disposal and water connections to the box-like buildings. Benjamin assisted him, often aided by Kelly, who divided her time between them and her mother, Gloria and other women at the newly established crop fields.

Lines of apartments began to materialise, in blocks of ten. Glass was a limited resource, dictating that only one small window be included in each apartment. Construction of attached houses around the loop road began. Beyond and adjacent to the crop fields, the clearing of connecting roads marked where individual houses would soon be started. These had the lowest priority, making for some conflict, but being busy helped keep resentments in check.

The Medical Centre, overlooking the beach, was the first important building to near completion. It was a large barn-like building cloistering small individual rooms at the back. Those not too busy flocked to the site to watch the crane lift roof trusses into position. With galvanised iron sheets nailed in place, the facility was almost ready, providing a boost to community morale. The sight of the water treatment and effluent processing plants, windmills, and a few spindly streetlights becoming established added to the sense of progress. The backhoe, working non-stop, excavated trenches for water lines, waste pipes and electrical cables. A rudimentary town was taking shape.

At last, they reached a decisive stage. With sharing, enough apartments were ready to begin permanent living above ground. A disorganised scramble for apartments ensued. For several days, the action was at fever pitch as cars and trailers transported everything useful for day-to-day living from the bunker and Bunkertown. The fair distribution of furniture caused strife, and an insufficient number of heating units due to an oversight in stocking the second bunker meant disappointment for many.

After transferring supplies and equipment to the Medical Centre, George opened the centre up for business. With everything but the heaviest machinery cleared and life-support systems closed down, Bunkertown became an empty shell. The final act was to close the control valve supplying water to it and open the other valve, to supply the newly laid piping for the rough but habitable town.

A huge cheer went up as water cascaded through the system; clean, safe water. The people rejoiced, playing in it, drinking it like wine. The euphoria was genuine, washing away doubts and anxieties in the certain evidence that sustainable life above ground was a reality.

The joy continued into the evening, unaffected by the onset of a bitterly cold night. The Medical Centre hosted a feast, supported by the remaining alcoholic beverages from Bunkertown. With all restrictions forgotten, the release of inhibitions followed.

Outside, a group of men were enjoying their prospects. Each held a glass, their consumption of alcohol already making up for lost time. Another imminent freedom was on their minds.

"Two and a half years of celibacy ends tonight," Fred announced, puckering his lips in anticipation.

"Good," a man with a gravelly voice replied. "Now I don't have to worry you might jump into my bed." They all laughed.

"The electricity isn't connected to our place yet," another commented. "I might not recognise my wife in the dark after so long."

"You can use the generous window space and streetlights," Fred suggested sarcastically.

More laughter, as they peered at a lighted pole a short distance away. The illumination was not brilliant, the windmills supplying limited power. Several couples hovered beneath the pole, one man pressing a woman against it, enveloping her in his arms.

"Who needs to see?" the man with a gravelly voice snarled. "It wouldn't worry me if I scored the wrong wife."

Again the laughter. He was not the only one feeling that way.

"That's right. Why not a new start in every way?" Fred encouraged. "I need more of this."

He held up his empty glass and moved towards the entrance. Most of the women had remained inside the centre, out of the cold. Fred's wife was not far away. Although they glimpsed each other, communication was noticeably absent as Fred received a refill of his drink and headed back outside.

Jocelyn returned her attention to the women in her group. "Fred expects to resume sex tonight," she said, the expression on her face reflecting disgust. "Well, it won't be with me, I'll make sure of that. Two years of peace is not going to waste. I'm looking for something better now."

"Me too," her friend responded. "My husband only ever thought of himself and what he wants. Now it's my turn."

Others sounded their support. Similar sentiments were evident in other groups. The free flow of alcohol was having its effect on everyone, adding to the embracing of new-found liberty and accelerating the release of inhibitions. The brief period of togetherness since emerging from Bunkertown was of little consequence in overturning two and a half years of dormancy in relationships. Now they were at the beginning again, and many felt unwilling to slip back into the former situation. By the end of the evening, several, with alcohol-induced impunity, had abandoned their spouses and entered into loose liaisons without commitment or responsibility.

Chapter 5

The reaction to freedom signalled a new direction for the community. With the pressure to establish life above ground disappearing overnight, selfishness and promiscuity took hold. A mentality of uncaring indifference had returned.

Self-policing under a one-status system was no longer workable. The Committee of Ten was defunct and unable to command respect. In an attempt to control worsening lawlessness and offer women protection against men who had gone wild, representatives from community factions formed a loose coalition. The only real authority they could exercise, however, was in town planning and other practical considerations. Try as they may, they had no impact in maintaining order or influencing the increasing aggressive behaviour.

Many people had too much spare time and little initiative or desire to contribute, causing dissatisfaction amongst those who did contribute. Inefficiency was a natural consequence. The further development of town, notably apartment construction, slowed drastically. The continued sharing of accommodation caused friction, which heightened whenever a newly completed apartment did come up for allocation. The most aggressive or intransigent usually won out. The coalition was unable to wield power in such matters.

On the high side of the main road, apartments extended almost to the Medical Centre, on the other to some way back from it just past the loop road. The first apartment there was used for administrative meetings. The large open space adjacent became a place of congregation for people with few places to go, and for distribution of food. Crude earth-cement benches were installed over a portion of it, creating the appearance of a ramshackle marketplace.

With construction at a low, the plant operators found another outlet for the active role they coveted. They steadily worked through the old town to demolish the ruins. Steel reinforcement, salvaged from the ruins, became a much sought-after building product.

Benjamin and his parents, like most family units, were fortunate to have an apartment to themselves, on the high side near the Medical Centre. Kelly and her parents had one at the other end, near the depot. Inconvenient as it was, the families often spent evenings together at one place or the other.

Benjamin and Kelly were teenagers now. Both were becoming more conscious of their bodies. Kelly was developing into an attractive young lady with her medium-length, curly blonde hair, smooth, well-proportioned features and winning smile. Her body was changing from the flatness of youth to womanly curves. Benjamin, as well as being aware of the changes in Kelly, could feel his own body filling out, and his voice was deeper. They were happy in each other's company.

Marcia's determination to be involved with Jean's group soured her relationship with Alec. Barely tolerated by him, she attended every group meeting, usually insisting Kelly go with her. It affected Kelly greatly.

Late afternoon one day, she and Benjamin were sitting on a piece of broken concrete at the front of a building site.

"I'll probably have to go with my mother to her meeting tonight," Kelly said despondently. "It's so creepy."

Benjamin was unimpressed by the group's influence on Kelly's mother and the pressure on Kelly. "What have they been talking about?"

"The usual stuff. They discuss how men have made a mess of things. They complain about how basic life is, the struggle to produce enough food and how cold it is in their homes."

Benjamin nodded, acknowledging the discomforts inherent in their lives. "It's not easy for anyone. But we all suffer the same. The men as well."

Kelly stared across the road at a deserted site. "I wish mother wasn't so taken in by it all. She's too easily influenced."

"Does she say much at the meetings?"

"Not much. She mostly listens and usually agrees with everyone. Last time, one woman was really nasty. She said all men are lazy and only want to chase after women and take advantage of them."

"A lot of men are doing that," Benjamin noted thoughtfully. "But there are women who want it, too. And not all men are bad."

Kelly smiled fondly at him and moved closer, clasping his hand affectionately. "Yes. But this woman seemed to think so. I'm glad you're not like that, Benjamin."

On an impulse, she kissed him on the cheek. They each felt the warmth of being together, in perfect harmony. They were lucky. Many people were separated from their partners, caring about no one. Benjamin put his arm around her, reassuring her. Kelly rested her head against him. Soon her father joined them and they left the work site. Benjamin rode home on his bicycle, Kelly and her father walking home.

Later, Alec, Marcia and Kelly drove to Benjamin's parents' home for an evening meal. As darkness fell, the cold set in. The air was clammy. They sat around the table near the cooking end of the apartment, making use of warmth from the stove. The apartment was basic but comfortable with its few items of furniture, including double bunk and single bed at the other end. Opposite the beds, an alcove hid the toilet and washroom.

They concentrated on their food in silence, each conscious of tension around the table. Alec in particular was unsettled. He was the first to speak, peering at his wife.

"Are you going to one of those meetings tonight?"

Marcia turned to her husband with a defiant look on her face. "Yes," she replied curtly.

The challenging tone of voice inflamed her husband instantly. His face hardened. "No doubt you'll come back with more fancy nonsense in your head."

Kelly gripped Benjamin's hand under the table, her body tensed, her mind confused. The beliefs driving the group of women made her fearful, yet she had to support her emotionally gullible mother. She hated being forcibly distanced from her father, although his stability ensured it never stayed that way for long.

Marcia was now able to stand up to her husband, drawing confidence from the women's example. "It might be fancy nonsense to you," she retorted, "but it makes sense to me. It's because of attitudes like yours that we need a women's group."

"Is that right?!" Alec shouted angrily. "And how do you think life would be if it wasn't for us men?"

Marcia's new found confidence took another leap. "Probably still as it was before any of this happened. Before Bunkertown."

Alec thumped his fist on the table. He glared at his wife. "We work hard to build a new town. And all the time you blame us for what's happened. These women you meet with are sick and they're making you sick as well!"

"If the women are sick, it's because of what men are doing to them. Look at the affairs and rapes going on. Men only care about getting what they want."

Alec looked at her with contempt then returned to derisive mode. "Not much chance of that in my case, is there."

"No, because I won't let you. Not while you've got that sort of attitude."

Kelly burst into tears, unable to take it any longer. Benjamin put his arm around her and she buried her face against his chest, sobbing and pleading with them to stop.

George cut in. "I think that's enough. We'll get nowhere like this. We have to depend on each other, so let's try to help each other."

Gloria leaned forward and took her husband's arm. "I agree. We have to think about the future and support each other."

Marcia turned away, a bold look of defiance fixed on her face. Acutely aware of her isolated position, she sought her only source of comfort. But Kelly was clinging to Benjamin, avoiding direct contact with her. No one spoke for some time. Finally Alec broke the silence, in control of himself again.

"We'll go home now."

His meal half-eaten, he stood. Marcia sprang to her feet, pleased to escape another circumstance of rejection. Reluctantly Kelly rose, looking helplessly at Benjamin. She followed her parents out.

That evening changed the relationship between the two families. Apart from Benjamin, Kelly and her father, they were no longer as close. To Benjamin, it was disturbingly symptomatic of people in general. He was intensely conscious of how lack of communication was estranging everyone, and the possibility of the rift similarly infecting him and Kelly troubled him.

As time passed, the community descended further and further down the destructive spiral of self-indulgence and self-interest. People had scant regard for each other or for individual rights. The lack of law enforcement contributed greatly to it. With little respect for relationships, more and more couples separated and carried on affairs. Some women enjoyed the freedom, no longer answering to their original spouse or any man in particular. Others took pleasure in exercising power over men by manipulating them while detesting them at the same time. Many, however, developed a culture of hatred or severe distrust, and withdrew from contact. Some men responded aggressively. Rapes occurred frequently, treated largely with indifference by the community at large. Other men developed a lack of confidence through feelings of not being needed.

For couples happy in a stable relationship, such as Gloria and George, life was very difficult, demanding great strength of character and a good deal of luck. They were no longer the norm and found rejection in every corner of their new town.

Women fell pregnant. Uncertainty in identifying the father was commonplace. The birth rate escalated, from zero almost a year after Re-emergence to 180 in the next. It was a drain on resources. The Medical Centre was constantly overloaded. To cope with it, construction work concentrated for a while on building more small rooms behind the main building. The demand on George's time was heavy.

Marcia and Alec continued to be alienated from one another, although they stayed together for Kelly's sake. Alec did not stamp too hard on his wife's frustrating involvement with Jean's group. They spent no more evenings with George and Gloria. Only Gloria and Marcia saw each other regularly, working the crop fields. Kelly kept on dividing her time between them and her father and Benjamin. At lunchtime one day, she and Benjamin sat on a twisted steel beam embedded in a pile of debris behind a site.

"They argued again last night," she said. "What can I do?"

"Was it about your mother's group again?" Benjamin looked at her pretty face; drawn and tired-looking. He wanted to take away her pain and make it his, but how could he?

Kelly nodded. "The group is getting stronger. Some of their attitudes are crazy. The other night, Jean talked about what they could do if women were in control of the community."

"That's interesting. How would they achieve that? No one has control of anything. People do what they want."

"It's scary. She said the only way to control a man is through sex." Kelly looked up at him. Her eyes were searching, trying to find an answer to what she had heard.

Benjamin looked at her curiously. Without realising what he was doing, he raised his hand and slowly, lightly brushed a lock of hair past her ear with the back of his fingers.

Kelly's colour rose and her heart beat faster. She sighed softly, raising her hand to smooth his dark wavy hair. Enchanted by his strong features and air of assurance, she moved closer. They came together, their lips meeting in a loving kiss. A natural act of commitment. Their hearts swelled with the thrill of it. They played with each other's hair and kissed again, and nothing else in the world mattered.

They continued for some time, discovering a new dimension in each other. Eventually, Kelly put her head on his shoulder, wrapping her arms around his chest. They sat in blissful silence until finally she raised her head.

"I have to go," she whispered reluctantly. "My mother is expecting me."

She kissed him again and stood, feeling safe and contented. Benjamin jumped up and they moved away, leaving their lunches untouched.

"I'll get your father." He looked for him, but Alec was out of sight.

"No, he doesn't have to drive me today. I feel like walking."

"He won't be pleased," Benjamin urged. "You know he never lets you go by yourself."

"I'll be okay. You can tell him."

With a lingering smile, she departed, full of confidence.

Benjamin sat in contemplation, caught between concern and a little guilt at letting her leave by herself, and enraptured by what had happened between them. They had kissed before a number of times, but never with so much feeling. Unaffected by the problems of others, he gave thanks to the fate that had given him Kelly.

He thought of what she had told him. He had no experience, but for a woman to suggest 'the only way to control a man is through sex' sounded insidious and calculating, not at all what he expected sex to be about. For a moment, he was worried. Her mother would continue forcing Kelly to attend the meetings. Then he reminded himself of what had just taken place. Feeling reassured, he returned to work.

As Kelly left him, she felt more secure than ever before. Cementing the bond between them satisfied a deep need in her, boosting the strength required to cope with her mother's demands. The promise of their relationship developing further on a physical plane was exciting, preoccupying her as she set out for the crop fields.

She passed a construction site, then apartment blocks, eventually turning left down the loop road. The number of people on the road was thinning out as she left behind more apartments and attached houses. She rounded the corner of the last building to start across the open ground towards the crop fields. Better standard house construction loomed in the distance.

Suddenly a young man confronted her, stopping her in her tracks. It jolted Kelly from pleasant thoughts. Instantly she was frightened.

He was rough and unwashed, with dirty, lank hair hanging shoulder-length. His clothes were filthy. He grinned hideously at Kelly, a gleam of malicious intent in his eyes. Kelly turned to flee, but he grabbed her arm, gripping it tightly. With a shriek of fear, she tried to pull away.

"I've seen you before," he drooled sadistically. "You must be looking for me."

"No!" Kelly cried, panic-stricken as she failed to free her arm. "Leave me alone!"

The man sneered, leering into her face aggressively. "Yeah. That's what all you women say."

Then the grin was gone, an ugly grimace taking its place as his lip curled with hate. He swung his hand, striking her viciously across the cheekbone. Kelly squealed as she stumbled backwards and fell to the ground.

"Benjamin!" she screamed, terror-stricken. "Help me!"

She tried to scramble away, but the man leapt on top of her, pinning her arms to the ground painfully with his knees. He struck her again across the face, and again, several times with both fists. Kelly screamed with each blow. Her body convulsed cruelly. Frantically she struggled, trying to break free, every muscle fighting him. But he was too strong. He lay on her, trapping her body beneath his. His heavy body pressed her into the ground, revolting her with its foul odour. Then he was tearing at her clothes, his greasy flesh against hers, forcing her legs apart, violating her.

Kelly fought him, frenzied as she strove to save herself. Then something inside her snapped, tearing at her soul, flooding her in evil. Gone were all her hopes and dreams.

Suddenly the weight of his body shifted to one side as more screams filled the air. The struggle intensified from a new source as two women tore at the man furiously.

"Get off her! Get off her!"

Marcia was fired by an insane rage. She and Gloria beat at the man with their fists, dragging him off Kelly, scratching at his face. Tenaciously they attacked him till he tired of it and ran off.

"My poor girl," Marcia whimpered, crawling to her daughter's side. "My poor girl."

She groped at Kelly possessively. Kelly lay immobile, frozen in shock. Her wide-open eyes stared straight up but unseeing.

Panting heavily, Gloria scrambled to her side. "We must get her to the Medical rooms."

They covered her with one of their coats. Each took an arm and lifted Kelly to her feet. They staggered to the road and began moving along it falteringly. No one helped them. Despite the nearby presence of people throughout the ordeal, no one had been interested in intervening.

The afternoon wore on steadily as Alec and Benjamin concentrated on laying pipes. Benjamin knew something was seriously wrong when he saw his mother dashing up the road towards them, waving her arms wildly. Alec saw her as well. Alarmed, they dropped their tools and ran to the road. Benjamin was aghast as she rushed to them in a state of distress. Her face and torn clothes were smeared with blood. Strands of hair flopped over her eyes, but she ignored them. Gasping for breath, she seized Alec by the arm.

"Come quickly. It's Kelly!"

She grabbed Benjamin's arm, tugging at them both. Fearful, they began running, following her back along the road. The Medical rooms were a long way. Out of breath, they reached them and sped through the main building to a small room out the back.

"What happened!" Alec shouted as they burst in.

George was hovering over the bed, where Kelly lay prone under a blanket. Her face was partly covered with bloodstained bandages, blonde hair plastered across her forehead. She was looking up vacantly with wide-open, glazed eyes, and registered no reaction as her father and Benjamin leaned over. Her breathing came in shallow gasps.

George stepped back to address them. "She's in shock at the moment. She's had a terrible experience, but she'll recover. We've taken care of her. She needs to rest."

Marcia was standing at the foot of the bed, her hands trembling as tightly intertwined fingers covered her mouth. Her appearance mirrored that of Gloria, clothes torn and stained with blood, hair dishevelled. She had been crying, and was still sobbing, her body shaking with fright. Alec turned to her.

"Tell me what happened! What's wrong with our daughter?"

Marcia was too overwrought to respond. Gloria, more composed now, came forward.

"A man attacked Kelly. She was on her way to join us in the fields, but she never got there."

"Attacked!" Alec bellowed, clenching his fists. "What did he do to her?"

"She's been severely bashed," George confirmed. "She has cuts and abrasions, not deep ones but she lost some blood, and she has concussion. The man raped her."

Alec and Benjamin stared at him then down at Kelly again; both stunned by the word they feared most.

"Raped!" Alec cried, his clenched fists raised, seeking an outlet of revenge. "How can this happen? Who did this?!"

George tried to calm him. "I've examined her. She has bruising and some bleeding, but will recover from that. She must have fought furiously against him."

"We stopped him," Gloria added, with a glance at Marcia. "She was late. We thought the car must have broken down. We found her pinned to the ground by this man. We dragged him off and fought till he ran away."

The room fell silent as the impact of her explanation sank in. At her reference to the car, Alec looked briefly at Benjamin then drooped his head in self-reproach. A hollow nausea gripped Benjamin in the stomach, and he cursed himself for letting Kelly depart by herself. Gloria brushed a strand of hair from her face and took his hands in hers, consoling him.

"Kelly will come through this, Benjamin," she said softly. "With your support, she'll be a whole girl again, and you'll be happy together."

Kelly made a full recovery from her injuries. She gradually came out of the shock, and was soon walking around again. However, the experience left her scarred psychologically. She was reticent and uptight in a way she never had been before, easily becoming nervous and uncertain under any sort of pressure.

She no longer joined her father and Benjamin during the day, staying close to her mother at all times. Marcia was determined to shield her from men. In a sick way, she seemed to gain confidence from having Kelly more dependent on her, as if to share a similar frailty was to somehow compensate for it. This was of no benefit to Kelly, her mother's increased possessiveness only stifling her progress.

Benjamin saw Kelly as often as he could, encouraged by her father but made more difficult by her mother. It was only possible at night, but even then was hampered by their parents not spending time together any more and by Kelly's regular attendance with her mother at the women's group meetings. As time went by, there were fewer evenings available to him and more for group meetings. The trend worried and frustrated Benjamin greatly.

Too often, he saw Kelly only in the presence of her mother, dearly treasuring any time they did have alone. Kelly was happy when with him, trying hard to be the girl she once was, even comprehending her own problems. However, when it came to any sort of close physical contact, she would tense up and shy away nervously. This upset them both, but she could not help herself.

Benjamin was patient and understanding, never trying to force anything. All he could do was persevere and hope for improvement. In the meantime, he felt as devastated as Kelly that something special had been taken from them.

Chapter 6

Four years after Re-emergence, the debauched attitudes rife in the community were worse than ever. People behaved individually, caring only about gratification of the moment. Couples staying together were in a decreasing minority. Children old enough to indulge themselves, and more becoming so, gave little hope for improvement.

As a consequence, the demand to construct more apartments had been continuous. The rate of completion was slow, with those doing the work begrudging the lack of contribution from those wanting the apartments. The end to demand was in sight, however, the youngest Bunkertown children nearly eleven years old now. After them, some seven years would have to pass before children born after Re-emergence began a repeat of the cycle.

Construction of houses beyond the loop road had been completed a short time ago. Women representing Jean's group, wielding strong influence within the coalition, had been the main driving force for accommodation reflecting a graduation in status. Most in the community did not care or comprehend it, paying little heed to formal allocation. Difference in status meant nothing in the scramble to grab a house, unsupervised like everything.

The people had become used to environmental restrictions, although the cold was difficult to live with. A light sprinkling of rain had occurred on just a few occasions, causing panic the first time as everyone dashed indoors. No radioactive contamination had resulted, though some of the crops were damaged by the acidic rain.

* * *

A man standing at the top of the rise beside the Medical Centre began shouting excitedly, pointing out to sea at a small shape.

"A ship! A ship!"

The news spread fast and soon everyone was crowding to the rise and spilling down on to the beach. Mesmerised, all watched as the shape grew larger.

Ominously, the ship crept into the harbour. It looked like a fishing trawler and was badly in need of maintenance. Its paint was flaking off and rust pitted the upper hull. As it anchored near the ruins of the wharf, people rushed along the beach, shouting and waving in an unusual show of unity. Consumed with self-interest, nobody had addressed the prospect of life elsewhere; not even in their own country, let alone the rest of the world.

Four characters marked on the rusting hull near the bow identified the ship as Asian, possibly Chinese. Crew rowed a small boat ashore, delivering two fit-looking men about thirty-five years of age and two attractive Chinese women. Ecstatic, the crowd swarmed and escorted them up the beach. They rallied at the open ground on the main road. Someone fetched a loud hailer. The four passengers stood on a bench, and one of the men greeted the people with a broad smile.

"Hi, everyone. I'm Jason. This is Bernard, Suchee and Tylin."

Jason indicated his companions in turn. He ran his fingers through a head of light brown hair and surveyed the crowd with confidence. He was powerfully built with hard lines to his face, a man moulded by harsh reality. Bernard was from the same mould. Standing together, they appeared a formidable pair.

"It's good to be back on Australian soil," Jason went on, with genuine sincerity. "I knew we'd make it one day. You're welcome is overwhelming, and we thank you kindly."

As the crowd cheered, Jason acknowledged them by raising a clenched fist and punching the air.

"It's seventeen years since Bernard and I left Australia, as young doctors with an aid group to the Balkans. We stayed in Europe after that. It seems a long time ago now."

He paused to reflect.

"War has been devastating everywhere. I can see it's the same here, although you're lucky to have avoided nuclear attack. Much of the world is uninhabitable because of radiation, including Europe. We left there three years ago, travelling by sea to South East Asia, where the chances were better. We lost the ship there, so we continued overland, trekking north using whatever means of transport we could find. Every day, the search for food was difficult. I would not describe what we sometimes had to eat. But we were lucky. Whenever it seemed hopeless, we'd come to an isolated pocket of survivors who helped us. Most places were unprepared for annihilation on such a scale, even though destruction was not by nuclear means in that region of the world. Only when we reached China, barely alive, did we find a community of any size. More people survived in China because they had extensive bunkers. These two ladies nursed us back to good health."

The Chinese women smiled briefly as Jason paid tribute to them, then reverted to a reserved, expressionless manner. Jason continued.

"I remember Darwin having a hot climate, and humid. Nowhere is like that now. Much of our travels, by sea and overland, were in former tropical areas, but it was always the same polluted atmosphere, and cold. The environment is barely sustaining the little population that remains. Of course, the big killer in the end was biological."

He hesitated, surveying the crowd as they watched him in stunned silence.

"Services we all took for granted years ago, like radio, television, telephone, computer link-up are no more. Interaction between survivors in different parts of the world is no longer possible. Air travel is a thing of the past, and even overland is too difficult for most. In China, they've resurrected some infrastructure. We obtained the ship, fuel and a crew, and set sail from Hong Kong. And here we are!"

He turned to Bernard, who joined him exulting in triumph. Bernard took the loud hailer and thanked the people for their hospitality. He praised the effort in building a new town and offered their expertise in the medical field for betterment of the community.

The crowd had been listening spellbound to the first real confirmation of what had happened to the world. A short pause followed Bernard's speech before they erupted in a rousing ovation. They led the four arrivals to an apartment near the Medical Centre, forcing a man to vacate. They brought food and extended all comforts available.

Jason, Bernard and their partners quickly settled into the community, satisfied it offered a future. The ship unloaded ten large unmarked boxes and departed for China. George, curious about what was in the boxes and pleased to have more medical staff, immediately became acquainted with the two men. He helped set them up at the Medical rooms. He was soon impressed with their wealth of knowledge, particularly in advanced medical research gained through years of work in Germany. He tried many times to see what they had unpacked from the boxes, but Jason simply shushed him away saying, "Just a little research we brought with us. Nothing to concern yourself about."

George invited them home for an evening. It was the first social exchange since Alec's family had ceased coming. Gloria put in a special effort and they sat around the table enjoying a fine meal. When Jason finished his, he leaned back in the chair.

"The food is good. I've never had soybean prepared that way before. You've done well to create a community here."

"Perhaps better than on your travels?" George suggested, proud of his wife.

"We'd have been here sooner if we'd known," Bernard remarked amusedly.

Suchee and Tylin remained impassive, showing not a flicker of emotion. The impression would have been of language difficulty, except Jason had previously mentioned they were fluent in English. Benjamin watched them, wondering what they were thinking. Gloria was quiet, knowing her husband, although different, was not unused to communicating with men like these.

"You were fortunate to leave Germany," George remarked.

The comment echoed Benjamin's thoughts. Conditions there must have been horrific, giving them powerful motivation to undertake an arduous journey. Oddly, both men were guarded, but in unspoken accord without looking at each other.

"We're Australian," Jason replied. "We wanted to come back."

He was a shrewd yet forceful character, strong in following a chosen path and undeterred by the prospect of hardship. George knew the approach to take.

"Were many nuclear warheads dropped on Germany?"

"Yes, quite a few."

"All over Europe," Bernard added. "Everywhere, there is nothing but devastation."

"Where did you stay when it was on?"

"We were bunkered beneath a research centre near the Dutch border; a sealed, self-contained unit. The Germans were well-prepared, huge bunkers ready for occupation all over the country. Many Germans were saved."

George was thoughtful. "It was different here. This was the only place with a fully prepared bunker. We've seen no one from other parts of the country."

Bernard glanced at Jason. "Looks like we'd better stay here, then."

"What were the facilities like in your bunker?" George asked, hoping to get a glimmer of what these men were up to.

"Very good," Jason answered. "Everything a person could want or need. We continued our research as if we were still above ground."

George was being careful, trying to assess what he could comfortably ask. "The Germans must have felt your research important to continue with it under such circumstances."

Jason hesitated before replying. "They did. They monitored the work closely, expecting results. The future was at stake, they said."

Bernard murmured his endorsement. "Others were working on it as well."

Both realised co-operation with George and other medical personnel would be necessary in establishing themselves here. The three men engaged in a brief discussion about more technical aspects of their research. Benjamin and Gloria did not understand the medical talk with its unfamiliar terms and language, but Benjamin noticed his father becoming strangely uneasy. And the two Chinese women appeared more focussed, evident in their dark but penetrating eyes, bringing no change in manner or expression, however.

"It was all to advance their national interests," Bernard explained. "The Germans have a deep-seated obsession about proving themselves. That's reflected in their plans for future development."

"They were using our skills to further their ambitions," Jason added.

"Is that why you left?" George queried, detecting another reason as well as environmental.

"We're not Germans," Jason replied. "Socialism rose quickly. Their ambitions were leading to organised expansionism, and we didn't like contributing to that. But the need was to find habitable land, the best prospect being South East Asia. The chance to get to Australia appealed to us. We hoped there'd be a place left standing that would enable us to continue our work."

"The Germans built a small ship at Rotterdam, using uncontaminated materials from storage," Bernard went on. "They needed doctors for the journey. It was not hard to be chosen, as we came from near Asia originally. And our bunker was one of the closest to Rotterdam. The short overland trip there was the most dangerous part, only possible by wearing fully enclosed protective suits till on board the ship."

"What happened when you reached South East Asia?"

Bernard gave a wry, humourless smile. "We arrived on the west Malaysian coast, at Penang. A group of local people were hostile. They wanted the ship, but there was a fight and it finished up in a ball of fire. Jason and I escaped with our equipment."

Around the table, all fell silent as they pondered the circumstances. Benjamin was intrigued at the implied connection between the men's research and their strong motivation to leave Germany. He wondered how they had managed to move all that equipment around by themselves. He began to share his father's uneasiness. The rest of the evening was pleasant if a little awkward, as if deeper issues were to remain unspoken.

After that evening, George did not talk about what the two men were doing, although it worried him. His relationship with them did not become overly friendly, and no more social evenings took place.

Time as always went by steadily, and the construction of apartments neared an end. Benjamin and Kelly's father more and more avoided talking about Kelly as they worked. She improved only marginally in the face of her mother's stifling possessiveness. Benjamin's visits to see her became infrequent, coinciding with her mother's increased obsession with the women's group. For the first time in his life, circumstances challenged his positive outlook and he struggled to reconcile the injustices of life. Gloria had to call on all her strength of character to maintain family stability, with Benjamin often low in spirits and George troubled by daily events at the Medical Centre. The many temptations rampant in the community constantly threatened.

One evening, as Benjamin sat with little to do after dinner, Gloria felt concerned for him.

"Are you seeing Kelly this evening?" she asked.

Benjamin shook his head. "It's one of their nights with the women's group."

His mother nodded. "The group is getting stronger. The two Chinese women are involved now as well."

George had been preoccupied, but heard what she said. "Really?" he responded with interest. "I didn't know that. But then, I don't have much to do with Jason and Bernard now, or their work." He paused, rubbing a forefinger across his cheekbone. "Their research is very technical. I know broadly what it's about, but I don't know what they hope to achieve by it. That bothers me. And if this women's group get interested through the Chinese women ...."

His voice tailed off and he fell into a distracted silence. Benjamin and his mother knew too little to pursue it.

"Can you find out more from Jason or Bernard?" Gloria suggested.

George shook his head. "I don't think they want others to be involved. Very little has happened so far. Like all of us, they're waiting for completion of the Administration Centre, where the new Medical Centre and laboratories will be far better."

Construction of the Administration Centre had started recently. Taking up much of the open space on the main road, it was by far the largest, most ambitious undertaking attempted. It would be the first two-storey building, made possible by a better grade of gravel now being excavated for the earth-cement mix. Steel reinforcement, scrounged from the ruins, would strengthen the structure. With no glass left, there would be no windows. The coalition, having discarded all pretensions of control over the wayward community, had decided to focus on an apparent need for a centralised point of decision-making and administration of services. A symbol of power. The impressive medical facilities planned were successful in generating community acceptance for the project.

Benjamin brightened at his father's mention of it. He and Kelly's father would be working there periodically, an exciting challenge.

"It'll take months to complete. When it's finished, it'll be like some of the buildings we used to have."

His mother and father smiled at each other with pride. George contemplated how his son had developed, handling himself and their tenuous circumstances in many ways better than himself. He knew it came from the strength of his wife. Life without her was unimaginable. A thought occurred to him. He went to the cupboard across the room, soon returning with a large folder. Benjamin recognised it from years ago, when it had been a source of great interest to his father.

George looked to his wife, who nodded encouragement. "Do you remember this, Benjamin?" He handed it to him. "If anything happens to me and your mother, you must look after this book, keep it safe at all times."

Gloria stood and bent to kiss Benjamin lightly on the cheek. "We'll go to bed now."

Left alone, Benjamin laid the book flat on the coffee table and smoothed his hand over the dark green cover, respecting the reverence with which his father regarded it. He adjusted the table lamp then opened the book slowly.

The scrapbook contained photographs, each with a short description beneath in his father's handwriting, and newspaper clippings. Presentation and upkeep were meticulous; each item was stuck firmly to the page. Some clippings were yellow with age. He leaned forward with mounting excitement.

The entries were roughly in chronological order. The earliest was a clipping, yellow and brittle, dated 27 December 1974. The headline read: TRACY DEVASTATES DARWIN. Pictures of the town levelled by a cyclone reminded him of his father's description years ago of the event. It had been traumatic for his father, as a nine year-old boy, and his family.

Other clippings included one dated early 1991, referring to war in the Middle East between Iraq and American-led forces, a 1997 report about the cloning of a sheep somewhere in Europe, one detailing advancements in genetic engineering, an article about increasing numbers of new and mutating diseases, and another on the development of genetically modified food.

He turned a page. A photograph depicted his parents looking radiantly happy on their wedding day. Another was of his mother proudly holding their newly born baby, with a caption beneath, 'Benjamin, born 29 April 1998'. The joy emanating from this photo made him realise how much they had wanted him.

More photos traced his development as a happy young boy growing up in a loving family environment. Captions read, 'Benjamin at the beach', 'Benjamin with his Mum at pre-school', 'Benjamin's first day at school'. Soon, from age six years, photos included a pretty young girl with blonde, curly locks of hair and a cute smile. The captions read, 'Benjamin and Kelly at the theme park', 'Benjamin and Kelly at Kelly's 7th birthday party', and others similar.

He paused, comparing in his mind Kelly's happy face in the photos with the sorry, damaged state she was in now. It saddened him, but the photos gave him strength.

Interspersed amongst them were more newspaper clippings. Most confirmed his father's interest in world events, particularly concerning medicine, public health, the environment and related political issues. They brought back fond memories of happier days when his father would sit with him and describe reports in the newspaper. Benjamin's eyes widened as he focussed on some of the more dramatic ones.

One was titled: EBOLA SPREADS IN THE US, and detailed the proliferation of a mutated strain of the killer virus Ebola through Florida, which was in quarantine. A phenomenon called the Greenhouse Effect was causing increasing concern, global warming encouraging viruses like Ebola to flourish, mutate and spread.

Another was headed: NUCLEAR BUILD-UP IN THE MIDDLE EAST. US Intelligence had obtained confirmation of nuclear expansion in Middle Eastern countries, involving a long-suspected transfer of materials and technology from countries of the former Soviet Union.

More clippings described disasters - earthquakes, floods and droughts - wars, political development and the consequences for people throughout the world. Alarm was deepening amongst scientists following evidence that global warming was causing accelerating expansion of the oceans, resulting in large-scale release of carbon dioxide, rising sea levels and greater pressures on the sea floor. Two disasters stood out as major events, instantly capturing Benjamin's attention as he turned a page.

In large headlines, one read: TSUNAMI HORROR HITS SOUTHERN NATIONS. A major earthquake in the seabed under the Southern Ocean had set in train a tsunami, which swamped islands, the southern tips of South America, South Africa, New Zealand and the south coast of Australia. Coastal cities had been decimated.

The second was headed: ICE SHELF PLUNGES TO SEA. The entire Ross ice-shelf had broken from the Antarctic continent, plunging into the Southern Ocean. The catastrophic event had not been totally unexpected; scientists for some time having monitored undermining due to the melting of ice support.

Later reports described the after-effects of both disasters, felt around the world and considered directly attributable to the Greenhouse Effect. Over time, the ice broke up, floated north and melted, cooling the oceans in a temporary relieving capacity.

Political consequences had soon followed. Faced with the escalating impact of global warming, the United States and European Union began enforcing a strategy of drastic reduction in causative fossil fuel dependence and greenhouse gas emissions, pressuring nations worldwide with threats of economic sanctions. The US led the way, replacing the traditional motor vehicle with the electric car, which used methanol fuel conversion to hydrogen with solar power backup.

Middle Eastern countries saw a booming US-based industry in electric car and components manufacture plus methanol production from waste material replacing demand for their oil resources. Tension amongst them and resentment of the United States mounted rapidly. A new Islamic leader, Mushud Ahmed, coming to power launched into aggressive rhetoric aimed at the US and other Western-aligned nations. The Chinese began moving fast, copying US technology to set up their own electric car industry.

Benjamin paused to reflect. Electric cars had been a part of life for as long as he could remember. Now he knew how they had come about. But four and a half years after Re-emergence, not many were around any more. Like everything, maintenance was a problem due to the dwindling availability of spare parts. His father had ditched their own car when he drove too fast over a nasty hollow in the road surface, damaging the suspension. Benjamin still had his bicycle, which he maintained conscientiously.

He looked at the next clipping, headed: CHINA INVADES TAIWAN. After years of diplomatic pressure, Chinese forces had finally taken over the island state. Efforts to return Taiwan to the motherland had greatly intensified following the successful return of Hong Kong in 1997 and Macau two years later.

The next clippings were on medical issues. One reported an unsuccessful attempt by doctors in Europe to clone a human being from DNA sampling, fusion with a female egg stripped of its DNA, and implantation in a woman. The attempt was in defiance of a worldwide ban following the successful cloning of a sheep several years before.

Another informed of scientific evidence condemning genetically modified food, describing the cumulative effects over time of many foods no longer performing as fuel to the human metabolism. Some were even destructive to it, due to altered structural effects and the creation of hitherto unheard-of toxins and carcinogens.

Another concerned the use of mobile telephones, following a similar pattern from enthusiastic short-term gain to eventual reluctant admission of disastrous cumulative health problems. Benjamin shook his head in wonder at the repetitive examples of human frailty, the ignoring of clear warnings by nature in the grab for political and economic edge.

Later clippings concentrated on escalating tensions between countries. In the Middle East, fierce competition for supplying the drastically reduced demand for oil was leading to confrontation. The aggressive Mushud Ahmed, from east of the Persian Gulf, was threatening neighbouring countries. Conflict exploded with dramatic consequences.

A clipping's headline read: NUCLEAR STRIKES HORRIFY THE WORLD. Two Middle Eastern countries, traditional foes from twenty years back, had finally resorted to the nuclear option. The smaller of the two, already hostile to its neighbours and the Western world, received no assistance and was decimated in a short time.

Mushud Ahmed exulted in victory, taunting and threatening other neighbours and the West. The devastating capability and will to use it threw the world into a state of fear, balanced only by the promise of mutual deterrence. Benjamin stared at the page, enthralled by the background that explained why their Government had embraced the NSP.

The next clipping was full of sinister connotations, describing the threat biological agents posed to mankind. With protagonist countries all possessing biological weapons, and the further proliferation unknown, the potential for total obliteration of the world's population was very real. Easily released by means undetectable, minute quantities could decimate people through the slightest contact. Larger quantities strategically placed and carried by air and water would be able to quickly reach every corner of the earth's surface. The catastrophic nature of it shocked Benjamin.

He turned the page and saw: WAR DECLARED IN MIDDLE EAST. A missile attack from east of the Persian Gulf, using conventional weapons, targeted Saudi Arabia, traditionally the largest oil exporter. The United States, on friendly terms with Saudi Arabia in keeping the oil option open, responded with an intensive air bombardment from sea and land-based forces in the region.

A few more clippings provided graphic insight into the worsening conflict. Another was about Australian forces, a medical corps, sent to support the US effort. War was spreading, drawing in ground forces. Muslim-led countries worldwide were aligning with the Middle East's Mushud Ahmed, who was constantly issuing warnings that all Western, European and allied interests throughout the world were potential targets. Mutual deterrence was holding back the nuclear option, but fear of it was a dominating influence.

Benjamin's eyes widened at the next clipping: POPE ASSASSINATED. The fifty-eight-year-old Pontiff, John Paul III, had been gunned down outside St Peter's basilica in Rome. Assassination of a man committed to peace with rare conviction was expected to greatly inflame passions around the world, a massive blow to peace.

A chilling article drew comparisons between recent events and the predictions of a sixteenth century prophet, Nostradamus. His mirroring of disaster, conflict, health and environmental problems leading to war had been so accurate that his final horrendous prediction for the world was generating great consternation.

The next page was full of photos. One was of him and his father in crouched, mock wrestling mode with arms entwined, both laughing with faces turned towards the camera. His father's military-style uniform included a cap emblazoned: AUSTRALIAN MEDICAL CORPS.

The next page was the last. He leaned forward, startled by the final newspaper clipping dated May 2008.

WAR TURNS NUCLEAR, WASHINGTON DECIMATED

With extreme hatred building to mindless insanity, conventional fighting had finally stepped over the threshold to nuclear war. A warhead had been detonated over Washington. The US responded with nuclear devices despatched to major targets in the Middle East. Heated rhetoric from Mushud Ahmed, promising annihilation of any country supporting Western powers, heightened fear throughout the world.

A chill ran down Benjamin's spine. For the first time, he understood how frenetic technological advancement of some societies had accelerated alienation from others and from an over-exploited environment. Social dislocation had run wildly out of control, culminating in the use of destructive technology, which had plunged the world back to the beginning at a single point in history.

Although starting with nuclear warfare, however, in the end it was biological warfare that had devastated the world's population. The only survivors were those cocooned from it, avoiding contact till the substances turned benign.

He checked the remaining pages, but there were no more entries. He closed the book and stared reverently at it, silently thanking his father for giving him the means to understand.

* * *

Several months later, construction of the Administration Centre was complete. Alec and Benjamin felt considerable satisfaction at their part in it. The building was imposing with its dominating size and height above ground. The grey earth-cement and lack of windows gave it a stark, impersonal appearance, like a man without a face, hovering menacingly over adjacent buildings and the surrounding environment. The impression was of morbid secrecy.

George and the medical staff moved there with all supplies and equipment from the centre overlooking the harbour, leaving that empty. Others involved in administration took up the rest of the building. The scene was set for what followed.

Alec and Benjamin were working at a site some way up the main road. People were running, shouting and pointing excitedly.

"There's trouble at the Administration Centre!" a man yelled.

Alec and Benjamin joined them. At the centre, the scene was ugly and confused. A mass of people moved chaotically in all directions amidst fierce fighting. Bodies lay prone on the ground, already victims of violence. Screams of panic filled the air.

Many men looked similar, wearing white shirts with black shoulder pads, and were fighting alongside each other against the rest. They carried weapons, heavy clubs. A number were wielding axes. Real fear pervaded the air with the evidence of an organised, deliberate attack. Alec stood poised like a cat ready to strike, but uncertain whom to tackle or what it was about.

"They've taken over the place!" a man shouted, frenzied as he staggered about aimlessly. "We have to stop them!"

The white-shirted men were gaining the upper hand as more bodies, bloodied and lifeless, littered the road. Alec moved forward, just as movement at the entrance of the building signalled more white-shirted men coming out to join the fray. A number of women were close behind them. Marcia was one, and standing half-obscured behind her, Kelly.

The violence eased as resistance waned and people fled in terror. The aggressors presided over a gruesome scene of dead and injured, ignoring the cries of anguish. They helped no one, waiting menacingly with weapons held ready. Benjamin stayed well back, frozen in disbelief. The sight of Kelly and her mother, involved on the side of hostility, horrified him. Alec started forward angrily, pointing at Marcia.

"That's my wife! I want to speak to her!"

Marcia moved into the open, as two white-shirted men pounced on him. A brief struggle ensued, then a man stepped forward and struck him a blow across the head with his club. Alec reeled backwards, stunned but not seriously injured. He was furious. Despite being held, he started forward again towards his wife.

"I want to speak to my wife!"

Marcia advanced to confront him. The man with the club moved in to deal him another blow, but she held up her hand. She spoke in a steely tone.

"Wait. Let him speak."

Alec glared at her, hardly recognising his wife as the woman he knew. "What's going on here?"

"We've taken over the centre," Marcia stated coldly.

"What do you mean? Who's taken over? Why?"

"Never mind that. Just do as you're told."

Her determined air was unlike anything Alec had seen in her before. A new confidence was in place instead of the downtrodden personality he had so often derided in the past. Her attitude incensed him.

"This is your women's group. I knew they'd mess you up eventually!"

With a big effort, he threw off the two men restraining him. But before he could do anything, the men overwhelmed him. Blows rained down on him and he fell to his knees. Then, as if in slow motion, a man stepped up and swung an axe. Alec's head burst open like a shattered egg and his body slumped lifeless to the ground.

PART 2
EVOLVING STOCK
Year 2030

Chapter 7

Benjamin sat quietly, his body tense, hands shaking as he struggled to dispel the last remnants of trauma. His mouth was dry. He thought of making a cup of coffee, but to lift himself from the chair required too much effort.

What a lucky escape! Many men before him had not been so lucky. He would have to be more diligent in future, make a special effort to prove his unquestioned compliance with the requirements of his job. He lifted his head and wiped the beads of perspiration from his forehead with the back of a sleeve. He slowly stood, stepped over and gazed through the small window. The hazy sun was about to drop below the roofline of the apartments across the road. The ruddy glow of the sky was fading. It was the start of another dreary evening.

The apartments in this once-proud town epitomised the all-pervading dreariness. Their grey appearance was a grim reminder of hasty construction twenty years ago. The needs were simple then, for people requiring accommodation in a hurry. Benjamin stared across the road and wondered if the occupants spent time staring at his apartment. Such a sentiment reflected how little he knew of even his closest neighbours.

He returned to the chair, put his feet on the coffee table and studied the far wall. A bleakly uninspiring wall. Faded yellow paint was flaking off the rough cement, typifying the state of the apartment. A picture of a horse hung there, contented in a paddock of lush green grass. He could see the irony of it in today's world. He stared at the only true alteration to his humble dwelling; a small doorway, cut into the flaky concrete. A small wooden door showed gaps of light through its ill fitting. It might have been rough but it was made by his hands and that was important to him. As he studied the weathered timber of the door, he couldn't help but wonder why he'd slaved those long nights to make it. He never actually used the door; only once had he opened it and even then it was just to see if it worked. With a sad smile, he turned from the door and its small significance and studied the rest of the room.

A single bare light bulb in the centre of the ceiling gloomily illuminated the sparseness of his life. The events of the day had focussed his mind on stark reality, forcing him to reassess his circumstances. The other two walls were bare except for a small clock, showing the time to be almost 6.00 pm. In the far corner was a single bed and mattress, covered with several old blankets. A chest of drawers, wardrobe, writing table and second chair completed the sum of his worldly belongings.

In the corner farthest from the bed, a built-in bench with stove and sink provided basic cooking and washing facilities. Benjamin rarely used them. Built-in cupboards gave refuge to a meagre supply of cutlery and cooking utensils. A larder next to the bench housed the few supplies he had bothered to obtain. He could recollect how indispensable a refrigerator had been when he was a young boy. No need for one in today's cold climate.

A shallow alcove in the wall opposite the bed hid the toilet, shower and washbasin. Lack of ventilation made it Benjamin's least favoured part of the apartment. Grimacing, he fixed his attention on the far wall again. He was calming. In moments, normality was restored and he became aware of the creeping cold. He went to the bed, grabbed a blanket and wrapped it around his shoulders. Returning to the chair, he began to reflect on his narrow escape.

The day had started as any other. Benjamin rode to the Clonesseum, arriving precisely on time, as usual, to settle behind his desk. He held a position of unusual responsibility for a man, although without any prospect of advancement. Apart from the Department Head, no one else worked in Records.

Benjamin had achieved his position by being meticulous in his duties and displaying unequivocal obedience at all times. He suppressed even the slightest doubt or resentment concerning anything he was instructed to do. This wasn't always easy for him. However, observance of what happened to others not so obedient had moved him rapidly up the learning curve.

Benjamin reflected on how easily he had found himself in a compromised position. The day was proceeding uneventfully, as always. He completed several tasks and turned to the final one. The case file revealed nothing unusual until he came to the name of the clone mother: Karla Mason. He knew her. She worked in the Laboratories Department, upstairs. Normally any woman in the community might be chosen as a clone mother, and most regarded the violating imposition of it as better than remaining in a state of insecure worthlessness. It at least moved them slightly ahead in the social order, and was their only hope of satisfying motherhood instincts. However, Karla was part of the system, having rare access to case files. That had always meant automatic exclusion. It surprised him.

He had met Karla twice, in the cafeteria where most workers in the Clonesseum gravitated for lunch. The first time, she was behind him in the queue for food. For some reason, she offered a brief greeting.

"Hello, Benjamin. Are you still working in Records?"

He wondered why she would choose to make contact with him. Even here, people knew each other only superficially. Everywhere, the stunted, distrustful mentality was the same. A result of fear and insecurity entrenched over the years since the Family took control. To begin with, Benjamin had been determined to maintain an open manner, even in situations others would treat with suspicion, but the endless suppression had taken its toll.

"Yes, I am. Are you still in Laboratories?" He was curious but kept it from his voice.

Karla nodded, offering a demure smile that was slightly flirtatious.

Benjamin felt ill at ease. Lacking experience of a meaningful relationship with a woman sometimes affected his ability to relate confidently. Unsure of her motives, he moved away with his food.

Two days later, she took a seat opposite him. He glanced at her but without showing interest, the fear of encouraging suspicion having taught him how to be discreet in his observations. Karla was appealing despite her conservative, unflattering dress typical of women. She was in her mid-twenties, with medium-length auburn hair, pleasant features and a well-proportioned figure.

"How many case files today, Benjamin?"

He paused, unnerved by her desire to engage in conversation. "It's been busy this morning," he replied finally.

Karla fell silent, appearing to lose interest in the conversation. Benjamin completed his lunch, excused himself and returned to the office. In the light of what would later unfold, it was obvious she had planned it beforehand.

Benjamin had put Karla out of his mind, until the case file arrived with her name as clone mother. Surprised, he set about processing it, first obtaining from the Green Files the green card for the DNA donor noted, who was unknown to him. However, when he looked in the Orange Files, he could not find the orange card for clone mother. He stared at the position in the file, maintained alphabetically, where the card should be. Why was it not there? Had he mislaid it? For the next hour, he searched through the entire filing system, but came up with nothing.

He felt the first stirrings of fear, knowing how little it took to be targeted for punishment. Nothing like this had happened to him before. He would have to tell his Department Head, Stephanie. Perceived incompetence in the Records Department could provoke a grim reaction from her, who could herself be punished despite being a woman in authority. He was mindful of this as he entered her room and stood before her.

"What is it, Benjamin?" Stephanie inquired in her usual bland way. Although uncommunicative, she was not difficult to get on with. She left him alone to perform his duties, indicative of indifference rather than reflecting confidence in his ability. No one cared what others did unless it affected them personally. She was mildly attractive for a woman in her mid-forties, with close-cropped blonde hair, medium height and build, and dressed in a suit befitting the conservative nature of her office.

"There seems to be an orange card missing," Benjamin offered, suddenly realising it sounded not as serious as he first imagined.

"I suggest you find it then." She barely glanced at him.

He handed her the case file. Impatient, she browsed through it as he waited. Benjamin was confident of his own thoroughness. "I've checked through all the files and anywhere it might have been misplaced, but I can't find it."

Frowning, Stephanie went to her filing cabinet, opened the middle drawer and thumbed through several files before closing it again. She returned to her desk.

Benjamin had no access to her filing system. Part of it contained a record of DNA donor and clone mother approvals, from which Stephanie made up the green and orange cards. Approvals followed a set procedure. The Investigations Department identified candidates from the community, interviewed them and sent those suitable to the Medical Centre attached to Laboratories. Subject to a satisfactory medical, approval was sent on to Records. Periodically someone from Investigations would come to Records to check if a card had been issued indicating approval, for someone they wished to use.

The existence of Records owed much to poor communication between Investigations, Laboratories and the Assessments Department. Rivalling each other, they readily accepted a neutral department to handle records with overlapping interest.

"I'll keep the file for now," Stephanie said, offering nothing beyond an impassive expression. "Look again for the orange card."

Benjamin opened his mouth to say something, but realised Stephanie had already dismissed him. He returned to his desk. Another search through the filing system and his working area proved fruitless. He finally concluded he must have mislaid the card.

The day dragged on, tedious as always. An hour before finishing time, two security officers appeared in the office. Distinctive in their white coats with black shoulder pads, they hovered menacingly over his desk. Both were big, tough-looking individuals, their arms hanging straight down by their sides but tensed ready for action. Benjamin was instantly alarmed.

"You are required at the office of General Manager Laboratories," one of the officers informed him, in a monotone reflecting the unfeeling nature of their duties.

A wave of panic stabbed through Benjamin like a knife. Many times, officers such as these had captured people, with punishment the inevitable follow-up. The grey office walls seemed to close around him. His heart beat furiously. His mouth was dry. He swallowed hard and stood. The two officers escorted him out, one on each side and slightly behind him.

General Manager Laboratories. What could she want with him? Contact with other Departments was uncommon. People found a rare solace in having their area of responsibility not shared by others. The thought ate at him as they moved across the dimly lit, windowless entrance foyer and up the stairs to Laboratories. They passed two closed doors and came to a third, accessing the main laboratory. Inside the rectangular room, workbenches projected from the walls and extended into the room. Equipment and paraphernalia suggesting experiments in progress littered the benches. White-coated assistants worked in silence. They showed no interest in Benjamin or the two officers. In one wall, three recessed doorways led to the Medical Centre, the Interview Room and a third place Benjamin did not wish to think about.

He had been here on two previous occasions, one just a few months ago when called to provide information about a man living in the apartment next to his. Benjamin hardly knew the man, only that his name was Fred. The man had been caught involved with a woman and was punished in the normal way with a Promart operation: removal of the prostate and main artery feeding the penis to render him impotent and infertile. Benjamin saw him in a state of abject misery soon after, and had not seen him since. The apartment next door was unoccupied now. Presumably the woman involved had also received normal punishment, the Prohyst treatment: a hysterectomy then lodgement at the Pro House.

Benjamin's first visit to Laboratories had been fifteen years ago. The memory of his mother and father suddenly flooded his brain. Usually he jammed it out of the conscious mind, but it took only an occasion like this for the horrifying experience to vividly reassert itself. He broke into a cold sweat and his step faltered as an overwhelming urge to run away from this hostile territory came over him.

"Through there," one of the officers ordered, prodding him towards a corridor leading from the far end.

A door to their right bore a nameplate, 'General Manager Laboratories'. The officers steered Benjamin to another door opposite, and they entered a room. More grey, windowless walls were devoid of decorations, the bare floor hosting no furnishings apart from a solid rectangular table in the centre and several wooden chairs against one wall. Another interview room. Standing at the far side of the table, between Stephanie and Karla Mason, was the General Manager of Laboratories. All watched him dispassionately as the officers pushed him forward into the room.

The General Manager was a humourless woman, about fifty years of age. Short and plump, she wore a dark suit buttoned to the chin. Her dark hair, turning grey, partly covered her ears in an even fringe encircling a rotund head. Her face was startlingly pale, as if the blood had been drained from it. Benjamin wondered if she was ill.

"I understand you know Karla Mason," she stated in a cold, deep voice. She inclined her head towards Karla.

Karla stood motionless, staring aggressively at Benjamin. Alongside the General Manager, she was an attractive figure despite her sourness. Benjamin felt unnerved. He braced himself, reassured by Stephanie's presence.

"Yes. I've seen her in the cafeteria," he said, as calmly as he could manage.

"Karla says you made improper suggestions to her and sexual advances," the General Manager went on, her thin lips barely moving. "Is that true?"

"No!" Benjamin cried in disbelief. "No, it's not true!"

Stung by the injustice, he swayed on his feet as another wave of panic made him weak at the knees. The officers behind him clamped vice-like grips on his upper arms.

"Karla says this happened twice in the cafeteria." The General Manager glanced at Karla, raising her eyebrows in inquiry. Karla nodded quickly and resumed her stolid stance.

"No!" Benjamin cried again. "It's not right! I, I ..."

The grip on his arms tightened, making him cry out in pain. Sweating profusely now, a horrible desperation clawed at his insides.

A deathly silence fell as all eyes bore into him. Without shifting her penetrating gaze, the General Manager reached for a case file on the table, holding it up for him to see.

"This is the case file with Karla as clone mother. You are familiar with it?"

"Yes," he gasped.

"Where is the orange card?"

As her voice hardened, she slapped the case file down on the table. Benjamin's mouth dropped open in dismay. He looked at Stephanie, expecting her to confirm their exchange earlier in the day. Surely she knew something from her own files! A ray of hope emerged, the new line of questioning seemingly unconnected to the initial accusation.

"I don't know. I couldn't find it."

Stephanie remained silent, exasperating him. Why did she not offer an explanation? Surely the card was lost; simple to make up a new one! Instead, it was the General Manager who spoke again.

"You removed the orange card from the files and destroyed it. Karla says you told her in the cafeteria that you were attracted to her and wanted a relationship, that you didn't want her to be a clone mother. You removed the orange card, so Investigations would assume approval had been denied."

Benjamin stared at her, numbed by the shock of such an accusation. He felt sick. Before he could respond, the officers further tightened their grip on his arms. The pain speared through him, his neck and shoulders aching unbearably. Nausea threatened to overcome him.

"No, it's not true," he implored, his voice choking. "I, I -- never saw it, the orange card. You must believe me."

"Are you saying Karla is lying?"

"I don't know."

The image of Fred flashed through his mind. The punishment meted out to him was the least he could expect, automatic for a crime of this nature. His heart was racing, his body tensed. The officers responded, twisting his arms behind him and forcing him to his knees. A knee bored into his back, levering against his arms. Benjamin screamed in pain. A hand grabbed his hair, jerking his head back viciously.

The three women surveyed him coldly. He looked up with bulging eyes at Karla, unable to comprehend her. She glanced away and her head dropped in the first sign of weakening resolve. Stephanie noticed and suddenly appeared uncertain. She whispered to the General Manager. After a brief exchange, the General Manager spoke to Karla then glared at Benjamin once more.

"We will deal with you shortly."

She gestured to the officers, and they dragged him to one of the chairs against the wall. He slumped into it thankfully.

The women left the room. Benjamin tried to calm himself, but the adrenalin rush was too strong. He was bathed in sweat, hands shaking, heart pounding. The two officers stood to one side, arms folded and waiting. The room was oppressively quiet as time passed agonisingly slowly. Eventually the door opened and the women returned. The officers pulled Benjamin to his feet and led him back to the table. He braced himself for what was coming.

The General Manager glanced at Stephanie then looked at Benjamin with contempt. After a long pause, she addressed him.

"You can go. You will look after the cards properly from now on."

Benjamin stood motionless. His mouth dropped open, his eyes widened as he gaped at her, uncomprehending. One of the officers nudged him in the ribs. Suddenly motivated, he stumbled towards the door then out to the corridor. He broke into a shuffling run, quickening as he put distance between himself and where he had been.

It was well past finishing time. He went straight to his bicycle at the racks by the side of the building, and managed to ride home.

Chapter 8

The first rays of morning light were peeping through the window as Benjamin woke from his cramped position in the chair. The blanket was still wrapped around his shoulders. An empty coffee cup sat on the table in front of him.

A headache thumped at his brain as he struggled to his feet. A faint nausea squirmed in his stomach. He went to the bench and made a cup of coffee. The first sips helped. He sat again and remembered the events of yesterday. He knew of no other man escaping a Promart under such circumstances. He finished the coffee, got ready and left for work.

His apartment was near the outskirts of town. Although the Clonesseum was not too far to walk, riding his bicycle was more exhilarating in the context of an otherwise dreary life. The road was dilapidated, no major maintenance done for twenty-five years apart from cement occasionally thrown down to patch bad hollows or broken-up sections. Benjamin was adept at weaving between the worst parts. Today, he rode slowly, more aware than usual of everything around him.

Men were leaving their apartments on foot or by bicycle. Many had mundane duties, others mindlessly filled in a day with whatever they could find to do. Their depressing manner and lack of real, personal interaction reflected the monotony of life.

A man disappeared between apartment blocks, heading for where debris had been pushed back in piles to make way for construction. It provided a vital resource for people to scrounge whatever they felt was useful. The sight was common all over town and beyond, a constant reminder of the town being a small, crude rebirth of the original.

Benjamin reached a road branching left, a detour route he often took if in the right mood. Soon he was passing more apartments. Women occupied these, deliberately separated from the men on the main road. The number of orange flags, displayed above the front door by an occupant during ovulation, was down this month.

Women walking along looked the same in their grey coats, eyes downcast, oblivious of each other. One woman was different, dressed in a grey suit depicting authority. With a business-like air, she was alternately referring to a clipboard of papers and looking up at apartments, performing for Investigations the daily ritual of identifying potential clone mothers by reconciling orange flags against the monthly record. Except under extraordinary circumstances, a woman would be punished for not displaying her orange flag when expected by the record.

The road swung right and became rougher, causing Benjamin to slow. The buildings were better now, individual houses linked together, but just as drab in appearance. Clone mothers lived here. Although better dressed and with more positive demeanour, there was still an air of resigned sadness about them. Some were obviously pregnant, others had babies carried against their chests inside a blanket tied tightly round the midriff. A few toddlers were walking, but none was more than two years of age.

A disturbance at one of the houses broke the monotony. Three people came rushing out and charged towards the road. A woman was carrying a young child, both screaming, the woman hysterical. The other two were Family Police officers. One of them caught her by the arm, spinning her round. The other began pulling at the child, trying to prise it away from her.

"No!" the woman screamed. "Don't take him. No!" She wrenched the child free. Benjamin had to stop as she dashed across the road in front of his bike.

"Please!" she cried out desperately to him. "Don't let them take my baby!"

Benjamin stared at her and the baby. The officers grabbed the woman, at the same time watching Benjamin for his reaction. He could do nothing to help her. No one had ever successfully defied the Family Police.

"I'm sorry," he murmured and moved away.

Soon one officer was holding the baby, the other the tormented mother, with arms pinned behind her. The officer with the baby left the scene.

Benjamin resumed riding, feeling a sense of guilt at not helping the woman. A ludicrous notion, one that no one would contemplate. He had witnessed such an incident several times. The relevant case file would reach his desk for final filing within a day or two, with Dump noted as the Action statement.

He passed a collapsed building. Dry rubble lay strewn around the truncated remains of four walls. Not uncommon to any part of town, it was indicative of insufficient strength in the cement. Anyone losing their home would move into another and scrounge new possessions if necessary. Despite being a regular occurrence, however, there was neither construction of new buildings nor reconstruction of collapsed ones going on. Yet no one was homeless, the opposite actually the case - some buildings were unoccupied.

Benjamin came to more of the attached-style houses. Women enjoying positions of worth in the community occupied these. Their status was above that of clone mothers, the absence of children an obvious difference. They represented the closest a woman could get beneath the elitism of the Family. Beyond the last building, a stretch of open ground marked the end of women's accommodation. Difference in status was as clearcut as the difference in housing, contrasting with the single lowly status of men in apartments on the main road.

The road improved as Benjamin passed the open ground. He weaved from side to side, doing an imaginary slalom course, then coasted with no hands, kicking his legs up. He relished his only opportunity to express some small defiance against the boring regimentation of his life and the people who made it that way. A fork in the road loomed. The left-hand branch plunged into a clump of trees lining each side from a short way along, then disappeared as it swung right further up. The trees were the only ones in town, specially planted fifteen years ago. No one dared venture down there, the idea of infiltrating Family or Family Police privacy striking instant fear.

He swooped to the right in racing mode. The road surface deteriorated again. Soon he reached the main road, turned left and arrived at the Clonesseum, a little late.

At his desk, he looked down at the tasks awaiting his attention. He felt different, in the same way he had last night in his apartment. The old timber desk pinning him to the end wall typified the life that condemned him every day. The lighting from two naked bulbs in the ceiling was dull. He stared past the steel filing cabinets lining one wall to where a photocopier sat at the far end beside the connecting door to Stephanie's office. With more than usual difficulty, he pushed down a feeling of resentment and forced himself to concentrate.

The case file involving Karla Mason was on top, with an orange card bearing her name clipped to the file cover. Benjamin wondered why loss of the original one had not been assumed lost in the first place instead of subjecting him to interrogation and accusation. He was hardly surprised, though. Those in authority were so paranoid they always jumped at conclusions suggesting subversion, real or perceived.

He obtained the green card again and entered the date and case file number onto the next line in sequence, and the new orange card the same. He took photocopies of the cards and attached them inside the case file. The last step was to record the details into the General File. He lifted down the large folder from on top of a cabinet and entered the date, case file number and names of DNA donor and clone mother, extending by one line the case-by-case chronology from the start of clone production. He returned the folder and filed the cards. Stephanie barely acknowledged him as he entered her room and dropped the case file in her In-tray.

Two more tasks remained. One involved a DNA donor who had died. A half-black, half-green card delivered from the Medical Centre bore the name, age and date of death. Benjamin obtained the corresponding green card, clipped the half-black one to it and filed them in the Deceased Files, kept alphabetically. Also kept there were the half-black half-orange cards representing clone mother deaths.

The other was a request from Investigations for the record of a DNA donor. It signified problems, perhaps an incompatibility, resulting in failed or flawed clone production perceived to be the fault of the DNA or its donor.

Failure happened far less now than it used to. When cloning first began fifteen years ago, there were few successes. It seemed the Family's ambitious program would become bogged down in technical complexity and unrealistic expectation. However, the Family were unperturbed, continuing with it ruthlessly, indifferent to failure. If a birth did occur but the clone proved defective, they dumped it then removed donor and clone mother from production. Gradually the success rate improved, and now failure was the exception not the rule. With the emphasis shifting towards mass production, Benjamin had become used to a steady stream of case files coming through.

He found a Donor Record Form, coloured green, in a drawer of his desk and obtained the relevant green card. Four entries were on the card. He entered the dates and case file numbers onto the Form. From the Case File records, where every case file finished up on conclusion, he found the first three. The fourth, still current, was not there. The first and third cases had been successful, but the second had 'FAIL' against the donor's name and included a comment about problems with the DNA. On the Record Form, he wrote FAIL against the second case and CURRENT against the fourth. With the fourth case probably a failure, the donor would be removed from the program, but he would wait for confirmation before processing the green card accordingly. Removal after two failures represented more tolerance than in the early days of cloning. The task complete, he returned the case files and green card to the files then dropped the completed Donor Record Form in Stephanie's In-tray.

Lunchtime arrived, releasing him from the tedium. He passed through the foyer and down the corridor to the cafeteria, where he joined the queue for food. A gruff, thickset man in white overalls was serving at a bench down one side. Beyond the bench, a door led to the kitchen. Benjamin knew it well, having started there fifteen years ago.

He indicated his choice of food; always the soybean and whatever leguminous foods were on offer, providing good sustenance from the range of vegetables grown at the crop fields. With his plate, he weaved between tables and chairs to his favourite spot halfway along the back wall. From there, he could observe people.

The cafeteria was filling quickly. Ralph, from Maintenance, joined him, carrying a plate piled high with food.

"Hi, Benjamin," he greeted and immediately attacked his lunch with typical exuberance.

Ralph was outgoing, with a carefree attitude towards all around him. He had youthful good looks, flowing medium-length blonde hair and a strong build. Benjamin enjoyed his company, finding him a refreshing exception to the sullen personalities of most. Ralph gravitated towards Benjamin, appreciating him for being unusually receptive to anything he felt confused about. They each drew comfort from being more open and honest with each other than was normally possible.

"What's new in Records?" Ralph asked after devouring several mouthfuls.

"Just the usual," Benjamin replied, not getting into what happened yesterday. "How about Maintenance?"

"Two light bulbs in the corridor outside Investigations and a leaky tap in one of the toilets. And I started on the new bench for Assessments."

Ralph had genuine pride in his ability to fix things, making him content with his job looking after the physical requirements of the building. Benjamin was envious of the way he simplified life, seemingly unconcerned about the traps a man could fall into and the crippling restrictions on ambition.

"I overheard them talking about clone assessments," Ralph went on.

"What were they saying?" Benjamin stopped eating as a spark of interest took hold. Updating the records after implantation was the only time he sighted a case file until final filing. After a successful birth, Assessments took it over from Laboratories. They inserted the clone's name, using a crude system retaining the name of the DNA donor with the number 1 appended, or whatever number clone it was from that donor. He knew little else about the role of Assessments except what was implied by the other insertion he saw at final filing, the one-word Action statement: TrainA, TrainB or Dump. For a Train, the date was always two years to the day from birth, when the clone would be taken from its clone mother and sent to a Training Centre. A Dump could be at any time within the two years. He listened keenly to Ralph's reply.

"Just talk about a couple of clones that didn't turn out right. One was born deaf so they dumped it. The donor had no problems like that, so they couldn't understand how it happened. They're sending the clone mother for re-examination, must be her fault."

"It shouldn't be. The clone mother only carries it. I'll see the case file when it comes back to Records."

He felt empathy for the unfortunate clone mother. "I wonder what will happen to her," he murmured.

Ralph shrugged his shoulders. "Plenty more where she came from."

Benjamin looked at him sharply. His callousness often disgusted but never surprised him. Ralph was only four years old when cloning started, so had become aware of no other system of reproduction. He had been too young to appreciate the horrifying violations suffered by people around that time, and had not endured the trauma of having his mother and father forcibly separated. Ralph had never seen his father, his existence the product of rampant promiscuity raging in the community prior to the Family taking control. Ralph's oblivious innocence reflected this.

"What were they saying about the second one?" Benjamin asked.

"It's an eighteen month clone giving his mother a hard time. He's prone to disobedience, so Assessments consider him unsuitable."

"What are they going to do?"

"They were going to dump him, then someone mentioned the B category of training, whatever that is."

The case files never explained the options, although TrainB was obviously an unsavoury one for a clone, an alternative to being dumped.

"They were critical of Investigations for using an inadequate donor," Ralph added.

Benjamin was not surprised. Another example of jealous protectionism between Assessments and Investigations, but they had to work closely together, with fear of displeasing the Family always the controlling force.

"That's interesting. How did you hear all this anyway?"

Ralph grinned mischievously. "I just get on with my work, making their new bench. They ignore me, don't think I'm smart enough to know what they're talking about."

Benjamin nodded, a smile creasing the corner of his mouth. With his straightforward personality, Ralph often confused people that way.

"How long to finish the bench?"

"Couple of days. I'll keep on listening, let you know what I hear. Now, what about tonight?"

Benjamin knew what was coming. Every now and then, Ralph asked him the same thing and he always gave him the same answer.

"The Pro House again?" he queried.

Ralph's tongue flitted across his lips in anticipation. "Sure, why not? Why don't you come with me?"

Benjamin usually blotted out such thoughts instantly, before they had a chance to rekindle the pain. However, after yesterday, his mind-set was different, more receptive. He considered it for a few moments.

The Pro House was a short walk from the Clonesseum, overlooking the harbour. After the Family took control, they wisely recognised the dangers of ignoring the needs of men prevented from having normal sexual relationships once clone production began. The horrific shock treatment associated with the way the Family ruthlessly tore apart society as it then was and forced their own system into place was no more starkly evident than in the way they set up the Pro House. They took by force women of questionable character, of whom there were plenty, gave them hysterectomies to negate the chance of pregnancy and installed them there. Backed by brutal policing and punishment, they eliminated sexual activity from the community at large, permitting it only with women of the Pro House.

Panic then terrible chaos swept the community as widespread rebellion ensued against the violation of basic rights. The Family were prepared, using a secretly established network of handpicked men who quickly gelled to form the powerful Family Police. They carried out practical enforcement, forcing all couples apart, removing children under two years of age never to be seen again, condemning pregnant women to abortions. People had no idea anything like this had been envisaged. Entrenched in a self-indulgent, promiscuous way of life, they were unaware of the influence a hardline group of women had established, seeing them merely as one of several groups contributing to a loosely formed coalition organising life after Re-emergence.

When they made their move, it was sudden and violent. The Family Police had great incentive to enforce the new order, being the only men permitted sexual relationships, with members of the Family only, elevating them to become an elite group amongst men. The Family women easily subordinated them, however, by cynically exploiting competition for sexual favour, making them work hard for it by proving themselves worthy in the area of enforcement. Any Family Police officer perceived as a troublemaker or straying outside the Family was punished by Promart and kicked out. The Family Police became a powerful, vigilant force, maintaining constant fear in the community.

As time went by, they broke down all of people's remaining resistance. Men had no alternative than a degraded, superfluous role. From fear developed suspicion, insecurity and an inability to form meaningful relationships, even of a non-threatening kind. The uncaring, oblivious mentality suited the Family Police, who now found it easy to control the community, knowing lack of communication between people meant no chance of mounting a concerted challenge. The power of the Family and Family Police reigned supreme, fear always the most effective tool, reinforced by examples of Promart for men or Prohyst for women, without exception, for anything perceived as subversive.

Benjamin gave himself a mental shake, irritated at allowing his mind to drift back, especially to the Pro House. He forced himself to concentrate on Ralph again.

"No, I don't think so," he replied uncertainly.

"Come on. What's the place there for? You've got to have fun sometime."

Benjamin hesitated. "Maybe some other time."

Ralph shook his head in disappointment. He finished the last of his lunch, wiped his mouth on a sleeve and stood.

"See you later, then." He departed.

Benjamin sat for a while longer, poking at his half-eaten lunch. His emotions were welling up, a lump in his throat choking him, his food swimming in front of his eyes. He swallowed, trying to push back the tide, but it made no difference. He was as low as he had felt for a long time. Raising his head, he noticed most people had left the cafeteria. He felt very alone. He hated himself for being this way. He struggled with his thoughts, desperate to avoid being dragged back to the terror and despair of those early days, when enforcement by the Family Police was most brutal. But the images flooded into his mind uncontrollably.

It had all begun on that fateful day fifteen years ago, when the Family and Family Police took over the newly completed Clonesseum, known then as the Administration Centre. For Benjamin, the savage murder of Kelly's father epitomised the violence. Kelly's mother had played a sick part in it, and even Kelly had been unfortunate enough to be there. The shock of it and loss of all contact with Kelly was very hard to handle then.

With the death of her father, there was little hope for Kelly, locked in to her mother's emotional possessiveness and the elitist separatism of the Family. The last image Benjamin had was of her standing forlorn and frightened behind her mother, at the forefront of the women's group controlling what happened that day.

Traumatic as that was, it was only the beginning. The Family appointed women to all positions of authority, in keeping with the subordinate role intended for men. Benjamin, no longer having Kelly's father to work with, was fortunate to gain a position as kitchen-hand at the cafeteria. His father held his position at the new Medical Centre, but no longer with any authority. Forced to carry out Promart and Prohyst operations under strict, Family Police supervision, he became more and more inconsolable every day. Their close family relationship came under terrific strain.

One night, it was their turn. They had been watching for it, knowing no couple would be exempt from separation. As the Family

Police descended on them, Gloria made it in time to a pile of debris behind the apartment where George had excavated a hiding-place. A foolish act, born out of desperation. The officers did not believe George's story that his wife had already been taken. They seized Benjamin, slamming him against the wall and threatening to execute him on the spot. Suddenly his mother rushed in.

"No! Leave him alone. I am here. Take me."

They led Gloria away.

Next morning, security officers at the Clonesseum were waiting for George. They ushered him upstairs to one of three rooms off the main laboratory. Benjamin followed, stricken by a fearful foreboding that something terrible was about to happen. An officer released Gloria, dressed only in a white, loose-fitting gown, from a holding cell at one end of the room. He pushed her forward to a white-clad table in the centre. The room was an operating theatre.

"No!" Benjamin screamed out, rushing towards his mother.

Two officers grabbed him and forced him to the cell. Locked inside, Benjamin gripped the steel bars as if to crush them, quivering with fright. His mother appeared resolute, with the inner strength he had always admired in her. A doctor injected her wrist. Soon she was lying prone on the table, the gown parted to reveal her abdomen.

George was sobbing openly, his head shaking mindlessly from side to side. An officer made him stand over her, then directed him to the instrument trolley. It was too much for George. His legs buckled and he slumped to his knees, head buried in his hands. Officers dragged him to the cell and threw him inside with Benjamin. The other doctor performed the Prohyst operation.

Those images would stay with Benjamin forever. His father never recovered from the ordeal, unable to cope without his wife. Two days later, Benjamin found him hanged in the bathroom. He was devastated, his world shattered, cast adrift in a sea of desolation.

He felt the same now, his hands clenching the sides of the table as if he was still gripping the steel bars all those years ago. The cafeteria was quiet, matching the emptiness gnawing at his insides. And still the images flooded through his mind.

After his father's death, Benjamin was disoriented for some time. His mind shut out the cruel experience. As a seventeen year-old living alone, he was vulnerable. He fell victim to the turmoil of people shifting apartments as the Family established separate areas for men and women. A man took advantage by ejecting him from the centrally located apartment his parents had made into a comfortable home. He found an empty one near the other end of town.

Several weeks passed before he had stabilised enough to venture a visit to the Pro House in search of his mother. Terrible strife had erupted there, as women, many previously well-respected in the community, were forced into hopeless, degrading circumstances. The Family Police had gained control by ruthlessly eliminating some, suppressing the rest. They were still present in numbers, ready to slam any signs of opposition.

The conditions inside were dingy, the lighting poor. Women sat at tables or lounged on benches around the grey walls of the barn-like building. The floor was bare and there were no adornments. A morbid, repressive atmosphere ruled.

Benjamin saw his mother sitting on a bench beside a younger woman. They had befriended each other. Like all the women there, she wore a long one-piece, tight-fitting dress he considered unsuitable for her. He was aghast at how drawn and weary she looked.

After pretending to the hard-bitten, unfriendly woman running the place that he wished to choose his mother, they went to her room out the back. A pokey room barely offering the basic essentials for minimum comfort. They broke down, sobbing in each other's arms.

"Benjamin, Benjamin!" she cried. "Did they do anything to you?"

"No. I'm okay."

"Where's your father?" No one had told her anything.

Benjamin stared at his mother as the emotion rose to choke him, stinging his eyes. Eventually he told her. She went limp in his arms then slumped on the bed like a wasted rag doll. She wept, on and on, draining the strength from her body. Benjamin sat on the bed and cried with her. Finally his mother clung to him, pleading.

"Please, Benjamin, look after yourself. Don't upset them. Look at me, it's not worth it."

Benjamin left shortly after, shocked by the harsh contrast of his mother to how he had always known her. He returned two days later, but she was gone. The woman he saw with her on the first occasion was very sad, telling him his mother had been taken away the previous day following complaints she was unable to perform properly.

"No woman taken from here by Family Police has ever returned. There is no further use for a woman who fails here," she had said.

Benjamin heard the words echoing through his mind as he sat alone in the cafeteria. The tears streamed down his face. The guilt was hard. Benjamin had felt responsible for his mother being taken away, the day after his first visit. Throughout the years since, he never really got over the guilt, learning only how to live with it as time went by. But the loneliness was something that never went away. The grinding pain of it was never-ending.

A kitchen-hand disturbed him, clearing away dishes. The cafeteria was deserted. The kitchen-hand hovered over him, on the point of saying something but changed his mind. He reached for Benjamin's plate.

"I have to clean up. Lunchtime is over."

Benjamin looked away, embarrassed. "I'm sorry," he murmured.

He stood and left, returning to the office in a daze. With little to do, he sat at his desk staring into space, unable to shake off the unexpected arousal of his emotions. What was the point of it all? What future was there, continuing day after day like this? He was feeling sorry for himself, a trait he detested, but he could not help it. He sat immobile, fighting to gain control. And then, slowly, a realisation dawned on him. Something had changed.

The events of yesterday involving Karla Mason had done it, jolting him like an electric shock. And now, facing perhaps for the first time what had happened to his mother and father, something stronger was stirring inside him. He was thirty-two years old! His eyes widened as it hit him. Was he going to drift on into middle age and beyond, feeling desolate and achieving nothing? He must do something, if only to rescue his self-respect. He felt himself teetering on a knife-edge, caught between slipping back into silent desperation with the system enclosing him in a straitjacket, and the as yet obscure potential for a better life. He had no idea what that would be. He only knew that, fundamentally, the Family had no right to violate people the way they did. They had taken it for themselves, so why could it not be taken back? But how?

He looked around the office, feeling angry. The last time he felt like this was years ago following his father's death, when he went through the full gamut of emotions. The anger was tempered with fear then, but now it stood alone as a powerful motivating force. It was strengthening. His eyes narrowed, a frown creased his forehead, his lips pressed into a thin line. Then, in a flash, something clicked inside his brain. Suddenly he felt better, stronger. He knew he had reached a milestone in his life. The change was irreversible, carrying him forward with a steely resolve.

He would do what he could. He did not know how or what, but he would try. He could find out more, understand more about everything happening around him. He would have to be careful, do nothing to arouse suspicion. He was amazed at how strong he felt, his sense of justice reactivating from dormancy, and without the fear.

The afternoon had slipped by. He waited out the remaining time then left.

Chapter 9

Next morning, Benjamin woke feeling buoyant. With a sense of purpose, he readied himself and left the apartment. Riding to work, he felt strangely detached from the cold, unfriendly environment, as if looking in from the outside. Men on the road, the buildings, the crumbling road surface all meant something significant today, although he was unsure what.

The second-to-last apartment block before the branch road loomed up on his left. A small number of women occupied this and the last one, deliberately separated from the women's areas after having encountered problems. They were not considered threatening so had avoided a Prohyst, but were only marginally above women of the Pro House in status.

A young woman was leaving one of the apartments. Brenda had only been there two days, after enduring a particularly distasteful ordeal. She was resolute, however, maintaining strong self-esteem, yet cautious, and instinctively perceptive of life around her. She had an undying belief that a greater force would one day cause the Family's demise, and she was determined to survive for when it happened. She noticed Benjamin approaching on his bicycle.

Benjamin noticed her. She seemed more poised than other women, despite the unflattering long grey coat with upturned collar. She projected a positive air, unlike the dull, unhappy women staying in those apartments. He stared at her, wondering what had gone wrong for her to be in this place.

The brief period of distraction was too long. The front wheel of his bike struck a rough spot on the road, twisting it sideways. Benjamin lost balance as the bike slid from beneath him. He crashed to the road, managing to cushion the fall by thrusting out his left arm and rolling on his shoulder. His face grazed the road surface, luckily avoiding a heavy bump to the head.

He lay stunned for a moment then propped himself up, embarrassingly aware of his ignominious position. Brenda came up and stood over him, a startled look on her face. She was unsure what to do, a little fearful since it was her presence that had caused it.

Benjamin felt foolish, exposed for paying her undue attention. He scrambled to his feet and dusted himself off. She sensed his humiliation, and a faint smile crept onto her face. Benjamin noticed it and reacted with a half-smile of his own. Before they knew it, they were laughing openly with each other.

"Are you hurt?" she asked in a soft voice.

"Only in my head," he replied, trying to regain composure.

They laughed again and a surge of warmth enveloped them. She was an attractive girl in her mid-twenties. She had a smooth, brown complexion with hazel eyes, and a full mouth exhibiting even, white teeth as she laughed. Her auburn-coloured hair, disappearing beneath the coat collar, enhanced classical facial features. There was depth and an appealing air of maturity about her.

Standing before her, Benjamin felt slightly nervous as a strange feeling stirred inside him. He fingered his left cheekbone, making him smart, leaving behind a smear of blood although the injury was only superficial. She offered a small handkerchief, which he accepted gratefully and held against the cut.

"You can return it to me sometime," she said. "I'm usually at the market before dark."

She started along the road with a spring in her step. The incident had been stimulating for Benjamin also, and he stared after her, his heart soaring, thrilled that she seemed to care. The dramatic effect made him realise how bereft of meaningful human contact his life was, despite being surrounded by people every day. But he reminded himself to be careful, recalling his near demise after relating to Karla Mason in a similar way.

He pocketed the handkerchief and remounted, his bike fortunately not damaged. He rode down the detour route and passed through the women's areas, coming to the fork in the road. A sudden idea made him stop, and he fixed a gaze to his left. A hidden force was daring him, the tunnel through the trees sucking him in. Should he risk it? He steeled himself. Buoyed with confidence and a touch of defiance, he angled his bike to the left and started cautiously towards the trees.

The road veered right then branched again at another fork. Staying right, Benjamin peddled forward warily. Around another shallow bend, a fence with an open-grille double steel gate came into view a short way ahead. Alarmed by abrupt exposure, he skidded to a halt. Luckily no one was at the gate. The road continued beyond it. Large, individual houses lined each side, better standard accommodation than any other he had seen, although made from the same drab cement. People were walking about; Family Police. He beat a fast retreat before anyone noticed him.

At the fork, he stopped and looked intently up the other branch. He drew a deep breath, determined not to weaken resolve, then started slowly along the tree-lined route. Again, exiting a shallow bend revealed a fence and double gate further up, this time of solid construction. And with two Family Police officers sitting outside as guards! Benjamin slammed on the brakes, but too late to correct the awful mistake he had made.

One of the officers jumped to his feet, pointing at him.

"You! What are you doing here?"

At the same time, the gate partially opened, distracting the officers. Two Family women walked out with a young boy. Benjamin caught a glimpse through, gaining a narrow sight of the road and part of a house. And, was it an electric car? He was astounded. He had not seen one of those for many years. Like everyone, he believed them to no longer exist.

Before the guard re-focussed on him, he swung his bike round and escaped. He reached the Clonesseum, late. For now, he was safe, but would there be reprisals?

Several mundane tasks kept Benjamin busy through the morning. By lunchtime, no one had visited him over his earlier misdemeanour, easing his sense of anxiety. In the cafeteria, he sat with Ralph, who wasted no time in tackling the mountain of food on his plate.

"Been working hard this morning?" Benjamin asked with amusement.

"Trying to get the bench finished in Assessments. They want it by tomorrow."

"Did you hear anything?"

"Sure did. They were arguing with someone from Investigations." Ralph paused to shovel more food into his mouth. "Both General Managers joined in."

Benjamin ate sparingly, his mind active. "It sounds important," he remarked, watching Ralph patiently.

"Yes. Assessments are not satisfied with the DNA donors chosen by Investigations. They're getting too many clones not up to standard."

"What sort of problems are they getting?"

"All sorts. They were talking about personality problems, physical, emotional, everything. They expect a high standard."

Benjamin tried to visualise the procedures Assessments followed, obscure as they were to anyone not involved. "So who's to blame for that?" he murmured.

"They blame each other. The argument got quite heated. Assessments blame Investigations for their choice of donors. Investigations blame Assessments for expecting too much perfection. Both are scared of the Family."

"Yes, of course."

"The GM Investigations tried to explain that it's not possible to find a donor with everything. A clone is just a copy of a person, she said, with all the good and bad things the person has."

"That's right. What did the GM Assessments think about that?" Benjamin asked, putting down his spoon.

"She agreed. But she was still critical Investigations weren't finding the best available, the highest percentage of perfection's how she put it."

Benjamin had never heard such a thing. *Percentage of perfection.* Whoever Investigations chose would have imperfections. What is perfect anyway? Surely a matter of opinion. They could improve a clone by training, and no doubt were doing so, but they could never change the fundamental traits and capabilities inherent in the donor. Evidently this was not good enough for Assessments. No wonder there was friction. The only common ground between Departments was their callous exploitation of the community.

Ralph paused between mouthfuls. "They were talking about something going on in Laboratories."

"Really? What's that about?"

"I'm not sure. They're doing experiments with DNA. They seem anxious to get results."

A cold shiver ran down Benjamin's spine. Were Laboratories trying to manipulate DNA? Perhaps to improve this 'percentage of perfection'? The possibilities were endless. The prospect filled him with a sense of dread. What did the future have in store?

Ralph finished his lunch, wiped his mouth and stood, looking at Benjamin with boyish enthusiasm.

"Want to come to the Pro House tonight?"

Benjamin smiled and opened his mouth to decline once again, but then hesitated. Ralph sensed the chance, after almost convincing him yesterday.

"Come on. Let's have a fun night out together."

Suddenly Benjamin felt more positive about the idea. A visit to the Pro House might give him insight into something.

"Well, okay. Let's go for a night out."

Ralph punched the air. "Yes!" he exclaimed. "A night to remember. I'll come to your office at finishing time and we'll go."

A huge grin lit up his face as he departed. Benjamin finished his lunch, lifted by Ralph's exuberance. He returned to the office. With no more tasks in the afternoon, images of the Pro House filled his mind again as he sat idly at his desk.

He had visited the Pro House only once more after the disappearance of his mother, about five years later. Someone he knew then, who was a bit like Ralph, talked him into it at a time when he was particularly low. At twenty-two years of age, instead of achievements he had only a void, or so he felt. He took the chance to do something different, no matter how futile, foolishly hoping the passage of time would allow him to override the acute pain the Pro House represented to him.

The only experience he had with women was with Kelly, but that had been severed when they were on the brink of developing it physically. He had not felt inclined to pursue contact with anyone since, either before or after the Family established the Pro House. The unwavering example of his mother had taught him a set of values based on respect for people. But that was out of step with the new order of things, and served only to heighten his frustration and loneliness.

He went to the Pro House on that occasion hoping for a little comfort, someone he could talk to. He did not find it, as no one was there for anything but sexual gratification. A woman with little to offer intellectually gave him a physical release, the first time for Benjamin. Although grateful for the experience, he knew something was missing. With no emotional content, he did not feel close to the woman in a sharing, loving way as he imagined it should be. The momentary physical sensation was mechanical and, overall, disappointing.

The next day, he felt grubby and disgusted with himself, having contributed to the demise of human dignity. And he had seriously underestimated the effect seeing the Pro House again would have on him. For some time after, his emotions ran out of control until he finally won the struggle to suppress the pain once more. He vowed then never to return to the Pro House again. Shortly after, he gained his position in Records. This sustained him for a while with its small measure of responsibility. However, the mindless tedium soon returned, day after day passing by, stretching into years. He survived by turning off emotionally and numbing his brain.

A sudden movement in front of his desk jerked him from his thoughts. Ralph stood there.

"Come on, let's go," Ralph said excitedly. "It's after finishing time."

"Already," Benjamin noted, surprised how quickly the afternoon had passed.

They left the building and turned left, soon passing the market, which was full of people bartering, exchanging and collecting their supplies. Anything needed to sustain life was obtainable at the market, or if not they would have to get by or do it for themselves. Those whose involvement in clone production left them no time were entitled to collect essential supplies by presenting their Food Card. The rest were left to their own devices. The market was the principle outlet for food grown at the crop fields. Benjamin went there once a week on his day off.

They reached the Pro House. Ralph strode towards the entrance. "Most come after dark. Means I get first pick."

Benjamin hesitated. "I'll take a look outside. I'll be in shortly."

Ralph went inside. Benjamin was in no hurry to follow, still mindful of what the Pro House meant to him. He wandered across the open ground and stood at the top of the rise, looking out at the empty sea. He contemplated how the surface hid all activity beneath it, just like the unfortunate community he lived in. Darkness began to fall. He turned away and headed for the entrance.

Inside, he immediately noticed differences from the last time he was here. Only two Family Police officers were present, one on the entrance door, the other opposite at the door to the back, the only other exit point. Disruptions, violence, even murder often occurred at the Pro House, creating an expectation of heavy security, as used to be the case. So few Family Police was puzzling, even disturbing.

Other differences were that no woman was in control now, and drink was being served at one end to his left, where men were congregating near a bar. Their conversation seemed restrained, as if awaiting a spark to justify them being there. Ralph was with them, sitting on a stool. He beckoned to Benjamin, who moved to a vacant stool beside him.

"Rice or vegetable?" Ralph asked, indicating the glass he was holding.

"Oh, I don't know. What's that?"

Ralph's drink had a lurid, green look to it. Benjamin cringed.

"Vegetable wine," Ralph said brightly, holding his glass higher. "Want some?"

"Maybe I'll try the rice wine."

Ralph leaned back and spoke to a man behind the bar. Benjamin accepted a glass containing a pale, cloudy liquid. Tentatively, he took a sip, grimacing at the bitter, acidic taste.

He looked around the rest of the place. The bare grey floor and walls and poor lighting made for an inhospitable environment. The women on offer were a depressing sight, sitting in sullen silence at tables or lolling on benches around the walls, waiting in limbo. Men were entering in a steady stream now, gravitating to the bar area or choosing a woman, then disappearing through the door to the rooms out the back. The officer at the door was standing stiffly with arms folded, one hand holding a long baton, an expressionless but alert look on his face.

The atmosphere was characterised by an undercurrent of submissive resignation in the women. The Family Police had done a good job in grinding down their spirit. The drinking end was a little different. A few women were prepared to make the best of their situation by joining in and drinking a little wine, generating a more sociable environment.

Ralph pointed at a good-looking woman sitting not far away on a bench. "What about that one?" he hinted.

Benjamin followed his outstretched arm, bemused by the callous disregard Ralph had for her other than as a source of physical pleasure. He saw a youthful girl who he estimated to be at least twenty-six years old but not much older. She was attractive with shoulder-length red hair and pleasant features but a sad, tired look on her face. She noticed them observing her and dropped her head self-consciously. Benjamin felt sorry for her.

"Why don't you go over and say hello?"

"I've had one already, before you came in," Ralph replied, indicating a woman a little further away. "Maybe after a couple more of these," he added, holding his drink up.

Benjamin ignored his reaction. Around the bar area, the men were all of similar type to Ralph, preoccupied with their own gratification. The noise level was increasing, regular laughter helping to intensify the scene. Benjamin began to feel out of place.

Ralph stood and started talking to a man. Soon they were laughing and gesticulating together. Ralph moved out of sight, returning shortly after with two women. One of them leaned against him in suggestive style, and the other moved close to Benjamin. She was reasonably attractive in a hard way, holding a glass of rice wine and obviously in tune with the action around them. Ralph was pleased with himself.

"Benjamin, that's Louise."

"Hello," Benjamin responded, glancing uncertainly at her.

"Louise can show you a thing or two," Ralph remarked, grinning.

Louise smiled, projecting a contrived coyness that Benjamin found disconcerting. She snuggled closer to him.

"I haven't seen you before," she purred, looking directly into his eyes.

"I haven't been here for a long time."

His heart was beating faster with nervousness, making his voice quiver slightly. He felt foolish, his lack of experience obvious.

"Have you been out the back yet?" she asked him, indicating the door through which couples continued to pass back and forth. Her quiet voice had a mesmerising effect, making his heart leap as he realised the implications of her question. He was unused to any woman treating him this way.

"No," he replied, his voice cutting short as the tightness caught his breath.

He glanced towards the door. The Family Police officer was still poised in waiting mode. Out of the corner of his eye, Benjamin noticed the red-haired girl observing him unobtrusively. He switched his attention to her, but she dropped her head again in embarrassment. He felt strangely intrigued as a warm feeling came over him.

"Do you want to see my room?" Louise offered, using soft tones again.

Before he could respond, there was a sudden increase in the noise level from a group behind them. A glass shattered on the floor, men shouted, a woman screamed. Benjamin jumped to his feet and backed away. Ralph leapt forward and moved around the periphery of the action to gain a better view. He punched the air, whooping with glee. Louise reacted swiftly, a hard look on her face now, in stark contrast to how she had just been projecting herself. She rushed over, shoving one man aside and yelling at the group in a shrill, piercing screech. The sudden change in her was astonishing, making Benjamin realise how little he knew of the people here.

The scene quickly turned ugly as other men joined in. The enlarged group soon spilled out beyond the bar area, making women scatter. Then it all erupted violently. A mass of torrid fighting broke out amidst a rising tide of shouting and screaming. Men wrestled with each other, crashing into tables and chairs. Bodies soon lay on the floor, getting trampled underfoot, glass smashing on walls and floor.

Benjamin staggered back in fear, looking to escape as the violence spread. At any moment, Family Police would be charging in to impose their power. They seemed slow in coming. A glass flew past close to his head and smashed against the wall. The shock of it made him fall to the floor. He scrambled on his knees towards the entrance door, crawling past bodies, some lying immobile, others cowering from the chaos. Pressing close to the wall, he felt for the entrance door. Suddenly he realised he was next to it, but it was closed. Horrified, he jumped to his feet and pulled frantically at the door handle. It would not budge. The door was locked!

He swung round, gripped by panic. The officer stationed there was nowhere to be seen. Benjamin looked to the other side. The door opposite was closed also, the officer there nowhere to be seen either! With a shock, he realised why the Family Police were slow in coming, because they were not coming. They did not care what people did to each other. He slumped to the floor, appalled by the situation he found himself in.

As he crouched against the wall, something tugged on his left arm. He turned his head and was looking into the face of the red-haired girl. She clutched his arm, her eyes pleading.

"Please, help me," she implored him.

She was petrified. Instinctively Benjamin put his arm around her and she clung to him, her body rigid with fright.

The violence raged on. The sounds of smashing, shouting and screaming continued unabated. Suddenly a small panel at the bottom of the entrance door slid open and a can rolled inside with smoke pouring from it. Within a short time, smoke filled the place. The sounds of violence quickly gave way to choking and spluttering. People ceased fighting and began flopping about helplessly. Benjamin struggled to his knees, keeping his head down, one hand clutching his throat as the acrid smoke clawed at his breathing passage. With a rasping cough, he fought for air repeatedly. His eyes watered, stinging painfully. His brain started pounding inside his head, making him feel sick.

The only sounds were of choking and retching. The struggle to breathe seemed to last an eternity before the entrance door opened abruptly. Everyone stormed the door. A stampede ensued as people rushed to embrace the fresh air outside. Benjamin stumbled out in a crush of bodies. He gulped in the cold air, panting and wheezing as he tried to clear his constricted throat. A cordon of Family Police was waiting, officers holding their long batons menacingly, ready for action. No one was in any condition to offer resistance.

The Family Police screened everyone as they came out, allowing only men to pass. Benjamin moved through without a problem and left the Pro House behind.

Chapter 10

Benjamin finished his coffee. The dull headache he had woken with was beginning to ease. Every week he looked forward to his day off work. Usually he would spend time at the market and beach, or just ride around feeling free. Today, he felt a need to do something different, something meaningful.

He left home on his bike, immediately enjoying the sensation of not being under the control of others. Without knowing why, he headed in the opposite direction to normal, out of town. Picking a path over the uneven road surface, he soon passed the last apartments then the disused shell of the construction depot on his left. On the other side of the road, the water treatment plant stood alone, the only service maintained along with the windmills and electricity generators. These were systems unable to be separated between supplying the Family and the community.

The road veered left and became even rougher, no maintenance done at all beyond the town limits. Benjamin rode slowly to avoid the worst of the crumbling surface. Piles of debris continued each side, with plenty of people scrounging amongst them, but it quickly thinned out to cease altogether. He was now alone on the road. The piles went on till he reached the countryside, where they, too, ceased abruptly.

He rode for what seemed a long time, although the distance covered was not great. Once, years ago, he had ridden out this way, having to turn back due to a barrier across the road. He had never bothered returning. The barren landscape, with no signs of life, stretched as far as he could see. He felt at peace. Although isolated, it was different compared to the isolation he lived in every day surrounded by people. Here it was expansive not restrictive, accepting not rejecting.

The barrier loomed up ahead. He stopped in front of it and dismounted. A waist-high rusty steel bar straddled the road, supported by a post on each side. A sign attached midway across read,

STOP

TURN BACK

Benjamin nodded in recognition. When he saw it years ago, he had immediately turned back. Now, he looked beyond the sign and wondered why it was here. Was it hiding something? The only route to other places cut off; why?

He stood peering down the road, trying to detect if there was anything worth seeing. Nothing, no signs of life at all. Why be fearful of going further? Determined to be positive, he wheeled his bike around the barrier, remounted and continued on cautiously.

Nothing was different about the road or surrounding countryside to suggest a reason for the barrier. For a while, Benjamin concentrated on the derelict surface, but began to feel he had embarked on a pointless exercise. Then suddenly, he saw something. A speck in the distance. Immediately his senses were alert. He dismounted. As he crept forward, the speck grew into the shape of a building, sited adjacent to the road. Another barrier was across the road, and on the other side of it something that instantly alarmed him - an electric car!

Benjamin stopped in his tracks and stared at it. A lookout post? Way out here? And guarded by someone still possessing electric car capability! For the second time in two days, evidence of that capability astounded him. He suddenly realised how exposed he was, with the open terrain offering nowhere to hide. Anxious, he turned his bike and retreated before someone spotted him, his mind filled with complex questions.

Relieved to escape detection, he headed back to town. As he reached the start of construction debris, he noticed the vague outline of an old, disused road leading off to his left. Barely hesitating, he turned down the road, which was rough with scrub tussocks pushing through the crumbling bitumen surface, but passable. Soon it began to dip. The slope became steeper as he descended. He dismounted and leaned his bike against the side slope then continued on foot. Before long, the steep-sided cutting towered above him on each side, a deep scar gouged into the rocky country. He knew what he had found.

The road ended abruptly at a gaping square black hole in a vertical rock face. Benjamin passed through and stood inside the entrance to the underground cavern of Bunkertown. Beside him, the thick concrete door was angled inwards in its fully open position. The seals around the portal frame were perished, everything decrepit and rusty. Nothing had budged for twenty years.

He moved further in, reverently surveying the cavern as a flood of memories cascaded through his mind. The light coming in illuminated solid rock faces enough to reveal the far end. Near the entrance, he could just make out the faded shape of a painted mural, diminished by dampness but still a reminder of the cavern's function - the Food Cavern. For a moment, he could visualise the cavern filled with tables and chairs and people engrossed in mealtime.

Down the left side, small openings in the rock led away. On the other side, four openings accessed another cavern; the Rest Cavern, as he recalled. He wished he had brought his torch with him. At the far end, he noted the dais from which the Committee Head had made announcements. High above it on the rock face, a series of empty frames offered no clue of their once-celebrated function as read-out screens.

Benjamin walked slowly back, feeling nostalgic despite the dark, eerie atmosphere. Even though the place was decayed and useless, he felt a great fondness for it. A haven for the lucky few chosen to survive, or a shrine for those who had not. But what was lucky then seemed unjustified now for the unworthy society that had regenerated. Inevitably, his mind turned to Kelly. They had been so close then, just twelve years old but already soulmates. The free-spirited certainty of their lives had overridden the uncertainty of circumstance. What had gone wrong?

At the entrance, he took a final look around then turned away. He climbed the slope, collected his bike and resumed riding at the top. Further along, another disused road led off the other side. The second bunker. Benjamin paused. Nothing was there now and it was getting late, so he continued on back to town.

He passed the Clonesseum and arrived at the market. He left his bike in one of the racks by the road and joined the bustling throng of people. Many went there to alleviate idleness, the process of barter and exchange necessitating interaction not otherwise likely. With life so basic, there was no monetary system. Instead, the incentive of survival motivated those capable and healthy enough to be useful. For those who were not, no one cared about them anyway. The market was the focal point in people's lives, operating the most basic form of communism imaginable.

Family Police were present in numbers, as always. Here, where the greatest contact between people took place, they were obsessive in looking out for subversive or sexual activity. These were the only crimes. Nothing else mattered, not even murder. Reflecting the single-minded ruthlessness of the Family, they did not care how people treated each other, as long as it did not affect the Family's interests.

Violence and would-be crimes, like stealing, were surprisingly low in the community. People had little of worth that was not available by scrounging from the ruins. Many incentives for stealing, such as greed or desire for status, did not exist. The Family decided status, greed had nothing like money by which to manifest itself. Violence only occurred out of frustration, notably at the Pro House, or the market occasionally. The lack of trouble was a symptom of surrender. With no improvement in living conditions for fifteen years, people no longer had ambition to attain something extra, even by fair means. Uncaring indifference was the worst consequence of all resulting from the stifling regime of the Family.

The market was unsheltered, rows of cement benches hosting the activity. People moved between them inspecting the goods and doing their business with a purposeful air, many carrying items procured or intended for exchange. An adjacent open area was available for larger items.

Benjamin rarely took part in barter and exchange. He had little time to be creative and could repair or adapt anything he needed, having learnt a lot from Kelly's father. He headed for the food section. A man was arguing with a woman, their barter not progressing pleasantly. The man was agitated.

"I make your chair and look at the food you give me. It's rubbish!"

A small wooden chair was on the ground between them.

"That's all I've got," the woman retorted. "Take it or leave it."

"Great! You'll have your chair even if I die of food poisoning."

He snatched up the food and stormed off. The exchange would have been amusing if not so poignant. People were always concerned about the food, as quality control was non-existent and there were no medical facilities if someone fell ill. Usually differences evaporated when one party, in a stronger position, was too intransigent for the other. Another man was pointing at a pile of food a woman had collected for him.

"That's not enough. I should get more than that."

The woman regarded him with disdain and did not argue, satisfied with her gain from their exchange. She waved him away. The man transferred the food to a basket and left without another word.

Benjamin showed his Food Card to a woman and gathered the few items he needed, in particular coffee. He returned to his bike and slipped the items into the saddlebag. He was about to remove his bike from the rack when a woman's voice sounded behind him.

"Did you bring my handkerchief?"

Benjamin swung round in surprise. The girl he'd met yesterday was standing close by, wearing the same grey coat. He stared at her, once again impressed by the air of reserved maturity projecting from her. Suddenly grasping her question, he fumbled in a trouser pocket and produced the handkerchief, stained with a dried patch of his own blood.

"Oh yes, here it is."

He handed it to her and tried to think of something to say, but his brain seized at the crucial moment. Brenda accepted the handkerchief, looking around uneasily as she put it away in her coat pocket. Anxious to avoid further contact, she turned to leave.

Benjamin found his voice at last. "I'm Benjamin," he blurted out awkwardly. "What's your name?"

She hesitated, on the point of ignoring him. "Brenda," she replied finally.

Nervously, she looked around again then walked off. Benjamin watched her mingle with the crowd, disappointed at her unwillingness to communicate. After relating warmly to each other yesterday, he thought she might have given more, the market being the one place where people could relate, if only for essential purposes.

Brenda had good reason to feel nervous. The stifling Family Police presence was a constant threat after harassment twice already since her problems with the system and her degrading, forced removal from the women's area. The apartment on the main road was grubby, unfit for habitation. She was burdened with bad memories, and Family Police intimidation always affected her in a particularly intrusive way.

The market and working with other women at the crop fields, although tedious, offered her some security. An unexpected encounter yesterday with a man falling off his bike had momentarily broken the tedium. At the time, she had been impressed by his unusually receptive nature in spite of the compromising situation for him. She had discerned an intriguing depth of character, as well as appreciating a certain physical attraction. She felt this again now, but walked away, sadly resigned to how life had to be. She joined a woman at one of the benches.

"Hi, Sasha. What have you got today?"

Sasha indicated the food spread on the bench. "Just the usual. You look sad today, Brenda. Are the Family Police still hounding you?"

Brenda nodded, taking a quick scan of the people nearby. Two officers were standing not far away, watching them.

"They're always looking for something," she whispered. "Anything they can use to impress the Family women. I'm a target because I failed at what was expected of me."

"What was it like? At Laboratories."

Before Brenda could reply, the two officers moved in. One pushed between them, glaring at Sasha and threatening her with his long baton.

"Don't talk to her," he commanded coldly. "She's a failed clone mother."

Brenda was instantly fearful. The officer's manner was horribly familiar, reminding her of another officer whose dark looks and vicious nature had been indelibly imprinted on her mind ever since the loss of her brother, Eric, fifteen years ago. Omar's inclusion in the Family Police and insatiable desire for power had incensed Eric, his only friend, to the point of confrontation. The consequence for Eric was a Promart. Soon after, her brother went off his head in a blind fury, and Omar led the group that mercilessly clubbed him to death.

For a frightened eleven-year-old, already devastated by their parents perishing in the violence of the times, it meant condemnation to years of torment. No longer was Eric, four years her senior, there to depend on. Over time she learned to cope, using it to strengthen her resolve. But the relentless loneliness never eased.

The memory was still vivid today.

Sasha backed away. The officer turned to Brenda. His arm shot out, shoving her backwards against the bench.

"Oh!" she exclaimed, as her arms flung sideways, sweeping away all within range in a shower of food and tin plates. Shocked, she fell to the ground. The officer stood over her, his baton raised. Then he pointed it at her face as she threw up an arm in self-defence.

"You be careful. We're watching you."

He moved away.

Brenda scrambled to her feet and dusted off her coat. Already her fright was changing to angry resentment at the unjust treatment and attempt to degrade her self-esteem. Others at the market had stayed well clear throughout and still kept their distance, too fearful to offer assistance. Even Sasha had disappeared. Normal activity gradually resumed. Brenda noticed Benjamin then, standing not far away. She wondered what he thought of her now.

Benjamin was angered. With difficulty, he had restrained himself from rushing to her aid. Now it was over, he was impressed at how she was handling it, her poise and dignity still intact as she regained control of herself. He came forward.

"Are you okay?" he asked.

"Yes. Don't worry about me. You don't want Family Police to see you talking to me."

"I don't care about that," he responded spontaneously, without realising what he was saying.

For an instant their circumstances were forgotten, but it was only a moment. Brenda smiled and turned away. She moved off to merge with the crowd.

Benjamin stared after her, his heart pounding, his whole being uplifted. He was unsure what had happened but knew it was meaningful. And futile!

The onset of darkness was close. He returned to his bike and rode slowly home.

In his apartment, he paced up and down restlessly. Many thoughts were jumbled in his mind; the lookout post, Bunkertown, Brenda. Yet most of all was an urge to do something more. He had positive momentum, unconducive to another lonely evening closed away.

He made a cup of coffee. Through the window, he watched the hazy sun as it steadily disappeared behind the apartments opposite. The cold quickly deepened with the darkness. He resumed pacing up and down.

He glanced at the clock. The evening was wearing on.

"I have to do something," he murmured finally.

He clenched his fist and lightly punched the air, his jaw setting firmly. He put on his black jacket and left the apartment on foot.

A Family Police patrol passed by, one of several that would scour the streets relentlessly all night. Over the years, they had caught many people that way, particularly couples trying to meet secretly. In recent times, patrols were not as prevalent. Like most people, Benjamin never ventured out at night, although the Family Police would probably assume he was merely visiting the Pro House. Watchfully he moved down the road. The gloomy illumination from streetlights was sufficient to see a fair way.

He approached the Clonesseum with caution. An officer was slumbering in a chair outside the entrance. No patrol was in the vicinity. Quickly Benjamin slipped down the side, merging into the shadows. He passed the bike racks and continued along the alleyway between buildings. It became narrow further on, and dark. The light improved marginally as he emerged at the rear of the Clonesseum. He stopped to look around.

The building had a morbid feel about it as it towered above him. A set of steps ascended the back wall to a landing that travelled half the length of the building. The landing gave private access to two doors at upper floor level, one coinciding with the Medical Centre off the main lab, the far one with the second or DNA lab. The doors explained why a Family woman was never seen entering the Clonesseum by the front entrance.

Turning his back on the place, Benjamin moved on. He linked with a rough but well-worn track leading away over the tussocky ground. He came to a tree, slid past it, then another and another. He continued on till emerging at a deserted road. The double gate entrance to the Family Police compound was a short distance to his right.

He darted across the road and plunged into more trees. Peering out from behind one, he could see along the other road, deserted also, to the solid double gate and fence concealing the Family area. Surprisingly, no guard was outside. Relieved, he crossed to the trees again and angled towards intercepting the fence. It was risky, but he was spurred on by the brief glimpse he had stolen yesterday. He chose a suitable tree, grabbed the lowest branch and began to climb. Gradually the inside of the Family area came into view over the top of the high fence. He settled on a solid branch.

Strong street lighting, from poles closely spaced, lit the large area, allowing a clear sight throughout. The well-maintained road ran straight through to another double gate and fence. Spacious-looking, generously separated houses lined each side of the road. Not quite midway through, a side road branched off, and another a short distance further up. Lined with houses, both reached out to the perimeter fence down the left-hand extremity. A single gate in the fence coincided with the end of the closer side road. A fence down the right-hand extremity completed the rectangular area, and was common to the adjacent Family Police compound.

All open ground between buildings and to the roads was cultured into close-cropped green turf, starkly contrasting with the usual rough, tussocky land. The combination of turf, roads and buildings presented a panorama of relative affluence.

After recent sightings, Benjamin was expecting to see electric cars again, but the number parked along the main and side roads astonished him. Not for many years, even well before the Family established themselves, had there been so many. Lack of spare parts had diminished the numbers initially. Then, soon after the Family took control, there was no more methanol fuel, at least not for the general community. But the evidence now before him suggested a plentiful supply of methanol, or were they relying on the solar power backup system? That had been inefficient after Re-emergence, with the sun's diffused rays offering a poor source of energy. What about spare parts?

He was looking at a different world, one divorced from the realities he knew, as if delivered through a time warp. An eerie stillness in the air and the idleness of cars suggested a place of sleepy contentment; an incongruous anomaly.

The time of night was not late, but few people were on the road. Those who were moved purposefully, their activity seemingly not of a social nature. Family women were dressed in their conservative, suit-like attire, Family Police officers in their white shirts, their sons and daughters nowhere to be seen. Then he noticed a difference he had never seen before. The officers' white shirts had red shoulder pads not black! Every officer he saw had the same, surely signifying different status for officers attached to Family women. Obviously only unattached officers, with black pads, were engaged on enforcement duties in the community. He wondered what the attached officers occupied themselves with each day, other than to periodically gratify the sexual purpose for which they were chosen.

At a spot midway between the two side roads, two officers were assisting a third towards a building on the left. The officer in the middle was hobbling with an injured leg. They disappeared inside. A while later, they emerged, the injured officer now unassisted and using a pair of crutches. His leg was bandaged below the knee. The three of them moved slowly up the road.

Benjamin was sickened by evidence of the privileged treatment the Family and Family Police accorded themselves. While he watched, several more visits by officers and Family women confirmed the building to be a medical clinic. People in the community knew nothing of this, aware only of the Medical Centre at the Clonesseum, and that was exclusively concentrated on clone production. The drugs and supplies left over from the almost limitless stockpile at Bunkertown were not available.

When people became sick or injured, they had nowhere to go, no option other than retreating to their homes, unlikely to know anyone caring enough to help. The sight of a dead body being removed from an apartment by Family Police was not uncommon. Always on the streets were examples of uncontrolled recovery from injury, people limping along, exhibiting a deformity or struggling to overcome an ailment. Men suffering Promart punishment were not hard to pick. How utterly insecure their lives were!

With little more to observe, Benjamin climbed down from the tree. He hesitated. Instead of returning through the trees, he went to his left, coming out over tussocky open ground again. He turned the corner of the perimeter fence and moved down the fence-line. Illumination from the town lights was minimal now, the weird silence and biting cold contributing to an outlandish sense of unreality. The edge of the crop fields, a short distance away, formed a shadowy outline. He groped his way to the gate he had noticed from the tree. With one eye, he peered through the thin gap between gate and fence, seeing a narrow strip of road surface. The gate was locked.

He reached the far end of the fence and swung left to skirt the crop fields, seeking an alternate route home across country. The ground was uneven. He stumbled into an overgrown heap of rubble. His foot slipped into a hole and he crashed to his knees. Cursing, he extricated himself then backtracked, finding solid ground further on. Twice more he bypassed construction debris then suddenly, his feet met a hard surface. A road, but where was he?

He started along it toward the distant town lights then stopped abruptly. A light further up was closer and brighter. Feeling exposed, he darted to one side and crouched next to debris. He crept forward then stopped again, alarmed. The hooded outline of an electric car was pointing down the road, parked in front of a building flooded in light. He shrank back and watched the activity in progress.

Family Police officers were wheeling out drums on trolleys and lifting them onto a trailer backed up to a set of wide-open double doors. They worked in silence, efficiently. Eventually all drums were loaded, the trailer full. The car headlights suddenly came on, blinding Benjamin for an instant. Recoiling, he lay low behind the debris. Shortly after, the car eased slowly down the road and passed him. He watched the headlights turn then disappear behind the Family perimeter fence.

The building was in darkness now. Benjamin came up to the double doors, which were closed and secured by heavy chain and lock. A low hum was sounding from inside, a faint odour in the air. The effluent processing plant.

He had never given the plant any thought over the years. Behind the women's apartments, it was inaccessible from town. He was not surprised it was operating, since effluent draining to it must be dealt with. Methanol production explained how electric cars were being powered, but the problem of maintenance was still a puzzle. And why did the community never have methanol fuel? Yet another example of suppression. Shaking his head in perplexity, he left the building behind.

Soon he came to a pile of debris. The improved light guided him behind more pushed-up piles, beyond which the vague shape of apartment blocks followed in parallel. Estimating where he was, he passed through to the main road and returned to his apartment.

Chapter 11

Benjamin looked pensively at the tasks on his desk, unable to concentrate. After recent events, uppermost in his mind was a pressing urgency to continue the momentum of discovery. It dawned on him that he had never really assessed in a critical way what he saw in a case file. Day by day, year after year, he had merely performed what was expected of him, like everyone too fearful to question anything. Now, however, his mind wandered, a determination to investigate replacing passive acceptance. He had plenty of time, only a few tasks to complete this morning.

One recent development nagged at him. It had even surprised him when it first happened. He went to the files. Scores of green and orange cards took up much of the space, but a small section contained just a few blue cards, for female DNA donors. The green cards were all for male donors. He pulled out the blue cards and checked each one. The earliest approval date, inserted at the top by Stephanie, was about two weeks ago. In each instance, the first date recorded for a case file was the next day or very soon after the approval date, and each already displayed several entries, suggesting some urgency. By contrast, many green cards lay dormant in the files or at least displayed infrequent case file entries.

One blue card held his attention. The name on it rang a bell, reminding him of a case file that had struck him as bizarre when it came through. Being recent helped him make the connection. In the Orange Files, he found confirmation; a card of the same name. The last entry showed the same date and case file number as on the blue card.

He stared at the two cards, dumbfounded. They had implanted the clone mother using her own DNA sample! It seemed an absurd notion, yet the nature of clone production suggested no technical reason why it could not be done. He filed the cards then checked in the General File. The entry was there, one of the latest, showing the same DNA donor and clone mother name with the date and case file number.

The implications were hard to gauge. Any woman could be a clone mother for any DNA donorship, with the same product resulting. What advantage was there in using a woman to clone herself? Perhaps it was merely a case of convenience that could happen from time to time. He expected the Family might try anything. Yet he knew there was always a definite purpose behind their actions. Something about it disturbed Benjamin.

Of even more concern to him was the start of female cloning. Two questions puzzled him. Why had the Family been interested only in male cloning until now, and what had happened to suddenly make them begin cloning females? The lack of even one female example in fifteen years suggested a deliberate, single-minded agenda, typical of the Family's ruthless efficiency. What could their vision be? Why the change in strategy? No one saw a clone beyond the age of two years, so it was difficult to gain insight into their intentions.

He thought about the way Investigations chose DNA donors, under pressure to achieve the greatest 'percentage of perfection' possible. A new Donor Assessment Form had been introduced just a week ago, to assess potential donors against a checklist of character traits and capabilities. The timing of it was pertinent in the light of criticisms overheard by Ralph the other day.

A flood of forms had come through for several days after introduction, indicating a crash course to complete assessment of all donors. More would trickle in for new donors and every new case file would have a copy of the donor's form included, for the benefit of Assessments later.

Benjamin pulled out some of the forms and began studying them. Each had the donor's name and date of birth at the top. Subdivided into several groups, a list of assessment traits offered the opportunity to tick one of three small boxes after each trait: PASS, FAIL or INCONCLUSIVE. The first group, sub-titled GENERAL, had only two boxes: PASS or FAIL. Here were three traits:

LOYALTY and OBEDIENCE
TRAINING POTENTIAL
ATTITUDE POTENTIAL

He checked each Form, noting all had a PASS tick for these, as if passing them was paramount to continuing any further with an assessment. The nature of them was a pointed reminder of Family priorities.

'Loyalty and Obedience': the keystone of Family expectation.

'Training Potential': gullibility to indoctrination?

'Attitude Potential': preference for a callous mentality?

A clone, by definition, was an exact replica of the donor. The Family were intent on producing the best possible, then bringing environmental influence to bear as soon after birth as practicable, by taking the clones away at two years of age.

The other groups were sub-titled MENTAL, EMOTIONAL, PSYCHOLOGICAL, SPIRITUAL and PHYSICAL. Each contained five assessment traits apart from PHYSICAL, which had ten. Benjamin noted the ticking patterns on each form. The handwriting style of the ticks intrigued him, in each case the same for every group other than PHYSICAL, which was distinctly different. He deduced that Investigations completed all but the PHYSICAL group then, if approving, passed the form on to Laboratories. The involvement of both Departments explained why the forms were filed at Records, following the same procedure as traditional approvals. Whoever from Investigations came to check a green card could also obtain copies of the Donor Assessment Form.

Benjamin returned the forms to the file. They hardly shed any light on the Family's vision or overall strategy, although they did provide a clearer picture of qualities preferred in DNA donors.

A thought occurred to him. Family Police were never used as donors, even though original recruitment of them suggested they had special qualities. Of course, there was nothing rewarding about being a donor. Taking the DNA sample, a quick and simple procedure, was all the donor ever knew. The rest was done in the laboratory. Neither the donor nor the clone mother would know who each other was, and the donor would never know his clone baby or even whether one resulted from implantation at all. The Family had deliberately set it up this way, so no unwanted liaisons could develop between people.

In the early years, Benjamin had often wondered if Investigations would call on him as a donor. They never did, he assumed because his mother's Prohyst and father's tragic reaction branded him as unsuitable. And after starting in Records, he saw case files, naturally excluding him from consideration. With faint amusement, he visualised the chaos he could cause by throwing open the files and tossing all case files in the air so people could see what donors were paired with which clone mothers. Then he thought of Karla Mason. She saw case files every day! Benjamin shook his head, uncomprehending.

The chance of unwanted liaisons explained why Family Police would never be donors. The Family ensured all officers were fully dedicated to the exclusive purposes for which they were chosen, eliminating diversionary factors that might dilute the controlling power they exercised through competition for sexual favour. Daughters the Family had with chosen officers would become Family of the future, sons future Family Police. Their regime would be permanently entrenched as a closed society devised from the narrow, self-appointed base of elite people with the commonly held views and prejudices that had drawn them together in the first place. This was why they treated the people the way they did.

Benjamin roused himself from the depths of thought. He went to close the General File he'd left on top of a filing cabinet, but hesitated. Instead, he lifted it down and laid it on his desk. Beginning at the last entry, he began perusing back through time, line by line. He had no idea what he was looking for, perhaps something like the DNA donor and clone mother being the same name, anything remotely irregular.

Every entry seemed in order. Benjamin shook his head, in awe of the number of case files that had passed through his hands. An entry a year ago caught his eye, no different from others except the donor's name had the number 1 after it. He looked at it curiously and tried to remember back, his suspicions roused. Then he noticed another the same, two days removed from the first. He checked further but found no more like this.

He searched in the Green Files for the first example. Two cards were there for that name! Fascinated, he noted one was with the number 1 after the name, the other without. The card without, for a donor thirty-five years old, had several case file entries, but the card with the number 1 had one entry only. The date of that entry was the same as in the General File. The donor would have been just thirteen years old then! Finally, he noticed the date of the first entry on the older donor's card - nine months before the date of birth on the other!

Benjamin stared at the two cards, stunned by the implications. The evidence was consistent with the older donor's first clone, produced in the early days of clone production, being itself used as a DNA donor a year ago.

He checked the second example. The same pattern was apparent from two green cards, one displaying the number 1, the other not. The dates were consistent and close to those of the first example.

The significance of clones producing clones was hard to judge. Two examples only were insufficient to establish a pattern, just three months of assessment too little for further commitment. Benjamin had no knowledge of what the Family envisaged, but one chilling conclusion occurred to him. If they pursued the use of clones as DNA donors extensively, then men in the community, already superfluous sexually and in terms of power and authority, could eventually become completely redundant. Perhaps the Family intended this, entrenching their elite society even more firmly. His eyes widened in alarm as the thought dawned on him.

He returned the cards then resumed perusing the General File. An entry two years ago caught his attention. Inserted above the clone mother name were the words 'Growth Trial'. Benjamin vaguely remembered it despite the time elapsed. A particularly insidious case, as he recalled.

Intrigued, he searched the Orange Files, but her card was not there. After a moment of reflection, he checked the Deceased Files.

The card was there, attached to a half-black half-orange one. The date of death was three months after the date entered in the General File. From the Case File records, he found the case file. Alongside the clone mother name were the words, 'Growth Trial'. Further on, he read, 'Growth Trial failure. Growth occurring too fast. Death of clone mother'.

He stared at the comments, remembering more clearly now. Using a special treatment, they had attempted to speed up growth of the clone baby. If successful, reducing the time of pregnancy could have led to faster turnaround time for clone mothers and acceleration in clone output. The trial had been so disastrous it had not been repeated since.

He forced himself to concentrate on the tasks on his desk. The first was a case file using a female DNA donor, advised by the letter "F" in brackets after the name. He processed it. A request from Laboratories for the record of a clone mother was perhaps the one Ralph had mentioned concerning the birth of a deaf clone. Benjamin completed a clone mother Record Form after referring to the records. Two case files returned from Assessments were for final filing. One was normal, with a birth date exactly two years ago and a TrainA Action statement. The other was a Dump for a clone born just over a year ago. It fitted the example he saw three mornings ago of a clone being wrenched from its distraught mother. He filed both in the Case File Records.

The second-to-last task was another case file. At first, nothing seemed different about it, until he looked for the DNA donor name. Startled, he leaned forward, gazing intently at the entry. Two names were there, not one! It had to be a mistake. How could there be two DNA donors for one case? This had never occurred before. He decided to check.

Stephanie barely moved as he entered her room. "What is it, Benjamin?" she inquired in a flat monotone.

Benjamin handed her the case file. "There are two DNA donors noted. Could it be a mistake?"

Stephanie looked up impatiently and took the case file. She glanced briefly inside then handed it back to him.

"There is no mistake," she said with a note of finality. "Process the file and cards in the normal way."

Benjamin felt like asking more but Stephanie, in her aloof way, had ended their conversation. He returned to his desk.

He contemplated the obvious conclusion. Of course, making a clone mother have twins would be a natural progression in the development of clone production, expediting output. Would they try triplets, quadruplets, or more? As many as a clone mother could carry! The Family cared only about efficiency, regardless of sacrifice. But the timing made no sense. Why had they waited fifteen years before trying such an obvious advancement? Benjamin shook his head in bewilderment. Dismissing it for now, he processed the case file, updating one orange and two green cards and the General File.

The final task was a case file accompanied by a request from Laboratories for removal of the clone mother from the program. Benjamin was curious, since completion of a clone mother Record Form invariably preceded such action, and the one he had just done was the first for a considerable time. He looked in the case file to identify the clone mother. Immediately his mouth dropped open in surprise. The name seemed to jump off the page to hit him in the eye. Her first name was Brenda!

He stared at it, instantly thinking of the Brenda who had impressed him twice recently in situations of compromise. Surely it must be the same person? Her precarious circumstances were apparent now. How inexplicable that someone with her poise and maturity should be treated this way.

Beside her name was the word 'Fail' and further down the page a comment he had seen before, 'Failed at Implantation'. He located her orange card in the files. The date of birth revealed she was twenty-six years old. The card was blank, not a single entry on it. Benjamin's eyes widened with astonishment. This was her first time! But the approval date was twelve years ago. Why had they not tried her before? And why were they removing her from the program after only one failure not two? Something had gone seriously wrong for Brenda.

He entered the details onto the card, stuck a TERMINATED sticker in the bottom right-hand corner and removed the card from the system to the Terminated Files. Also the case file, with request, to the Case File records.

All tasks complete, he dropped those to be passed on in Stephanie's In-tray.

At lunchtime, Ralph joined him at his favourite table in the cafeteria, in ebullient mood as he attacked his food with enthusiasm. Eventually he paused.

"You remember that red-haired one watching us the other night?" he asked mischievously.

Benjamin pictured the self-conscious girl who had seemed so out of place at the Pro House, terrified as she clung to him, cowering from the violence.

"Yes, I remember her."

"She asked about you."

"Me? Why?"

Ralph gave him a roguish look. "She likes you. I told her you work in Records. She was interested in that. She said she was working in Laboratories but something happened. She's only been at the Pro House a few days."

"Really? What was she doing in Laboratories?"

"Why don't you come tonight and ask her?"

Benjamin had an irresistible urge to talk to her. "Yes, why not? Let's go tonight."

"Great! I'll come to your office at finishing time."

Benjamin watched him attacking his food, amazed at his single-minded approach to whatever was of immediate interest. Ralph seemed unaffected, physically or emotionally, by the violence at the Pro House. Just part of a typical day for Ralph.

"I see you avoided getting hurt the other night."

Ralph grinned. "Sure. I got out of it."

"You were right in the middle to begin with."

"The trick is to leave before they close the doors. Just the right time for a lady."

Benjamin was incredulous. Ralph's insensitivity even extended to a callous disregard for people getting injured or worse. He was sharp though, always a step ahead of the action at grassroots level. He was unaware of how Benjamin regarded him, focussed only on shovelling food into his mouth as fast as the spoon could lift it from his plate. Benjamin felt vaguely disgusted.

"What about the people inside? A lot were injured."

Ralph nodded. "Three people killed. I don't know how many injured. Lots were affected by smoke."

What a sorry indictment! Three killed by a degrading environment that succeeded only in giving vent to underlying frustration.

"What happened after?" Benjamin asked, dismayed. "What did they do with the bodies?"

Ralph stopped eating, looking puzzled. He shrugged his shoulders. "I'm not sure. Family Police take away the dead ones but I don't know where to. Does it matter?"

"And the injured?"

"Oh, the Family Police don't bother with them. They just want the place cleared. The injured have to get out the same as everyone else."

How insidiously calculating the response had been. The Family Police were not only uncaring of people injured or killed, they seemed actually to welcome what had happened. Why did they lock everyone inside and wait so long before taking steps to end it?

Ralph's plate was empty. "See you at finishing time." He departed.

Benjamin finished his lunch and left the cafeteria.

With his hand about to push open the office door, he stopped as a disturbance suddenly broke in the entrance foyer. Two officers were hauling in a woman from outside. Twisting her arms behind her back, they shoved her towards the stairs leading to Laboratories. She was resisting furiously, but in their unfeeling, forceful way, they were far too strong for her. She screamed at them, defiant.

"Leave me alone! I haven't done anything wrong!"

Brenda had been at the market, contributing her efforts. After yesterday, she was even more wary of Family Police, but had no other outlets than the market and crop fields. Her concerns were well-founded.

The same two officers as yesterday noticed her talking to Sasha. The more aggressive one, with a self-indulgent smirk on his face, moved forward and without warning struck her with his long baton. Fortunately, Brenda caught a glimpse of it coming and swayed quickly to one side. The blow glanced off her head, but the force of it sent her sprawling to the ground. The officer stood over her.

"I told you we're watching you," he declared, glaring at her coldly. "Failed clone mothers don't try subverting others. Now you will pay."

They dragged Brenda to her feet. Her coat was torn, hanging off one shoulder to release a cascade of hair, which blew across her face. She was bewildered but angry.

"I've done nothing! Leave me alone!"

Resolute as always, her every instinct was to resist. People in the vicinity, including Sasha, cleared away to a safe distance, leaving her to fend for herself. The officers twisted her arms behind her back savagely, making her yelp with pain. They led her away.

At the bottom of the stairs, the two officers responded to her screams viciously, twisting her arms back further. She was a mess, her hair dishevelled, plastered across her contorted face. But angry defiance was turning to despair now, as the horrifying spectre of a Prohyst loomed large. She could do nothing.

With his hand against the office door, Benjamin watched aghast. Then, with a shock, he recognised Brenda. She noticed him, and in a desperate plea tried to fling herself in his direction. Their eyes met for an instant. Benjamin felt her despair, mirrored in fear-struck eyes. She cried out as the officers began forcing her up the stairs. Then they disappeared from view. The entire scene took a few moments only and she was gone.

Benjamin stared at the base of the stairs, the image of her vividly etched in his mind. He felt sick in the stomach as a horribly familiar feeling hit him. Although only knowing Brenda briefly, he knew he was about to lose something precious. A crazy urge to rush upstairs and fight for her gripped him, but the moment passed as he realised the insanity of it. He pushed open the door and moved slowly inside.

He stood in the middle of the room, frantically grasping for inspiration. Time was the enemy. Every second brought Brenda closer to her fate! He rushed to the files and began flailing through them aimlessly. The cards, case files, Donor Assessment Forms. He stopped. In a flash, an idea struck him. A remote chance, but it might work.

A blank Donor Assessment Form was there. Benjamin seized it. He obtained a photocopy, took a completed Form as an example then retrieved Brenda's orange card from the Terminated Files. At his desk, he worked quickly. Every moment was crucial.

From the card, he printed Brenda's full name and date of birth at the top of the blank form, copying as best he could the printing style on the example. Similarly he ticked the three PASS options under GENERAL then filled in a reasonable pattern of ticks for the assessment traits under the next four headings, choosing a predominance of PASS options. He left blank the last ten assessments under PHYSICAL.

The task took a few minutes only. The form appeared authentic. He wiped at the perspiration on his brow, his hand shaking. Before he had time to reconsider, he left the office and made his way up the stairs to Laboratories.

He entered the main laboratory, the adrenalin flowing strongly through him, negating fear. White-coated Assistants worked at their benches, oblivious as he moved through to the far end of the lab. Inside the corridor now, no one around. The door to the GM's office was open, no one inside. But voices were faintly audible, coming from behind the closed door of the interview room opposite. Fate was playing a kind hand this time.

In a trance, he stepped inside the GM's office. An In-tray was there on her desk. In it another Donor Assessment Form; part-completed the same as the one he held, with the last ten PHYSICAL assessments blank! Thrilled at the vindication of his efforts, he dropped Brenda's form on top and backed quickly out of the office.

Still no one in the vicinity. Moving fast but maintaining composure, he returned past the Assistants to the main corridor and relative safety. Back in his office, he felt elated yet amazed he had done it so easily.

Relieved, he slumped into the chair, his mind still buzzing. Would the form make a difference? Would Brenda's apparent worth as a DNA donor override the desire to punish her? He had no idea. Was it in time? He could not have done it faster. No repercussions would follow as long as lack of communication between Departments held true. The form would come to Records and sit dormant in the files, never to be accessed by an unknowing Investigations Department.

Finishing time was approaching. Ralph appeared in front of his desk, looking down at him nonchalantly.

"Come on, let's go. It's finishing time."

Benjamin was confused for a moment then remembered. "Oh yes, of course. Let's go."

Chapter 12

Benjamin sat on a stool near the bar, holding a glass of rice wine. The area was filling gradually. Ralph returned, leaving a girl at the door. He re-joined Benjamin.

"That was a good one. I needed that," he commented, looking satisfied.

Benjamin was conscious of the red-haired girl sitting at a table not far away, part of a group with three other girls. Although young and attractive, she had the same sad, tired look as the previous time he saw her. He was aware, from her furtive look when they first entered, that she had noticed him. He felt a buzz of anticipation.

Ralph saw where his attention was focussed. He jumped to his feet and went over to her. After a brief moment, he beckoned eagerly to Benjamin, who joined them.

"Benjamin, this is Natalie."

"Hello, Benjamin," Natalie greeted in a soft, welcoming voice.

He returned her greeting and sat in the spare seat beside her.

Natalie took the initiative. "Ralph told me you work in the Records Department at the Clonesseum."

"Yes. He told me you worked in Laboratories."

"I did. Till a month ago."

Before he could reply, she was speaking again. "I'd like to ask you something. But not here. Can you come to my room?"

The prospect of being alone with her affected him a little. She stood and led the way to her room.

Natalie's room was small but private. She had added a few feminine touches to soften the starkness of her environment. The living conditions were basic, however, with just a table, one chair, a cupboard, wardrobe, small larder and a bench with sink and tap. A single, rumpled bed was against the wall farthest from the door, beneath a small window. The room was depressingly inadequate for anything other than intended use. Eating, washing and toilet facilities were all communal, a short walk from any of the rooms.

Natalie projected a more favourable image than most women of the Pro House. Despite her cruel circumstances, she retained a dignity lacking in others. It stamped her as a person of strength. Her sadness was in sharp contrast, however, exposing a vulnerability that made Benjamin want to reach out to protect her. Nothing would help though, or shield her from the regular physical violations for which the women were installed here.

She sat on the edge of the bed, Benjamin on the chair next to it. He had not been alone with a woman in secluded circumstances for a long time. The proximity of the bed made him uncomfortable.

"What were you working on in Laboratories?" he began.

Natalie leaned forward, attentive. "I was in the Medical Centre. Working with the clone mothers from ovulation to implantation, monitoring them during pregnancy and birth. I also did medical examinations for DNA donor and clone mother approvals." Some of her defences dropped immediately, as his question had targeted her interests rather than indulging in talk centred on sexual pleasure.

"You must know all about clone production procedures," Benjamin commented excitedly, impressed at the significance of her responsibilities and the brightness that now filled her eyes.

"Not entirely. I only know what I was involved in. Laboratories is divided into sections and there's minimal contact between them."

"That's their way with everything. The less people know, the less of a threat they can be."

"Yes. For instance, I never saw what happens with the donors or their samples. That's all done in the DNA lab. The first I'd know of a case was when I received the DNA and case file. When the ovulating clone mother arrived, I'd complete the process, extracting and processing the egg, injecting the DNA, fusion then implantation. All clinical and very efficient."

Benjamin listened intently. A thought occurred to him. "Who gave you the sample and case file?"

"Always the General Manager."

"She controls everything," he murmured, picturing the plump, humourless woman who had terrorised him several days ago.

"Yes, everything goes through her. When I get the case file, it already has the names inserted under DNA donor and clone mother. When I've completed implantation, I insert the time and date, make any comments and hand it back to the GM."

"And the GM sends it on to us at Records. When I receive it, I update the record cards, attach copies of them to the case file and give it to Stephanie, my Head. She returns it to your GM for the pregnancy period and birth."

"That's right. I had it until birth then the GM passes it on to Assessments. I don't know what happens after that, unless the clone baby needs medical attention."

Benjamin nodded. "It comes back to Records eventually, when the case is concluded. Usually after two years. I know nothing after that. The clones are sent away for training."

They fell silent, each contemplating how the system worked. What stood out to Benjamin was the deliberate secrecy from one section or department to another, and particularly how the GM completely controlled the incoming and outgoing of every case file to and from Laboratories.

Natalie kept her eyes on him, appreciating the chance to be near a man who respected her. He was different from others coming to the Pro House. Becoming engrossed in talking about the system was leaving little room for personal intimacy to develop, but she could feel herself hoping. She desperately needed comfort, to be close to someone in a sharing way, not the degrading way taken by men normally. She sensed Benjamin was capable of more.

He became conscious of Natalie watching him. Although alone with her next to the bed, something held him back. Before the silence became awkward, he turned his thoughts to the reason for being here.

"You said you want to ask me something?"

An intense look came onto her face. "Yes, about the medical examinations for approvals." She paused before continuing. "I'd complete a medical report and hand it to the GM. Where do they go from there?"

Intrigued by the question, Benjamin took up the train of thought as she paused again. "Approvals are received and retained by Stephanie. She makes out a new card, green for DNA donor, orange for clone mother. The cards are part of the filing system I work with."

"I thought it must work something like that. So you can confirm the approval of any DNA donor just by finding the card in your files?"

"Yes."

"Good. If I give you the names of a couple of donors, can you check them for me?"

"Sure, but why?"

"Because I strongly suspect some donors are used that haven't been approved in the normal way. I started getting suspicious some time ago but could never prove it. I only had memory to go by, but so many approvals have gone through. I had no access to the files, which the GM keeps locked in her room."

"I see. But if non-approved donors were being used, I'd have received case files with no green cards for them. I'm certain that's never happened. Only once has there been no card and that was orange for a clone mother."

He thought of Karla Mason again. Natalie stared at him for a moment then her head drooped forward in disappointment.

"I see what you mean," she whispered unhappily. "I was so sure, but I must have been mistaken."

She slumped forward, face in her hands, and burst into tears. Benjamin moved closer to comfort her. She clutched hold of him and all the pent-up emotion released from inside her. It poured out, her spirit broken. Benjamin felt of no use, having told her something that only destroyed her hopes. They sat that way for some time, until gradually the sobbing subsided. Natalie looked forlornly at him and tried to compose herself.

"I'm sorry. I didn't mean to involve you in my problems. But thank you for understanding."

"Why did they do this to you?"

She wiped at the tears. "I asked too many questions. I should have kept it to myself and just continued doing what they expected of me. They felt threatened so gave me a Prohyst, and here I am." She sobbed quietly again. "That was a month ago. They allow three weeks to recover. I've only been here a few days. It's horrible."

Benjamin looked at her in sorrow. He could do little to help her. "Can you give me the names? I might as well check them anyway, you never know what I might find."

"Yes." Natalie went to the table and opened a drawer. She extracted a piece of paper, handing it to Benjamin as she returned to the bed.

He glanced at the two names scribbled on the paper. Instantly he was staring hard at them. Something was not right.

"What's the matter?" Natalie asked diffidently.

"These are names of women. Are you sure they're DNA donors, not clone mothers?"

"No, they're DNA donors. Why? I don't understand."

"And they're only first name plus initial," he added, still looking hard at them. "Is this how they were in the case files?"

"Yes," Natalie confirmed, perplexed. "All female donors are noted that way. I'm not sure why. You must have seen that in Records."

"No, never. I've never seen a case file with anything but full names."

"Really? That's strange."

"It's as though they want to obscure identity from anyone who doesn't know for sure who the donors are. But more than that, there have never been cases using a female donor until two weeks ago. All previous clone production has used male donors."

"What!" Natalie exclaimed, leaning forward with a look of disbelief. "That can't be right! Female donors have been used plenty of times, starting years ago. Not many compared to male ones certainly, but you say there have been none? No, that's not right. There must be a mistake."

Benjamin was incredulous. "There's no mistake. Just two weeks ago, Stephanie introduced the first blue cards for female donors. There are still only a few of them in the files."

They stared at each other in amazement, both grappling with the anomalous situation. In vain, he tried to rationalise it.

"There's something strange going on. Until the blue cards, your GM can't have passed on any case files involving female donors. Maybe she kept them briefly then handed them back to you, so you wouldn't know the difference. Except they wouldn't have copies of our record cards attached when you got them back."

He looked at Natalie inquiringly.

"That did happen sometimes," she responded. "I assumed it was the first case for that donor and clone mother, so no previous records."

"Right. But that only confirms it. There's been no case where I didn't attach copies of the cards, even if it was their first case."

"So it must be as you say. The GM didn't pass on case files involving female donors."

"Yes." Benjamin was convinced of something devious now. "And she didn't pass them on to Assessments after birth either. Otherwise we'd have ended up with them at Records on conclusion, which is only two years at the most. That certainly hasn't happened."

"That's right!" Natalie agreed.

"And Investigations know nothing of them. If they did, they'd expect our cards to be kept up to date. Their involvement is why Laboratories send us the case files after implantation, so I can update the cards. Investigations might want to use the donor again."

They were both excited now, realising how deliberate the secrecy was.

"Not only that," Benjamin continued, "Investigations couldn't have chosen them in the first place. If they had, they'd have come to Records to check for a card and seen there was no approval, no cards for female donors at all, even."

"Of course! So this means no one outside Laboratories, outside the GM in fact, knows about clone production from those female donors. And what I suspected is true, about donors being used that weren't approved!"

"Right. All female ones before the blue cards."

"That's what first made me suspicious. Female names were appearing in case files under DNA donor that I couldn't remember examining for approval. Maybe all of them, as you say. I couldn't be certain because an examination is the same for donor or clone mother. When I questioned it, the GM told me someone else had done examinations as well. It was confusing, too many inconsistencies. I should have kept quiet."

She drooped her head again. Benjamin continued to concentrate, trying to make sense of it.

"But why? Why should it be different from other clone production? There's more to it, something missing. But what?" He frowned, focussing on why the approval process had been bypassed. Suddenly, he realised. He looked up grimly at Natalie, who was watching him closely once more.

"If Investigations had nothing to do with it, then how were the female donors chosen? Who chose them?"

Natalie stared at him wide-eyed as the pertinence of the question struck her. "I've no idea. My section had nothing to do with that side of it. I only did the medical examinations."

"There's only one answer. The Family chose them directly. Who else if not Investigations?"

"Yes, of course. But why not do it in the normal way? I don't understand that."

"Neither do I," Benjamin admitted with a sigh of exasperation. "Their intentions must be different, a secret kept from Assessments. What happens to those clones after birth? If they were sent for training, Assessments would have to be involved, wouldn't they?"

The question hung in the air.

"I also wonder about the first ones starting two weeks ago, with blue cards," he continued. "They had full names inserted, not just first name and initial. Why use normal procedures now? Or is this something new? Perhaps the other secret method is still being done. Too many questions and no answers." He rubbed his eyes, his concentration easing as they reached the limit of what they could deduce. He went over it in his mind again, frustrated. Then suddenly, the reason why it did not add up crystallised.

"Wait a minute. Why would the Family bother hiding something like this? They do whatever they like. Many of their actions are evil, but they don't try to hide them. They don't care because no one can touch them. So why the secrecy? It doesn't make sense."

Another question unanswered. He shook his head, bewildered. Then a steely determination gripped him.

"I will find out what it's about," he declared. He was still clutching the piece of paper with the two names on it. "Can I keep this?"

"Yes." Natalie was heartened. "But don't let anybody see it, or know where you got it from."

Benjamin put it away in his pocket. "Safe," he said softly.

Natalie leaned forward again, with more on her mind. "Do you know anything about the other two labs at Laboratories? The DNA and the third lab."

"No," he replied, his curiosity roused again. "I've seen the two entrance doors along the main corridor, but I've never been inside either one."

"Neither have I. The doors are always locked. There's access from the internal corridor off the main lab, but the door at the end of that is always locked too. I'm sure donors are in and out of the DNA lab as quickly as their DNA can be extracted. Apart from them and essential personnel, no one is allowed in there."

Benjamin nodded, remembering the two recent occasions he had glimpsed down the internal corridor, but without time to notice what was further along.

"They make sure people know as little as possible. So what's the third lab for?" he asked.

Natalie slowly shook her head. "I've no idea. I've never seen anyone go in there. I don't even know anyone who works there."

"Really!" he exclaimed, surprised. "That's interesting. I wonder what it could be."

"I'd certainly like to know. I'm sure things are going on in both labs they don't want people to know about. If only it was possible to get inside." Her suggestion was far from guarded.

She looked at him intently.

Benjamin understood clearly. He had already begun to consider it. The thought of gaining access to the labs was exciting, but to actually do it was a perilous prospect.

"Are you suggesting I should try to get inside?" he queried.

Natalie felt embarrassed. She hesitated, but was hopeful. "It would not be easy," she said eventually. "Very dangerous. If you were caught, the punishment would be severe."

He contemplated the idea. Curiously, it was not fear that daunted him, since he was committed to doing anything he could regardless of potential consequences. However, defying authority did not come naturally to him, despite the circumstances firing his sense of justice. This would be a truly subversive act and calculatingly so, unlike what he had done for Brenda in the emotion of the moment. But he knew he would do it.

"Ralph might help," he offered. "He works in Maintenance. He'd know how to gain access, maybe with keys even. At least he'd know about security, although that's probably not much. Everything non-medical is so basic."

"That's right. There's only one guard patrolling the main corridor outside Laboratories at night. You could have a diversion, something to draw him away." The prospective action excited her.

"They rely on fear to maintain control," Benjamin commented. "And it certainly has worked. But they're getting complacent after so many years of successful suppression."

They fell silent again. Natalie continued to watch him, feeling satisfaction at having imparted what she knew to him. It gave her a small measure of hope. Benjamin was the first man she had met with the will or capability to try and make a difference. In her desperate circumstances, she needed something to hope for. "I know things are happening that are very bad, evil," she added. "If you decide to go into those labs, I'm sure you'll find something."

Benjamin nodded, respecting how close Natalie had been to the heart of the system. "In Records, I don't see anything actually happening. I only see what appears in the files. Today, a case file came through with two DNA donors for the one clone mother. It's the first time I've seen that. They must be trying for twins, double the output. I wonder why they didn't start it years ago."

Natalie raised her eyebrows in surprise. "They did try it before. About three years after clone production started. As soon as they were achieving a high success rate, they looked to increase output by any means possible. I don't know the details. It was all before I started in Laboratories. But I know it was disastrous."

"Really! I never knew that." He wished he had perused further back in the General File this morning. "Why was it disastrous?"

She surreptitiously looked about the room and lowered her voice as if the room had suddenly grown ears. "I only know what someone in my section told me. Apparently they even tried triplets as well. It failed every time, and violently. Something to do with the implantations being hostile and destroying each other. The process poisoned the clone mother. The Family kept pursuing it for a while, but it was always the same."

"Wow," Benjamin murmured, dismayed. "Every time a dramatic reaction. There must be something about cloning that's different from natural reproduction. Maybe a clone is more individualistic, intolerant of sharing."

"Yes, that's the conclusion they came to. It suggests there's something fundamentally lacking in the cloning method, a missing ingredient. But they could never find a medical reason for it."

"Maybe the reason is non-medical."

A cold shiver ran down his spine as the bizarre thought occurred to him. If not medical, then what, spiritual? He shuddered and glanced at Natalie. She was staring wide-eyed at him; comprehending the same thought.

"It was too diabolical even for the Family. They had to give up on it. Instead, they moved to increase output by whatever other means they could. They targeted any girl who was ovulating, no matter how young. I had two clones before starting in Laboratories, the first when I was sixteen." She looked away. After a few moments, she continued. "Some women, those with strong motherhood instincts, can accept being a clone mother. But I never could. I felt used, my body not belonging to me, no longer available to nature, just a recycling bin producing something belonging to no one. Women more accepting find it hard when the clone is taken away after two years. For me, and others, it was a blessing. When the second one ruined me and I could have no more, they put me in Laboratories."

Benjamin was silent, aghast at her horrific experience. Natalie went on quickly, anxious not to dwell on it.

"When they began concentrating on output, the youngest girls were about fourteen. Then a seven-year gap to the oldest of the other children, meaning a long delay for new clone mothers. That made the Family ruthless. They wasted no opportunity. Three women I knew of had problems of not ovulating. One was implanted as a surrogate, using an egg from another woman. That failed too. The clone mother died violently, just like those tried with twins. They had no idea why."

Benjamin was flabbergasted. "Did they try it ag…"

Suddenly the door crashed open. "Ay wheris she!" A man, gripping the handle, swung inside as the door slammed against the adjacent wall. The jolt made him lurch forward, his arms flopping about groping for support.

Benjamin stiffened with shock, then jumped to his feet to intercept him. The man was oblivious. Short and thickset with a paunchy belly, he was stark naked. His hairy body was sweating and he was breathing heavily. Lank strands of hair were plastered across his forehead, a residue of green smeared around his mouth and down his chin.

"I wasavin fun," the man slurred. "Wared she go."

Benjamin winced as he caught the smell of vegetable wine on his breath. "Out!" he yelled at the man, grabbing a flailing arm and pushing him towards the door.

The man staggered backwards, coming up against the bench with a thump. He lolled back across the sink, presenting a full frontal view of a smallish member hanging limp below the ample belly, giving the lie to his earlier claim.

Benjamin seized the man's arm again. "Over there!" With a big effort, he shoved him through the opening, then threw the door closed after him.

Disgusted but relieved, he returned to the chair. "You okay?" he asked Natalie, clasping her hand tightly. His own was shaking.

Natalie nodded, but her face was tight with fear and urgency. Benjamin could barely imagine the horrors she and all the girls here had to endure, raped every night by strangers. "We can continue this another time," he suggested.

"No!" she cried quickly, anxious for him not to leave yet. Gradually she relaxed as they sat in silence, eventually withdrawing her hand from his. "This sort of thing happens regularly. I'm okay." Her eyes held his for a moment and she smiled faintly.

Benjamin glanced at the door. "I can arrange for a lock," he offered.

Natalie shook her head. "There are no locks. I asked one of the girls on my first day here. She said no girl would want to lock her door. A woman once did, but didn't live to regret it. A man got violent with her, and by the time other girls broke through the door, it was too late."

Benjamin's eyes widened and he said nothing.

"You were asking if they tried using a clone mother as a surrogate again," she resumed.

"Yes."

"They tried it once more, but the same thing happened. The clone mother died violently. They didn't bother after that. But they made certain every woman was a clone mother as soon as she started ovulating."

"I see," Benjamin muttered. "The repeated failures obviously upset the Family."

"I believe so. They lost patience with anything deviating from basic clone production. Clone mothers dying meant inefficiency. They changed focus to concentrate on quality and efficiency, to maintain the high success rate established before."

"And it's been that way ever since. So why are they trying for twins again? Have they discovered something to overcome the problems?" Benjamin was puzzled.

"Perhaps. I'd be surprised, though. There was no interest in it or signs of a discovery when I was there."

"It must be very recent. I'll find out as more case files come through." Inwardly, he resolved to continue secretly investigating, and find out what he could to help Natalie.

Natalie began wondering what other opportunities his unique position might offer.

"What else have you seen in the case files?" she asked. "Anything irregular?"

"Not really," he replied thoughtfully. "Irregularities don't happen, only developments. Except for a few days ago. An orange card was missing."

"You mentioned that before. Who was that?"

"You'd probably know her, she's in Laboratories. Karla Mason."

"What! Karla Mason! Are you sure?" Natalie sat bolt upright and glared at him.

Benjamin was astonished at her reaction. "Yes, Karla Mason. I'm sure. Why?"

"Because she's not a clone mother. She's having a real baby."

"What!" His mouth dropped open. A real baby! The words echoed in his mind and he shivered involuntarily.

Natalie peered at him. "You seem upset by it. Is there something more?"

Benjamin paused to gather his thoughts as questions began hammering at him. Then he told her the full story of his contact with Karla. By the time he had finished, Natalie was shaking her head in amazement.

"That's incredible! I knew Karla better than anyone. We worked closely together. When she learned she was pregnant, she told me, but kept it secret from everyone else. She still hadn't told anyone by the time I was gone. But that couldn't last."

Benjamin stared at her, trying to reconcile it. "Do you know who the father is?"

"Yes. A doctor in the DNA lab. You remember the two doctors who started all this; they came from China about fifteen years ago? It's one of them. Jason."

"Really!" Benjamin exclaimed. Suddenly the reasons clarified for how events had unfolded. "That explains why they can escape without punishment. Jason must have tremendous influence with the GM. Obviously the Family doesn't know about it. Even though he's vitally important to them, that wouldn't save them, or not Karla at least."

"That's right. The two Chinese women who came with them are leading members of the Family. Jason would have been very careful to hide having an affair, let alone a baby, from his woman."

"Of course. So they fabricated a cover-up by processing a case file through the usual channels. Karla can have the baby and no one will know the difference from clone production. Jason probably picked out a DNA donor's name without Investigations knowing anything."

The potential for factions of self-interest to affect the Family was an electrifying prospect. Benjamin could not recall seeing any such signs of weakness before.

"Jason can fix things how he likes," she said, as she shifted closer to him. "But they'll have to be careful. The pregnancy and birth must progress exactly as for clone production. Karla is vulnerable.

The Family doesn't need her as it does Jason. If he cares about her, he'll have to keep up the deception. He must be scared as well. His Chinese woman is capable of anything if she finds out."

"How would they explain Karla being a clone mother when she's in Laboratories and sees case files?"

"Actually that's not a problem any more," Natalie replied. "Availability of clone mothers is a limiting factor, so no woman is excluded nowadays. Anyway, very few women see case files, so it's hardly an issue. And they can make sure a clone mother doesn't see her own case file. Years ago, a clone mother found out who the DNA donor was and tried to meet him. They were both punished. It's never been a problem since."

"I see," Benjamin murmured. Another thought occurred to him. "I wonder how they got the GM to cover up for them. Jason must have promised to do something special for her. And Stephanie was a problem, too. She wouldn't believe Karla's orange card and her approval had both been lost accidentally."

"So they thought of sacrificing you with an appropriate accusation. Very clever."

Benjamin could visualise Stephanie whispering to the GM in a precursor to his release. "Stephanie had suspicions. So they were forced to tell her the truth. Once she became part of the cover-up, there was no reason to frame me. And to give me a Promart might only have attracted the Family's attention unnecessarily."

"Now they can let the clone production process run its course."

"They'll have a problem with Assessments later," Benjamin noted. "But they've got at least the pregnancy period and even two years after that to work out something."

Both comprehended the full picture now. Bit by bit, the deceitful world that oppressed them was being uncovered.

They had been in Natalie's room for a considerable time. At various moments, he had been aware of Natalie watching him, as she was again now. The silence was comfortable, except with nothing immediate to discuss, he again became conscious of being alone with an attractive girl in the privacy of her room. They had developed an in-depth rapport in their common quest for answers. At first, he had been acutely aware that a sexual encounter might develop. However, the idea of being another hungry male using her for physical gratification was at odds with the respect he held for her.

Although Natalie had been regarding him with growing intensity, she realised he was preoccupied and not thinking about her in the same way. She left any move up to him.

"We'd better get back," Benjamin said finally. "We've been gone a long time."

"Yes." Her low voice betrayed her disappointment.

They returned to the main building. It was getting late. Fewer people were in the place than earlier, and more were leaving. The night had been trouble-free. Benjamin left Natalie at the girls' table and joined Ralph at the bar.

"That must have been sensational," Ralph cried with a huge grin on his face. "She'll be no good for anyone else now."

Benjamin smiled. He leaned closer, glad to be alone with him.

"Have you ever been inside the labs?" he asked quietly.

Ralph looked surprised. "I've been inside the main one and the one next to it, for maintenance. I've never been inside the third one. Why?"

"Natalie and I are suspicious about what happens in there. The labs could reveal a lot," Benjamin replied, hoping to bait Ralph's interest.

Ralph considered that for a moment. "I was in the DNA lab once, but a fair while ago. I had to fix plumbing, attach some new fittings. It's the same as the main lab, equipment and stuff on benches."

"What about the third lab?"

Ralph shrugged. "I don't know. I don't even know of anyone working there."

Benjamin shivered as a cold sensation passed over him. Natalie had said the same.

"When you worked in the DNA lab, how did you get in?" Benjamin pushed on.

"I had to wait outside in the corridor. A doctor let me in, and watched me all the time while I did the work."

Benjamin looked around the bar area, making sure they were not being overheard. He leaned still closer and kept his voice low.

"If I wanted to get inside those two labs without anyone knowing, how could I do it?"

Ralph stared at him in mild alarm, surprised he would consider endangering himself that way. The idea roused his curiosity though, and his enthusiasm for the prospect of exciting action. "By getting hold of the keys, I suppose. There are no alarm systems. Construction was basic when the place was built, and there haven't been any improvements since. What are you planning?"

The culture of fear had guaranteed no security breaches. In an unprecedented moment, Benjamin felt favoured by the passage of time, Family Police complacency unwittingly opening up opportunity.

"I'll fill you in later. Can you get the keys for me?"

Ralph smiled broadly, the prospect appealing to his sense of adventure. "I know where the keys are. Maybe I can get access to them. I'll see what I can do."

Benjamin gave him a return smile then headed for home. The night had been very interesting, offering some hope.

Chapter 13

Brenda sat quietly in the waiting cubicle, thankful for the chance to calm herself. It had been a harrowing ordeal. She looked around the small space, which contained nothing but the short bench seat on which she sat, alone. The four grey walls crowded in on her, broken only by the narrow, doorless opening opposite. She pulled her torn coat over her shoulders and tried to suppress the shiver that had settled in her muscles.

She knew of no one avoiding a Prohyst once that punishment had been decided. She suspected fate had played its hand in her favour through Benjamin. He was the only one seeing what was happening who would care enough to help. Perhaps he had done something. She resolved to find out if given a chance to see him again.

A young Medical Assistant in a long white coat appeared at the opening, holding a form.

"Come with me," she ordered.

Brenda followed her through a section of the adjacent room, noting with distaste the white-padded table on which she had lain for the failed implantation procedure. Beyond, an opening in the sidewall led to the delivery and recovery rooms. They walked around a partition to another section. The assistant, Karla, directed Brenda to a seat by the consultation desk. On the desk were several medical instruments. Karla took a seat behind the desk.

Brenda vaguely recognised the room from her only other time here many years ago. Around the cement walls were benches strewn with instruments and equipment, plus washing facilities. At the far end, another white-padded table partly obscured several pieces of exercise apparatus. Shelves covering most of one long wall were sparsely littered with a few bottles and minor items of medical supply. The room was unremarkable but served the purpose of carrying out approval examinations.

Karla laid the form on the desktop. Brenda recognised it. They had strapped her down on the operating table with the doctor about to inject her wrist when an older woman arrived brandishing it. A heated exchange had ensued, after which they released her.

With a face blanked of expression, Karla looked up from the form and took a few moments to study the woman who had been brought to her. She recognised her.

"You're the clone mother who failed implantation at the first attempt a week ago," she remarked.

Although not directly involved, Karla knew about it, since it was an unusual case. Brenda acknowledged her comment with a quick nod and said nothing.

"Why did it fail?" Karla asked.

Brenda shrugged her shoulders. "My body wasn't receptive to it. I don't know why."

Karla paused. Strangely, she felt some affinity for her. Brenda was almost the same age as herself, and projected an aura of natural yet non-threatening defiance. It appealed to her.

"Don't you want to be a clone mother? It's better than what you are now."

"It's not the right way to have a baby," Brenda retorted before realising what she was saying. She regretted it instantly. The assistant's reaction surprised her, however. Spontaneously, Karla glanced down at herself, her hand involuntarily moving to cradle her stomach, and she squirmed in her seat self-consciously. Brenda intuitively recognised the signs.

"You're pregnant. You're a clone mother yourself."

Karla looked up quickly, thrown off-guard. Their eyes met just as she opened her mouth to reply, causing her voice to catch in her throat. Brenda's sharp intuition worked once more and she knew the truth. She could see it in her eyes.

"It's not a clone baby, is it? It's a real baby."

Karla nodded defensively, deflated by her own foolishness. She said nothing but simply stared down at her stomach as yet showing no outward signs.

"But you're not part of the Family," Brenda pursued with genuine concern for her. "Do they know?"

Karla shook her head disconsolately. "No. We've fixed it to appear as clone production." She felt helplessly vulnerable. The struggle with insecurity had intensified since the sudden demise of Natalie, the only person she had confided in. Conscious of how dispensable she was compared to Jason, she was unsure he would remain faithful to her.

The fear had built up intolerably, eased only when Jason used the GM's dependence on him to force the cover-up. Framing the man in Records was an action foreign to her nature, motivated by self-preservation. It had worked out fortuitously for all, including Benjamin. But she was still out on a limb, without the stabilising support of Natalie. Inexorably she felt drawn to Brenda, who seemed to possess similar qualities.

Brenda resisted the temptation to take advantage, feeling empathy for the girl, whose situation was not hard to identify with. "I know what it's like to be afraid." She offered her hand across the desk. "The Family Police have been harassing me ever since the failure."

Karla was aware of how Brenda had come to her. "You're lucky to escape a Prohyst," she commented, responding by touching the back of Brenda's hand with the tips of her fingers. "I don't know anyone else that's happened to. It's only because of this." She indicated the form in front of her.

"What is that?" Brenda asked, intrigued now. "What does it say?"

Karla was surprised. "Didn't Investigations show you? It's the Donor Assessment form you did there. They've approved you to this point, so now I test your physical capabilities for final approval, as a DNA donor. You're lucky it came through in time."

Brenda looked at her blankly. She had no idea what the reference to Investigations was about. "Did you say I'm down as a DNA donor? I thought only men were donors."

"Oh no," Karla replied, baffled by her reaction. "Most are men, but not all."

Brenda knew too little to dispute it. However, out of the women she had lived with, she could not recall one who had been a DNA donor.

"How long have they been using women as DNA donors?"

"Quite a few years now, but there's been a sudden increase in the last two weeks."

"Why is that?" Brenda asked, concerned about her new classification.

Karla paused, but welcomed the chance to confide in someone not wanting to take her baby away. "The Family are concerned about running out of clone mothers. The numbers are continually decreasing. So they've started concentrating on producing more for the future."

Brenda felt too far removed to comprehend the implications, but something about it was disturbing. No woman would be overlooked now.

Karla had learned a lot from Jason, although he refused to talk about some things, claiming even he did not know much of what the Family ultimately envisaged. His alienation from them on a personal level, particularly Suchee, at least made her feel his faithfulness was more likely, although not assured. Relating now to someone the way she used to with Natalie was uplifting. She was still conscious of her duties, however.

"I have to complete this form. You've been here for clone mother approval before, so I'll just fill it in." She completed the form quickly, inserting a favourable pattern of ticks for the ten PHYSICAL traits.

Having avoided serious recriminations, Brenda was hopeful of her prospects now, especially with her surprising new status as a DNA donor. And to strike up a rapport with the assistant was unexpected. Feeling close to someone was a rarity, to be embraced despite the dangers.

"I won't tell anyone about your baby," she assured her. "I hope we can talk again. I think we both need that."

Karla nodded, her sense of vulnerability eased a little. "We can't meet here. I go to the market once a week, usually tomorrow, late afternoon."

Brenda hesitated, fearful of the market. Instead of the haven that had always represented survival, it now loomed as the most dangerous place she could be. The Family Police officers hounding her would not appreciate her escaping a Prohyst and walking about unscathed. With a shock, Brenda came to a horrifying realisation. Nowhere was safe any more! An awful feeling of isolation overwhelmed her. Would she be an outcast?

"I'll see you there," she murmured uncertainly.

Karla stood, signalling an end to the interview. "There's nothing more required of you for now. With final approval, this form goes to Records."

"I don't know your name," Brenda queried as she followed her out.

"Karla." They parted, each offering the other a smile of reassurance.

Brenda left the building. Late afternoon would normally find her at the market, but that now brought with it fear. She also feared the roads and even her apartment. She adjusted her torn coat and turned the collar up as high as it would go. She turned down the side road and was soon angling across the open ground towards the crop fields. Darkness was approaching, but some women still milled about. Two days a week, a special group put together and delivered supplies for the Family. Today was one of those days. The women were busy packing a number of large baskets. One of them looked up.

"Hi, Brenda."

All stopped and crowded around Brenda, eager for news.

"We thought you were taken for a Prohyst," another said.

"I was lucky," Brenda replied. "But I can't attend the market any more. Can I join your group?"

"You can take my place," one offered, stepping forward.

A cautious camaraderie existed amongst women working the crop fields, although it did not extend deeply. The Family Police were likely to suspect subversion at any time.

Thankful, Brenda joined in packing as the other woman departed.

Darkness fell. They carried the baskets to the gate and waited. At the appointed time, a lock clicked across and the gate swung open. Two Family Police officers escorted the women through. Silently they moved up the road, two women to each basket, grasping the cane handles.

In the early days, the Family had been overly paranoid about anyone seeing inside their compound. Officers would pick up the baskets from outside the gate and deliver them themselves. Some years ago, six Family women fell ill after a foolish attempt by several women to poison the food. They survived. The Family Police chose six women at random from the crop fields and punished them by Prohyst. No further attempts on the Family were made again.

The group reached an intersection. The main road was a scene of restrained orderliness, with Family women and Family Police passing by regularly, many with young, well-behaved children. Brenda and her partner took their turn delivering the basket to the first house along, placing it on the floor just inside the entrance. They waited outside as each pair completed delivery.

A group of five Family women and one man emerged from the next building and drifted towards them. The women looked authoritative in their smart suits; their seniority evident. Each held a document folder. It appeared they had just concluded a meeting. The man was middle-aged, physically strong and with slightly greying hair, his face etched with lines of experience.

Their business had given rise to heated exchanges and was still consuming their attention. The friction amongst them generated a tense atmosphere. One woman, incensed, addressed the man in sharp tones.

"We expect immediate action, Jason. The Memory Storage Project must proceed without further delay."

Jason was on the defensive. "I'll find a subject," he replied, making no attempt to justify his failure to perform.

Another woman was looking up the road irritably. Her thin-lipped, downturned mouth was a depressing feature. Her lined, sunken face was topped by short, spiky hair. A younger woman came and stood beside her. She was attractive, with curly blonde shoulder-length hair and a smooth, fair complexion. A deep sadness marred her beauty, however. Her pale blue eyes were as though something had died inside her.

The older woman took charge. "Kelly, where have you been? I expected you to wait for me here." Her manner was that of a woman never disobeyed.

"I know, Mother," Kelly replied, eyes downcast. "I didn't know when you'd be finished."

"I'm finished now. We must go home. I have things to tell you. You're not due at the clinic yet."

The women ignored Jason now, and he parted company from them. He wandered up the road, a solitary figure although his posture revealed a stubborn streak.

Brenda had overheard the exchanges, which provided a rare, revealing insight into prevailing Family mentality. The two officers were slow in reacting, but soon began herding Brenda and the others back down the side road. The women returned through the gate, which was locked behind them.

One by one, as they passed through the women's area, they peeled off to their separate apartments. In moments, Brenda was alone. She stood in the centre of the road, desolate, then made her way slowly towards the main road, towards an emptiness greater even than the empty lives of the others she had once shared.

At the intersection, she pressed herself against the end wall of the first apartment block. Cautiously she peered round the corner and up the road, her eyes searching through the gloomy light. Family Police were there! Not a patrol but two officers hovering near her apartment, waiting. Instinctively, Brenda knew they were waiting for her. The same two officers who had terrorised her at the market? She shrank back behind the wall. What could she do, where could she go?

She moved back behind the apartments, then beyond the debris piles and began running along behind them, putting as much distance between herself and the officers as she could. Reaching towards the end of town, Brenda switched back between apartment blocks and squatted against the wall; panting, sucking at the cold air.

Hidden in the shadows, she clasped her coat tightly about her. She peered around the corner of the building. Back down the road, the officers were still there. Would she have to spend all night outside? And if tonight, then what about every night? A chilling thought, cast adrift by the relentless oppression of the Family Police!

As the night wore on, she continued to check, but the officers remained, persistent.

It was very late now. The road was deserted. Except for someone approaching on a bicycle. Brenda watched as the figure drew close, and suddenly she recognised him. Benjamin! The sight of him thrilled her, offering hope. As he came alongside, she stepped from the shadows and called to him in a hushed voice.

Benjamin was concentrating on the illuminated pool of road surface dancing ahead of his bike. His mind was abuzz with intrigue after his talk with Natalie.

"Benjamin. Over here."

Startled, he pulled on the brakes and skidded to a halt. His head jerked around, searching the half-light. A figure in a long grey coat was standing just out from the shadows of an apartment block. He looked around cautiously then wheeled his bike over.

"Brenda! Is that you?" He recognised her face in the dull light. "Are you okay?"

"Yes," she replied urgently. "They released me." She darted back into the darkness, beckoning him to follow.

Benjamin leaned his bike against the wall. He focussed on the darkened outline of her face and thought of his ploy with the Donor Assessment Form.

Brenda wanted to embrace him, to confirm he was responsible for her escaping a Prohyst, to see a sign that he cared. "There was a form they use for assessing DNA donors. It saved me. Do you know about it?"

Benjamin broke into a triumphant smile. "We receive those forms in Records. When I saw you taken upstairs, I did one quickly and left it in the GM's office. I didn't know if it would work."

"Oh, it worked!" she cried, moving closer then clutching his arm, elated.

Benjamin's heart swelled with pride. He drew her to him, feeling a deep warmth for her; a burning desire to protect her, and more. But the reality of her plight reminded him and his thoughts plummeted. "I passed two Family Police officers outside your apartment. Is that why you're here?"

Brenda nodded. "I can't go home. I'm sure they're the same officers who took me before. They'll have heard I escaped the Prohyst."

Benjamin checked around the corner of the building. "They're still there," he noted, pulling back. "My apartment is a block further up. You can stay with me till they're gone." He glanced towards the road. "There's a patrol coming."

"Are you sure? It'll put you in danger." She moved into his arms again, as a feeling began burning inside her.

"Don't worry about that. We're all in danger all the time. Go to the back of the next building, halfway along. Wait for me there. Quick, before the patrol gets here." He smiled reassuringly at her and they parted.

Brenda disappeared into the shadows. Benjamin emerged onto the road and rode to his apartment. He stowed his bike and dashed inside. The rear door he had opened but once was stiff. He pulled at the makeshift handle and the door swung narrowly open, as far as its bottom edge scraping across the floor would allow.

"What do you think you're doing?" a deep voice sounded behind him.

Benjamin jumped. He turned to face one of the patrol officers striding across the room. His heart thumped, his throat constricted.

"You up to something?" the officer demanded to know, glaring at Benjamin's crude creation. "Why were you out so late? The Pro House closed long ago."

"My bike broke down," Benjamin replied, holding his nerve. "The wheel jammed. I had to fix it on the side of the road."

The officer smirked. "What's this for?" He pointed his long baton at the rear door. Stooping, he squeezed his head and shoulders through the narrow opening. Tense, Benjamin waited for the worst. A few moments later, the officer pulled back and straightened.

"I keep spare parts outside," Benjamin said, silently applauding Brenda for staying hidden.

The officer stared at him then abruptly turned and left, slamming the front door closed.

Brenda peeked through the rear opening. "That was close." She clambered inside and Benjamin pushed the ill-fitting door back in place.

She took off her coat and draped it over the coffee table. A cascade of hair fell around her shoulders. Benjamin was once again struck by how attractive she was. Her appealing maturity transcended the look of tired anxiety on her face. She moved to him, needing to be close, feeling a small measure of security for the first time in many years since losing her brother. Benjamin possessed the same indomitable spirit as him, but tempered with better judgement. She looked up at him.

"I'm not sure what I can do. I can still help at the crop fields, but I can't attend the market any more."

Benjamin drew her into his arms. "You've just escaped a Prohyst. That's enough to think about for now."

She rested her head on his shoulder. "It was horrible in the operating room. They held me in a cell and made me wear a white gown. When they strapped me down on the operating table, I thought I was finished. I've never been so frightened. Then that old woman came in with the form."

"Yes." Benjamin remembered the terrifying occasion involving his mother. He told Brenda about it. As the memory flooded back vividly, his emotions welled up and he struggled to hold back the tears. Brenda listened, nodding with understanding. They held each other, sharing a common pain.

She wiped a tear from his cheek and kissed him lightly. Then again, several times as Benjamin responded. They kissed longer, passionately, then embraced, both starved of close contact for too long. Their arousal swept them up on a quickening wave of desire. She pressed her body against him and he caressed her firmly. Their passion rose higher, sensationally, their breath coming in quick gasps as the need for each other escalated wildly.

She tore at his shirt. They stumbled to the bed, discarding their clothes. Brenda opened herself to him and he slipped easily inside her. Ecstatic, he thrust deeply. A tide of emotion surged through them both. From far within, a sensation gathered strength and he exploded inside her in a euphoric climax, racking his body in waves of shuddering pleasure. In the same instant, Brenda cried out as a warmth flooded through her and her body pulsated in all-consuming rapture. They collapsed in each other's arms, panting. Brenda rolled to her side as Benjamin slid from her body and nestled into the crook of her arm. She reached down and drew a coarse blanket over them as their passion heat dissipated into the cold night air.

"That was powerful," Brenda whispered. "Is there nothing you can't do?"

"Not sure about that," Benjamin mused dreamily.

Brenda soon had his blood boiling again and they made love once more, longer this time and with a depth of feeling neither had imagined possible. When their bodies were spent, they lay side by side in a state of exhaustion.

A while later, Brenda raised herself to a sitting position. She looked down to marvel at the strong, athletic form she had given herself to, then leaned over and kissed him lightly. She stood by the bed, stretching herself. Benjamin was enchanted, her large, firm breasts and curvaceous hips providing new pleasure.

He lifted himself from the bed. They got dressed, the cold cutting short each other's viewing pleasure.

"I usually drink coffee. Would you like one?" he offered, moving to the bench.

"Yes, I need something," Brenda responded happily.

With their coffee, they sat side by side at the coffee table - the first use Benjamin could remember for his second chair. He began contemplating their circumstances, feeling responsible for them both now.

"We must work out what to do, so you'll be safe from the Family Police."

Brenda nodded, settled now but knowing it could not last. "Maybe one day we can stay together. But the Family Police are too good at detecting this sort of thing." She smiled, wishful, then continued. "I can't hide from them all the time. My only chance is to make them accept me."

"How?"

She thought for a moment. "I met an assistant at the Medical Centre after they released me. It was her job to complete that form. She told me about her own problems and we agreed to meet at the market late tomorrow. Maybe she could tell those officers I'm wanted as a DNA donor, and they might leave me alone."

"Are you sure she'd help you?" he queried, sceptical. "People don't help each other normally. It'd be very dangerous if it didn't work out."

"I have no choice. I don't want to put you in danger." She kissed him on the cheek and rested her head against him as he put his arm around her.

"I'll come to the market tomorrow as well," he assured her. "In case something happens."

Brenda snuggled against his neck and they fell silent. Something she had said was in Benjamin's mind.

"You said the Medical Assistant has problems. What problems?"

"She's having a baby. Not a clone baby, a real one. I guessed it from her manner and she confided in me. We're about the same age. Her name is Karla."

"Karla! You met Karla Mason?"

Brenda looked up quickly, surprised at his reaction. Benjamin told her how he was interrogated and almost punished because of Karla's accusations, and the problems in processing her case. He mentioned how Ralph introduced him to Natalie at the Pro House, who told him about Karla's affair with Jason.

"Jason is one of the instigators of clone production. He has a lot of influence, enough to fix their baby as clone production without the Family knowing."

Brenda was astounded, and also concerned. "If Karla is capable of doing that to you, then I can't trust her. It's too risky to meet her at the market."

"That's right. We must think of another way."

Benjamin's mention of Jason suddenly excited Brenda, reminding her. "I've seen Jason. Early this evening. I helped the women deliver food supplies to the Family." She recounted what she had observed. "It must be the same Jason. He seemed important to them. Important but under their control, of course. A woman mentioned something called the Memory Storage Project. She was dissatisfied because of his lack of progress in finding a subject for it."

Benjamin was intrigued. Many small pieces were dropping into his lap but as yet he couldn't put it all together. "There's a lot going on that no one outside the Family knows about. I'm finding out what I can."

His determination to make a difference appealed to Brenda. "I believe one day we'll be free of the Family and their oppression. Evil destroys itself in the end."

"I've discovered a lot already," Benjamin added, feeling his resolve strengthen as Brenda expressed her belief with haunting conviction.

"And more every day." He told her all he knew. It was good to share with another soul. He felt like he was building a network of solidarity. "There's a lot more to uncover yet. But just knowing is not enough." He looked at Brenda. "What can we do with the knowledge once we've got it?"

"With knowledge comes opportunity," Brenda replied firmly. "We must be patient."

Benjamin thought for a moment. Brenda might hold one of the keys he was searching for. "I saw your case file this morning. It showed failure at implantation, and only the first attempt. What happened?"

"I hated it!" she replied angrily. "Being forced to have a baby that way is a gross violation. When I have a baby, I want it to be a real baby, made the right way." She looked at Benjamin meaningfully. "I didn't fight against it, just that my body was so tensed up it rejected the implantation. They got impatient and tried to force it, but it was no use. In the end, they discarded me in disgust. I was lucky they didn't give me a Prohyst then and there."

Benjamin nodded, realising why she had been removed from the program without a second attempt. It failed to explain another anomaly, however.

"Why did they never call on you before?" he asked.

Brenda shook her head. "I've always had problems ovulating. Ever since the early years when the Family first started violating the natural order of things. I was eleven then, just heading into womanhood. All my life, my body has been sensitive, reacting like a barometer to right and wrong. Perhaps one day, circumstances will be right." She looked at him again strongly.

In a flash, Benjamin recalled what Natalie had told him. "Were you ovulating for the recent attempt, or a surrogate for another woman's egg?"

"I was a surrogate," she replied bitterly. "I don't know if it's been done before. Not many women don't ovulate. I always thought they'd try me sometime. But I think Investigations had me left out of their records, so they never looked for an orange flag at my apartment. And I never displayed one. Finally they did try me. You know the rest."

Ruefully, Benjamin noted the occasional value to be gained from lack of departmental communication. The woman checking orange flags merely followed the record blindly. Had Brenda been fortunate? Was she the third of three not ovulating that Natalie had known of? More unanswered questions; not the direction he had wanted to head in.

"The process was tried twice, about twelve years ago," he told her. "Both women who were implanted died violently. No one knew for certain why. They forgot about it then."

"Died!" Brenda exclaimed, going white in the face. "You mean I could have died?" She was angry. How nearly had she fallen prey to a fatal violation! "My body must have reacted to the danger," she asserted. "That's why the implantation failed." She grasped his arm firmly. "My body's instincts saved me."

Benjamin held her tight. His respect and feelings for her were continuing to grow. She was strong despite her elusive quest for security, which was never more challenged than now. He shook his head, bewildered, but feeling honoured by the twist of fate that had brought them together.

Brenda contemplated how fragile her situation was. She thought of Karla and her problems, and the rapport they had struck up. A development Benjamin had mentioned struck a chord in her mind.

"You said female cloning only began recently," she said, intrigued. "Karla told me they've used female DNA donors for years. Only small numbers, but there's been a sudden increase lately. I thought it was strange because I don't know any women who've been donors."

"I know," Benjamin acknowledged. "But only the most recent cases have come through Records. Talking to Natalie, we concluded the Family have been choosing female donors directly and no one outside Laboratories has known about it. The recent cases must have a different purpose. That's what we must find out."

"Karla said the sudden increase is because clone mother numbers have been continually decreasing. The Family are concerned, so they've started concentrating on producing more for the future. I'm sure she's right. Availability of clone mothers explains why they finally tried to use me."

Benjamin listened, spellbound. Suddenly the start of female cloning using blue cards was logical! And the reason for Brenda's belated inclusion was now clear. But unaccountably, a cold shiver ran down his spine.

"What is it?" Brenda asked, concerned at his reaction.

"The whole population is decreasing!" he pointed out, abruptly sitting up in the chair. The revelation was firm in his mind. "It's been happening ever since the Family put their system in place. Why did they smash all existing relationships? Why is it a crime to form relationships or have any sexual activity except at the Pro House? Because they only want children created within the Family, developing their elite society. What happens to the community then? With no children being born, the population decreases every time someone dies! Only the old will remain, then…" He looked Brenda in the eyes, searching for comfort in his moment of painful revelation. "Only the Family regime will be left!"

Brenda reached out and grasped his hands. Her touch was warm, far removed from the chill that had settled into his bones.

"The Family has deliberately encouraged this to happen," he continued. "Promart and Prohyst punishment leaves people half dead. There are no medical facilities for us, no law and order to protect us from each other, nothing available to give hope or incentive for the future." He shook his head in sorrow. "No effort is made to improve living conditions, no maintenance done on decaying or collapsing buildings or the roads or anything. And that's just how the Family wants it."

"The Family is already planning for the entire population to die out!" Brenda added, incredulous.

"It certainly is. I now know, from the records, they can use clones as DNA donors. They tried it a year ago and, as far as I know, it was successful. This means men in the community won't be needed as donors any more, or for any purpose. Women will only be needed until enough female clones are old enough to be clone mothers themselves. When that's proven, production of clones will be self-perpetuating."

At last, the wider picture was clear. A horrifying scenario for the community! But something fundamental still made no sense. A burning question remained.

"Wait a minute. What's the point of clone production anyway? The Family is creating its own elite society, so why do they need the clones? What are they for?"

"I've no idea," Brenda admitted. She looked helpless before him.

"I must find out more. Knowledge creates opportunity, as you say. Natalie is suspicious of the two other labs at Laboratories, particularly the third lab. She's never been in either one even though she used to work in Laboratories. I have to try and gain access to them."

Brenda was anxious. "How?"

"The Family Police are smug these days, relying on old fear tactics. Ralph works in Maintenance. He said he'd try and get the keys for me."

"Please be careful," she urged him. She kissed him on the cheek then snuggled closer against his neck.

"Would you like more coffee?" he offered.

"No, it's very late." She roused herself. "I have to leave before dawn. If those officers are gone, I can go home."

They stood. Brenda put on her coat, turning up the collar. Benjamin pulled the rear door open as far as it would go. He slithered through to the outside and moved to the corner of the building. The full length of the road was deserted. He returned to the opening in the rear wall and called out to Brenda. "They're gone."

Brenda scrambled through and stood beside him. "During the day, I'll be with the other women at the fields, so I should be safe," she assured him. "At night, it could be dangerous. I'll just have to be careful." She paused. "I'll be okay. Don't worry."

Once again, her strength impressed him. "If you have a problem, wait for me at the back here. I'll look for you every night."

She smiled and they kissed. Brenda disappeared into the shadows.

Chapter 14

The morning passed amidst repetitive routine. The completed Donor Assessment Form for Brenda was on his desk. He filed it. He checked the green and blue cards, but did not find one for either name on Natalie's piece of paper. He tucked it away in his shirt pocket.

At lunchtime, Ralph joined him in the cafeteria with a cheerful greeting and immediately launched an attack on the mountain of food on his plate. After devouring a few mouthfuls, he looked up.

"You had a good go with Natalie last night. How was it?"

"We talked."

"You were gone a long time," Ralph persisted. "I bet you weren't talking all the time?"

Benjamin shrugged. "She told me enough, but I need more." He leaned closer and lowered his voice. "That's why I want to get inside the labs."

Ralph turned serious as he looked around casually at nearby tables. People were paying them no attention. He reached into his shirt pocket and placed an object on the table, keeping his hand over it as he looked around again. Slowly he withdrew his hand to reveal a small bundle wrapped in cloth.

"Three keys. You can keep them, they're copies."

Benjamin realised the danger Ralph had put himself in. "Did you have any trouble?"

"Getting hold of the originals took some work, but making copies was easy. I'm usually alone in the workshop."

Benjamin nodded, appreciating there was more to Ralph than the breezy, superficial exterior. Ralph possessed a natural cunning, having learned how to survive in his own way.

Ralph finished his food, wished Benjamin luck and left. Benjamin slipped the cloth-wrapped keys into his shirt pocket, ate most of his lunch and returned to the office.

The afternoon passed without incident. At finishing time, he rode straight home. He settled into his chair with a cup of coffee and waited until darkness fell. The evening wore on and Benjamin waited, feeling calm and resolute in what he would do. He watched the clock. Eventually the time felt right: 11.00pm. He changed into black trousers, pulled on his dark jacket and slipped into soft cloth house shoes. He dropped his torch into a pocket and zipped up the jacket. He was ready. He stepped out of the apartment and left on foot.

Benjamin approached the Clonesseum with caution. The front door was never locked, as some facilities could be required at any time. A Family Police officer, slumped in a chair outside the entrance with his head drooping forward in slumber, depicted a state of normality. Benjamin crept up quietly then slipped past and through the entrance without disturbing him. Now inside, his heart began racing as the adrenalin coursed swiftly through his body. His muscles tensed in anticipation. Fear churned inside him, the thought of meeting a security officer or someone else uppermost in his mind.

With a deep breath, he calmed himself then started up the stairs. At the top, he looked cautiously around the corner of the wall. Lighting down the corridor was poor, reduced to a minimum after working hours. No one was in sight. Light was coming from the main laboratory two-thirds of the way along. Was the building officer on guard inside? He saw his chance and darted past the first door to stand outside the second. He inserted one of Ralph's keys in the lock, lucky first time as the lock slid open with a dull click. In a flash, Benjamin was through to the other side, closing and locking the door behind him. He stood in the haunting quiet of the DNA lab.

His heart pounded. He stood still, trying to relax; relieved to escape being exposed in the corridor. A moment of panic gripped him as he stared into the room. The lab had light! Someone was in the lab! He swivelled round, searching the full extent of the immediate lab area. No one. The weak light, tinged green, was emanating from a glass cabinet against the far wall. He stared at the cabinet, listening to his blood course through his veins; feeling his heart try to break through his ribs and run away.

Calming himself, he moved amongst the equipment. He paused at the end of a bench, the first of three in parallel extending from the near wall to halfway across the room. Unsure what to look for, he reached for his torch and played the beam over the clutter. The benches were strewn with apparatus and innocent-looking devices. Close to his left, in the short wall adjacent, was a door. Access to the corridor connecting the main lab? He tried the handle; it was locked. He swung the torch beam slowly around the room. In the long wall on the far side were two doors, one either side of the glass cabinet. He rested the beam on the second one, a door of heavy steel construction and closed against thick, rubber seals around a steel frame. It was probably a coolroom. At the far end of the lab, a square opening in the short wall led into darkness. A shiver ran down his spine as he stared into the black hole. The third laboratory, maybe? He felt a chill throughout his body; his nerve was giving out. He must act now or run for it.

He tried the door without the seal. It gave easily. The room beyond was dark, the dull half-glow from the lab not penetrating. The torch beam intercepted a long, narrow table covered by white cloth in the centre of the room. An operating table. Beside it a trolley carrying an array of instruments. Along the wall a bench with more instruments, below it a row of cupboards. Another bench against the back wall contained a double sink. Next to it was another door. Was this the rear wall of the Clonesseum? The same door as the one he saw along the outside landing the other night?

He checked the cupboards without knowing what he was looking for. Nothing there looked likely to be promoting evil. He tried the door; locked. Concluding that the room was where DNA extraction took place, he returned to the lab.

He stopped in front of the lighted cabinet. Rather than a cabinet, it was a watertight glass encasement, filled with light green fluid.

His interest triggered, his eyes searched deeper into the tank. Six objects, strips of biological material coloured dark brown with a slightly pinkish tinge, lay on two glass shelves. Each strip had thin tubes attached. The tubes ran to the top of the tank and disappeared through a sidewall just below the top access lid. A black cabinet, twice the height of the tank, was attached at the side, accepting the tubes. There was a single locked door at the front of the cabinet.

He placed the flat of his hands against the glass and noted the warmth. He guessed it was an incubator. On the back wall, two thick vertical tubes were emitting the light and warmth. Benjamin shook his head, perplexed. What the hell was all this?

Still confused, he tried the heavy steel door on the other side of the tank and cabinet. With a deep breath, he pulled at the handle. The door swung slowly towards him, releasing a sudden blast of cold air that stung his face. Bracing himself, he squeezed through the narrow gap, playing the torch beam ahead.

He shivered as the cold, crisp air closed in around him. He breathed frosty clouds into the white mist of the coolroom. Through the floating ice he saw steel shelves, three tiers high, lining each side. There was enough width to walk down the centre and touch the shelves with bent arms. The shelves to his left contained small, glass containers with blue screw tops. The torch beam revealed something inside the containers. He looked closer. Each container was filled with light green fluid in which floated a piece of dark material the size of a thumbnail. All looked the same, but the name on a label identified each as different. Several names he recognised as those of DNA donors from the case files. Some were female names. The names were printed in full. He reached in his pocket, checked each name plus initial on the paper Natalie had given him then studied each label. None of the names matched. The sight of what he presumed was extracted DNA enthralled him.

As he slowly swung the torch beam back, he noticed a few containers near the entrance, separated from the rest. He examined one of them closely. He was shocked. Two names were on the label! The sample appeared no different from any of the others, yet it represented two DNA donors. He checked the four containers adjacent. They also had two names, and each sample was again a single entity.

Benjamin thought of the case file with two DNA donors he had processed yesterday. The evidence he was now looking at had implications far more insidious than the production of twins. He recalled what Ralph had overheard concerning experimentation with DNA. Were these examples of DNA manipulation sitting on the steel shelf in front of him? Combining samples from two donors to form one improved sample?!

The possibilities were horrifying. What sort of clone might they produce? And what if the technique did not work properly, or partially worked? They were manipulating nature itself; a disaster in the making. Benjamin shuddered at the thought.

But what was disaster to the Family? They would merely dump the failure, no need for reprisals; just continue trying, or something else. Their disrespect for life, other than within their own closed circle, was sickening. Benjamin felt heat rush through his face, even in the chill of the coolroom.

He checked the shelves along the other side. They appeared empty, but the torch beam rested on several objects at the far end slightly hidden by the shelves' depth. He approached warily then stopped and took a step back, aghast. Human brains! Benjamin stared in horror at a number of steel trays, each bearing a brain. Each brain was a complete specimen, lifted out intact from the skull. Each had a globular texture, light grey and crisscrossed all over by a myriad of bright red blood vessels. Nausea gripped him and he reeled back, unprepared for anything like this.

At the rear of the coolroom, beyond the shelves, were a few metres of space where a sunken floor was shaped towards a drain-hole in the centre. A length of hose coiled up to one side was attached to a tap in the wall. Several large plastic bags lay folded on the floor. Just below the ceiling, a steel rail ran from wall to wall, with several steel meat hooks hanging from it. In a flash, Benjamin saw in his mind the picture of a body wrapped in plastic hanging from a meat hook.

The reality was too much. He stumbled backwards and lurched out into the lab. He pushed the heavy door closed as fast as he could. He stood staring at it, breathing heavily, struggling to understand the nature of what he had seen. It went far beyond the basic concept of clone production. This was something else, something more sinister; something evil in every sense of the word.

Benjamin turned his back on the door and its horrors. He stared at the black hole in the end wall. Like a magnet it drew him in. Surely the entrance to the third lab? A sense of foreboding closed around him and he shivered. To break his focus, he looked away, trying to ignore his imagination. Again his torch found something startling. At the last bench, at bench level, stood two steel hemispheres a couple of metres apart, each the right size to fit over a person's head. Leather securing straps hung from their bottom edges. Small holes liberally punctured each hemisphere, and through each hole was a thin steel probe. Wires led from the probes along the benchtop to a series of steel boxes against the wall. Each box had a small screen with knobs and dials at the front. The blackened screens glistened under the torch light, like black eyes waiting to be awakened.

Playing the torch lower, he noticed that each hemisphere was suspended above a solid, high-backed leather chair. The chairs had leather straps for securing around legs, waist and chest. With horror, Benjamin visualised the hideous function of the probes, reaching halfway through a hemisphere from all angles. The reason for powerful restraints was not hard to imagine.

The chairs were facing the lab's end wall, where a large white screen was fixed. On the benchtop, a projector pointed between the chairs at the screen. Benjamin felt revulsion. Perhaps it was just an experiment, but one that would surely inflict great pain on a subject. For what purpose? For an instant, he wanted to smash the equipment to pieces, but it would only be a futile gesture. Disgusted, he moved away.

Once again he stood at the opening and contemplated the blackness beyond. He steeled himself, fighting to control an unaccountable feeling of dread. The torch beam threw shadows around the bare corridor walls. Taking a deep breath, he started through the opening. This was why he was here; the real reason he had asked Ralph to risk his neck.

On the right was a door; an office? There was no nameplate and it was locked. He tried each of the keys but none fitted. The corridor was short, the beam exposing a door at the end. He tried the handle;

locked again. He wiped his brow as he fumbled with the keys. The first key failed. His heart pounded and he fumbled again, breaking into a full sweat as he fought the urge to run from this place of horrors. He slid the second key in and the lock clicked. His heart leapt and his hand hovered shakily over the handle. Something unknown awaited him on the other side. His mouth was dry. He swallowed hard and turned the handle. Slowly he pushed open the door.

The room was pitch dark. Creeping forward, he swung the torch around in a full sweep. Swallowing again, he slowly closed the door behind him, isolating himself from the other lab.

The room had a musty smell. There was a staleness in the air from lack of circulation. He advanced further in, playing the torch around continuously. The room was smaller than the other labs and simpler in content. He could see no benches but there was another door; access from the main corridor.

The beam flicked across a form in the centre of the room. Benjamin moved closer and came to another table covered in white cloth. Next to it was a trolley holding medical instruments. Another operating theatre! He wondered what was different about this one to warrant so much secrecy.

He backed away from the table and began skirting to his left. Reaching the back wall, he noted a bench running a short way along from the corner. Within the bench was a double sink with taps. Beneath were two cupboards. He checked them, finding only a few items for washing.

He continued along the wall, passing the end of the bench. His foot struck an obstacle on the floor and he tripped, crashing face first onto the object, managing to fling out an arm in time to protect himself. Cursing and shaken, he scrambled to his knees and cradled his throbbing elbow. Luckily, the torch was in his other hand. He flashed it at the object.

A shallow wooden box, just a foot high, was fixed to the floor. The box had a lid, hinged to lean against the wall when open. It had no catch. Benjamin opened it. A foul, pungent stench struck him, making him reel back as his stomach churned. Resisting the temptation to slam the lid closed, he leaned over gingerly and flashed the torch inside.

He quickly realised it was not a box at all, but rather the opening to a deep well.

Holding his breath, he shone the beam down, noting the rough cement walls plunging into blackness, too deep for the beam to reach the bottom. He closed the lid and stood, the smell making him hold his breath longer before releasing it in a short burst.

He moved on, more careful now. Ahead was the base of a steel ladder, which slanted at an acute angle to a platform constructed at two-thirds height towards the ceiling. He could just make out a number of vague shapes sitting on the platform. Storage? He decided to take a look up there later.

Benjamin played the beam on the sidewall. Vague shapes began to materialise - a row of objects sitting side by side on the floor lining the wall. The eerie silence and mustiness of the room was getting to him. Wiping his brow, he came up close to one of the shapes and shone the torch at it.

In front of him was a large round glass jar, waist high, filled with light green fluid, and suspended within were a number of body parts. He knelt down and stared in dismay. Most of them he recognised: a heart, two kidneys, what he thought could be a bladder, a liver and a few others he was unsure of. The parts looked raw and alive, a rich pink colour. The heart was pulsating with a regular beat. Tubes were connected to each organ and thin wires held each in position. Could the wires transmit electric current? The tubes and wires disappeared through the jar's flat-topped lid. On the outside of the jar, a label displayed a name. He stood and gazed wide-eyed at the set-up, questions racing through his mind as he began comprehending the third lab.

Above the jar was a shelf on which sat a square black box, the same width as the jar. The tubes and wires entered through holes in the shelf. On tiptoes, Benjamin could just see the top of the box, which had a hinged lid. He tried it - locked. He stepped back and paused to wipe his brow again. Feeling exhausted, he wanted to lay down and sleep; perhaps to forget all he had seen. In spite of the sinister implications, however, he was impressed at how highly sophisticated the system must be to feed and stimulate body parts in a living state.

He walked slowly along, following a line of black boxes. He reached the corner of the room and continued around the front wall. Halfway along, he came to the last box. Angling the torch down, he started back, noting each box had its own glass jar beneath, all the same size and shape. Many of the jars were empty, awaiting future use. He came to one full of fluid but no body parts, tubes and wires dangling loosely inside. Kneeling down, he studied the name on the label then began shuffling along on his knees. Abruptly he stopped, staring at a name. He reached for Natalie's piece of paper. A match! One of the names on it coincided with the full name on the jar. Startled, he sat back. What was going on here? He was piecing things together now.

He shuffled to the next jar. The name coincided with the other one on the paper. He put the paper away and continued along, studying every name now. Soon he came to the start of jars complete with body parts. The sets here were small compared to the first he saw. As he worked around to the side wall, a trend of increasing size, consistent with growth time lengthening from latest to earliest take-up of jars, became apparent. All the names were female. He stopped. Martha Hendry. He could remember a Martha from years ago. Could it be the same one? He moved on. The name Jocelyn was there, then Tylin, Suchee. His mind was racing as he began studying all the names on the jars. He froze - Marcia Winters! If Kelly's mother, then what of Kelly? He kept shuffling along. Almost back to the first jar. Cynthia, Jean. But no Kelly.

At the first jar, he stood and rubbed his eyes wearily. With a final look and shake of his head, he turned away. At the base of the ladder, he paused to shine the torch up. Although sick of the place, he was determined to see everything. He climbed the ladder and crawled onto the platform. Black boxes and empty glass jars were sitting there. He knelt between two boxes and lifted one of the lids. Inside was a bunch of the tubes and wires. He closed the lid and rested his arm on it. The air near the ceiling was especially stale and heavy. He twisted around to lean against a box and rest for a moment, switching off the torch.

* * *

Benjamin jerked awake. Something had disturbed him. Alarmed, he realised where he was. How long had he been here? He found the torch. But instead of switching it on, he cringed back behind the black boxes, alert. A light had appeared below. He could hear the muffled cries of a young child. Tense, he inched forward till he could peek past the first box and observe below.

Two women and a small child had entered through the door from the main corridor, where the light was coming from. Suddenly bright light flooded the room. Benjamin winced as the backs of his eyes hurt. At the same time, a low hum started up and the swirling circulation of fresh air began.

One of the women closed and locked the door. They were wearing long white lab coats. One carried a suitcase. The other gripped the arm of the child, a girl; two years old? She was distressed, digging her heels in as she tried to pull away. A gag around her mouth was choking off her cries. The woman ignored her anguish as she dragged her to the centre of the room. She began pulling the little girl's dress up over her head, an awkward task amidst the struggles and muffled cries intensifying.

The other woman laid a large plastic sheet over the operating table. She took hold of the little girl, who was standing naked now, and injected her wrist. The little girl stopped crying as her body went limp. They laid her on the operating table on her back.

The women scrubbed their hands at the sink, returned to the instrument trolley and pulled on surgical gloves. They moved about in silence. One bent over the prone figure on the table. Soon the body was covered in blood. Methodically, the woman removed parts and placed them on a large tray held by the other. When they were finished, the woman with the tray took it to a glass jar at the front wall.

The other wrapped the plastic sheet over the remains of the body. Pulling the four corners together, she carried it to the box-like opening Benjamin had tripped over. She lifted the lid and dropped the bundle down the well. Benjamin caught the foul stench again as she returned for the little girl's clothes and dropped them down the well also. She closed the lid then joined her colleague at the glass jar.

They worked quietly and efficiently, using equipment and materials from the suitcase. One obtained a stepladder from beneath the platform and used it to gain access inside the black box. Eventually their work was complete.

One returned the stepladder while the other collected their gloves and used instruments, dropping them into the suitcase. Satisfied, they moved silently to the entrance door. Suddenly it was dark again and the low hum of air circulation ceased. Light from the main corridor showed briefly then everything went black.

Benjamin remained on the platform, shuddering with shock. The image of the little girl's remains being tossed down the well like a bag of rubbish was indelibly etched in his mind. Devising her existence for this purpose summed up how the Family regarded life outside its own circle. Using clone production to provide the insurance of future transplants without medical rejection. Benjamin shook his head, appalled. The reality he imagined was coming true.

Panic gripped him. How long had he slept? Could he get out? He had to get out, to escape this room of horrors. He flicked on the torch. The beam shimmered over the ghost-like proximity of the back wall. The silence was crushing. He descended the ladder quickly and stumbled to the door by which he had entered, fumbling for the keys. Thankfully, he passed through to the internal corridor, locking the door behind him.

Relieved, he ran to the DNA lab, embracing the dull glow of light from the glass encasement. He moved through and cautiously unlocked the entrance door. A Family Police officer was slumped in a chair further up by the main lab, his head drooping forward in repose. Benjamin slipped out, shut and locked the door then hurried away. Gratefully he reached the stairs. The officer outside the main entrance was nowhere to be seen. Benjamin crept out and ran for home.

It was late. Few people were on the road. There were no officers outside Brenda's apartment. Reaching his own, he checked at the rear of the building. Brenda was not there.

Chapter 15

Another tedious morning. Benjamin processed the tasks, including several case files with female DNA donors and another with two donors for the one clone mother. He studied this one, aware now of what it meant. He noticed how the two Donor Assessment forms complemented each other. On both, most traits were ticked with a PASS, but if a trait had a FAIL or INCONCLUSIVE on one, it invariably had a PASS on the other. The impression was of higher overall quality when combined, the same obviously expected to manifest itself in practice.

At lunchtime, he sat with Ralph in the cafeteria.

"Have you tried the keys yet?" Ralph asked, unusually serious.

"Yes, last night. I saw both the other labs."

A smile of satisfaction fleetingly creased Ralph's face. "And?"

Benjamin paused, unsure how much to tell him. "Natalie was right. A lot's going on that the Family wouldn't like us to know about. You were right, too. They're doing experiments with DNA. Manipulating, combining samples, that sort of thing."

Ralph grunted. "What else is happening? In Records."

"I've seen things," Benjamin replied, glad to shift focus. "Like the start of female cloning, using a clone mother's own DNA, even using a clone as a DNA donor."

"What! Why are they doing that? Don't they want men any more?"

Benjamin cringed, instantly regretting telling Ralph too much. His reaction was a warning. With his open exuberance, Ralph could easily say the wrong thing to someone.

Benjamin tried to make light of it. "It's nothing really. They're only experimenting."

Ralph resumed attacking his food.

"Are you going to the Pro House tonight?" Benjamin asked after a while.

Ralph grinned, snapping back to his usual self. "We'll go at finishing time."

He finished his lunch and departed. Benjamin followed soon after. At finishing time, they went to the Pro House. Ralph found himself a girl and they disappeared out the back. Benjamin joined Natalie, sitting with the same three girls as last time.

"Hello, Benjamin."

He returned Natalie's greeting and acknowledged the others. Several girls were hovering near their table, creating an impression of more than usual interest in their group. Natalie stood, seeking the privacy of her room. Benjamin followed her and was soon sitting in her chair by the bed. He noted the deep sadness in her face, her eyes hollow and wearied.

"Your table seems popular with the other girls," he said, offering a positive thought.

Natalie smiled wanly. "I've got to know some of them. Most have a story to tell, many worse than mine. A lot of the women were once prominent in the community. They could be helpful with their knowledge. Some want to talk to you. They see you as their big hope. I feel the same, too." She put a hand on his knee, looking into his eyes. For a moment, they were close, a moment when it could happen between them. Natalie very much wanted to be with him, and Benjamin sensed it but he thought of Brenda.

Natalie sensed his reluctance and removed her hand, trying to hide her disappointment. "Have you found out anything more?" she asked.

"Yes, a lot. Ralph got me keys and I saw inside the labs last night." He described everything he had seen. Natalie leaned forward, amazed.

"I never knew anything like that was going on!" she exclaimed when he explained what was in the coolroom. She confirmed the containers held DNA samples.

"It appears that a case with two donors is not for producing twins after all." He went on to describe the third laboratory and horrific operation on the little girl. Natalie was dismayed. She broke down and cried.

Benjamin sat on the bed beside her and offered what comfort he could, even shedding a tear of his own, his mind having now had time to process what he'd seen.

"That explains the years of secret female cloning," Natalie observed, as she pushed herself slowly out of his arms. Her eyes were red welts.

Benjamin fortified himself with a deep breath. "I saw the names you gave me," he concurred. "On glass jars with fluid only; awaiting body parts. All the names on jars are of Family women, cloning themselves for future transplants. They obscure their identity by only inserting first name and initial in a case file, and rely on clone mother approvals to confuse that process. Secrecy is the easiest way of ensuring no one else can do it. Otherwise they wouldn't care."

Natalie nodded as the picture clarified for her. She was thoughtful. "It might be useful if you talk to some of the girls," she suggested after a pause.

Benjamin agreed. As they moved to the door, she threw her arms around his neck and clasped him in a heartfelt embrace. He was shocked at how thin her body felt, and the way it shook with anxiety. She released her hold and wiped the tears from her cheeks.

"Good luck, Benjamin. Please be careful."

When they returned, Natalie spoke to the three girls in her group, then Benjamin went with each in turn to their rooms. Each had a dreadful story to tell.

Patty had been caught in a sexual involvement. The man was her husband, and they had been happy together before the Family takeover. They saw each other one day and made secret plans to renew contact, but made a mistake.

Ruth had enjoyed a position of considerable authority, in the top bracket of women below the Family. The Family promised acceptance into its circle of any woman from this bracket proving herself worthy. According to Ruth, it was merely a cynical ploy to defuse resentment at reaching a ceiling. She knew of just two women who had gained acceptance that way, enough to maintain the policy as credible. Ruth had been ambitious but pushed too hard for inclusion and upset someone. Her ambitions were very different now.

Janine used to spend much of her time at the market. Just before dark one day, when few people remained, a Family Police officer molested her, demanding sexual satisfaction. Janine panicked, rejecting his coercion. The officer was indignant, then became scared as the scene developed. He pretended she was causing the problem. Other officers arrived and dragged her away for a Prohyst.

Benjamin shook his head in amazement as he listened to Janine's story, unable to find anything to say. He looked around her room. Janine had made it as homely as its basic facilities and cramped space allowed, and it reflected her personality. Although not as soft and feminine as Natalie, she was an attractive woman with dark shoulder-length hair and pleasant features.

Something about her story nagged at him. Puzzled, he tried to rationalise it.

"The Family Police can have relationships with Family women. Why would an officer feel the need to try something like that?"

Janine smiled grimly. "It's not so unusual. There are plenty of examples like mine. Life's not as rosy for the Family Police as you might expect. There's a lot of frustration and jealousy, resentment at being dominated and used as pawns to satisfy the whims of the Family women."

"Really? I never knew that."

"Oh yes. Some come here for satisfaction. I've seen a lot. And heard a lot, too. My room is at the end of the main building. The Family Police compound is only a short distance away. Sometimes late at night, I walk outside and hear shouting and sounds of violence coming from there."

Benjamin was enthralled at the prospect of strife within the hierarchy. "I'd like to see that," he murmured excitedly.

"There's a narrow track around the end of the building. In the dark, you can reach the Family Police area without anyone seeing you. It's best to wait till late."

Benjamin relished the idea. They re-joined the other girls. He went to the bar area.

"You're popular tonight," Ralph cheered spiritedly. "Four ladies already! I've got some catching up to do."

Benjamin smiled, thankful for some light relief. He waited out the evening in Ralph's undemanding company till late. At last, Janine gave him a signal and he followed her to her room. In the poor outside light, she pointed out the rough, narrow track disappearing around the corner of the main building. Benjamin started along it.

He felt his way along the end wall and emerged at the front corner, not far from the top of the bank overlooking the beach. The entrance light to his left faintly illuminated the open area of ground, which he crossed quickly to reach the tussocky scrub on the other side. He continued towards a well-lit area ahead, and soon came to a high wire fence defining the perimeter of the Family Police compound.

The adrenalin was flowing through him now. He dropped to hands and knees, inching up behind a bushy shrub against the fence. Lying flat on the ground, he peered around the shrub into alien territory. A cauldron of intrigue, and he was teetering on the edge.

The strong street lighting created a sharp contrast with the outside surrounds, and dark buildings. They loomed large, running parallel to the fence with their rear walls just a few metres from it. The building closest to his right was larger, separated from the next to his left by a stretch of ground wider than was typical. The space afforded a good view of the road and buildings beyond. Faint sounds of revelry were audible, reaching him through an open window in the wall of the large building. A recreation centre. Benjamin settled behind the shrub, prepared to wait.

Periodically, an officer moved along the road within his scope of vision. Several times, two passed each other, on each occasion neither stopping to even acknowledge the other. Seemingly their demeanour was that of indifference, as bereft in their will to communicate as people in the community. Was it a mentality resulting from the jealousy and resentment Janine claimed was rife amongst them? Despite their better accommodation and prospects, the atmosphere was hardly different from along the town's main road. He saw no women. The Family's involvement with chosen officers would only be within their area. Every officer he saw was unattached, with black shoulder pads on his white shirt. No attached officers with red pads would come here.

It was very late now. The Pro House must be closing soon. His position on the ground was uncomfortable. Still the revelry continued inside the recreation centre. But suddenly there was an escalation in the noise. Men were leaving, white shirts coming into view at the front. The merriment continued - shouting, laughing and moving about drunkenly.

Benjamin lay low behind the shrub, alert.

Two men were arguing. One was more aggressive, pointing his finger into the chest of the other as he shouted at him. The target of his anger backed off and the two separated from the rest. They shifted across the open ground towards the fence. The aggressive man suddenly grabbed the other by his shirt, almost lifting him off the ground as he shoved him backwards. Shouting wildly, he slammed him against the fence close to Benjamin's position. The fence shook and rattled. Benjamin shrank back in fear.

"You think all the women love you, don't you! You make moves on my girl again and I'll kill you!"

With his chin thrust forward, their faces were barely inches apart. His rival was cool. He responded with a sneering, arrogant laugh, goading his aggressor as he glared straight back into his face, unflinching.

"Who's your girl? Why don't you ask her whose girl she is?"

"I'll show you who!"

He was incensed, letting fly with his fists as he exploded with fury. The two engaged in a furious brawl, shouting and slamming against the fence repeatedly. Other men moved in then to break it up. Some were laughing.

"Come on, you fellows," one joked. "She loves me anyway, so there's nothing to fight about."

More laughter. The aggressor did not appreciate it. Consumed with rage, he swung round, intent on fighting anyone. For some moments, the brawl engulfed several before the two protagonists were forced apart and overpowered. A brief lull ensued, broken momentarily by more shouting and finger pointing. The anger was finally quelled and the men shifted away from the fence. Accompanied by more laughter, they moved to the road and disappeared from view.

With the sudden calm fell a deathly silence. The recreation centre was closed now. No one was on the road. Benjamin stood, relieved at escaping detection but stiff from prolonged discomfort. He brushed bits of undergrowth from his clothes then sidled to his left, bringing more road and buildings into view. He was next to a gate in the fence. A well-worn track leading into darkness towards the Pro House and a worn patch on the other side indicated its regular use. Not locked, it was held closed by a rusty catch. Yet another example of Family Police complacency. And easy access to the Pro House! That explained why only two officers were stationed there normally. But the gate was irreconcilable with their long delay in taking action against the violence several nights ago. Benjamin shook his head in disgust.

Two officers appeared on the road. They turned off, heading across the open ground. Benjamin was alarmed. Exposed! In an instant, he threw himself to the ground and scrambled into the scrubby undergrowth. His heart was racing as he shrank back behind a shrub. The officers passed through the gate and continued up the track.

Benjamin admonished himself for his carelessness. A timely reminder of how watchful he had to be at all times. He stood and moved through the undergrowth, keeping away from the track. As he reached the cleared area, two more officers appeared through the entrance of the Pro House. Once again, he dropped to the ground. They passed down the track and disappeared, completing a change of guard.

The Pro House was quiet now, confirming how late it was. Benjamin crawled past until well beyond the entrance, then stood and returned to the Clonesseum for his bike.

* * *

For the next two days and nights, nothing happened to increase Benjamin's knowledge or understanding of the Family's vision, or to better explain the discoveries he had made. In the office, several case files featured recent developments but shed no light on the intentions they represented. Lunchtime punctuated the tedium, although Ralph had nothing further to offer either.

He felt frustrated. Despite the satisfaction of discovery, it seemed of little consequence in terms of making a difference. The Family women were secretly cloning themselves for spare body parts, but so what? What could he do about it? He knew the non-secret use of female DNA donors just started was to alleviate future clone mother shortage. The possibility that men could become redundant if clones were used as donors and the reality of DNA manipulation by combining samples were emerging twists all too clear. He knew about Karla Mason's affair and baby with Jason, even of jealousy and resentment amongst unattached Family Police. However, none of it was of any use in forcing a change to the system or the ruthless, dominating oppression practised by the Family.

Despite the dangers, Benjamin felt on the verge of achieving something worthwhile, but he needed a breakthrough, a revelation of some sort. He had one more avenue to pursue, again a matter of discovery rather than influential action, but for now it would have to do.

Each night, he stayed in his apartment and regularly checked at the back door for Brenda. She did not show. He had no idea if she had waited for him on previous nights when he was out till late. Having found out all he could from Laboratories and the girls at the Pro House, he had no reason to go out anyway.

* * *

The first sign of dawn was reddening the sky as Brenda started across the open ground towards the crop fields. It was a relief after surviving another night out of the hands of the Family Police. Each morning, she escaped from her apartment before first light. For two nights after her night with Benjamin, she had waited for him in vain at the back door of his apartment. She was disappointed, feeling a need to be with him, to feel safe in his arms. But she knew he was moving stealthily around town, probably until late night, trying to discover what he could. And it was dangerous, anyway, to continue

196

seeing each other the way they had. Strength and patience were vital to survival. One day something would happen to change life. Brenda was more certain than ever about that.

The first night she waited, the two Family Police officers were again hovering outside her apartment. It was late when they finally gave up, allowing her to return home. The second night, they were not there, and nor were they last night. She had taken the risk of returning home early.

She reached the crop fields, thankful, feeling more distanced from the Family Police. As the first morning light strengthened, other women began arriving. They set about their work. The familiar environment was welcoming, giving Brenda a sense of belonging. The women did not talk much but were united in their beliefs. They afforded each other more trust than in other sectors of the community, although practical support would quickly give way to fear if Family Police action threatened.

By late afternoon, Brenda had settled in, even beginning to feel a cautious optimism that a return to the life she knew and needed might be possible. Absence of the officers from outside her apartment for two nights helped. She either had to test her chances at the market, the closest to a social outlet a woman could expect, or remain ostracised.

A woman approached. "Brenda, they've started getting supplies ready for the Family. Do you want to take my place again?"

Brenda paused from tilling the soil. She hesitated, wiping at the perspiration on her brow. Time for a decision. She made up her mind.

"No. I'll go to the market."

"Are you sure?" The woman sounded surprised.

Brenda nodded, resolute. The woman moved away.

The day's work done, Brenda picked up her supplies wrapped in cloth. She left with others, for the market. She was watchful as she moved to a bench.

"Hi, Brenda," Sasha greeted. "I heard what happened. It's good to see you back."

Brenda appreciated the welcome. "I was lucky."

"Is it safe for you here?" Sasha looked over her shoulder, fearful.

"I don't know. But I have to find out. I can't live a life in hiding. If the Family Police want to catch someone, they will." Brenda looked around uncertainly, feeling vulnerable but determined not to weaken her resolve. As she took in the scene, her eyes settled on the same two officers hounding her before. A chill ran down her spine.

The officers had noticed her. One spoke to the other and pointed his long baton straight at her. They started toward her bench. Brenda tensed; she was frightened. There was no escape. She had to stand her ground and convince them to leave her alone. They came up close, both leering at her arrogantly.

"There you are," one proclaimed, smirking. "We've been looking for you."

Brenda took it as a reference to their night vigil outside her apartment. Her heart sank as she realised her awful mistake in returning to the market.

"I suppose you think you're lucky," the officer went on in a sinister tone. "We're going to show you how lucky you are."

The smirk on his face deepened as he raised his baton. Brenda thought fast.

"They want me as a DNA donor."

The officer kept leering at her, unmoved. "Who wants you? Investigations? A dead person can be a donor, too."

Both officers laughed sadistically. Then he struck at Brenda with his baton. Instinctively, she ducked, taking the baton across her face in a glancing blow. With the force of it, she lost balance and stumbled against the bench, crying out. One arm swept the bench, sending food and containers flying.

Before she could recover, the officer planted the point of his baton painfully into her chest and shoved her to the ground. Then she saw that the other held a knife. A long, sharp blade. As if in slow motion, he swooped on her. Brenda screamed. Her leg was on fire! She flung her arms out, scrambling away, desperate. He stabbed at her repeatedly.

She rolled away. Frantic, she staggered to her feet, crashing against the bench. Faintly, she could hear the officer's sadistic laugh.

"Let her go," he crowed. "I got her a good one. Let her suffer. She won't last long."

Brenda clutched her leg above the knee; it burned with pain. She ignored it, driven by terror, casting around blindly, careering into benches. The world was spinning, a blurred sea of people far away. No one helped. Where was Sasha? She lurched aimlessly onto the road, forcing her legs to move. The adrenalin propelled her, fuelling her body frenetically.

Where was Benjamin? She must get up the road! Her own apartment waited a crushing distance away. She drove herself, crumbling continually to the ground, her legs failing. She passed the branch road. Still no one helped. Mercifully, she recognised her apartment through glazed vision. Gasping for breath, she crawled to the door, straining for the handle. She staggered inside and pushed the door closed, collapsing to the floor. She dragged herself to the bed and pulled herself up to click on the lamp. With her last strength, she discarded her heavy coat.

"Benjamin," she murmured hoarsely, crawling onto the bed.

Chapter 16

The case files revealed nothing unexpected and another dreary day passed offering no opportunity for new discovery. Lunchtime with Ralph followed the normal pattern. Benjamin deliberately ate a big lunch.

Throughout the day, he could not shake a feeling of disappointment or a strange sense of anxiety concerning Brenda. He was certain he could not have missed her at the rear of his apartment on either of the last two nights, if she had come. At finishing time, he rode straight home with greater than usual relief, anticipating the night ahead and his day off tomorrow.

In his apartment, he gathered a few items; torch with his jacket, binoculars, a parcel of food and bottle of water in a shoulder bag. The binoculars were a powerful set he treasured as a legacy from his father. Benjamin placed the bag and jacket on the coffee table, changed into dark clothing, then relaxed with a cup of coffee. The clock showed not yet 6.00 pm. He set the alarm for midnight then lay on the bed.

* * *

He jumped as the alarm pierced the air. He rushed to turn it off. Excited, he put on his jacket, slung the bag over his shoulder and slipped quietly out of the apartment. The cold made him shiver. In the gloomy light, he could see no patrol.

He set off up the road, concentrating, walking quickly. He was fearful. His movement in this direction at this time of night would undoubtedly be suspicious to a patrol. From his apartment, the end of town was not far, however, and he soon passed the last apartment block. The water treatment plant slipped by, and shortly after he was beyond the sphere of influence from the town lights. Blackness was ahead, all around and above. With nothing to guide him, he stumbled over the crumbling surface, feeling for the road with each step.

He paused to assess his progress, clicking on the torch and keeping it pointed down with his hand hooded over. Piles of debris showed in the periphery of the glow. He switched it off and kept walking, falling into a regular routine with the torch. Eventually he no longer saw the debris. He was alone in the barren, lifeless wilderness he could feel but not see.

It seemed to take an eternity to reach the barrier. With the torch, he finally found it; ghost-like at first, then the rusty steel bar was directly in front of him. He was relieved. It was a welcome sign of reality in the absolute blackness. He passed around the post and continued on with heightened awareness, straining his eyes to see ahead.

Progress was slow. He dared not use the torch now. The derelict road surface caused him to stumble several times. Twice he nearly walked off the edge. The further he went, the more tense and expectant he became.

At last, he saw a pinprick of light. Gradually it grew in size as he crept closer. The light was attached to the lookout building, faintly illuminating it and the road stretching to it. An electric car sat idly behind the barrier, just as last time.

He could see no one outside, but kept a safe distance. Why was a lookout here? Determined to find out, he turned off the road, darkness now his ally. He skirted the lookout in a semi-circle. Scrubby tussocks hampered him. The dry, sandy ground was uneven and difficult to walk on, sucking at his shoes. Relocating the road, now on the other side of the lookout, he glanced back with satisfaction and pressed on. Dawn was still some hours off. He needed to see what was out here then escape far away, the barren countryside unlikely to offer much of a hiding place.

Once again, he entered a blanked-out world; a black hole drawing him into unknown territory. He felt the road through his shoes. The surface was better, uneven but without the holes. Maintenance had been done for vehicular use.

In the distance, he saw a tiny light. He blinked, unsure. Was it really there? He pushed on further then stopped, his heart leaping with excitement. Another light, then another, several. He moved forward slowly, tense and alert. The lights grew closer, and more numerous. Vague shapes materialised - buildings! The road went straight towards them, leading to a scene enshrouded in a faint, hazy glow that gave a minimal sight of the surrounding area.

Was it a settlement of some sort? Although it was nestled in a natural undulation, he was too far away to detect signs of life. Nervous, he looked around. The topography to his left was more elevated. He moved off the road and climbed gently until coming to where the ground formed a dome-shaped mound. An ideal spot. Thankfully, he dropped behind it, laying his bag beside him.

Lying on his stomach, he looked over the top. From his elevated position, he could observe the settlement and feel relatively safe from detection, even in daylight. The prospect excited him. Instead of fleeing before dawn, he would stay; watch and learn.

He rested, waiting for the first rays of dawn. At last, the sky began to lighten. He watched behind him as a diffused ball of red rose slowly from below the landscape, creating a vivid impression of the dust-filled atmosphere. As the sun rose, it exposed the countryside; dry, devoid of trees and empty of life.

Further around, the lookout post was a small blot in the distance. Next to it, a road branched off, snaking towards the sun now climbing into the sky; the route south. Midway between the lookout and settlement, another road formed a V with the one on which he had approached.

The normal light of day was gaining strength. Benjamin eased the binoculars from his bag and began observing the settlement. It was a fair-sized town, very similar to his own. The main road was a continuation of the approach, penetrating straight through town and beyond. In the foreground, one either side, were two single-storey, barn-like buildings of impressive size. Past them stood rows of apartments stretching along in continuous lines. All the apartments had two-storeys, a sign of better-quality construction. Their boring uniformity suggested the same narrow, regimented way of life Benjamin knew so well. The number of them showed a good-sized population lived here. Like his own town, lining the smaller roads were individual, better standard houses. The set-up seemed familiar, elite residents separated from the rest occupying low-class apartments.

In front of each large building were areas of ground cleared of scrub and nurtured into grassed fields. Their greenness starkly contrasted with the adjacent harsh, red-brown landscape and drab buildings, defining the leading edge of town.

Benjamin focussed his attention on one of the lesser branch roads. Electric cars were parked along it and some were beginning to move. The number of cars once again surprised him. He traced the road to where it ended at the coastline. Beyond, the shimmering blue sea was clearly visible. He stiffened, concentrating the binoculars at a point just past the last buildings at the coast. A ship! His mouth dropped open in astonishment. He had not seen a ship since Jason and Bernard arrived with their Chinese partners more than fifteen years ago. No further contact from outside the community had occurred since. Yet it definitely was a ship. Questions without answers flooded his mind. They were not alone.

The sun was low in the sky and plenty of activity was under way. The town was emerging from sleep. People on foot, electric cars buzzing the streets, the ship's presence, all gave the impression of an active, progressive community. How had it come to be here without anyone from his town knowing?

A car passed between the fields and left town, making its way to the lookout. When it arrived, two figures jumped out and entered the building, replacing two others who returned to town in the other car.

Suddenly, there was a dramatic increase in activity at the nearer large building. A set of double doors flew open and two lines of people came jogging onto the field. One line wheeled to the right, the other to the left. The regimentation was instantly apparent, portraying a highly disciplined unit about to undergo an exercise.

Their single colour, one-piece, full-length uniforms reinforced the perception, those on the left in light grey the others dressed in darker grey uniform. All figures had identical close-cropped hairstyles. The sameness from one to another was as if they had rolled off an assembly line of mass production. Each carried a long, stiff rod.

The two lines spread across the field and came to attention, facing each other on either side of a centreline. They stood rigid, left hand behind the back, right hand in front gripping the rod planted with one end on the ground. Each stared fixedly at his opposite number.

The figures in dark grey were angled towards Benjamin. Moving the binoculars slowly along the line of faces, he was amazed at their similarity. Each was totally expressionless, with no movement of eyes or mouth, devoid of emotion as if nothing registered to the senses. The sameness of it was as stark as that of their uniforms and hairstyles. All appeared the same youthful age, seemingly late teenagers or early twenties, and physically powerful. The impression was that of programmed machines rather than people. Benjamin was stunned by the military aura that surrounded them.

They waited, twenty in each line, as more figures came out of the building and took up positions behind the lines. Family Police! The white shirts with red shoulder pads stood out like beacons. Each carried a thin cane or short, flexible whip.

A Family Police officer stood near the double doors of the building opposite the centreline. He reached into a box at his feet and withdrew a small object, which he held in the palm of his hand. A shrill blaring sound cut through the still air like a knife, reminding Benjamin of a klaxon his father had when he was a child.

"Ha!" Shouting in perfect unison, the two lines instantly swung into action. They grasped their rods in both hands and charged forward to engage each other.

The action was furiously intense. Fierce one-on-one battles, rods wielded at great speed and force, lightning reflexes on full display. Bloody injuries soon showed on their faces and clothing as the ferocity of attack continued unabated. To ensure this, officers regularly moved in behind fighting couples, using canes and whips to thrash any combatant showing signs of slowing. Benjamin was shocked at the brutality of the event.

The conflict raged on, the air filled with the sounds of clacking rods and the smacking of canes and whips. The klaxon blared twice, echoing across the field.

"Ha!" Instantly every combatant stopped and stepped back to re-form the original lines, left hand behind the back, right hand planting the rod in front.

Benjamin moved the binoculars along the line of dark uniforms again. Each face was as expressionless as before, unwavering in discipline and lack of emotion. Blood smears, ripped clothing, heaving chests and heavy perspiration evidenced the action that had taken place.

Three officers moved in behind, targeting two light uniforms and one dark. Each officer grabbed the collar, jerked the combatant out of line and marched him inside the building. No resistance, only passive compliance.

The exercise had required no instructions or discussion, the sound of the klaxon sufficient to start and stop proceedings. A regular, familiar routine. The physical fitness of combatants was awesome. Benjamin was bewildered as to the ultimate purpose of it.

After a brief pause, officers took up positions evenly spaced down each side of the field and across each end. The effect more clearly defined the perimeter. They waited, canes and whips ready. An officer ran onto the field and placed a large box on the centre spot. Two others ran out, one to each end to plant three flagged sticks in the ground. The near flags were light grey, the far ones dark grey.

At a sweeping gesture from an officer, the combatants darted to the sideline, discarded their rods, then returned to spread over their respective halves of the field in inverted arrow formation. Light grey once again stood rigidly to face dark grey.

The klaxon again. Instantly the two groups engaged in a furious onslaught of unarmed combat. Each side tried to burst through the other, wrestling, tackling ferociously, some breaking free, chasing, crashing opponents to the ground. They swarmed over the field. Officers regularly dashed on, administering punishment to under-performers. Early on, a combatant fell against the box in the centre. An officer grabbed him by the collar. The figure stood straight to attention, in a flash changing from a state of violence to compliance. The officer marched him into the building.

The exercise entered a new phase as they gradually split into separate packs concentrating towards each end. Half of each group attacked the other's flags, the rest defending their own at the other end. As each side gained opposing flags, the violent combat intensified, tackling, blocking, shepherding, surging towards the centre again. Soon they surrounded the box. Then the klaxon blared again, twice. The action stopped and the combatants leapt to attention, staring straight ahead. The abrupt transition was bizarre. Benjamin was astonished at the extreme nature of it.

An officer moved to the box and reached inside. He held up three light grey flags and one dark grey. An eerie silence prevailed, no decisions or instructions given. The officer found the other dark grey flags nearby on the ground, then went to the far end and planted the three of them again. Another officer replanted the light grey ones at the near end. They returned to the sideline.

At a signal, the combatants re-formed into inverted arrow formation. The starting officer sounded the klaxon. The action repeated with the same fury and intensity as before. When it ended this time, two dark grey flags and one light grey were in the box. The process was repeated two more times until the officer held up three light grey flags only. The exercise was over.

At another signal, the dark grey victors left the field, dismissed. The light greys remained. Officers herded them into the large building and the doors closed behind them.

Benjamin stared at the empty field, astounded by the harshness of what he had witnessed.

At the field on the other side of the road, another exercise was finishing. The participants looked identical to the first in uniform and appearance. The brutal combat and control by Family Police had been the same.

Benjamin scanned further afield with the binoculars. The town was bustling with activity, electric cars ferreting around the roads busily. Light and dark grey uniformed figures, all with close-cropped hairstyles, were everywhere. Family Police in their distinctive shirts stood out but their numbers were few by comparison. An even fewer number of others, in groups of two or three, projected an air of authority. Family women?

He watched the movement of cars. Many towed an open trailer carrying equipment and materials. The branch road to the coast was alive with action as cars ferried goods from the ship into town. Several construction projects were hives of activity. Cargo was disappearing into the buildings at the coast. Storage? The operations all enhanced the impression of a progressive, military town. Benjamin focussed on the ship, perplexed. He could only imagine where it had come from.

From the centre of town, a car passed down the main road, continuing south beyond the last buildings. Fascinated, Benjamin followed its progress until it became a diminishing dot in the distance then vanished. What could be down there to attract a visit? Later, the car returned. It would happen three times during the day.

Several cars left the near side of town. Each towed a trailer packed with light and dark grey uniformed figures. At the road midway to the lookout, they swung off and gradually disappeared into the distance. Some time later, the binoculars could just pick out some kind of operation taking place far away.

After a brief lull, action resumed at the fields. New groups of light and dark grey combatants followed the same format of brutal exercises; one-on-one combat with long rods then a flags-in-the-box battle for supremacy. The level of violence, Family Police discipline and machine-like motions of participants again had Benjamin watching in awe.

The routines repeated throughout the day, enough times to suggest the entire grey-uniformed population of town was involved. As the day wore on, successive groups were younger and younger, the late ones mere toddlers. The very last group seemed little more than two year-olds. Regardless of age, however, the exercises and mentality were the same, lessening only in physical harshness not commitment.

Benjamin realised that not one combatant had been female. Throughout town, all light and dark grey figures were male, consistent with every case file he had processed over the years. This was the Training Centre. The reality was enlightening, the brutality alarming, the degree of development astounding and galling. What a contrast to his own town!

One impression confused him. The oldest clones must be no more than fourteen years of age. Yet they seemed older, their faces depicting later maturity. They were dauntingly powerful, physically beyond expectation for that age. Perhaps the punishing training regime explained it, but he could not shake a feeling there was more to it.

The consequences of taking clones for training just two years from birth were apparent in their regimented mentality. Early indoctrination would naturally result in easy control later. The behaviour of all clones under Family Police domination was evidence of that.

Benjamin wondered what education or intellectual stimulation the clones received, if any. All indications suggested there was none. Their physical superiority was what commanded fearful respect. They would be unchallenged, even at such youthful ages, if involved in confrontation with anyone. What sort of confrontation and with whom? A chilling question! Questions within questions. Was he really getting any closer to an answer? To a point of action?

These clones were destined to spend their lives in a void, with no love or close emotional support. Benjamin surmised that severely stunted development both intellectually and emotionally, even without the treatment they had to endure, would be an inevitable consequence of the clone production system. An essential ingredient was surely missing. Processing a DNA sample with a female egg and implantation in a woman using cold laboratory techniques was mechanical in conception and implementation. The method had no place for love, no meaning such as being the product of a loving union between man and woman, nothing on which to establish bonding or the fundamental fulfilment of belonging as an integral part of a family, no true mother and father foundations. None of that existed under clone production. Instead, the process was that of systematically turning out products from a factory by copying the originals. With no emotion or love involved, it followed that emotionless, loveless products would result. The behaviour of clones throughout the day had been an exact portrayal of this scenario.

The low position of the sun indicated late afternoon. The electric cars earlier transporting clones for their operation returned to town. Activity slowed, the movement of cars lessened. Light and dark grey figures, some leaving from the large buildings in the foreground, were finding their way to the drab apartments in a steady stream. All cars gravitated to the branch road, where Family Police officers and the few Family women were retiring to the better class accommodation.

Benjamin watched until the sun dropped below the horizon. He braced himself against the cold as darkness overtook the last tinge of red. A car left town, its headlights pointing the way to the lookout. Another returned shortly after. The lights of the Training Centre were on. The scene Benjamin saw when he first reached the mound was back in place. He put the binoculars away and rolled onto his back, his muscles stiff.

Chapter 17

Feeling hungry, he reached in his bag for the packet of food and water bottle. A movement of light caught his eye. He twisted round to peer over the mound. Several electric cars were leaving town, headlights ablaze. They took the road midway to the lookout and gradually faded into the distance until the black night swallowed their light.

Down at the Training Centre, the movement of car lights heading along the road to the coast betrayed the only activity. Continuation after dark suggested some kind of urgency. He pondered it for a moment before moving away from the mound.

Keeping just beyond the range of illumination from the centre lights, he crossed the road and traversed the tussocky field. Eventually he came to the coast, standing at the edge to look out over the faint shimmer of light dancing on the water. He slid down the bank until his feet sank into soft sand, then moved up the beach to a suitably concealed observation spot.

The ship was moored on the far side of a brightly lit jetty jutting out over gently lapping waters. The ship was an old, rusty vessel. It didn't appear large enough for handling the open sea. He crouched against the sandy bank and watched, trying to make sense of the activity.

Cars were arriving at a parking area and clones, dressed in the fashion of those he'd seen earlier, were disembarking from the trailers. Two ordered lines strode along the jetty, up a short plank and onto the ship. Family Police stood watch, ever ready with their canes. The operation proceeded in silence, no verbal instructions.

The clones carried nothing with them, seemingly treated only as part of the cargo. Some trailers were delivering other cargo; bags of identical size, style and brown colour, combat gear and the long, thin rods used during the day's exercises. Officers had their arms full of clubs, which were also loaded onto the ship. Each club was a rounded shape, honed from a thin handle to the bludgeoning end as thick as a man's leg. Benjamin's eyes widened in awe as he visualised the damage such menacing weapons could inflict.

The loading reached completion. The ship's crew appeared on deck. Startled, Benjamin stared at them. They were Chinese! He turned his attention to the ship itself. The hull was very rusty, yet close to the bow he could just make out four Chinese characters. He had seen this ship before. It was the same one that had brought Jason, Bernard and their partners from China nearly sixteen years ago!

With haste, the ship was being readied for departure. A return trip to China? Was a regular trade going on? Delivering clones in exchange for goods? That would explain the high level of progress and construction around this separate town. And the electric cars! So many here and back at the Family area. Spare parts would not be a problem coming from China, which must have survived the worst of the bombings relatively unscathed.

Benjamin was incredulous. His own town so suppressed and deceived!

The ship and jetty were quiet now. The last car left and the jetty lights were dimmed. Benjamin moved away, retracing his steps along the beach.

Back at the mound, he sat by his bag and took a long drink from the water bottle. It was only early evening; the cover of darkness offered a vital opportunity. Refreshed, he set off in a new direction. Staying in the shadows, he skirted the Training Centre, heading for the far end of town. He reached the road and, with a glance at the faint outline of the last apartment buildings, he left the town behind.

The road was in good condition, expected after seeing three return visits by a car during the day. What was down here to justify that? Determined to find out, he plunged into blackness again. On and on he walked, each step feeling for the road surface, substituting for sight, the torch too risky to use.

A light broke through the darkness unexpectedly. Surprised, he ducked from the road into the low scrub. It was several moments before he realised the light was neither approaching nor moving away. Cautiously he returned to the road, his senses sharpened by fear. The light grew larger as he continued his approach. Two more appeared. Soon a faint circle of illumination unveiled vague outlines - the ghost-like shape of buildings and the road leading to them. It looked just like the Training Centre.

Confused and tired, he moved off the road. He needed to stop and rest but nervous energy pushed him. Stumbling through the scrub, he advanced on the buildings. A high wire fence encircled the collection of hut-like structures. Razor wire attached glinted along the top. The approach road led to the fence, where a gate was secured by a heavy chain and lock. No guard. No visible signs of life. Over the thump of his heart, Benjamin thought he could hear the faint sounds of wailing. A morbid atmosphere of inhuman suffering enveloped him. His skin crawled as he tried to imagine what could be making such a sound.

The lighting around the buildings was poor. He felt anxious. Should he run or stay? Had he already seen enough or was this a secret he needed to know? Benjamin dropped to his knees and inched forward, closer to the wire mesh. He lay on the ground behind a tussock and peered through the gloom.

He was looking down sandy and uneven ground. To his left, two lines of single-storey apartments ran down one side. Opposite them were three buildings, each an identical circular shape, constructed as one piece. The domed roof was their true oddity. Each building had a heavy steel entrance door, sitting flush against the wall surface. They looked like cocoons. Two steps provided entry from ground level. A square-shaped room was attached to each building, with its own access door. Control rooms? The specially constructed facilities looked fearsome for whatever function they served. What were they for? No road, no electric cars, just the heart-wrenching wailing. Benjamin shuddered as he broke into a cold sweat.

The wailing was getting to him. Long, drawn out sounds of despair, of someone in great pain or at the edge of insanity. The sounds came from the apartments. Suddenly, a small figure dashed from one, arms waving wildly. The wail became a scream. It pierced the air, a scream of unspeakable horror.

The figure careered across the open ground. It was a young boy, no more than five years old. Desperate, his hands were to his face, scratching. He stumbled and fell, then back on his feet, unaware. Several times it happened. Driven by hidden demons, he plunged towards the fence. Oblivious of his surroundings, he cannoned into the fence, close enough for Benjamin to see his tortured face clearly in the gloom. The boy's clenched fingers grasped the wire. His vividly outlined face, with wide-open mouth, gave a glimpse of hideous, yellow pockmarked skin. The skin was scarred, broken by bleeding scratches. His eyes were sunken and unseeing, the whites inflamed red. Benjamin tried to sink into the ground, horrified by the grotesque disfigurement of that face. Then the boy screamed again, expending the last air from his lungs, challenging Benjamin's own sanity.

The young boy broke from the fence. Another darted from an apartment, screaming and flailing his arms crazily. Then another and another. Soon a number were dashing about, their erratic, tortured behaviour triggered by the first. Several times they crashed into each other, but were unaffected, ravaged by torment. A shrill cacophony invaded the air.

The oldest boy seemed about six or seven years old. Each wore a one-piece, full-length uniform similar to clones at the Training Centre, except they were a lurid green. Were these the failed clones? In a flash of perception, Benjamin pictured a completed case file with the TrainB Action statement, a designation he knew to be unfavourable. He was certain he was looking at the TrainB clones now. Without any moderating influence or controlling authority, they had been left here to rot.

As he gazed at them, he came to a realisation that the domed buildings were a part of their terror. Was it some kind of experimentation? Testing how much pain and suffering they could tolerate? The choking horror of it galvanised him. He jumped to his feet and backed away, unable to witness such an evil hellhole any longer. He ran, stumbling straight through tussocks till he reached the road, relieved to distance himself from the place of tortured souls. A feeling of great helplessness weighed on him. He felt tired, emotionally bankrupt.

Benjamin plunged along the road, feeling for every step again, blinded by what he had seen as much as by the blackness. Eventually the lights of the Training Centre were ahead, jolting him back to reality, pulling him back from his own visions of hell. When he reached the mound, he sat by his bag and drank the last of his water.

The night was advancing. Rejuvenated, he stood, shouldered his bag and moved away from the mound. The Training Centre lights were invitingly close but offered nothing further worth risking himself for. With a final glance at them, he headed back up the road he had first arrived on. All around was black once more. He felt his way along the left edge. When it changed direction, he stopped, glimpsed the lookout light then swung down the alternative road. As he progressed, the light gradually shifted behind him, diminishing until eventually he was alone with his thoughts again. The road was good, maintained for the cars. He resumed periodic use of the torch, feeling comforted by brief sightings of the road surface. Slipping into a routine, he began peering ahead with anticipation.

He saw lights again, faint at first, but many of them. He drew closer. Surely his own town, but where was the road coming in? He was almost certain of the answer after seeing cars disappear down here at nightfall.

He walked onward, acutely aware of the possibility that people were close by. He entered a sphere of illumination that dimly revealed the road ahead. Piles of debris lined each side. He came to a fork and took the left branch. Up ahead, the lights were gaining strength. Soon they revealed a double gate and fence a short distance away. He leapt to one side and dropped to the ground. He could see no one, no guard on the gate. Highly alert and keeping behind tussocks, he crawled up to the fence and lay flat behind a large shrub. Wary, he looked down the road continuing straight through the well-lit Family Police compound, noting the individual houses lining each side, double gate and fence at the far end. More than halfway down on the left was the large recreation centre. No cars. Those leaving the Training Centre after dark must have gone to the Family area.

The road was deserted. Then he saw the reason for it. Not far to his right, between houses, stood a raised platform with a grandstand rising behind it. Three Family women sat along one edge of the platform. A Family Police officer stood in the centre facing the grandstand, which was full of officers sitting in silent attentiveness, all in their white shirts with black shoulder pads.

The officer on stage moved his arms about, as if making a speech. He seemed intent on giving a forceful account of himself. The crowd of officers was non-reactive, as if to move was to be conspicuous. The three women were scrutinising the speechmaker. Their strict control over proceedings was evident from their regular switch of attention to study the crowd. The only sound was a faint drone from the officer, rising and falling as he strove to impress. His speech, delivered methodically, seemed to follow a written script or expected routine rather than expressing ideas of his own.

The officer finished his performance. A brief pause ensued then the crowd erupted into chanting. The loud shout came in two short bursts, perfectly in unison. The controlled discipline of it was startling, not as submissive as that of the clones but just as willing. Another pre-arranged format. They repeated it twice following a brief pause each time. Then silence. A longer pause, then the three women stood, stepped down from the platform and disappeared around the far side of the grandstand, speaking to no one. The atmosphere seemed to relax. The crowd dispersed, spilling out from the grandstand onto the road. Many headed for the recreation centre, another night of revelry about to begin.

Benjamin stared after them, suddenly seeing them in a new light. In fundamental terms, they were really only one step better off than men in the community, although that step was a big one. Lured by the prospect of relations with Family women, they accepted the strict terms that subordinated them or else fell that final step. Their regimented obedience was in stark contrast to the jealousy and resentment rife at unsupervised times.

He roused himself. Few officers were in sight now. No one was near his end of the compound, still no guard on the gate. He backed away on hands and knees then stood when a safe distance away and returned to the fork. The road continued straight ahead to the Family area.

The light was enough to outline the fence and double gate some distance on. No guard again. The solid construction blocked any view beyond, making further progress pointless. Close to his right, a narrow road led off through a gap in the debris. He started down it; the same road he had stumbled on a week ago after crashing through rubble.

He hesitated, then changed his mind. The corner of the Family perimeter fence was near. He diverted to it and moved along the fenceline, reaching the corner nearest town. He darted through the trees, across both approach roads and up to the rear of the Clonesseum. He came onto the main road and walked to the Pro House.

Ralph was at the bar with a group of men. Benjamin returned his wave as he joined Natalie, Janine, Patty and Ruth sitting together.

"Hello, Benjamin," Natalie greeted him welcomingly. "You look a little tired. You okay?"

He sat next to her and acknowledged the others with a smile. "Been a long day," he said softly, taking a sip of someone's drink that happened to be in front of him.

Janine, on the other side of Natalie, leaned forward. She spoke in a low voice.

"Did you see anything at the Family Police area the other night?"

Benjamin paused to look around, conscious of their exposure to being overheard.

"There was a disturbance when they left their recreation centre. Some kind of jealousy between two of them." He tried to keep his voice low.

"I heard it, too. It happens often," Janine affirmed.

Natalie appreciated the need for privacy. "Janine knows more about the Family Police than any of us. Why don't you go to her room?"

Grateful for her understanding, he followed Janine out and was soon sitting on her chair, with Janine seated on the edge of the bed.

"You're right about the Family Police," he said. "I was surprised at what I saw." For the first time in a day and two nights, he felt his body relax a little, relieved to be in familiar circumstance. He longed to return home to his bed but forced himself to concentrate.

"Many aren't as satisfied with their lives as we might expect, considering how much better off they are," Janine replied.

Benjamin was thoughtful. "It's ironic, but perhaps they'd be better off without something to compete for, like the rest of us."

Janine smiled bleakly. "The attached officers are the lucky ones, as long as they do what's expected of them. The others are still trying to be chosen."

He nodded. "You must have seen a lot to understand them as you do."

"Officers come here sometimes, when they're frustrated. I even have to entertain the one who caused me to be here in the first place." Her head dropped and she wiped at tears in her eyes.

"I saw them again tonight, from the other end of their compound," Benjamin continued, in an effort to distract Janine from her own horrible life.

Janine looked up with interest. Benjamin described his excursion. Janine was enthralled, her admiration for his efforts obvious.

"You've been getting to the right places!" She reached out and touched his face. "No wonder you look tired."

"I wish I could have heard what was said at that weird meeting."

Janine gave him a strange look then slipped off the bed and went to the cupboard. She pulled out an item and held it up. It was a Family Police shirt, white with black shoulder pads. "You could have been there if you'd been wearing this."

Benjamin stared at the shirt with a mixture of excitement and apprehension, recognising the opportunity it gave him, perilous as it was.

"How did you get hold of that?"

"As I said, officers visit us here."

"Are you suggesting I could wear it and infiltrate the Family Police?"

"It would be very dangerous," she replied. She was all suggestion.

Benjamin felt a growing enthusiasm for the idea. "I could join them for one of those gatherings. There's enough Family Police there to not notice a stranger, and they don't talk to each other while it's on. All I have to do is keep out of their way before and after."

"You can take it with you," Janine offered, placing the shirt next to him.

He accepted, stuffing it inside his jacket. Committed, he followed Janine back to the table and the others. She and Natalie talked for a few moments, then Natalie led Benjamin to her room. She listened intently as he told her what he had seen.

"Janine said she gave you a Family Police shirt," Natalie said, looking into his eyes. "Please be careful, Benjamin."

She hugged him to her. Benjamin held her close, buoyed by her overwhelming support. They returned and he joined Ralph near the bar.

"You must know everything about those girls by now," Ralph commented, grinning. "I'll have to introduce you to some variety."

Benjamin was glad to relax in Ralph's crude but uncomplicated company. He stayed till late then walked home.

Chapter 18

Finishing time arrived at last.

Benjamin rode to the market, having missed his usual visit yesterday. He wandered around, in no hurry to collect his supplies. The later he returned home, the less would be the frustrating wait till later. The sight and sounds of active people provided some comfort. He looked for Brenda, but as expected, he did not see her.

With darkness approaching, he collected coffee and other supplies at the food section and returned to his bike. A woman approached as he loaded the saddlebag.

"Hi, I'm Sasha," she greeted. "Have you seen Brenda?"

Benjamin looked at her curiously. About the same age as Brenda, she was plain by comparison and a little hard around the edges. She seemed like someone who had accepted her lot and was making the best of it.

"What makes you think I'd see her?" he said bluntly.

"I saw you talking to her before. She likes you."

Benjamin nodded and glanced around cautiously. The Family Police were showing them no interest. "I don't think she'll return to the market. It's too dangerous for her here. The Family Police keep targeting her."

"You don't know then? She was attacked here three days ago by two officers."

"What! Was she hurt?" Benjamin grabbed her by the shoulders.

Sasha nodded, pulling away slightly. "One had a knife. They hurt her but let her go. She escaped up the road. I haven't seen her since. She hasn't been at the fields, either."

Benjamin was aghast, his mind a whirl of possibilities. He had to find Brenda! Suddenly nothing else mattered. He grabbed his bike from the rack and took off up the road. He did not care about Family Police now. Brenda needed his help, whatever the consequences.

The light was fading as he reached his apartment. He dashed inside with his supplies then changed into dark clothing and pulled on his jacket. He headed back down the road.

Warily, he approached Brenda's apartment. The dull streetlight cast fat shadows around her building. There were no officers lurking about. Risking everything, he moved to the door and knocked. No answer. With mounting trepidation, he knocked again. Still no answer. He pushed open the door and entered, closing it quickly behind him.

Dim light exposed an apartment even more basic and sparsely furnished than his own; a table, one chair and a wardrobe. A foul odour in the air warned him something was not right. He moved to the centre of the room.

To his left, a lamp stand next to the bed was aglow. Then he saw her. He rushed to the bed, stumbling over Brenda's discarded coat on the floor. He leaned over, anxious. Brenda was in a serious state. She offered no recognition, eyes glazed and unseeing, lips quivering, body squirming feverishly. Her face and body were bathed in sweat, her breathing a struggle coming in shallow gasps. She was uncovered, unaware of the biting cold in her delirious state.

"Oh no," he murmured. "What have they done to you?" He put his face to hers. She was burning up, yet her sweat felt cold. Quickly he turned to her wounds.

Her dress was torn. A number of cuts and abrasions were plastered with congealed blood, smeared with the glistening sweat. One of them caught his eye. A deep gash in her left leg above the knee! The flesh around it was yellow, oozing an ugly brown fluid. Benjamin was aghast. The foul smell of advanced infection stung his nose.

He hurried to the sink, filled a bowl and clean glass with water and snatched some towels from the bench. He returned to the bed and began wiping away sweat from her face and neck, trying to cool her feverish temperature. He bathed her wounds, concentrating on the nasty gash in her leg. With his arm behind her neck, he lifted her head and eased water from the glass between her quivering lips. Every drop was a victory against dehydration. Bit by bit, he persevered till the glass was empty. He laid her head back gently. At the bench, he refilled the glass and bowl then laid a fresh towel across her forehead.

Brenda remained unchanged. Just the continuous shallow gasping for breath. She was very sick, in desperate need of more help than he could give her. The wound in her leg needed urgent medical care. Without drugs, the fight against infection was hopeless. Benjamin gazed down at it, despairing. With another towel, he kept bathing it, but could only clean the outside. What about the inside?

He felt a horrible fear for her, and for himself. A debilitating feeling, all too familiar despite many years since he last felt it. The fear of inadequacy, of seeing someone precious being taken away, the likelihood of losing her completely. A crazy panic overtook him as he stared at the wound in her leg. The infection was already critical, threatening her life. Yet there was nothing more he could do.

Lifting her head, he eased more water between her trembling lips. He sat in the chair next to her, periodically resuming the bathing. He did his best but it was not enough.

Time passed slowly with no change in her condition. Benjamin thought of the plans he had for tonight. He did not want to leave her, but to continue helplessly watching her was futile, and a tiny voice inside his head told him to go. Brenda must fight the infection from within, bleak as the prospect was. "I'll be back," he said as he kissed her softly on the lips; was it for the last time?

With a final look at her fever-racked body, he left. The road near her apartment was deserted. Benjamin hurried home, grabbed his bike and rode to the Clonesseum. He pulled the Family Police shirt from the saddlebag where he had left it, slipped it under his jacket and walked to the Pro House.

Skirting the building entrance, he soon reached the Family Police perimeter fence. With no one around, he put on the shirt and hid his jacket behind a shrub. Steeling himself, he lifted the rusty catch holding the gate and passed through, closing it behind him. He was inside the Family Police compound!

Trying to appear calm, he proceeded to the road. A few officers were wandering along. They ignored him. The culture of indifference was as prevalent here as anywhere else. Benjamin knew, however, they would act swiftly and harshly given the chance to expose an impostor and impress the Family.

He passed the empty stage and grandstand to his left and came to the far double gate, unguarded again. The road disappeared into darkness, past where he had lain last night. Disappointed a gathering seemed unlikely to be on tonight, he turned to make his way back.

He was immediately surprised. The scene had been developing behind him. Many officers were on the road now, all heading for the grandstand. Some had already taken up seats. Maintaining composure, Benjamin moved in and took a seat at the edge about two thirds of the way up. The grandstand quickly filled. No one spoke. A glum-looking officer took the seat next to him, offering no acknowledgment, no sign he had even noticed him. A tense silence hung over the crowd as they waited.

Benjamin glanced down to his right. A track ran back beside the grandstand to a gate in the fence common to the Family area. He snapped his head to the front as three Family women approached along it. In silence, they took up their positions along the edge of the stage. They looked hard and unfriendly, acknowledging no one, their expectations of obeyance clear. Without introduction, an officer from the front row of the stand made his way onto the stage. He glanced at the three women before turning to face the crowd.

His speech started uncertainly, but he gradually gained in confidence as he proceeded with no apparent disapproval from the women. He began with a description of his own performance in enforcement over the last month, recounting actions taken against people in the community. Included was a Promart punishment he considered himself responsible for bringing about. The further he went, the more his pride in himself swelled, bursting forth in pathetic, nauseating self-gratification. The performance was a grovelling justification of his continued existence with the Family Police, submitting to his perception of what the Family expected.

A brief pause followed then he launched into a new phase, amounting to little more than a repetition of the previous. The officer expounded his support for the system perpetrated by the Family, urging all officers to uphold established method and principle. He pledged a continuing commitment to seeking out subversive or threatening behaviour in the community. Finally, he threw himself at the mercy of the Family women, expressing the hope his performance was adequate in their eyes.

As the speech progressed, Benjamin felt increasingly disgusted by such a pandering, self-degrading example of indoctrination. Its predictability suggested a standard routine, a script to be followed. Throughout, the three women studied the officer closely, moving only to glance occasionally at the grandstand and scrutinise the crowd. The atmosphere was tight and oppressive.

After a short silence, the chanting began. All stared straight ahead, unflinching as they shouted in strict unison. A stirring sound; two short bursts, three times.

"Loyalty is Security, Dominate and Eliminate; Loyalty is Security, Dominate and Eliminate; Loyalty is Security, Dominate and Eliminate."

Another pause. The Family women offered no reaction. Ignoring the masses, they stood and left the stage, returned down the track and disappeared through the gate.

The tension immediately eased. Some officers began talking to each other as they left the grandstand. The officer next to Benjamin displayed a completely changed manner.

"That's another one survived. Had your turn this round yet?"

Benjamin was startled, unsure what to say. "No, not yet," he replied evenly.

The officer grimaced. "Me neither. Better brush up on the routine."

"Yes, I'm sure."

Benjamin descended the grandstand steps and followed the others gravitating toward the recreation centre. He looked around, anxious. Escape was too risky with so many officers standing around. Yet where could he hide? He was trapped. With no better options, he joined the milling officers and tried to blend in. Steadily, small groups began to form and enter the centre. Soon the numbers would thin out and he'd be left on his own.

"No use hanging about out here," a voice close behind said. "The action's inside."

Benjamin turned, trying to remain calm. The officer who had sat beside him in the grandstand was gesturing towards the entrance. Suddenly he was being carried along with the others. The flow pushed him to the entrance. In moments, he was inside!

For one horrifying moment, he felt caged. He had just made a crucial mistake. He steeled himself, trying to remain outwardly calm. Pushed from behind, he moved further inside and looked for somewhere unobtrusive, away from the mainstream.

Small tables, each surrounded by four or five chairs, filled the open hall. Already, groups of officers had taken up many of them, settling in for another night of revelry. Benjamin weaved through to an empty table towards one corner with only three chairs. He sat facing the main body of people, trying not to draw attention or to make eye contact.

An officer, behind a bar that ran parallel to the side wall from near the entrance, served the men, many as they entered the hall. Some gathered at one end of the bar. No one asked to see identification. The atmosphere seemed relaxed. Benjamin decided the safest way was to conform, and perhaps he might learn something while he was here. He found a route back to the bar. The barman stared blankly at him, waiting for his order.

"Rice wine," Benjamin blurted out awkwardly, without knowing the choice.

The officer was a burly, hard-looking individual. The thin slit of a mouth and cold eyes remained unchanged as he poured the drink from a bulk container beneath the bar. A small splash leapt over the side of the glass as he planted it on the cement surface. Hands shaking slightly, Benjamin lifted the glass and returned to his table.

The drink was pungent and tasted sour, even worse than the concoction served at the Pro House. He tried to relax, taking in the surroundings. There was little to take in; tables, chairs, bar and officers bantering, gesticulating and slowly getting drunk. The grey walls were bare and depressing, the cold floor the same. The impression was of a place established merely to herd people together for whatever they felt like doing. An opening in the far sidewall, delineating the toilet area, was a busy thoroughfare.

Throughout most of the hall, conversation was humming, punctuated regularly by bouts of laughter. Periodically, the noise level escalated as someone became excited or shouted to make a point. A number of tables, like his, had just one officer occupying it. This helped ease Benjamin's sense of being out of place.

An officer sitting by himself two tables away was looking directly at him, studying him. Benjamin felt unnerved, the possibility of being exposed making his heart pound. His hands shook, causing him to spill some of his drink. The officer was vaguely familiar. Benjamin pretended not to notice.

Three officers moved through and settled at the table closest to him. One was considerably younger than the other two.

"I can't believe it," he complained. "I thought I was chosen. Now she doesn't want me any more." The young officer stared down at his drink.

"Yeah, the same thing happened to me straight after my speech at the Racktrap. I don't think they liked it," one of his companions offered.

"It must be the same thing. My speech two nights ago wasn't good. I was too nervous."

"What can you expect with three of them sitting there, waiting for a mistake," the second said. He sculled his drink. "One mistake and you're finished, forget about a relationship."

"I thought I already had a relationship. I thought she loved me." The young officer looked up, saddened by his cruel awakening.

The second officer stood, getting ready to obtain another drink. "Ha! Love? What's that? They use us when it suits them. You might think you're in love, Mike, but to them it's power and control, forget about love." His voice took on a sneering tone, making no attempt to conceal his antagonism.

"But there are plenty of relationships with Family women that are working," Mike reasoned. "We don't see them because they live in the other area."

"You think they're working? A relationship only happens if a Family woman wants children, or because they use sex to control us, and through us the community. Neither reason has anything to do with love. They have no feelings for us. Ask Jack, he knows." He nodded at the other older man, who spoke for the first time.

"Brad's right. I lived in the Family area for a while with one of them, but I was kicked out when we had no children."

"No children, that was unlucky," Mike responded.

"Nothing to do with luck," Jack replied, smirking with disdain. "I'm not the only one. A couple of others have been with her too. Why do you think we call her White Ice?"

They laughed. "Perhaps you should have a go with her, Mike," Brad suggested sarcastically. "With your theories about love, the ice might turn to steam and you'll be an example to all of us."

They laughed again, more raucously. Jack threw his head back with hilarity, enjoying a buzz of avenging satisfaction. Mike was more circumspect, his sense of humour clouded by the rocky learning process he was going through.

Benjamin sat quietly with his drink, trying to appear uninterested. The exchanges were amusing but confirmed the unhealthy nature of Family-to-Family Police relationships. How could the women possibly gain satisfaction from them? For the younger ones, no romance, just arrangement probably orchestrated by the senior women.

In a moment of cynical insight, he saw the Family women's elitism for what it was. They used themselves sexually for unprincipled gain. Surely, in the final judgement, it put them even lower than the Pro House women, who would not choose their plight wilfully. Who would be seen as the most degraded?

He finished his drink. The centre was abuzz, officers absorbed in their own small circles. He was anxious to get back and do what he could for Brenda. He made his way to the entrance and exited the place, relieved. Outside, the road and surrounds were void of officers. He focussed on the gate in the fence not far away and headed across the open ground.

Suddenly, a hand clamped onto his shoulder. His heart leapt and his breath caught in his throat. Spinning round, he found himself face to face with an officer. The same officer who had been studying him inside the building.

"You're not a Family Police officer." His voice was menacing. "What are you doing here? Why are you wearing that shirt?" His grip strengthened on Benjamin's shoulder.

Benjamin stared at him in shock. A feeling of disaster overwhelmed him. The officer spoke again.

"Come with me," he ordered.

Benjamin felt weak at the knees as panic shot through him. "Wait!" he blurted out hoarsely.

The officer hesitated. Benjamin's mind focussed on the impression of familiarity he had felt before, and again now. The officer was strongly built, middle-aged with greying hair. An underlying confidence in him was that of someone who had overcome adversity with strength and toughness. In a flash, Benjamin recognised him. The facial features were more lined now, but unmistakeable.

"You're Jason," he stated with a sudden calm certainty.

The officer was surprised. "Yes. Why? How do you know me?"

Benjamin felt a glimmer of hope. They stood glaring at each other, sizing each other up. Time seemed suspended as a mental tussle developed, an imaginary pendulum being tugged back and forth.

"I know about your affair with Karla Mason and the baby she's having," Benjamin declared incisively, seizing the opportunity to take the initiative. It was all he had; would it be enough?

The pendulum swung Benjamin's way. Jason stood stunned, his face paled. Benjamin knew he must capitalise by taking the next step.

"You're right. I'm not a Family Police officer. I work in the Records Department at the Clonesseum. My name is Benjamin."

Jason snapped back to life sharply, striving to seize control of the situation. Then he nodded slowly. "Yes, I know you. Karla told me about you." He looked over his shoulder at a small group of officers exiting the building. They headed in the opposite direction. Jason's voice lowered a fraction. "It's been a long time since I saw you with your father. What are you doing here?"

Benjamin's mind whirled as he sought a suitable reason before precarious mutual deterrence collapsed. A flash of inspiration came to him. "I need medical supplies," he said boldly, a small ray of hope for Brenda giving him courage. "Someone is sick."

"People get sick all the time," Jason replied scornfully. "Why does that concern you?"

"She's got a deep wound in her leg. It's infected. She's got a high fever."

"So it's a woman," Jason noted with a half-smile. "You're taking a big risk getting involved with a woman. I'm sure you know what can happen. It is very foolish."

"As foolish as you've been?"

Jason scowled at him, irritated. Then a twitch of amusement flickered at the corner of his mouth and he looked away in a faint admission of weakness. "There are no medical supplies here," he replied finally.

Benjamin felt a surge of momentum now as the urgency of Brenda's situation drove him. The chance to obtain what she needed was standing in front of him. He had to press Jason for it, whatever the risk.

"In the Family area," he persisted, reminded of what he had seen from up a tree. "There must be supplies there."

"Yes, there are. But that's not for your use."

Benjamin took a step towards him and looked him directly in the eye. "You get me supplies and I'll keep quiet about you and Karla and your baby."

Jason stood in silence, his face hard as he tried to wrest the pendulum his way. He broke into a relieving half-smile again. "What makes you think Karla and I are having a baby?" he asserted, aware he had not openly admitted it. "It's clone production. You've seen the case file."

Benjamin snorted. "I went through an interrogation because Karla tried to hide it, as you know. I work in Records. You think I don't know the truth?"

Jason hesitated, his mind working fast. He dropped the bluff. "Someone must have told you. Who told you?"

"No-one," Benjamin refuted. He had no intention of mentioning Natalie. "I found out myself."

"I don't believe you. Was it Stephanie? You must tell me who else knows."

"Stephanie told me nothing. There's no more I can say." He was determined to hold firm, certain he had Jason on the back foot. Jason's mouth twitched in uneasiness, but it was only momentary.

"It doesn't matter," he said, thinking of another angle. "No-one would believe you over me. I could put you in a lot of trouble if I had to."

"I don't have to tell anyone," Benjamin retorted, holding his nerve steady. "Through Records, I could make it obvious what happened without involving myself. I'm sure Investigations would be interested in how Karla became a clone mother, without selecting or approving her. And Assessments too, after the baby is born. I wonder if it'll be male or female. I'm sure you've got it worked out, but you don't need complicating factors, do you?"

The pendulum swung irrevocably in his favour as Jason looked slightly deflated.

"All you have to do is give me medical supplies," Benjamin went on. "Then nothing else needs to happen. We both know each other's secret, mutual deterrence. I didn't keep my job in Records by talking about what I see and don't see."

Jason watched him intently, a new respect emerging. He nodded slowly, appreciating an acceptable outcome. "Okay, I agree," he conceded. "I can get what you want."

He glanced at the black pads on Benjamin's shirt then started back. They passed the still lively recreation centre and moved up the deserted road, swinging left at the stage and grandstand. At the fence, Jason produced his key and gained them access to the Family area. He locked the gate behind them.

Benjamin walked beside Jason across an open, short-grassed area. He could barely contain his anxiety and fear, yet he felt excited. He was doing something; a chance to save Brenda! They sidled between two electric cars, the closest he had been to one for many years. The cars appeared unchanged. They emerged midway between where the two side roads branched off the far side of the deserted main road.

The time was late. Unlike the unattached Family Police, the Family women and attached officers were not partying. Jason led the way across the road, angling between cars then over the grass verge towards a building, the same one Benjamin had observed from the tree. They passed through the entrance.

They stood in the middle of a reception room. The grey walls and floor belied the clinic's prestigious function. A bench reached two-thirds of the way across the back wall, stopping short of a closed door. Behind the bench, shelves covered the wall from ceiling to at least bench-top level, filled with a wide-ranging array of medical supplies, many small bottles and packets of drugs. Benjamin was astonished at the quantity of supplies.

Jason moved behind the bench. The door in the rear wall opened and a woman entered. She exchanged a brief greeting with Jason then glanced at Benjamin. Instantly she froze, her pale blue eyes widening as the colour ran from her cheeks.

Benjamin caught his breath in shocked surprise. "Kelly!" he exclaimed, as an intense sensation surged through him.

"Yes," she whispered. "Hello, Benjamin."

They stared at each other. Briefly their eyes met and a powerful message passed between them. Kelly cut it short, quickly dropping her head and looking away in nervous self-consciousness. A deep sadness was glaringly apparent in her, giving Benjamin a strong urge to reach out. Many questions flooded his mind, but he could only stand transfixed.

"Are you okay?" he asked eventually.

Kelly nodded but said nothing. Her head stayed down as she gazed at the floor. Her downturned lips quivered. Then she lifted her head and looked directly at him, her eyes swimming with tears as she sobbed quietly, unable to hide her feelings. Putting a shaky hand to her mouth, she looked away in miserable embarrassment.

Benjamin felt powerless, his throat constricted with emotion as he agonised. No reaction seemed worthy. Too much time had passed. How could he help her now? They remained silent, both struggling to cope with the moment. At last, Kelly wiped at her tears and offered an encouraging smile.

"I'm sorry. I wasn't expecting this."

"It's been a long time," he murmured.

He marvelled at the changes in her. She was a beautiful, grown-up woman now, different from when they were teenagers together.

Yet he easily recognised unmistakeable characteristics in manner and appearance uniquely hers, giving him a warm feeling of closeness. The smile was still the same, captivating him even now, just as it had in younger days. Her wavy blonde hair with curly fringe across her forehead was largely unchanged. The smooth, even facial features were as enchanting as ever, but with greater depth from the passing years.

Kelly recognised in him the emotional security missing for so long. Without it, she had plunged into a state of unfulfilled passivity, the only way of surviving the traumatic death of her father and role reversal with her demanding mother. Now, seeing Benjamin reactivated her need. And his strong physical appearance was just as she remembered, except for a more lined, experienced face.

Becoming more composed, she moved to the end of the bench. Benjamin came forward, glancing at Jason who had paused in collecting items from the shelves to watch them.

"I want to speak to Benjamin in private," Kelly said, addressing Jason.

She beckoned Benjamin to the door in the back wall. He followed her through and she closed it behind them.

The room was for consultations, set up with normal facilities for medical treatment, including a hard-based, bench-like bed, cupboards, several benches strewn with equipment and a double sink with taps. Shelves covered one entire wall, filled with more supplies. Benjamin was again amazed at the sheer quantity of it all.

They took seats at a desk, facing each other. With the initial shock behind them, each felt a strange awareness of the bond that once held them. But it was disconnected now, suspended in a different time. Kelly's deep-seated sadness reflected the loss. She was the first to speak.

"I didn't think you were part of the Family Police."

"I'm not," Benjamin replied with apprehension. "Someone gave me this shirt."

He felt comfortable confiding in her, although unsure what she would tell her mother. It seemed unlikely their relationship had changed much over the years.

"You're taking a big risk," Kelly responded with concern.

Benjamin nodded. "Somebody has to do something."

"Yes. Life is very bad now."

He felt closer to her then, encouraged by an outlook seemingly at odds with her being part of the Family.

"Life is controlled by the Family." He paused in reflection then asked, "How is your mother?" Instinctively, he knew her mother was a major cause of Kelly's sadness and lack of confidence. He thought of her troubled state fifteen years ago and wondered what else had happened in her life.

Kelly looked forlorn and tired. "My mother is one of the senior women in the Family. She has a part in making decisions. She tells me what they want to do, but I can't understand why they do such horrible things to people. She treats me as if I'm still a child, controlling everything. I have no freedom." Her voice tailed off as she retreated within herself.

"What about others?" he asked. "Is there anyone you can talk to?"

Kelly shook her head morosely. "Most believe in what the Family is doing, particularly older ones like my mother. No-one dares question anything or challenge the system. Those not too old concentrate on having children with chosen Family Police officers. Our time is dedicated to learning and advancing the Family's visions."

Benjamin listened intently. A burning question sprang into his mind. He paused, struggling with what the answer might be. "Do you have children and a Family Police partner?" he asked eventually.

Kelly dropped her head as her mouth quivered with emotion again. Her hands were shaking. "No," she whispered unhappily. "I have neither."

Benjamin leaned forward to take her hands in his. Suddenly, she broke down. Jumping from her chair, she flung her arms around his neck, crying openly. He held her, sharing the same pain as suppressed feelings released from them both in a strong surge. So much lost by the passing of time. At last, Kelly loosened her hold and sat back on the edge of her chair. She dried her eyes.

"I wish life could be like it was. I don't know why it had to be this way. I never forgot you, Benjamin. One day, I knew I would see you again." She smiled meekly, and they fell silent; the warm, easy silence of two people comfortable with each other.

Benjamin observed her curly blonde hair and the appealing outline of her face. How unthinkable someone as attractive and intelligent as Kelly could be so alone and isolated. She sensed his interest and their eyes met for an instant, a powerful message again passing between them. As before, Kelly looked away, nervous.

"How has life been for you, Benjamin?" she asked.

"I work in the Records Department. I've been at the Clonesseum since the start of clone production."

He described his duties, the way he lived, the dreary monotony of each day relentlessly accumulating into years. Kelly was unhappily conscious of her own place in the Family, where ultimate responsibility lay for conditions in the community.

"I heard what happened to your mother and father. I'm so sorry."

"And your father, too."

A buzzer sounded above the desk, breaking the mood. Benjamin jumped in fright. Kelly went to the front, returning a few moments later.

"It's Jason. He's waiting for you."

"Oh, of course."

He stood and faced Kelly. Then she was in his arms. They held each other, her taut body pressed into him tightly.

"I need to see you again, Benjamin," she cried, releasing him.

He was pensive. "How?"

"I finish here at three o'clock every morning." She was suddenly determined. "I'll meet you that time tomorrow night, outside the gate near the crop fields. Do you know it?"

Benjamin nodded and smiled. He kissed her lightly, her lips soft and giving. He left her then. Jason was standing by the entrance door, impatient.

"How long do you expect me to wait here?" he demanded to know.

Although irritated, he could not contain a glimmer of amusement. He handed a cloth bag to Benjamin.

"Everything you need is there."

Benjamin accepted the bag gratefully. They left the building and returned to the gate. Jason let him through. No one was on the road, but the recreation centre was still alive with the sounds of revelry. He hastened past and through the gate beyond. He retrieved and put on his jacket, then returned to the Clonesseum. After changing out of the Family Police shirt, which he stored in the saddlebag of his bike, he rode home as fast as he could.

With Jason's bag tucked inside his jacket, he walked to Brenda's apartment. Avoiding a patrol, he was soon inside, closing the door quickly behind him.

The foul odour struck him instantly. The dimly lit scene was exactly as he had left it. He hurried to the bed and knelt down. Brenda's face was bathed in sweat, her breath coming in short, agitated gasps. The delirious fever was raging with frightening intensity. Her body writhed back and forth in tortured fervour. He felt her forehead, noting the soaring temperature. Brenda was in a critical state.

He took the towels, bowl and glass he had used before to the sink, soon returning with clean towels and refills. He dampened her forehead, wiping the sweat away. Lifting her head, he eased water from the glass between her trembling lips.

Inside the bag was a small bottle containing dark fluid and two bottles of tablets. One was marked 'For Infection: Take two then one every 4 hours'. He took out two and managed to wash them down her throat with water from the glass. Then the same from the other bottle marked 'For Fever: Take two then one every 3 hours'.

He focussed on the wound in her upper left leg, wincing with concern. The oozing yellow flesh was frightening, the foul smell giving him real fears. What if it went gangrenous? He washed it as clean as he could with a fresh towel. The bottle of dark fluid was marked 'For Open Wound'. Using the dropper attached to the cap, he liberally invaded the wound with droplets of the fluid. A red stain immediately spread along the edges, alleviating the yellow ugliness a little. Encouraged, he eased the flesh back on each side, exposing the gaping depths to which the knife had plunged. Quickly, he injected the fluid deep inside and throughout, watching it react with congealed blood and the oozing infection. Already, the wound began to look a little better.

He tended to the other cuts and abrasions in the same way. None were serious injuries. The one to her leg was the major concern, and he came back to it with more fluid.

Brenda remained oblivious to everything he did. He gave her more water and continued applying damp towels, feeling a huge relief now. He had helped her in every way possible. Now he could only wait and hope.

He sat in the chair, watching her fight a grim battle against the debilitating infection and fever. Her tenacity had continually impressed him. She needed every bit of it now. With everything in him, he willed her through the crisis.

Time passed slowly. He stood and walked around, noting the decrepit state of the apartment. Bare walls, no pictures or adornments, not even a clock. Soul-destroying. Patches of cement were crumbling from the walls, lying in small dirt-heaps around the floor. It crunched under his feet as he paced up and down. On the spindly-legged table were a number of items, mostly essentials, a few trinkets the only feminine touch he could see.

He picked up a framed picture and wiped away the dust. The photo of a boy in school uniform, grinning and brandishing a hockey stick, gave him a fleeting moment of escape to his own school days. A lifetime ago. He angled the photo towards the dim light. Hand-written scribble was all over it. He peered closer and realised it was more than scribble - the name Eric overlaid numerous times!

Startled, he moved back to stare down at the writhing figure on the bed. In a vivid flashback, he saw the image of a four year-old straining for her older brother's attention at a game of table hockey. With Omar then befriending Eric, he had not mixed with them after that. Now, twenty-two years later, here she was! What had happened to Eric? Incredulous, Benjamin returned the photo to the table then knelt beside her again, gazing at her tormented face, wondering what other torment she had endured.

He gave her one each of the tablets, washing them down with water. He dropped more red fluid into and around the wound in her leg then wrapped it with a gauzy bandage Jason had put in the bag. There was a hastily scrawled note written on the bandage's paper wrapping: 'Change regularly and keep wound clean'. The fever was still raging, but Brenda's torturous writhing had eased and her breathing seemed slower, deeper. Her lips were no longer trembling.

Encouraged, Benjamin sat back in the chair and closed his eyes. Gradually, he fell into a semi-slumber.

* * *

With a jolt, he became aware as the first light of dawn showed through the small window. He leapt out of the chair, fearful of losing the cover of night.

Brenda looked the same. Her face still glistened with sweat as she fought the fever. He gave her two more of each tablet, dropped more red fluid into the wound and rewrapped the bandage. Slipping the bag of medical supplies under his jacket, he left the apartment. Dawn was breaking and the road was deserted.

Chapter 19

Benjamin was glad to be passing the time with mundane duties again. He was looking through the next case file. In an instant, his eyes fixed on the space for DNA donor. Two names again, as he had seen before, but one had the letter F after it! One was male, the other female.

Although only names on paper, he was shocked; this was surely a dramatic development. What sort of clone would eventuate by combining DNA in this way? Would it be half male, half female and which parts of its make-up would be which? Or some sort of bizarre hybrid, unrecognisable as male or female? What was the Family up to? Did they know what the outcome would be? But they would not care. The TrainB camp would be home for the rejects. Or Dump.

He tried to envisage what purpose it might serve. Family intentions were always ruthlessly efficient; a reason for every action. Was it just the beginning? Combining and manipulating DNA had endless possibilities. What did that mean for evolution of the human race?

He studied the two Donor Assessment Forms. The ticking patterns were not unusual. Both forms showed strong physical traits, almost all assessments with a Pass tick. The physical capability of the resultant clone was obviously of high priority. With a resigned shake of his head, Benjamin processed the case file, cards and General File.

Lunchtime came and went, and a tedious afternoon followed. Finishing time drew near, bringing on a sense of anticipation. Soon he could check on Brenda. And looming closer was the prospect of meeting Kelly again. Both had been at the forefront of his mind all day.

Suddenly, Jason appeared in front of his desk, the first time he had ever come to Records. He was agitated. He leaned across, pointing his finger at Benjamin's chest.

"You said you wouldn't talk about Karla's baby if I gave you those supplies."

"What!" Benjamin exclaimed, bewildered. "What do you mean? What's happened?"

"She's at Investigations now," Jason replied angrily. "They sent for her. Why else would they want to see her?"

"I've said nothing," Benjamin retorted, indignant. "Why shouldn't Investigations want to see her? Maybe they're considering her for clone motherhood, or they've found out about her baby some other way. But not from me! Your GM and Stephanie know about it. What about them?"

"They wouldn't say anything. Investigations could only find out from you. I saw Karla before she went there. She's very frightened. She thinks you've told them, to get back at her for what she did to you. I think she's right."

"That's nonsense. Investigations are considering any woman now. Clone mother numbers are decreasing. I'm sure you know that. Has she been displaying her orange flag?"

"Of course not. She's already in the system as a clone mother."

"Investigations don't know that. That's why they sent for her. No orange flag."

Jason hesitated but remained angry. He was determined to lay the problem with Benjamin. Leaning further across the desk, he looked him hard in the eye.

"It makes no difference. If they want her for clone motherhood, there'll be a medical examination. They'll soon know she's already pregnant. If Investigations realise it's a baby through sex, they'll punish her and look for the father. Well, let me tell you something. I'll let them find out you're the father. They'll believe that because of your interrogation before." He straightened, letting his words sink in.

"What do you expect me to do?" Benjamin refuted, fuming. He tried to remain calm, determined not to give Jason the edge.

Jason pointed his finger again. "You make sure the records are fixed so there's no doubt it's clone production. If Investigations think a mix-up occurred in the system, confusion over names or something like that, nothing further will happen. Karla can have the baby as if it was a clone. The Family need not even know. Investigations would have no reason to tell them. There's not much time. Now do something."

"Too many people are involved in the process," Benjamin protested, feeling sick with his prospects. "Anyway, the records are already fixed as much as they can be. There's nothing more I can do. And we don't even know what's happened yet. You have to find that out from Karla first."

"No, you have to find out. Remember, if something goes wrong then you're the father. Karla goes to the market today after work. You can find her there."

"But Karla won't talk to me."

"Then you'll have to talk to her."

Jason turned and stormed out. Benjamin stared after him, flabbergasted. The man was unscrupulous. Yet he was also afraid. And he did feel for Karla and her predicament. Jason could easily have turned away from her and the problem entirely. Benjamin respected him at least for that.

Finishing time had passed. Uppermost in his mind now was to find Karla then work out what to do. He left the office and rode to the market.

He searched through the crowd for Karla. Had she been detained and already punished? Then he saw her as he came back to the Food Section. Relieved, he eased his way along the bench, trying to appear interested in the goods. She had already obtained her supplies and was on her own.

"Hello, Karla," he greeted in a muted tone.

Karla was startled. "What are you doing talking to me?" Her voice was strained. She began moving away.

"Wait. Jason sent me."

Karla glared at him. "Why?"

"He told me what happened with Investigations." He looked around. Enough people were present to screen them from Family Police. "Jason wants me to fix the records more, so Investigations believe your baby to be a clone. But I need to know what happened this afternoon."

Karla was silent, guilt and embarrassment evident in her manner. "Who else knows about me and Jason?" she asked, mindful of the encounter last night Jason had told her about.

"No one. And I won't tell anyone. I know you must be afraid."

Karla nodded and dropped her head. After a lengthy pause, she looked up, a little more trusting.

"When Investigations sent for me, I thought you must have told them. But they wanted to interview me for clone motherhood. Women in positions like mine are being included now. I had the medical examination and now they know I'm already pregnant. Everyone in Laboratories and Investigations are talking about it."

Benjamin cursed quietly to himself, his worst fears confirmed. "You're lucky they let you go. What are they doing about it?"

"I told them it's clone production. Investigations are very suspicious because they have no record of it. There is the case file though, so they accept for the moment there could have been a mistake. Enough doubt to let me go at least. They're investigating further."

"I don't think there's anything I can do," he concluded. "It's progressed too far."

"I don't know what will happen to me now." Karla sniffed back a tear.

Benjamin wished he could reassure her, but her prospects were not good. "Have hope," he said then moved away. Karla turned away as if he'd said nothing.

Benjamin returned to his bike. With darkness nearing, people were leaving the market in numbers, drifting down the road with their produce. Two officers were coming up the road. He watched them with growing concern as they turned in and began mingling, looking for someone. Soon they emerged with a woman, one on each side and slightly behind in standard formation. Karla!

The three figures moved away and headed towards the Clonesseum. Benjamin stood gazing after them, helpless. Being pregnant would not save her from a Prohyst. Compassion like that was never shown. He wondered what Jason would do now. Feeling powerless in the face of pending Family justice, he rode slowly home.

It was dark now. He slipped the bag of medical supplies inside his jacket and left the apartment. As he neared Brenda's, a patrol was passing, forcing him to continue past, wait in the shadows further on and return later. With caution, he made it inside without a problem. The scene was unchanged, the lamp's dim light holding the room in a state of suspension. He went to the bed and knelt beside Brenda. The bed stank; he would have to clean her and lay out fresh bedding.

Her face was more at peace now. Instead of the heavy sweating and delirious torment, only a light perspiration glistened on her brow. Her forehead was still warm, but with nothing like the raging temperature of before. The fever had broken. She was in a deep sleep, her breathing more regular.

He un-bandaged the wound; it appeared improved, no yellowness or oozing fluid, and no foul smell as far as he could tell amongst the other smells. A dried residue of red around the edges gave the wound a healthy colour. Benjamin reached in the bag for the small bottle and dropped more red fluid along the length of the wound. The evidence of steady recuperation was a great relief. The contents of the bottle, unknown to him, were working a heaven-sent miracle.

He washed the towels and refilled the glass and bowl. Gently, he undressed her and washed her body, then stripped the bed while she lay naked on top. It was hard work, slow work, but soon he had the bed re-covered and Brenda in clean underwear and dress he found in the wardrobe. Several times, she showed signs of vague awareness and Benjamin stopped to encourage her, but she was not yet ready to surface. When he was finished, he piled the soiled linen in a bag.

Carefully, he lifted her head, eased one of each tablet down her throat and trickled water between her lips. She began to stir. Her lips parted, helping the flow of water. Her head turned slightly towards him, her eyelids flickered then partly opened and her moist lips moved imperceptibly, a faint murmur escaping. It lasted a few moments only, then her eyelids closed and she fell back into sleep.

Encouraged, Benjamin laid her head back. He placed a damp towel across her forehead and retired to the chair. With a lot to think about, it was difficult to relax, but gradually sleep crept over him.

He shook himself awake. Brenda was in a deep sleep. Benjamin went to the small window and peered out. Gloomy darkness. He gave Brenda another round of treatment, left her with refilled bowl and glass and found a blanket, which he spread over her. He bent and kissed her lightly on the lips.

"I'll be back," he murmured. With a slight twinge of emotional pain, he headed into the night, to get ready for another encounter. An encounter with the past and long forgotten feelings.

Benjamin arrived back at his apartment just after 11.00 pm. He set the alarm for 2.00 am and lay on the bed.

The shrill buzz jangled him to consciousness. He groped across the room and turned off the alarm. With excited anticipation, he tidied himself and slipped out of the apartment.

His intention was to disappear around the end of the apartment block then make his way via the more secluded route. At such a late hour, walking towards town would be more difficult to explain than returning home from the Pro House. Before even reaching the corner of the building, however, a patrol was there; two officers walking straight towards him. As they came alongside, they beckoned him to stop. One shone a torch into his face and leered at him.

"Where are you going at this time of night?"

Benjamin thought quickly. "I was at the Pro House earlier. I left something there."

The officer's leer turned into an arrogant sneer as his upper lip curled. He played his torch up and down, resting the beam at a point below Benjamin's waist.

"I'm sure you did."

Both officers laughed, gaining pleasure out of maligning him.

"We're watching you," the second officer said, smirking. "The Pro House will soon be closed. Not much time to leave something else there."

They laughed again. Satisfied, they moved on.

The contact meant he had to walk into town now. Another patrol stopped him and accepted the same explanation. At the Clonesseum, an officer slumbering outside the entrance was the only nearby presence. He darted down the side of the building. Taking a familiar route through the trees and across the roads, he was soon at the gate in the Family fence.

Kelly was not there yet. The time was surely close to 3.00 am. He leaned against the fence and waited, watching the rippling movement of crops faintly outlined a short distance away. The cold night and eerie silence seemed to ridicule the idea that Kelly would appear through the gate. Doubts began eating at him.

A clicking noise made him jump. Then the gate was swinging open. He stepped back as a figure crept through from the other side. The faint light silhouetted the outline of a face and fringe of curly blonde hair, partly obscured by the upturned collar of a coat.

Benjamin came forward. "Hello, Kelly."

"Oh!" she uttered, momentarily startled.

With a relieved smile, she dropped a bundle of blankets and pillows on the ground and closed the gate. She moved closer to him. But self-doubt made her hesitate.

"Blankets," Benjamin said approvingly. "That's a good idea."

Her uncertainty eased, she broke into a broader smile. It touched his heart, as only Kelly could do. He took her hands in his, then she was in his arms, hugging him, gaining much-needed comfort. After a while, she drew back.

"Come on, Benjamin. It's cold."

Eagerly, she knelt and began spreading a blanket, laying it with two pillows against the fence. She sat, propping against the fence and pulling two more blankets over her outstretched legs. She looked up at him playfully. He settled beside her under the blankets.

Both relished the moment. A feeling of belonging was still there, unable to be erased by the passing years. The fundamental bond formed in early childhood was stronger than anything the Family could do.

"I never forgot you, Benjamin. I knew we'd see each other again one day."

Their eyes met. Her tears were of sorrow mixed with tentative hope, if only for the moment. Benjamin felt his heart swell. A natural inevitability was bringing them together. He put his arm around her shoulders and drew her close. Kelly rested her head against him and they lay quietly together.

He thought of the risk she was taking. "Your mother might wonder where you are. Will she miss you?"

Kelly hesitated. "I'm not sure. When I first started at the clinic, she was always awake when I came home, but I've been doing it for a while now and it doesn't worry her so much. Sometimes she's awake, sometimes not. It's a risk I have to take."

"She'd be upset if she knew."

Kelly nodded. "I don't care."

She smiled mischievously and snuggled closer, burying her face against his neck. Benjamin's heart fluttered as an excitement stirred inside him. He turned his head and kissed her lightly, then again, several times. She responded lovingly, trying to push through the tension persistent in her body. Their feelings flowed and their lips pressed together searchingly, more passionately. Benjamin's spirits soared. But unaccountably, the tension in Kelly heightened, until suddenly she pulled away as it escalated beyond tolerance.

"Oh!" she gasped frantically, catching her breath as her body stiffened and began to shake uncontrollably.

Benjamin was astounded. He held her gently and stroked her hair. The extraordinary reaction went on for some time, then gradually the panic began to ease and the violent shaking subsided. She clung to him, panting heavily.

"I'm sorry," she whispered, her voice quivering with fright. "I can't help it. It's always the same, whenever I get too close. I always think of what happened before."

Her bulging eyes, filled with emotional agony, pleaded with him. Benjamin was appalled. Her distress, the dreadful legacy of a violation imposed by a lawless age, had seethed untreated for sixteen years! How inadequate her self-centred mother was for the task of helping her. He held her tighter, comforting her, trying to ease the stress in her body. As she sobbed, he stroked her hair and gently wiped the tears from her smooth cheeks. Slowly, she regained control as her body relaxed a little more.

"Is this why you have no children or a Family Police partner?" he asked, remembering what she had said last night.

Kelly nodded. "My mother was determined to find the right partner for me. Three times she pushed me into a relationship and every time it failed. I could never respond properly. Whenever it came to making love, I'd get tense and frightened. I'd always think of the time I was attacked. Then I could do nothing."

Her voice tailed off haltingly as she struggled to contain her emotions.

"Wasn't there anybody who could help you?"

Kelly shook her head. "Mother only cares that I'm close to her and following the correct principles of the Family. When my relationships failed, I think she was secretly pleased. When the men were sent back, I was more dependent on her again."

Her mother's attitude hardly surprised him. "What about the men? How did they feel?"

Kelly grimaced as a bad memory returned. "The first was Omar."

"Omar!" The name struck him like an iron fist. "Why Omar?"

"He already knew me from school. Mother liked him at first. He's quiet but aggressive. He proved himself in the Family Police. But he got violent when I couldn't perform. Now mother hates him."

"Really!" In a moment of bitterness, Benjamin visualised a boy whose personality had been obscure at best, particularly in relation to Kelly.

"I know you never liked him," Kelly added, despondent. "But I had no choice. My mother decided."

"What happened after? Was he punished?"

"No. Other senior women like him, because of his effectiveness in enforcement. He's with someone else now. Mother resented the lack of support, even feeling the other women were scorning her. It affected her standing. She and Omar have stayed out of each other's way ever since."

"I see," Benjamin muttered, noting her mother's frailty as again a pertinent factor. "What about the other men?"

"I was even worse after that. The others didn't last long. They were relieved to be sent back without consequences. I know they make fun of me. They call me White Ice."

Benjamin was startled, recognising Jack's description in the recreation centre.

"What about now? Is there anyone?"

Kelly shook her head. "No. After the third time, mother gave up. I was appointed to the clinic through the night hours, since I don't have anyone to be with at night."

Benjamin understood her circumstances better now. But he knew Kelly could only break from her torment by finding the right feelings within herself, not due to pressure he might put on her. Had too much time passed them by? Entrenched in different worlds, he could do little to help. He needed to be positive, to divert their thoughts.

"What else do you do besides minding the clinic? What about during the day?"

"I sleep till late morning. Mother tries to involve me in Family activity and their plans for the future, but secretly I don't agree with it. No one has the right to do what they're doing. I have to listen though or she'll be upset with me."

Benjamin's mind focussed as he realised Kelly must have valuable knowledge of Family intentions and their ultimate vision. Her opposition to their beliefs spurred him on.

"What has your mother been telling you?" He felt they had re-established enough trust now for him to ask.

Kelly was thoughtful. "I'm not sure of the details. I don't listen that closely. But I know things are going on that are very frightening. There are regular meetings, always dominated by the senior women. They try to involve us younger ones, though. They're always thinking of the future."

"Do you go to the meetings?"

"Sometimes. When mother pushes me. I don't enjoy them. I haven't been to one for a while."

"What things are going on?" he asked, feeling on the brink of something momentous. "What are they planning for the future?"

Kelly reflected for a moment. "The manipulation of DNA has just begun," she went on. "You must have seen examples of it in Records already, but there's a lot more to come. They're constantly devising ways of producing better clones. There's no limit. I don't know the technicalities, only what mother tells me. Jason is at the forefront of it. He's always at the meetings."

Benjamin was intrigued, Jason's important role reaffirmed. And Jason was a man! How inconceivable he would create conditions that were making men redundant. Benjamin shook his head in amazement.

"They're doing other studies as well," Kelly continued. "Looking further ahead. Mother is very excited about it, but she hasn't told me much yet. Jason would know."

In his mind, Benjamin tried to rationalise what he knew, to formulate an overall picture. Kelly's inside knowledge was vital, but first he had to share his own with her. If they helped each other, the fight he had taken on might one day bring some reward.

"My position in Records gives me opportunity. I've found out a lot recently. And seen a lot, too." He told her everything he'd seen and heard. Some of the images in his mind again disturbed him.

Kelly gripped his hand and listened intently, nodding at things she already knew. However, the idea of clones supplying DNA, making men obsolete, surprised and concerned her.

"What can we do? Please, Benjamin, tell me how I can help." She looked into his eyes with conviction then buried her face against his neck again. He held her close. Her pledge strengthened his resolve. But his feelings were confused in another way, distracting him for a moment; what about Brenda?

"There's a lot I don't know yet," he admitted, re-focussing. "About the clones, for instance. What's the purpose of them? Such a powerful combat force, why?"

Kelly lifted her head quickly. "I know the answer to that. When they're ready, clones are shipped to China, to build up an army there as fast as clones can be produced. You said you saw some being loaded at the Training Centre. That's why Jason and Bernard instigated clone production in the first place. To counter the Germans. Jason knows what the Germans can do, already with a head start before he came here. I'm sure it's why he continues to do what he's doing."

"I see, I see," Benjamin murmured, nodding slowly, enthralled. "Of course, clone production is a fast way of replacing population. With clones made to order according to the DNA chosen, or manipulated, they're easily trained and have no emotional family ties that would impede or complicate their effectiveness. Jason knows the Germans would follow the ship he and Bernard left their nuclear devastated region in with other ships, to populate the habitable Asian region.

They could expand fast. Jason sees China as the only place from which to mount meaningful resistance, and quickly. There's been no evidence of significant survival in any other parts of the world."

The purpose of a combat force was clear now. It certainly explained Jason's motives. But it failed to justify oppression of the community, perpetrated in order to achieve the rest of the Family's evil system. Did Jason not care about that?

"I've been to the Training Centre," Kelly said. "With my mother when she had duties there. It's a busy place."

"Yes. There's a trade going on, goods and electric cars for clones. The centre is progressing with new construction. And the town here falls further into decay."

They fell silent, each contemplating where the years had brought them, their prospects as bleak as those of the town. They might steal moments together, but no future could come of it. Benjamin visualised the physical power of the clones he had witnessed, created to enhance a future only for the elite Family.

"I was amazed at how strong and developed the clones are," he observed, staring at the faint outline of the crop fields. "Even though the oldest can be no more than fourteen years."

"They're boosted artificially. With special growth hormones. As soon as they reach the centre, they're put on a treatment program to accelerate physical development."

"Really! I thought many looked older than fourteen. Now I know why. So they're all younger than they look, even the youngest. Wow! That means they can be trained harder and made ready sooner!"

"That's right. And there's more research going on too, at Laboratories."

"Yes, of course. I've seen it in the DNA lab."

He visualised the glass encasement with strips of material in green fluid and tubes attached. He wondered about the long-term effects of prolonged treatment. Surely interference with natural growth would have consequences; medical problems, premature ageing, excessive stress on organs and body functions? The Family wouldn't care, as long as the clones remained effective.

"They treat the clones as if they're not even human," he added. "Mechanical objects, manufactured by a laboratory process and indoctrinated for a single purpose. There's no love or emotion in them because the method of creation has no love or emotion."

"It's horrible, Benjamin. I can't understand it and I don't want to." Kelly tried to bury her face deeper into his neck.

"And what about the ones at that other place south of the Training Centre? The cruel torture inflicted on them is something I never expected to see."

The heinous degradation of the young clones there was still vivid in his mind; the ugly yellow blotches and bleeding scars on the tormented face of the one hurtling into the fence, all of them cannoning into each other in mindless oblivion. And the screaming. The incessant screaming that permeated the air; nothing could compare to the insane horror of that screaming. Kelly knew about it, but had not seen what Benjamin saw.

"It's ghastly," she agreed. "Experiments are done to find out what they can tolerate. They're exposed to radiation, chemical and biological agents. Their reactions are monitored. The idea is to manipulate DNA to create natural immunity in future clones."

"Right," Benjamin muttered, comprehending the perverted logic. "A combat force immune to these things would be a huge advantage."

The TrainB clones depicted more than anything the depth of Family ruthlessness. But the role of Jason was amazing. Being a man surely put him fundamentally at odds with Family ambition, yet his actions belied that.

"I don't understand why Jason helps perpetuate the system. The combat force could be done without oppressing the community."

"Jason is afraid of the Family women," Kelly answered, looking up at Benjamin. "He's even afraid of Suchee. She's one of the senior women. She has a lot of influence because she and Tylin have the contacts in China." She paused. "I'm afraid of the other women too. Sometimes even my mother," she added pensively.

Benjamin nodded slowly, understanding it now. "This is all about power. The Family women want their exclusive society, to dominate not only over men, who they blame for destruction of the world, but in other places too, starting in China. That's why they jumped at Jason's idea of a combat force through clone production. But for them, it's not only to counter the Germans. Clone production, with its natural subordination of men, is the chance to dominate absolutely. We see it already in the community here."

"And there's nothing Jason can do about that," Kelly affirmed.

"I wonder what they'd do if he suddenly refused to help any more."

"It'd be a setback, but only in time not principle. They've forced Jason to teach some of the women about his work. Without him, it would continue, although without his special expertise, of course. Jason knows he's not indispensable now. They could even punish him then force him to continue. And he's already seen what happened to Bernard."

Benjamin looked at her sharply. Bernard! Where was he? All their talk had been about Jason. And Jason had been alone in the recreation centre.

"What happened to Bernard?"

Kelly was quiet for several moments before answering. "Bernard is dead. They killed him. You've seen the third lab. Bernard set that up. He was working on a special cloning technique, producing just a body with no head or nervous system. Spare parts farming, he called it. But when the lab was ready, he hadn't quite perfected the process. His program was scrapped and they forced him to proceed using normal clone production. Bernard was very upset. There was a bad scene and they killed him."

Benjamin stared at her, stunned. It put Jason's position in a new light.

"Jason must have been devastated. They went through so much together."

"Yes, he was. He's been alienated from the Family ever since."

Suddenly he felt as though he knew Jason a lot better. They fell into silent contemplation. Kelly rested her head against him again, feeling comfortable. Sharing what she knew with him had greatly eased the tension in her body.

"What else can you tell me?" Benjamin asked.

"I know what's happened up till now, because Mother tells me, and from the meetings I've been to. But I don't know much about future plans. I could find out more, by attending the meetings again. There's one tomorrow afternoon. Do you think I should go?"

"Good idea!" Benjamin responded enthusiastically.

She lifted her head and smiled impishly then kissed him happily on the cheek.

"Then I will," she decided with sudden assurance. "And we can meet here tomorrow night at the same time. Can you come? I'll tell you everything that happens."

They chuckled together, both enjoying the prospect. Kelly felt some hope, with a positive action to think about.

Benjamin became more conscious of their surroundings. They had been sitting under the blankets talking for a considerable time. The crop fields were still faintly outlined, no sign of dawn yet. In their heightened state, they had barely noticed the biting cold.

"You'd better get back. Your mother might notice you're gone."

"Yes, you're right." Kelly looked worried again.

They stood and she wrapped up the blankets and pillows. They went to the gate.

"I might have trouble with my mother," she considered. "If I'm not here tomorrow night, it's because of that. So I'll come the next night, or the next. Every night!"

She kissed him and they hugged. She opened the gate and disappeared through. The gate clicked as she locked it behind her. He stared at it before eventually moving away.

He reached the far end of the fenced area and continued on, taking a wider arc than last time to avoid debris. Intercepting the narrow road, he swung left and made his way back. The effluent processing plant was in darkness. As before, the double doors were secured by heavy chain and lock, the low hum from inside betraying plant operation. He left it behind and headed for home.

Chapter 20

Another dreary morning passed, typified by Stephanie's lack of interest as Benjamin dropped completed case files in her In-tray and left. Lunchtime was a welcome relief.

In the cafeteria, Ralph attacked his food, eventually surfacing to look curiously at Benjamin. "Haven't seen you at the Pro House lately. Natalie was asking about you."

"I'll come again soon," Benjamin replied.

"I bet you will." Ralph laughed laconically, lacking his usual spark. "A new lady started. More variety." He sounded almost bored, distracted. He paused then leaned closer to Benjamin to speak what was really on his mind. "What else have you found out? About Laboratories?"

Benjamin hesitated, wary of Ralph's antagonistic attitude last time they discussed the subject. "Nothing more. It's hard to find anything out." He sat back in his chair.

"I don't like what you told me about getting DNA from clones. Why should they be used instead of the men here?" It was as if the idea somehow threatened his masculinity.

Benjamin cringed at the possibility of Ralph being too forthright and saying the wrong thing to someone.

"I don't think it means anything significant," he replied, trying to play it down.

Ralph pushed his tray away and stood, examining Benjamin for a long moment before leaving to resume work.

Benjamin noticed Karla sitting by herself on the other side of the cafeteria. Her back was to him. She looked a forlorn figure. He had no wish to approach, relieved just to note that her forced removal from the market late yesterday had not led to drastic consequences. Did that mean Investigations accepted a foul-up in the system or paperwork? Or were they still delving? Would Jason name him as the father? Convinced there was nothing more he could do, Benjamin resigned himself to a wait-and-see course of action.

Time passed slowly in Benjamin's office, when around late afternoon, a woman he had never seen before emerged from Stephanie's office and approached. She stood at his desk and peered down at him. She was middle-aged, dressed conservatively and not particularly attractive.

"I have taken over from Stephanie," she stated formally. "Everything you did for Stephanie you will now do for me. My name is Miriam."

Benjamin was astonished. What had happened to Stephanie, the only Head of Records he had known? Before he could ask questions, Miriam departed and returned to what used to be Stephanie's office.

* * *

A mood of quiet anticipation hung over the room as they settled into their seats. The last woman arrived and closed the door, shutting out the late afternoon light. The large room was part of a building commanding prominence in the Family area. The walls were painted light yellow, alleviating cement greyness, and were decorated with hanging adornments, but there were no windows. The artificial light was good. Floor coverings and a long, solid rectangular table in the centre of the room contributed to an air of prestige.

Along one side of the table sat thirteen Family women. Attired in sombre suits, they collectively presented a stern front of authority. In front of them, folders containing papers were like a neat row of tablemats. Facing them on the other side sat the three General Managers: Investigations, Assessments, Laboratories. Jason was also present, seated nearest the head of the table. Each had a similar folder in front of them. At the head, a stony-faced woman surveyed the scene before her. On her left, a woman held a pencil, poised ready to take notes on a pad.

At the far end of the room, women of all ages occupied chairs in rows facing the table. They waited and watched in silence. Kelly sat in the front row with a clear view of the active participants around the table. No men were present in the room apart from Jason.

Kelly was alert, but making a conscious effort to remain still in her chair so as not to attract the wrong kind of attention. She was determined to learn as much as possible this time. She stole a glance at her mother, who was seated just one up from the nearer end of the table in keeping with her relative standing. Not returning the look, the hard-set face and thinly pursed lips were typical signs her mother was upset. A blazing row had followed Kelly's eventual return from the clinic just before daybreak. Kelly's unconvincing explanation of falling asleep had not placated her mother's suspicions.

An atmosphere of tense expectancy prevailed throughout the room. The meeting was a monthly review and would be more detailed than other regular meetings. The stony-faced Head gave a barely perceptible nod to the first woman on her right.

"Cynthia," she uttered, her thin lips hardly moving.

"Thank you, Jean." Cynthia cast an austere look down the table. "The meeting will begin with a review of current matters. Donor and clone mother activity."

A woman three along from her, distinctive with a paucity of wispy white hair barely covering her scalp, fixed a gaze across the table. "GMI, I understand numbers are down this month," she asserted sourly.

The General Manager Investigations, a short, thin woman with hollow cheeks, looked uncomfortable. "Introduction of the Donor Assessment Form has slowed the choosing of donors," she responded, glancing pointedly at the GM Assessments next to her.

She opened her folder and began presenting a report detailing the number of cases processed, difficulties encountered and removals from the program. Several problems gave rise to incisive questioning of the GMI. Decisions were made, sometimes superseded by the

Family further along the chain of command, until endorsed by Jean. Two issues of a more serious nature were deferred to later in the meeting.

"The new form should improve efficiency from now on," the GMI concluded.

"Should?" the white-haired woman snapped. "We expect a higher percentage of perfection immediately. This has not been satisfactory."

She shifted her steely glare briefly to the GM Assessments then returned it to the former. "What about clone mother numbers?"

"We are identifying all women for clone motherhood now," the GMI replied hastily. "Even those with previous problems and in positions of authority. Diminishing numbers have contributed to the lower number of cases."

"It is too slow. Unsatisfactory. You will expedite the process, or there are others who can."

The GMI cringed, her downturned mouth accentuating the gaunt face.

"And this Karla Mason case yesterday," the white-haired woman demanded of her. "Why did Investigations select a woman who is already pregnant?"

A gasp of surprise sounded from women at the far end of the room.

"We will discuss that with deferred matters," Cynthia cut in, impatient. "And the problem with numbers in future planning. GML, your report."

Everyone's attention diverted to the GM Laboratories, sitting next to Jason. Her face was drained of colour, off-white patches shading parts of her skin. Her hollow eyes were those of a tired, listless woman, accentuating an impression of illness. She was always this way to some degree, but worse lately. With an effort, she lifted her plump body higher in the chair and set her mouth firmly.

"We have processed every case delivered from Investigations," she began tactfully.

She went on to report statistics, cases of interest, failures and any clone mothers no longer suitable or capable. The GML held the hushed audience captive for a considerable time, several times interrupted by Cynthia speaking harshly in reprimand, followed by strict instructions. One issue was deferred.

"Failures are foreseeable," Cynthia stated coldly at one point. "Here is a case of implantation failure in a woman never tried before. Why is that?"

"The woman never ovulated. Years ago, cases failed using such women."

"This is a waste! We do not want Laboratories run by someone unable to make proper use of resources. Continue."

The GML completed her report. "We are constantly trying to boost efficiency," she claimed in conclusion, breathing heavily after her exhaustive effort. "New developments will further improve this."

"DNA research and development. Yes." Cynthia glanced at Jason. "We will discuss this with future planning matters. Now, GMA."

The GM Assessments, a tall woman with jowl chin and thick, pouting lips, began delivering her report.

"TrainA clones represent 84% of cases coming to us, TrainB 6%, Dump 10%. Of the 84%, 10% are considered marginal, of the 6% TrainB, 4% are later dumped, of the ..."

"Stop!" From across the table, a woman distinguished by a set of square-rimmed glasses that appeared to dilate her pupils, glared at the GMA. "This is like last month. We expect your report to identify patterns, to establish the level of perfection reached. Your statistics do nothing."

The GMA's lips quivered. "We have discussed the choice of DNA with Investigations. Many times. Our statistics show some improvement, but problem clones still occur frequently." She went on to detail examples and answer questions regularly fired at her. Several times, the exchanges drew a defensive GMI into justifying her Department's methods. Heated exchanges flared between the two GMs, becoming irritating.

"Enough!" Cynthia put a sudden end to it, fixing a hard look at each GM in turn. "You will work together to improve clone outcomes. Next month, each of you will present a detailed report of every case processed in the last three months, complete with trends and future projections. You will provide full information or there will be severe consequences."

A deathly silence followed.

"The Training Centre," Cynthia declared, finally shifting her attention. She glanced at Suchee, seated next to her.

Suchee and Tylin were jointly in charge of the Training Centre. Their contacts in China gave them elevated status, which they coveted by controlling information about progress in China arriving with the ship. No one else was familiar with the Mandarin language. Their positions of seniority were incontestable.

Suchee cast a searching look down the table. A woman next to Marcia opened her folder and cleared her throat, then launched into a report covering the performance of the clones in their training, including statistics on age groups, their readiness for combat and compliance to discipline. She also covered the development of the centre itself.

"Three clones from the oldest age group had seizures and died," she reported.

A murmur of interest passed around the table, but no reaction from Suchee or Tylin.

"Is this because of the growth hormone?" another woman asked.

Attention focussed on Jason. He gave a brief description of the effects and possible stresses imposed on the body, and provided an update of the quest for more effective growth hormone through experimentation in the DNA lab.

The woman next to Marcia continued with an assessment of Family Police competence at the centre. "Two officers were identified as excessively influential with the clones, beyond normal controlling signals. They were returned here immediately. Even this month's Starter has been suspect."

"Yes." Suchee reacted for the first time. "Absolute control by the Family will be maintained. The Police administer day-to-day training, but no more. And next month, we must have the strongest, most dependable Starter available."

All in the room watched her with acute interest, aware of how important the issue was. The report ended with confirmation that a shipment of clones was ready for departure.

"I have been delayed today." Suchee gave Jason a fleeting look and her eyes narrowed. "Soon I will go there with my final instructions."

A brief lull was taken up by Tylin, who delivered her account of progress in China - short and deliberately unspecific, despite the keen attention of everyone in the room. After that was a report about the experimentation on clones at the compound south of the centre. Brief discussion followed and continuance agreed as nothing of note had developed since the last meeting.

In conclusion, Suchee peered down the table to a woman halfway along. "Martha, you will control the new team for next month at the centre, from the start of next week. The new Starter will be Omar Sharooq. He is the best of those we have had before."

Marcia glanced at Kelly, reacting with some pleasure at Omar's imminent removal to maximum distance from them. She failed to catch Kelly's eye.

Discipline and enforcement were next. A general discussion ensued, with no Family woman overly interested or specifically responsible - any would order instant punishment if appropriate. Suppression of the community, achieved long ago, was easy to maintain by the propagation of fear and normal punishment procedures, with Family Police incentive to perform still as strong as ever. Longer-term goals concerned them more now.

A woman detailed three Promart punishments for the month, two under the sex category the other under subversion. Only one Prohyst had been done, in line with a policy change last month connected to dwindling clone mother numbers. The number of violent deaths and suspect elements known to be forming at the Pro House came under brief scrutiny. The rate of decline of the community population attracted particular interest, reviewed as always in a favourable light apart from the problem of clone mother resources.

"Police attachments," Cynthia announced. "Jocelyn."

Sitting next to Martha, Jocelyn opened her folder and commenced an overview of Family Police movements for the month. Three attached officers, inadequate sexually, had been returned to the Police compound. Attachments begun since last month's review were analysed. Jocelyn then embarked on an in-depth assessment of unattached officer's speeches on stage each night in front of her and the two other overseers. Discussion followed, failures confirmed, new attachments decided.

That completed the agenda for current matters. Throughout, Kelly was determined to remember everything, although little new or unexpected had arisen. Pleasingly, the eligibility of unattached officers did not affect her as it used to. Smiling to herself, she savoured the wonderful contact with Benjamin. Correcting herself before her mother noticed, she concentrated on the meeting again.

Next was a return to deferred matters. The first two were resolved after lively exchanges. Then the Karla Mason case resurfaced. The white-haired woman glared across the table at the GMI.

"What's going on with this case? How did Karla come to be pregnant?"

A murmur rippled along the table. Jason squirmed uncomfortably in his seat. All eyes switched to the GMI. She puckered her lips, unnerved, her sunken cheeks drawing in even further. She gathered courage. "We have no record of her being a clone mother already. At first, we thought it must be through sex, not a clone. But then we were made aware of her case file, which appears to be in order. We are investigating further. If it's a failing in my department, then whoever is responsible will be identified."

Her words hung in the air and the tension mounted, her explanation obviously inadequate. Jason felt his stomach knotting up. He glanced furtively at a stoic GM Laboratories. The white-haired woman addressed her.

"What do you know about this?"

The GML had her position worked out. "We received the case file in the normal way," she replied, cleverly shifting the burden back on Investigations. "Karla was then processed."

"This girl works in Laboratories, does she not?"

"Yes. But all women are eligible now."

The white-haired woman stared penetratingly at her, suspicious. She returned her attention to the GMI. "What have you got to say about that?"

The GMI wriggled nervously in her seat. "We are investigating it. I will find out how decisions were made. Last evening, I discussed it with the Head of Records. Stephanie would not allow me to see her files and check Karla's approval. I'm not sure why she refused." She paused, gratified to have diverted suspicion to Stephanie. "We interviewed Karla again last evening, but did not learn anything more from her."

A tremulous silence followed as they reached an impasse. The white-haired woman continued to glare at the GMI then leaned forward threateningly. Her face hardened, but just as she opened her mouth to speak, another voice cut her off.

"I have handled the issue today."

All heads turned in surprise to look at Suchee. She offered not the slightest emotion. Her deadpan expression never changed. It matched the exact symmetry of her countenance. Straight black hair bordered a moon-shaped face, falling neatly down each side to just below the chin. Her narrow brown eyes peered cuttingly at Jason for a brief instant, then swivelled to take in the women around the table. Her commanding presence affected everyone, achieved through steadfast resolve rather than aggression. She spoke in a clipped monotone.

"Yes. I have talked to the Head of Records today. I am satisfied the fault is hers. She has been dealt with. There is nothing further to discuss. The meeting will resume with the next item."

A stunned silence held the room in suspense. No one would dare dispute Suchee's authority, regardless of how odd the situation and her treatment of it was. Jason was inwardly relieved, yet he knew her calculating mentality.

The meeting recovered direction. They handled the final deferred matter then moved on to future planning. Kelly shifted in her chair and sharpened her concentration.

Future planning was prominent in the interests of Marcia. She fixed her eyes on Jason, who was the focus of everyone's attention now, and spoke for the first time.

"I would like to know when we can expect better clone production through the manipulation of DNA."

Jason disliked having to justify progress on what was groundbreaking research. The Family did not appreciate the difficulty in assessing when a goal would be achieved or a breakthrough attained. They just expected answers. He paused before replying.

"So far, we've only tried crude combinations of DNA. Combining two samples. And one male-female case. We must confirm viability in principle before proceeding further."

"How long before we know these cases are successful?" Marcia pursued.

"Implantation in a clone mother has been successful in each case. But problems could occur through the pregnancy period, and we don't know what clone products, if any, will result at birth. In the meantime, we continue with the next stage. As we've discussed before, if we can identify how characteristics are represented in DNA, and isolate them individually, we can replace them with better examples from other samples."

"And through effective planning, we can expand the principle to perfect future clone production," Marcia concluded.

"Yes." Jason glanced along the line of Family women. Each was watching him intently, searching for any weakness.

At the far end of the room, Kelly was inwardly excited.

A woman next to Jocelyn joined in. "How is progress with this next stage?"

Jason was thoughtful. "There are different aspects to it. I've made strong progress in identifying physical characteristics. Body parts and organs are tangible, their origins in DNA easily identifiable. Replacement of physical characteristics will not be too difficult. A basic DNA sample, possessing as many desired characteristics as possible, would be used and specific characteristics for which a better example is available replaced, keeping the basic sample otherwise undisturbed."

The woman next to Jocelyn gave a quick nod. "This means we can proceed with male-female clones," she stated, impatient to pursue practical development.

"Yes. Hybrids." Jason squirmed. "One method uses a suitable male donor to provide the basic DNA, then specific female characteristics used in replacement, such as ovaries, uterus, breasts and so on. The other uses female basic DNA with male replacement."

"And either clone product will have male characteristics of greater strength and physical capability, but also capable of ovulating and being a clone mother."

"If it works," Jason agreed, with reservation.

The white-haired woman spoke again. "Can you guarantee such clones would be trainable to the same level as male clones at the Training Centre?"

"The male-based clone would be better for combat, but the female-based one would be more certain to ovulate. However, I cannot guarantee anything till we have actual results."

"But this is what we want," the white-haired woman responded, barely giving Jason time to finish. "One package clones. They must be physically capable of enhancing the combat force while able to be a clone mother at any time. This means greater efficiency in clone production. A recent case involved implanting a clone mother using her own DNA. And we know a clone can be a DNA donor. This means a hybrid, as you call it, could supply its own DNA to itself and reproduce itself. Is this correct?"

"In theory," Jason replied warily. "But we won't know for some time if hybrid clones can evolve to reproduce by using hybrid DNA directly, instead of requiring separate male and female DNA sources."

"We can test that," the white-haired woman replied coldly. "As soon as we have a hybrid clone. We can use its DNA to implant any clone mother and see if the same hybrid reproduces. We must proceed with both male-based and female-based types equally, to cover every contingency. You say male-based is better. Therefore, you must concentrate on achieving ovulation by that type. As soon as one is old enough, we can try it for clone motherhood. That is years away. Till then, we use separate male, female DNA with replacement. But eventually, hybrid clones will reproduce themselves self-sufficiently, with no input from other donors and clone mothers. This will be our future combat force."

A murmur of consent sounded around the table, followed by a few moments of silence. The woman next to Jocelyn spoke again.

"We must keep all options open. Normal clone production must continue at the maximum rate possible."

"Yes," the white-haired woman agreed. "This is why we started female cloning. To boost future clone mother numbers. As for DNA donors, we can use clones at any stage."

"We need to start a program for that," Cynthia added. "To coincide with our plans for the community."

At the head of the table, Jean made a rare entry to the regular workings of the meeting. "We will discuss that in Closed Session," she declared. "Move ahead."

Her word was final.

The white-haired woman moved to wrap up practicalities. "The co-ordinating Team will meet after Closed Session to set ratios and quantities of clone products for the next month," she concluded, glancing along the table at the woman with square-rimmed glasses, another next to her and the GM Investigations.

Jean nodded her approval.

The woman next to Jocelyn looked across the table at Jason and resumed. "We've discussed replacement of physical characteristics. What progress have you made with mental and spiritual?"

Jason shifted uncomfortably in his seat. "That's a lot more difficult. Mental characteristics are intangible. To identify the processes that generate the senses, feelings and emotions controlling us has mostly been an unrewarding exercise. The brain studies have been helpful, however, and I recently made a breakthrough. I've discovered how to recognise in the brain an emotion or thought process, by analysing electrical and chemical patterns. By identifying these individually, making them tangible, I can tag them to intangible activity like anger, pleasure, fear, confidence, jealousy, intelligence, every mental characteristic. The next step will be to recognise it all in DNA by linking to those tags. Then it will be possible to isolate and replace mental characteristics in DNA just like physical ones."

"This is vital in perfecting clone production," Cynthia reminded him. "We need to produce instinctively obedient, easily trained clones with the right attitude to perform as required. You must concentrate on these factors."

"How long before you perfect this replacement technique?" Marcia asked quickly, determined to be involved again.

"It's difficult to estimate," Jason replied. "There are many mental characteristics. It will take time to identify them all."

"And spiritual characteristics. What about those?"

"Yes," the woman with square-rimmed glasses added. "We want to know what makes every person different, the individuality, the spiritual identity that is never duplicated. The soul. These characteristics must be identifiable, just like others. This is important to us, as you know."

"This is much more difficult," Jason replied, trying to think of how to dilute their interest. "It's an unknown domain. I believe spiritual characteristics are unique to an individual. Because of this, they're not transferable through DNA, unlike physical and mental ones. And I believe the soul is assigned on a one-off basis."

"Your beliefs are not helpful. We know the idea is not to replace them with better examples from other DNA. The process involves direct transfer from subject to clone."

"And you have the process set up," Marcia interjected, looking penetratingly at Jason. "What progress have you made with the Memory Storage Project?"

Jason hesitated, his uncomfortableness clearly showing. "Finding a suitable subject has caused a delay. It must be someone with the right sort of memory, for when I check that it's intact after transfer to and from storage."

The woman with square-rimmed glasses leaned over the table, more intense. "You've been delaying the project because of your feelings about the effects on the subject."

"The process will be highly invasive," he admitted defensively. "Trauma could alter or even destroy the memory, making it a self-defeating exercise. If I could use a dead subject and re-stimulate the brain with electrical impulses, as I've done for the other brain studies, then this would be avoided."

"No. It must be done on a live subject because this will obviously be the case when the project is adopted." She adjusted her glasses and glanced along the table, seeking endorsement from the other women. A rumble of consent sounded amongst them in an unusually animated reaction, an indication of their personal stake in the project.

Jason tried once more to convince her. "I believe the process is so invasive it could kill the subject. The act of transferring memory might destroy the brain. It's inconceivable a memory could exist in separate places at the same time. I believe it cannot be copied, only removed, leaving behind an empty shell."

"It doesn't matter what you believe. This is why you must do the studies. You will refine the process till it is no longer invasive. You will transfer a memory without affecting the brain at all. We expect you to find a subject immediately and begin the project without further delay."

Her abrupt comments bore a note of finality. Jason looked shaken by the questioning and the decision handed down.

Unusually, Jean rose to her feet, instantly holding the attention of everyone in the room. She fixed a hard glare at the women gathered at the far end. A lengthy pause heightened the dramatic effect before she spoke. "This subject will remain secret from all in the community and all Family Police." She paused again to drive home the point, then resumed her seat as a deathly hush fell over the meeting. "Continue with further business," Jean ordered.

Martha raised one more issue. "Earlier we discussed the declining number of clone mothers. As well as starting female cloning, there's another way to help with this problem. Two years ago, we did a trial using growth hormone on a clone mother, to accelerate growth after implantation and reduce the pregnancy period. We could try this again."

A murmur arose amongst the women.

"Yes, I remember it," the white-haired woman responded. "It was a disastrous failure and never tried again. It was only experimentation, of no urgency."

Several others acknowledged their recollection of the horrific consequences. The clone mother had died in excruciating agony, her body ripped apart from within by out-of-control acceleration in growth of the clone baby. It had shocked even the most hardened of Family women at the time.

"Jason has informed us of the successful use of growth hormone on clones at the Training Centre," Martha pursued. "With his ongoing research, perhaps it would be more successful now. We could achieve faster turnaround time for clone mothers. I think we should try it again."

The idea was met with scepticism - the first sign of uncertainty in any of the business handled by the meeting.

"Jason could investigate it," the white-haired woman suggested eventually, not entirely convinced. "It would be useful if it worked, but we don't want to lose more clone mothers. Anyway, clone mothers will be plentiful once female cloning develops. And male-female hybrids will multiply themselves quickly once that's established further on."

"Jason, you will investigate the matter," Cynthia ordered finally.

The meeting came to an end, signalled by Jean who announced the commencement of Closed Session. The three general managers and Jason stood and left, followed by women from the end of the room, leaving just the senior women at the table to discuss further business in private. Marcia watched Kelly depart, the hard set to her face unchanged. Kelly glanced at her while trying to hide her excitement. Pacifying her mother was crucial to her chances of sneaking away to see Benjamin.

Outside, the night was well advanced. The meeting had been a long one. As the women dispersed, Kelly saw an opportunity while her mother was still occupied. She moved alongside Jason, who was walking slowly by himself, deep in thought.

"Jason. The meeting was interesting."

Jason was surprised. They stopped beneath a streetlight. "Do you think so? You're not usually interested in the meetings. Did your mother push you harder today?" He had sympathy for Kelly's situation with her mother.

"No," Kelly replied with a quick smile. "I wanted to attend today."

She rarely talked to Jason, although they had always got on amiably. She knew the other women rode him mercilessly, but she regarded him more as a possible father figure, except he was too remote for that to eventuate in reality.

Jason noticed the difference in her; there was a sparkle in her blue eyes. "I know what it is," he noted with amusement. "I remember you and Benjamin were together years ago. The other night at the clinic was special for you."

"Yes, it was," Kelly whispered, her eyes filling with tears. "I hope nothing happens to him."

"It would if your mother knew. The other night was the first I've seen of him also. I never go to Records. He knows how to handle himself. He'll be okay."

Kelly nodded, flashing another quick smile as her eyes sparkled again.

"Did you want to ask me something?" Jason asked.

"Yes, about the meeting. Where is clone production leading us, Jason?"

Jason turned his head away to stare past Kelly into space. He was silent for some time. "I used to know the answer to that," he replied at last. "Now, I'm not sure."

Kelly was pensive. "All the talk about replacing characteristics in DNA. And this Memory Storage Project, what does it mean? What's the purpose of it?"

"I'm sure your mother will tell you. She's particularly keen on this, especially the Memory Storage Project. If it happens, it could benefit Family women in ways you've never dreamed of. Or they think of it as a benefit. I'm not sure it would be."

Kelly was surprised at the depth of concern in him, unexpected considering how entrenched he was in his research. She opened her mouth to ask another question, but was suddenly interrupted as Suchee pushed between them. Closed Session was over. Suchee glared at Jason coldly. "I want to talk to you."

She ignored Kelly, moving away and expecting Jason to follow. They left Kelly to wait for her mother, and returned to their house in silence. In private now, Suchee turned on him with a look as hard as anything he had ever seen in her. It meant trouble.

"I know about you and Karla Mason," she declared incisively but without emotion.

"What!" Jason exclaimed, shocked. "What do you know?"

"I found out today. From the Head of Records."

Jason gaped at her, struggling for something to say.

Suchee continued. "Stephanie knew she was in trouble after discussing the problem with the GM Investigations last evening. She asked to see me today. She told me the truth, hoping I would treat her with favouritism for informing me." She let her words sink in, giving Jason time to feel as uncomfortable as possible.

"But at the meeting, you said you handled it," Jason replied, gaining a hold on himself. "You said you dealt with Stephanie, for not keeping the records properly."

A flicker at the corner of Suchee's mouth was the first hint of a smile. "Yes. I have dealt with Stephanie. She covered up in the records for your involvement with Karla Mason. I am not sure why but it does not matter. Stephanie has been punished. She is gone."

Jason felt a sinking sensation - disaster looming! Denying it was useless. He searched for some semblance of control.

"How do the other women feel about that?"

The corner of her mouth flickered again as a sinister gleam came into her eye. "Only I know the real reasons for her punishment. Only I know it is not a problem in the clone production system."

An awful silence followed, the gulf between them never wider than now. For the first time, alienation from her struck real fear into Jason. He waited for her to reveal what action she would take. Suchee moved slowly to one side, keeping her steely eyes fixed unwaveringly on his face, as if circling for the kill.

"What are you going to do?" he asked at last.

"No, it is what you are going to do." She paused, savouring what she was about to say. "You will terminate her pregnancy. Then you will implant her as a clone mother. The DNA donor will be me."

"What!" Jason cried with repulsion. "I can't do that!"

"Yes, you will. It is very suitable. You planted your seed inside her. Now I will plant my seed instead. Yes, it is very suitable. Karla's baby will be Chinese."

Jason reeled from her, horrified at the workings of her mind. "And if I refuse?"

Her eyes bored into him. "I am sure you know it is a better option for her, and for you also. After Prohyst, she will not have a baby or a clone. She will only have men at the Pro House. And after Promart, you will not be one of those men."

Jason felt sick, her words striking to his heart. He was trapped! He tried to calm himself, to think of a way out. Instead, he felt only dread.

"Why? Why do you want a clone of yourself?"

Again her mouth flickered as she relished her hold over him. "In the meeting, there was talk about the Memory Storage Project. You are to concentrate on this, refine it, perfect it. Now you will have more incentive to do so."

"Why?" The word almost choked him.

"First, you will work with my DNA sample. You will perfect it to my requirements, using the concept of replacing physical and mental characteristics. When Karla produces my clone, you will test it for perfection. You will work again with my DNA, achieving more perfection. You will implant Karla again and produce a better clone once more. The process will be repeated as many times as necessary, and until you have perfected the Memory Storage Project."

Jason was aghast. "That will take years!"

"It will take as long as you take. You will refine the Project till transfer of a memory to and from storage is a simple, no-risk process. You said in the meeting memory cannot be copied, only removed to leave the brain destroyed. You must overcome this so the brain is not destroyed. You will perfect the process until transfer of a stored memory to replace that of a clone, then back to original subject if required, can occur many times without damage to the memory or original subject. You will test the process using a suitable subject and a new clone, any clone. The tests will confirm the clone with transferred memory has the individuality, personal awareness and soul of the original subject. If not, you will continue till it does, using new subjects if necessary. When it can be said the clone is the original subject in a new body, only then is the Project perfected." She paused again.

Jason seized on an opportunity to refute her, his reservations about Family ambition unchanged despite her conviction. "I said at the meeting I believe the soul is assigned on a one-off basis. It cannot be transferred. Perhaps other characteristics as well, spiritual ones."

Suchee responded instantly, harshly. "I do not believe that. Everything is identifiable. Brain activity happens because of what is there. If it is there, it can be identified. What is the soul anyway? I remember weeks ago when a meeting first discussed this, you said memory gives people awareness of themselves. From birth or even before, we develop individuality from experiencing our environment. It is all stored as memory, always there, formulating us. This is what you told us. If memory contains spiritual characteristics like awareness and individuality, then of course the soul also. When a memory transfers to a clone, it will all transfer with it."

Jason shook his head, amazed at the obsessive hold the Project had on her. He knew he could not sway her - she had too much at stake, too much power over him. He felt compelled to try, however.

"Maybe some. But not the soul. I believe a spiritual source unknown to us assigns the soul. We cannot influence that. Perhaps the source regards clone production as fundamentally alien to humanity, and does not assign a soul to any clone."

For the first time, Suchee's hard resolve cracked. Her eyes darted from Jason's face for an instant, the corner of her mouth taking a minutely downward turn. A brief instant only. Her eyes narrowed again, returning to penetrate into Jason's as she wrested back control. A cold anger took over.

"I do not believe what you say. But it does not matter. When you transfer a memory to a clone, you will test everything. You will continue the process until I am satisfied with the results."

"And then?" Jason responded, gratified to note her brief moment of weakness.

Suchee allowed herself a half-smile of satisfaction. "Then, all will be ready for me to transfer to my new body. When the time is right. When I am older and weaker or near death, you will transfer my memory to the last clone produced from Karla - the best one, the one most perfected by replacement of physical and mental characteristics. I will begin a new life. I will be in a new, better version of my body and with all the knowledge and experience from my old life. And soul. I will be the first woman to achieve this."

The gleam in her eyes declared her naked ambition. He had to live with it every day, but could never shake it.

"What if something goes wrong? What if it doesn't work properly? What if you don't like your new clone body? Or there are problems with it? And if transfer is irreversible?"

"This is why you will test everything with other subjects first. You will perfect the transfer process so return to the original subject is assured if required." She was resolute, fixated on her vision.

Jason stared at her in disgust and said nothing.

"I have discussed everything with Tylin," Suchee went on. "You will do the same for her, using any clone mother. At all times, you will keep us briefed on all progress. We will know as much as yourself at all stages. When the time comes to transfer, Tylin will supervise for me and I for her. There will be no mistakes. Only Tylin knows of this, and of Karla. No one else will know."

Jason felt a sick despair, shamed by having ever become involved with her. And the terrible consequences for Karla! The pending loss of their baby was just the beginning. A quiet desperation overwhelmed him. He moved to the door, thinking only of drowning himself at the recreation centre. Suchee was speaking again.

"Wait. I have not finished. At the meeting, there was discussion about growth hormone. You are to try this again. You will use Karla. It will be suitable if Karla produces clones quickly. Yes, very suitable. Karla will be my vehicle for future life, just as she was your vehicle. Tomorrow, you will begin. You will terminate her pregnancy and I will be there to ensure it is done."

Jason pushed open the door and left.

Chapter 21

Benjamin put his hand to Brenda's forehead. It felt cool. She was no longer sweating and her face was at peace. Her breathing was shallow, but even and settled as she slept.

He treated the wound carefully. The glass of water on the floor was almost empty, indicating Brenda had woken and found it. Heartened, he refilled it then sat in the chair to wait.

At last, Brenda's eyelids fluttered and her lips puckered as she slowly surfaced. Benjamin leaned over the bed eagerly. Falteringly, she opened her eyes. They gradually focussed and she smiled faintly as she looked up at him.

"How do you feel?" he asked.

"Tired," she murmured. For some moments, she struggled to clear her head. "Have you been treating me?"

"I obtained medical supplies. There's a wound above your left knee, but it's healing now. You were in a high fever for days."

Her expression set grimly as the memory returned. "I was attacked by those two officers at the market. How many days have I been here?"

"I found you two nights ago. Sasha told me what happened."

"I'm thirsty."

Benjamin held the glass and supported her with his arm as she took in the water. She smiled weakly but with warmth, and tried to raise an arm towards him. He took her hand.

He refilled the glass and another container, enough to last her next day. In the larder, he found food. Brenda ate a little, her first for days. She lay back, exhausted by the effort.

"I need to sleep."

Benjamin leaned over and kissed her on the forehead, then lips. "I'll be back tomorrow evening."

She tried to respond but her eyelids dropped closed and she drifted into slumber.

He left the medical bag by the lamp stand and returned to his own apartment. After setting the alarm, he retired to the bed. His last thought was for Kelly at the Family meeting, which was probably over by now.

* * *

He leapt off the bed as the alarm sounded. Soon he was ready and on his way. Avoiding a patrol this time, he took the route behind debris piles and past the effluent plant to the Family area. Time passed slowly as he sat propped against the fence, watching the faint outline of the crop fields, listening for the gate to click open. He visualised Kelly's curly blonde hair waving gently in the cold night air and her enchanting smile.

The time slid by. Surely Kelly had left the clinic by now! He tried to push his doubts aside, but a sinking feeling grinding in the pit of his stomach became more persistent. Kelly was not coming. He waited longer. Finally, he left reluctantly and returned to his apartment, cursing Kelly's mother for her stifling possessiveness.

* * *

Next day, Benjamin went about his duties in a mood of frustration.

Miriam was little different from Stephanie, and they soon slipped into the same sort of uncommunicative relationship. When nothing more developed and no further contact with Jason occurred, he assumed Karla's problem had been resolved by Investigations accepting the explanation of a mix-up.

After dark, he tended to Brenda. Her condition was improving rapidly, the colour returning to her face. She sat up in bed, eating hungrily and drinking copious amounts of water. Her positive, mature demeanour quickly resurfaced, defying the circumstances.

Her leg needed time to strengthen. The wound would heal as an ugly wide scar. They shared moments of amusement as he helped her from the bed and she hopped to the bathroom. She listened intently to his alarming descriptions of the clones, the DNA and third labs, the Family Police compound, and Karla. The rapport between them continued to build. For her, he was the strong figure desperately missed since the crushing loss of her brother. For Benjamin, the heart-warming lift to his spirits was a rare gift after many years bereft of meaningful contact with a woman. An unwelcome feeling of guilt plagued him, however. He now had two women to think about, neither knowing about the other. He would have to be more honest with both at some stage.

Brenda fell asleep mid-evening. Although in need of sleep himself, he walked to the Pro House, the best chance of gaining inspiration until he could see Kelly again.

Ralph was at the bar, laughing and gesturing with the men there. Benjamin returned his wave as he joined Natalie's group.

He went with Janine to her room. She looked particularly sad and tired, as if something had upset her. As she sat on the edge of the bed, he noticed a dark swelling beneath one eye. She had tried to cover it by rubbing a light-coloured powder over.

"Are you okay?" he asked.

Janine began nodding her head then shook it instead. "No. It's that officer, the one who caused me to be here and visits me sometimes."

"Did he hit you?"

She nodded, instinctively lifting her hand to finger the swelling. "He's jealous. And frustrated because he can't get a Family woman. The shirt I gave you was his and he wants to know what I did with it. He thinks I gave it to another officer."

"I see," Benjamin murmured guiltily. "How often does he come here?"

"It's his turn on duty at the entrance door. So he's here every evening for a while, starting yesterday."

"Really. That must be hard."

"Yes. But I want you to have the shirt. At least you're trying to do something."

She dropped her head in quiet misery and they fell silent. She brightened a little when Benjamin told her of the Family Police gathering and officer's speech, and the action inside the recreation centre. They returned to the other women.

He went with Natalie to her room. She also looked more tired than last time, under strain, as though the continual degradation was breaking her down. He told her of the latest developments. Natalie was dismayed at the male-female hybrid case, agreeing it was undoubtedly just the beginning of endless possibilities to manipulate DNA.

"I had no idea of this when I was in Laboratories!"

"It's only very recent."

He told her of meeting Jason and events involving Karla. When he suggested Investigations seemed ready to accept Karla's pregnancy as a mishandled clone production case, she leaned forward with sudden intensity.

"No," she asserted bluntly, much to Benjamin's surprise.

She slipped off the bed and went to open the wardrobe. A figure stepped out from inside.

"Hello, Benjamin." A sullen Karla came forward.

Benjamin was astonished. "What happened?"

Karla sat on the bed beside Natalie. She looked pale and worried, but defiant. Benjamin could see how Jason had been drawn to her. No outward signs of her pregnancy were showing yet.

"Jason told me my baby must be terminated," Karla stated bitterly. "He said I'll be a clone mother, with that Suchee as DNA donor. I had to get away. I can trust only Natalie." She looked at her hands. "And you."

"What!" Benjamin exclaimed, bewildered. "They found out about your baby? How? And what's Suchee trying to do?"

"Stephanie was afraid of being exposed or blamed for the system breaking down, so she told Suchee the truth. Suchee told Tylin but no one else, and got rid of Stephanie. She wants everyone to think it was a fault in clone production procedures and that Stephanie has been punished for that."

"Really! Why?" He could now see the reason for Stephanie being replaced, but little else.

Karla's jaw was set. "The Family have a new scheme called the Memory Storage Project. Suchee wants to use me, secretly, to benefit herself through that. Otherwise it's a Prohyst."

The Memory Storage Project! Brenda had mentioned that, after overhearing the Family women castigating Jason for lack of progress on it. Suddenly, he felt daunted by it. To be the preferred punishment to a Prohyst gave it a fearsome aura.

"I've heard of the project, but I don't know what it is."

"Jason says the idea is to transfer a person's memory to storage outside the brain, then to a clone of that person. It's like starting another life in a new body but still being the same person as before. Because memory is what makes a person aware of who they are." She explained Suchee's obsessive ambition, as Jason had detailed it.

"Hell!" Benjamin stared at Karla, horrified and amazed.

What an incredible vision the Family had! Images of the DNA lab suddenly flooded his mind, of human brains on steel trays in a coolroom, and space to hang bodies on meat hooks. Equally as vivid was the image of two hemispheres with thin steel probes designed to penetrate the human brain. Evil and torturous, they would surely inflict great suffering on an unfortunate subject. Jason had not found one yet, but the equipment was ready for when he did! And the long-term implications - horrifying, not only for Karla.

"So Suchee wants to be first to achieve this, with only Tylin knowing. If successful, they could command the highest standing of all Family women, or so they think."

"They already hold high standing amongst the women. They want more, much more." Karla put her face in her hands. "I don't want to have her clone. I want to have my own baby. And it's repeatedly, not just once."

"Repeatedly?"

"I'll be a human incubator for all the trials it'll take to perfect her clone. I'll be forever with her clone in me!" She began to sob, quietly at first, then in a flood of emotion as the terrifying reality of her situation overcame her. Natalie clasped her hand, comforting her.

Benjamin felt powerless. Suchee would take retribution in the most personally satisfying way imaginable. He knew the work of the

Family had evil consequences. Was this to be the first full act of horror on another fellow human? The first of many? Perpetually producing and dumping clones, striving for ever greater perfection. And the Memory Storage Project - surely it would take years to perfect! He was aware of the two girls looking to him for hope. He stared at his own hands. They were empty.

"This Project will require many trials before a successful transfer of memory occurs. It'll be a long time before the process is proven and reliable. It's a highly dangerous concept, especially for the poor subjects chosen for testing. Jason will have to refine it until it's painless before Suchee subjects herself to it. Suchee will be impatient for results, but ultimately she can wait for as long as it takes."

"And what about me?!" Karla cried, sobbing again.

He had no answer. Natalie and Karla sat huddled together, both forlorn and frightened.

"What can we do?" Natalie asked.

Benjamin slowly shook his head. "Karla can't hide here for long. The Family Police will track her down, then we're all in trouble." He paused, as an idea formed. "Wait a minute. Only Suchee and Tylin know about this. The other Family women think your baby is a clone and the system broke down. If they found out Suchee is deceiving them, it could cause a serious split in the Family hierarchy."

"That's it!" Natalie was excited, a small ray of hope emerging. "But how would they find out?"

"I'm not sure, but I'll think of something. It has to be subtle, so they think they're finding out for themselves. Jason won't help. He's satisfying Suchee to protect himself."

"I can't trust him any more," Karla added, bitter again. "He's too close to the Family, always doing what they want. He doesn't know I'm here."

"The idea is very dangerous for you, though. If the Family finds out your baby is not a clone, they'll punish you by Prohyst."

"I can hide," she replied defiantly.

Benjamin nodded. "If it's done right, it could be a big opportunity. I'm certain one day the Family and clone production system will break down. It's fundamentally wrong. Maybe we can cause the beginnings of a crack, then anything might happen."

The prospect filled him with new intensity. A weakness in the Family set-up of any kind was unheard of. Suddenly he thought of a possibility - foolproof and courting little danger. But it involved someone he wanted no one else to know about, even the two girls.

"There is something that might work. I'll let you know what happens," he promised, finally offering the women a slither of hope.

Karla leaned forward. "Can you really do something?"

"I'll try," he reassured her, as he grasped her hands in his.

She gave a quick half-smile and they fell silent. Then a look of guilt came onto her face. "I'm sorry, what I did to you, before," she uttered, struggling to express herself. "The interrogation. I hope you don't hate me."

He was touched by the huge concession for her, and her genuine sincerity. No one had apologised to him that way before. In an instant, he saw good cause for Jason's attraction to her, which undoubtedly was more than surface-deep.

"I understand your reasons," he replied finally.

Heartened, he followed Natalie back to the main building. He spent time with Ralph then left the Pro House. On the way out, he glanced at the officer on entrance duty – a powerfully-built individual with a humourless, uncompromising look about him. Benjamin could easily imagine him treating Janine roughly. He walked home.

He managed a short sleep before the alarm once more sprung him, sending him off on another attempt to see Kelly. Again, she did not show.

* * *

Benjamin struggled to concentrate on case files. Morning dragged into afternoon. He expected another visit from Jason, who would surely be searching for Karla. How would Jason threaten him this time? Or would he merely rely on the Family Police to track her down? No doubt Suchee would have the pressure on. Time was against Karla. Her impulsive actions were a consequence of fear rather than logic. Fear even of Jason, who had failed to convince her that he cared. Ultimately, however, his entrapment by the Family would mean having to sacrifice her. Perhaps Karla realised that.

By finishing time, Jason had not appeared. Benjamin rode home. He spent the evening with Brenda. She could tentatively put weight on her left leg now and hobble about for short periods. After little sleep, he again waited for Kelly outside the gate, but for the third night running, she did not show. He wandered home, feeling more than the cold of night in his heart.

* * *

The next day was the same. Until he could meet Kelly again, there was little more to achieve or discover. Still Jason did not appear. Was Karla still hiding in Natalie's room? It seemed her best chance, but for how long? He decided to stay away from the Pro House, sensing his association with Karla would only lead to trouble. The only positive thought he had all day was at finishing time, with tomorrow being his day off.

After seeing Brenda, he returned to his apartment mid-evening. She was still sleeping a lot, conveniently; a guilty sentiment Benjamin felt ashamed of. He would have to tell her about Kelly some time. But for now, he welcomed the chance to catch sleep himself, wearied by the nightly vigil waiting in vain by the gate.

The alarm sounded. It was 2.00 am. He clambered to his feet and soon left the apartment, hopeful once more. At the gate, he waited propped against the fence, braving the cold and dark but with expectations not high. Suddenly, the sound he wanted to hear was there. The gate clicked open and a shadowy figure appeared from the other side.

Benjamin jumped to his feet. He caught a glimpse of a curly blonde head of hair as the gate closed with another click.

"Kelly!" He moved forward excitedly.

Kelly swung round, dropping the bundle of blankets and pillows to the ground.

"Oh, you're here!" she cried joyfully. She leapt into his arms, thrilled to embrace him again. Eagerly, she began arranging the blankets and pillows on the ground in the same way as last time. Soon they were side by side against the fence, blankets covering their outstretched legs. Kelly snuggled close, enjoying a rare sense of peace. The last few days had been particularly harrowing.

"Have you been here every night?" she asked, looking into his eyes appealingly.

"Yes," he replied, smiling with affection. "Are there problems with your mother?"

Kelly nodded. "Last time, she was awake when I got back. She was very angry. I told her I fell asleep at the clinic, but I don't think she believed me. Next night, she was there to take me home before I even finished. She's been waiting every night since. Only tonight she was asleep, so I had to come."

They chuckled together, each relishing the chance to steal time from their oppressive circumstances. Kelly rested her head against him as he held her.

"What happened at the meeting?" he asked.

"There's so much to tell you." She began describing the first part, concerning current matters. Benjamin listened keenly. He knew most of it already, but confirmation of how the Family maintained a dominating influence at the Training Centre was particularly interesting, especially the overall control by Suchee and Tylin.

Kelly remembered the case about mishandled documentation of a clone mother. "For some reason, Suchee dealt with the problem. Your Department Head, Stephanie, was to blame. She's been punished. Do you know about it?"

"It's Karla Mason. I know all about it. But there's more to it than that."

Kelly looked at him searchingly, impressed at his awareness. She had missed that. It strengthened her now though, resurrecting feelings long suppressed, even ones she believed were beyond her. She kissed him on the cheek.

"What else?" Benjamin asked, anxious to know everything.

Kelly continued. She described future planning - the manipulation of DNA by replacement of characteristics, the purpose intended for self-perpetuating male-female hybrid clones, the possibility of another trial using growth hormone.

Benjamin shook his head in amazement, at last gaining a clear picture of the Family's vision. He understood the methods now as well as the facts. How ideal it was for Suchee's secret intentions, using Karla's body repeatedly and indefinitely!

"This is far more advanced than the crude mixture of two samples tried so far. And mental characteristics as well as physical. Wow!"

"Jason has been doing studies on the brain to identify mental characteristics and learn how to isolate them in DNA."

"Really," he murmured. An image of human brains and steel hemispheres flashed through his mind again. "There's no end to what they can do."

He contemplated the implications. What adjustments would the Family consider suitable? The three GENERAL traits on Donor Assessment Forms - Loyalty and Obedience, Training Potential, Attitude Potential - all defined suitable mental characteristics, vital to producing clones gullible to indoctrination and motivated to perform. But would nature have the final say? Would there be reactions no one could ever predict? Humanity violated! Benjamin shuddered.

"There must be a big danger of weird distortions and deformities. A hybrid is a deformity in itself. What if a clone goes haywire mentally? Imagine the havoc if clones went berserk, behaving in ways never heard of. The Family is delving into something they have no knowledge of. They only have ambition."

"But they don't care." Kelly again felt acutely uncomfortable at being a part of them.

"That's right. Efficiency and domination are their goals. First here, next in China. A race against the Germans. Growth hormone can make it happen faster; make clones even stronger. But while they're doing it, what else is happening? Their actions are irreversible."

They fell silent, each reflecting on where life was heading. Isolated within her elite world, Kelly had never been excited by Family goals. Only now, with Benjamin's arm around her, did she feel a force igniting her. But it was stolen time, all too brief. She huddled closer, burying her face against his neck.

Benjamin turned his head and lightly kissed her. Kelly responded and they kissed several times. A warmth flowing through her body transmitted itself to him, stirring him deep inside, swelling his desire. He longed to carry it further. But he knew physical contact too intimate would cause her torment to resurface. He was content to enjoy their closeness as it was. And to share their knowledge.

Kelly resumed describing future planning. "They talked about spiritual characteristics as well. They want Jason to identify the cause of individuality, a person's awareness of who they are, even the soul. Apparently, these are in the memory." She mentioned the Memory Storage Project and the pressure Jason was under to find a suitable subject. "My mother is very excited about it, but she hasn't told me much yet."

"I know about it," Benjamin responded, remembering Karla's descriptions. "But the soul? I can't imagine even the Family believe they can influence that."

"They do. They believe nothing is impossible."

He shook his head in amazement. Transfer to a new, perfected clone was bizarre enough, but surely everyone's soul was unique! Yet the Family believed they could shift it around as a matter of convenience. He thought of his promise to Natalie and Karla.

"You mentioned the problem of Karla Mason. There's a good reason why Suchee stepped in to handle that." He explained how Karla's baby was a real one by Jason, how Suchee found out and what she intended, using Karla. Kelly stared at him, her eyes widening in dismay.

"None of the Family women know about that! If they knew, there'd be big trouble."

Benjamin felt encouraged. "That's what I was thinking. Suchee told only Tylin. They're deliberately deceiving the Family women. Suchee wants to be the first to benefit from the Memory Storage Project."

"That's unbelievable!" Kelly exclaimed, incredulous.

"Do you want to do something?"

"What can I do? Please tell me, Benjamin. I want to help."

He paused to reassess an action that could have dramatic consequences. His conviction for it was firm, however.

"Tell your mother. You say she's excited about this project. If she knew how Suchee was deceiving them, she'd tell other senior women and there'd be big trouble, as you say."

Kelly caught her breath, stunned by the proposition. Then her mouth creased into a mischievous smile as the idea took hold. A chance to strike a blow against the oppressive evil that trapped her.

"I'll do it!" she cried, and kissed him impulsively on the cheek.

"You must give no clue about how you found out. You can say you overheard Suchee and Tylin talking about it, with each other or with Jason."

"That's easy. I know how to handle my mother."

Benjamin felt pleased. The opportunity to use her mother's insecurity against the Family appealed to him. Could they etch a small crack in the Family's impregnable barrier of dominance? Catastrophic events often started from something small.

The consequences for Jason and Karla could be disastrous, of course. He had little sympathy for Jason, whose efforts were largely responsible for everyone's circumstances. But Karla was different, an innocent victim. Relief from Family despotism was at best a bleak expectation, let alone in time to save Karla. She had accepted the risk, but how long could she hide?

Kelly pressed her face against his neck again, wanting to be close, to give everything she could of herself. She wrapped her arm around his midriff.

Benjamin felt his excitement stir once more. Their faces were inches apart. He kissed her lightly then more firmly. She responded. Their kisses became more urgent, lasting longer, intensifying as a surge of passion carried them higher. He knew he must be sensitive to her, but his blood was pulsing through him in quickening waves, the desire for her building, the aching excitement arousing him further. Kelly felt his desire. She longed to give herself. But suddenly, she stiffened and broke away.

"Oh!" she gasped, catching her breath frantically.

Her body seized then began to shake cruelly. The old torment was invading her again, ripping at her heart with an awful sense of inadequacy and failure. She began to sob despairingly, the emotional agony overwhelming.

"I'm sorry," she whispered desperately, her voice quivering with fright.

"It's all right," he consoled. "I understand."

He held her close and stroked her hair, comforting her. He kissed her again, repeatedly, trying to draw her out, to wash away her pain. Her sobbing eased. Gradually, her body stopped shaking as she responded to him again. He brushed the side of her face lightly with his fingers and kissed her more firmly but gently. The tension in her body slowly subsided. They kissed for longer, more passionately. Kelly felt the invasion again, but this time she fought it, resisting the urge to pull away. Benjamin soothed her, aware not to push over the brink of her capability. But he wanted her like he wanted nothing else, and he could feel the desire was mutual.

They slid down to lie full-length under the blankets, their faces close, bodies pressed together. He caressed her. The turmoil raged inside her. She struggled against it, her body tensing and easing as the cruel cycle repeated. Gradually, it lessened in intensity as she worked it out of herself. Her confidence grew, her feelings for him gaining ascendancy.

They kissed again, a loving kiss. Benjamin's blood coursed hotly through his body, swelling him. He loosened the chord around her waist then slipped his hand inside her shirt. Her smooth skin was soft, sensual. His heightened excitement pushed against her. Kelly stiffened, but her passions were inflaming her, at last taking her beyond the torment suppressing her for too long. Suddenly, she broke clear of it.

"Please, Benjamin, please!" she gasped, a burning need driving her now.

She was frantic, kissing him, clawing at him. Benjamin slid his trousers off as Kelly did the same. Their legs entwined, her moist desire against his thigh. He rolled on top of her and slipped easily inside. Then he was pushing deeply, slowly. Her body writhed beneath his, frenzied as their passion swept them higher and higher. Suddenly she cried out, ecstatic as her body shuddered with a surge of pleasure that rose and flooded her from deep within. He felt the sensation of it, and his own pleasure as it gathered from every part of his body and exploded inside her. Their bodies were spent. The promise of bygone years was finally consummated, the warmth of it lying close in each other's arms.

They lay as one, clinging to each other in sublime fulfilment, their hearts beating furiously. Gradually they descended from climax, their breathing returning to normal as the passion subsided, wonderfully satisfied. He withdrew from her gently. He kissed her lovingly and looked into her eyes. Kelly's eyes sparkled, a huge burden lifted from her.

"I did it," she whispered blissfully. "I did it with you, Benjamin."

They chuckled quietly together, enjoying the afterglow. They slipped their clothes on and Kelly lay close against him, her head on his chest.

Benjamin was the first to become aware of their surroundings again. He had an uncomfortable feeling dawn was not far off. Lying inactive, the cold night air was biting, the blankets affording minimal protection. Kelly slumbered contentedly, hard against him, her arm slung across his chest. As he stirred, she pressed closer, tightening her arm.

"It'll soon be light," he said, concerned.

Kelly lifted her head. His face was inches away. "I'd better get back," she murmured, anxious now.

They scrambled to their feet and Kelly gathered the blankets and pillows.

"I'll come tomorrow night if mother is asleep. Can you come?"

Benjamin nodded with an amused smile. "I'll be here."

They kissed a final time, then Kelly opened the gate. With a lingering look at him, she passed through. The gate closed behind her.

He dragged his eyes away and started down the fenceline. At the far end, he paused. The approaching day was his day off. He was standing on the brink of a large expanse swallowed by blackness. Feeling buoyed, he moved away from the fence and angled to his right.

Chapter 22

He peered through the murky light. A short stretch away, small waves broke along the shore, a peaceful swishing sound repeating as each expended itself on the sand. As he watched, thoughts of Kelly swam in his heart. And thoughts of Brenda played through his mind.

Behind him, the town lights shimmered in the approaching dawn, giving a false impression of peace and tranquillity. Beyond, a faint ruddy glow had begun taking the edge off the black sky. How long had he been standing here?

Benjamin dropped to the ground as a moving light grabbed his attention. A row of headlights was moving slowly along the road from the direction of the Training Centre. He stared in surprise as they approached then stopped well short of town. Was it clones being brought for their training exercises? He remembered at the Training Centre, it was well into the day when he had observed clones being transported to this location.

He was on open ground; he had to hide. Before someone could spot him, he slid down the shallow bank to the sand and moved up the beach, staying as close as possible to the bank. The sand was soft and yielding, and tiring. To his right moved the huge expanse of open sea. Its vastness epitomised how alone and isolated their community was within the remnants of the world. He felt daunted. Despite the actions of people to devastate the environment, it was indestructible, adjusting at its own convenience, perhaps drastically for human and other life. Would human evolution adjust accordingly?

Estimating how far he'd travelled, Benjamin stopped and lay against the bank. He eased himself up on his stomach until he could peer over the top. The morning was light enough to see clearly now. The line of cars and trailers had not travelled far across an area of cleared ground.

Adjacent, clones stood stiffly to attention in rows. They wore their one-piece, full-length uniforms of light or dark grey. Their close-cropped haircuts, sameness of features and faces like expressionless masks were as if they'd been cloned from each other rather than different sources. Age was difficult to assess, obscured by the distorting effects of growth hormone, but the youngest seemed about eight.

Family Police, distinctive in their white shirts with red shoulder pads but comparatively few in number, stood around casually, thin canes and short whips at the ready. Several officers were setting up two parallel lines of dummies, about ten metres apart, down the cleared area. Each dummy, life-size with body and head shaped like a human, was held upright by steel frame driven into the ground. Eventually, the task was complete, the dummies covering a significant area of the open ground.

A pile of clubs, the same heavy weapons Benjamin had seen loaded on the ship at the Training Centre, was stacked neatly in front of the first line of clones. An officer standing next to them reached inside the box at his feet and withdrew a whistle. He blew a long, shrill blast.

"Ha!" The shout was instant, loud and in unison. From the front row, clones burst into action, each darting forward to grab a club then heading for the dummies.

A fierce assault followed, one clone to each dummy. With single-minded intent, they wielded the clubs with blinding speed and ferocity. In a blur of action, dummies' heads thrashed from side to side, the air continually resounding with deep thudding sounds. The size and weight of the clubs had no effect on the furious pace. Benjamin watched in awe. These were vicious creatures to be feared.

Officers regularly administered punishment to perceived under-performers. The smacking of canes and whips on their backs could easily be heard over the thudding of clubs. The clones, utterly focussed, were undeterred by the beatings.

The whistle blew again.

"Ha!" Instantly, the next clones charged forward as the first group ceased their onslaught and dashed from the area. The assault resumed, the thudding and smacking unrelenting, the focus extreme.

The exercise went on until every clone had performed his training. Several times, the thick leather of a dummy split open or the head was severed, causing its filling to burst out and over the ground. The clone would stop immediately and stand to attention, while an officer lifted the useless dummy off its steel frame and replaced it with another.

Finally, two blasts of the whistle. The last clones ran off to join the others standing in rows adjacent to the road, hands clasped behind their backs, faces unchanged despite the exertion. The clubs lay discarded on the ground, next to a pile of black jackets. An officer stepped past the first row and held his cane out at arm's length. The indicated clones moved forward and each put on a jacket. The jackets looked heavy, weighted in some way. Again, the whistle blew. The jacketed clones sprinted off, fanning out in different directions across country.

The starting officer held a stopwatch. After a time, he blew the whistle once more, pointing with a sweep of his arm towards the fleeing jacket-clad figures. The remaining clones took off after them. Officers used binoculars to follow performance widely spread over the flat, sparsely scrubbed terrain. It reminded Benjamin of the guerrilla-type operation he had observed from afar a week ago.

The Starter regularly checked his stopwatch. Some time later, a group of four clones returned with one of the jacket-clad prey. A steady stream of small groups soon followed, each escorting a jacketed clone. The Starter, his arm raised, eyes glued to the stopwatch, sounded a short blast on his whistle and dropped his arm.

Two groups returned after the whistle blast. The two jacketed clones from these groups, singled out as the fastest, were stood to one side, separated from the main body of clones who had again formed into rows.

The exercise resumed using new jacket wearers. And so it went on until all clones had worn a jacket.

As a final test, the accumulated group of fastest clones was now the quarry again, and pursuit restarted. The explosive speed never wavered, increasingly drawing on fitness and stamina from endless training. And, Benjamin suspected, hormone treatments. At last, the Family Police were satisfied.

The clones re-formed adjacent to the trailers, standing to attention with heads held high. Each gripped a rod, one end planted on the ground in front. At a sweep of an arm by a directing officer, they sprinted to the cleared area, where dummies and steel frames had been removed. Now the light uniformed faced the dark uniformed clones. The Starter returned the whistle and lifted a small object from the box in front of him. A loud shrill rang out. Benjamin recognised the sound from the Training Centre; the klaxon.

"Ha!" A new onslaught commenced. Clone versus clone, light against dark. Rods flashed with lightning speed, uniforms being ripped, splattered with blood as the maelstrom intensified.

A clone fell to his knees and took a blow across the head, quickly standing to resume the fight. But not before an officer struck him across the shoulders with his cane. It happened several times, whenever a clone was downed, ensuring there was no lessening of focus. Once again, Benjamin was horrified by the brutally violent spectacle, played out in a cacophonous clatter of clashing rods accompanied by smacking canes and whips.

The action gradually shifted towards Benjamin's hiding spot as the dark greys began to dominate. The Starter sounded the klaxon twice. Instantly, every clone stood to attention. Victory to the dark greys. Despite the cuts and abrasions and heavy sweating, all maintained an unwavering, expressionless countenance.

The directing officer pointed with his cane to the cars. The dark grey clones made their way there, the exercise over for them. For the others, it was a change of uniforms for half, the klaxon blared once and the battle started again in earnest. The spectacle was repeated until the officers were satisfied.

Finally, the klaxon sounded twice for the last time. Four losing clones were in a state of exhaustion, bloodied with their uniforms almost torn from their bodies. Yet they stood to attention, not a flicker of pain or emotion displayed on their battered faces. Officers moved in then. With their canes and whips, they thrashed the four losers until they fell to the ground, spent. The clones made no attempt to resist, totally submissive. When it was over, the officers hovered briefly then dragged them off to re-join the others. The harsh regime was in abeyance for now.

The officers cleaned up the area, packing the gear onto the trailers. The clones boarded. As silently as they had come, the cars and trailers headed back to the Training Centre.

Benjamin watched them disappear, mesmerised by the fearsome capability and harsh treatment he had witnessed. Each violent action started by the simplest of commands; one whistle or klaxon blast. Such speed of movement by the clones, fighting with such ferocity, stoppable only by two blasts. And the unresisted extreme control by the Family Police.

It was mid-afternoon. He slumped down the bank on his back and lay there, staring across the sand at the huge expanse of the sea. Musing and dozing, he waited for dark.

* * *

Benjamin woke with a start, shivering. Darkness was falling quickly. A flaming glow on the horizon was all that remained of the day. He headed back slowly to town, following the deserted beach. He thought of Brenda, who would be expecting him. He thought of Kelly. To deliberately deceive someone was not in his nature. Brenda would quickly detect any change in him, and she was steadily regaining strength. A physical involvement with both at the same time was unthinkable. Confused, he decided to postpone the problem by not seeing Brenda tonight.

The sky was black now, offering no comfort, an endless void. An impenetrable blanket. The lines of small waves guided him. As he reached closer to town, a diffused light began to expose the surroundings. He continued around the foreshore, skirting where the brightly lit Family Police compound threw a pool of light across the beach. The double-gated fence stood a little back from the bank. Soon he was opposite the Pro House. He scrambled up the bank. After brushing tell-tale sand from shoes and clothes, he walked purposefully to the entrance.

He waved to Ralph near the bar and joined Natalie, Janine, Patty and Ruth sitting at their usual table. He sensed tension in the girls, their sombre mood contrasting sharply with the social activity at the bar.

"Is there something wrong?" he asked Natalie.

She was on edge, her fingers fidgeting nervously, the lines on her face stretched taut with anxiety. Her wide-open eyes were fixed on the door to the back and the Family Police officer standing there impassively. She said nothing.

Patty broke the silence. "It's Family Police. They're out the back looking for someone."

He leaned close to Natalie, anxious. "Karla?"

Natalie nodded. "They've been before," she muttered, without shifting her gaze. "They look more determined this time. And more of them."

Around the main area, activity was no different from normal. Girls sat at tables and benches or leaned against a wall, waiting until a man approached. An uneasy awareness was evident, however. At the bar area, Ralph was enjoying himself in a group of mostly men. With no immediate likelihood of talking to Natalie or Janine in their rooms, Benjamin excused himself and joined him.

"Not going with one of the girls tonight?" Ralph greeted him with boyish enthusiasm.

Benjamin smiled. Ralph's preoccupation with sexual gratification was relentless. But although the environment he grew up in had moulded him, he was still young. Expectations of a meaningful relationship with a woman might yet develop in him, futile as that would be. Ralph took his silence as encouragement to pursue the subject.

"I had a good one tonight. That one over there."

He pointed past Natalie's table to an attractive but sullen girl leaning against the wall. The corners of her mouth trembled as she noticed them observing her, then she looked away in embarrassment. Ralph burst into laughter.

The noise level increased as a man took offence and shouted. More shouting followed, then more laughter. The ingredients for violence were thick in the air tonight.

"I need a drink," Benjamin said. He received a glass of rice wine from the bar. On return, he found Ralph had merged with others.

"Hello, Benjamin."

Standing at his shoulder was the girl Ralph had introduced the first time.

"Louise!"

"You remember my name." Her voice purred with obvious pleasure. She was looking him up and down. Then directly into his eyes, smiling flirtatiously, her body language encouraging closer contact. Her strong facial features, light brown short hair and penetrating brown eyes gave her a hard attractiveness.

Benjamin felt uncomfortable, looking to move away.

"Ralph tells me you're a man of action. What sort of action do you like?" Louise ran her hand down his chest.

Benjamin had no ready answer, affected by the double meaning in her question. He regarded her with reservation, put ill at ease by her lack of sincerity and artificial mannerisms.

"What has Ralph been telling you?" he asked warily, with a quick smile to hide his inner turmoil.

Louise hesitated then moved closer and nudged him, as if about to share a confidence. "He says you've been finding out things. Is it true about Laboratories manipulating DNA? Do the Family really want to use clones for DNA instead of men?"

Benjamin looked at her sharply as a feeling of dread came over him. He cursed himself for having told Ralph too much. Who else had he talked to in his exuberant way? He glanced at Ralph, who was laughing with another man as they watched him and Louise, seemingly congratulating himself on initiating a sexual liaison.

"I don't know what you mean," Benjamin murmured defensively, shuffling slightly away from Louise. "I think Ralph ..."

A hush suddenly descended around them, as if a switch had cut all lines of communication. Even Ralph changed, a look of dismay replacing the boyish grin as he stared past Benjamin. Others reacted similarly. The quiet was only momentary, overtaken by screams of anguish coming from the main area. Benjamin spun round, alarmed.

Family Police were pouring in from out the back. Two dragged a distraught woman across the floor, taking over the centre as others scattered. She was a mess, hair and clothes dishevelled and a look of terror on her face. She screamed again.

It was Karla!

The number of officers was unusually large. They quickly formed a ring to keep people back, scrutinising everyone menacingly. Long batons were poised ready to deal with trouble. The leading officer glared at Natalie's table and pointed with his baton.

"There!" he ordered in a harsh tone.

Officers charged forward. They cast the table aside, scattering the four girls to the floor.

"She's the one," the leading officer shouted, indicating Natalie. "Take her!"

Natalie squealed with fright. An officer jerked her to her feet by the arm then swung his baton, striking her flush across the cheekbone and sending her reeling in a shriek of terror. Another grabbed her and flung her across the floor into the centre, where she sprawled next to Karla.

Janine, after crashing to the floor with Natalie, staggered to her feet. "No! Leave her alone!"

A powerfully-built officer with a cruel face rushed at her. Janine's long-time tormentor.

"I told you before! You do what I tell you!"

He was out of control, driven insane by his blinding obsession for her. Fired by the action already, he raised his baton and struck her a full-blooded blow across the temple. The brutal force of it lifted her off the floor, then she plunged to the cement surface. Her head struck it with a resounding crack. Two officers threw her lifeless body into the centre with the others.

Patty and Ruth were more fortunate, thrown to the floor away from the others. With the focus on Natalie and Janine, they scrambled back and cowered with the other women. At the fall of Janine, men from the bar area began shouting and pressing forward, incensed. Mortified, Benjamin did the same.

"No! Stop!" he cried out.

He tried to push through. Suddenly Ralph shot past him, yelling in enraged wrath as he bullocked his way to the front. Louise charged forward, her shrill screech heard above others. The ring of officers responded, swinging their batons in a flurry of strikes, beating the men back.

The leading officer fixed his eyes on Ralph. "Him, too!" he ordered, pointing at him. "He's the one who's been talking!"

Family Police swarmed around Ralph, who immediately began kicking out. His uninhibited nature was now his downfall. Batons flashed and he crumpled to his knees, easily overpowered as the blows rained down on him. Officers dragged him to the centre of the room.

The place erupted then. The pressure was too great, the treatment of Ralph the final spark. Men surged forward and a terrifying burst of fury released from them. All the pent-up hatred and frustration of many years could no longer be suppressed, pouring forth now in crazed violence. The rage spread fast, threatening to engulf everyone. Petrified women desperately tried to escape. Family Police wielded their batons ferociously, sparing no one. Terror-stricken, people fought for their lives as the scene escalated quickly to a crescendo of screaming, smashing glass, crashing furniture and the thudding of batons on flesh.

Benjamin was caught in the middle. He fought with the others, anger fuelling him; hidden, dark anger. It bubbled up and out like the sea and he struck an officer as if all the evil had possessed him. Something struck his head, then struck him again, and again.

Chapter 23

A vague awareness came to him, a cold, wet sensation against his face. Benjamin tried to lift his head but couldn't. He groaned, remaining still. His eyes flickered and partially opened. Everything was a blur. The cause of the cold wetness was hard - a cement floor.

Something was close to his face, and it came into focus briefly. A foot. He pushed himself up on one elbow, fighting to rise above the pulsating headache and nausea squirming in his stomach. The reaction made him retch and he vomited down his chest. He took several deep steadying breaths to stop from throwing up again.

The foot belonged to a body sprawled unmoving on the floor. All around were more bodies, some stirring but most lying prone. The floor was littered with shattered glass, pools of water and blood. Broken tables and chairs were strewn everywhere.

Women were moving amongst the injured, assisting. A woman knelt in front of him and looked into his face.

"Benjamin, how are you?" Patty asked anxiously. "Can you stand up?"

He scrambled to his knees and tried to get up but instead hunched over, hands to his head in agony. A lump on each side left his fingers wet with sticky blood.

"What happened?" he croaked.

Patty soothed him. "It's all over now. Let me help you."

With a damp towel, she dabbed at the lumps on his head. Benjamin winced, the skin tender. He rose shakily to his feet and looked around. The Pro House women were doing their best to help men staggering about in recovery or those on the floor showing signs of life, including even some Family Police.

"Some of us escaped to our rooms before they closed the doors," Patty told him.

Their selfless compassion was a sobering contrast to the physical degradation many they now tended had imposed on them over the years. The most abused and desperate also the most caring and humane.

"Did they use smoke?" He detected a faint residual odour.

Patty nodded. "It soon put an end to the fighting."

He remembered the choking horror of it last time, bringing on a fresh wave of nausea. He steadied himself until it eased. A fearful anxiety gripped him.

"What about the others?"

Patty slowly shook her head and her eyes filled with tears. "The Family Police took them away when the violence broke out," she whispered. "I don't think Janine survived. I don't know what will happen to Natalie and Karla. And Ralph, too."

Words spoken to him fifteen years ago were hard in Benjamin's mind: 'No woman taken from here by Family Police has ever returned. There is no further use for a woman who fails here.' The words were now hard in the reality of his world. Would Karla be returned after a Prohyst? Or would Suchee succeed in using her for her vision? Where did Jason stand now?

"Ralph," he murmured bitterly. "Natalie."

The terrible finality of a Promart was too horrendous to contemplate for Ralph, still only nineteen. What interest would he have in life after that? Benjamin cursed in angry, helpless frustration.

Patty felt his pain. "Don't blame yourself, Benjamin. We all know you're trying to do something. It's our only hope for the future. We do what we can, whatever the risk."

Benjamin surveyed the lifeless bodies amongst the shattered debris, people who had tried to do what they could. "I must go," he responded, feeling an urge to move on.

With a look of reassurance from Patty, he departed. Outside, the first signs of dawn were showing. He walked slowly home.

The morning light was strong by the time he left the apartment, washed and change of clothes, feeling a little better after a cup of coffee. He rode to the Clonesseum.

Case files awaited him, as if nothing had happened. Still unwell, he struggled to complete them by lunchtime. In the cafeteria, he sat dejectedly picking at his lunch. No Ralph. For as long as he could remember, Ralph had always been there for lunch. He choked on his food. Spluttering, he coughed it up and pushed the plate away in disgust. He returned to the office and dropped wearily into his chair.

The enormity of what had happened suddenly hit him. In one devastating blow, he had lost Ralph, Natalie, Janine - most of the few people he had forged a meaningful rapport with, against the odds. Was it the destiny of anyone he came close to? Only Brenda was left, and Kelly for the fleeting moments she could steal away. There would not be many of those, her mother already suspicious. But then, there was no future with Brenda either, or anyone. The slim window of opportunity to cause destabilisation in the Family was a forlorn hope. But what else? Jason was no help. Was he an ally or an enemy? Certainly he could not be trusted. Benjamin stared blankly at the desktop, all the positive momentum gained over recent days evaporated.

He looked up in surprise as two security officers hovered menacingly over the desk.

"You are wanted at the main Laboratory," one informed him in a cold, gruff tone.

Words he had heard before! Fear clawed at his insides. The spectre of another torturous interrogation, implicit in the latent physical threat the officers posed, loomed large. Had his luck finally run out?

The officers escorted him to the main Laboratory. They passed the benches to reach the Interview room. A sense of pending doom strengthened as they entered and an officer on guard closed the door behind them.

Benjamin stood at the long table in the centre of the room, facing four people on the other side. The officers remained behind him, poised to administer physical persuasion if needed. Testimony to their effectiveness was the absence of equipment for torture. Ultimately, Promart and Prohyst deemed intermediate steps inefficient. The floor without coverings, grey walls devoid of decoration, room bare of contents other than the table and several chairs against one wall were horribly familiar.

The four people opposite were two Family women, the GM Laboratories and Jason. All glared at him, unnerving him further. The woman on Jason's right Benjamin recognised as Suchee, even though he had not seen her for many years. The other woman, tall with short hair framing a hard, humourless face was also vaguely reminiscent. Both wore dark, featureless suits buttoned to the chin.

Cynthia glanced behind and gave a quick nod. Two officers carried forward another person, his feet barely touching the floor. Benjamin stared at him, horrified.

Ralph was in a sorry state, his head lolling back and forth. His face was drained, as grey as the cement walls, his expression vacant as if the very life had been squeezed from him. Revealed, through a slit in the white, loose-fitting gown he wore, were bandages around his lower abdomen. He was stooped, in pain, his hands cradling the stricken part of his body below the waist.

Benjamin felt a boiling anger inside. He hated the Family now as never before. He glowered across the table, silently vowing to make them pay for their actions.

The two women were unmoved, their supremacy unable to be challenged. A Promart was close, but he felt defiant. They could destroy him physically but not totally.

Ralph was propped against the end of the table. Cynthia gestured towards him. "I believe you know this person."

Benjamin nodded. She was barely interested in his response.

"He was caught inciting subversive behaviour in others," she went on in a monotone. "We know you see much of him, every day in the cafeteria. We want to know what you talk about."

An implied accusation only. A small ray of hope glimmered for Benjamin. Perhaps they had no firm evidence of his involvement, other than by association.

"We talk about how the day is going. Ralph enjoys his work."

A look of scorn came onto Cynthia's face in the first sign of emotion. "Two girls at the Pro House have been behaving the same way. We've dealt with them. We know you spent time with them. We want to know who else you've been inciting to behave this way."

The glimmer of hope vanished. But they could do what they liked, he would not betray Brenda, the only one he had left!

"There's no one," he replied.

Cynthia signalled to the officers behind him. They gripped his arms, twisting them viciously behind his back. He cried out in pain as they forced him to his knees, one shoving a knee into his back and jerking his head back by the hair, forcing him to look up at the woman. Her scornful expression deepened to a pitiless contempt.

"We know you've been moving about town late at night and early morning. Who else?!"

A strangled yelp escaped his throat as the knee bored deeper into his back, his head and arms contorted further. Then a large hand cuffed him across the head, bringing on a blinding pain that speared through his brain. Again, the throbbing headache and a crippling wave of nausea hit him.

Cynthia glanced at Suchee, who spoke in a flat, clipped tone. "Perhaps you have been visiting your woman friend."

Benjamin stared at her helplessly, his worst fears striking at his heart. Then another blow around the head. His ears rang, his stomach churned. At a signal from Suchee, the officers lifted him. He wobbled on his feet, the room spinning. Suchee gestured to the guard, who left the room. All waited in silence. Soon two officers brought in a woman and stood her next to Benjamin. Then suddenly, his head cleared and his eyes widened in astonishment. It was not Brenda! Instead, Karla was beside him!

Karla looked pale, her face showing the strain. She glared at Jason in barely concealed accusation. Jason tried to remain impassive, but a small twitch pulled at the corner of his mouth. He jerked his head away guiltily.

Suchee took control. A gleam in her narrow eyes betrayed her relish for the circumstance. In a steely tone, she addressed a bewildered Benjamin.

"We know Karla's baby is yours. You tried to hide Karla at the Pro House with one of the girls. We found her. You tried to disguise her pregnancy as clone production by creating a case file through your position at Records. Stephanie has been punished for her part in it. Now you will be punished also."

Benjamin was appalled by her distorted view. Then, in a flash, he comprehended her. How insidiously clever she was! Of course, Karla's sudden disappearance and recapture threatened to alert the Family to the real truth. If Jason became known as the father, she would lose power over him and her evil ambitions would be exposed due to personal involvement. So she would nail someone else. Benjamin saw it clearly now.

Suchee's eyes bored into him, stamping her will. A slight flicker touched her lip momentarily, a rare sign of emotion. She glanced at Cynthia, who stood united with her, unknowingly confirming the success of her clever ploy. Now the Family would know about Karla's baby in a way that suited Suchee.

Benjamin stared at Jason, disgusted by his treacherous silence and collaboration with Suchee. What a shocking betrayal of poor Karla! Jason's mouth twitched again and he looked away quickly. Karla bowed her head in misery, devastated by Jason discarding her. She could say nothing - anyone would be believed before her.

Suchee let her words hang in the air before speaking again, her cold gaze once more fixed on Benjamin. "We have decided Karla's punishment. Her pregnancy will be terminated. Karla will be used to produce clones, experimental clones we are developing through DNA manipulation. And for growth hormone trials. We will learn much from Karla's body. It will be used for as long as it is capable. Jason, you will organise this."

She switched to Jason, nailing him with a meaningful look. Then to Karla briefly, despising her. Finally to Cynthia, who nodded her approval. Suchee felt immensely satisfied at establishing Karla's fate openly as suitable punishment. The secrecy of her own ambitions would now be easy to preserve, and personal retribution assured.

Benjamin watched her, amazed, as she fortified her position. He had no chance of influencing the outcome after being depicted as the father. All prospects were hopeless, including the ludicrous and now pointless notion he could somehow cause disunity within the Family through Kelly telling her mother the truth. He felt a desperate helplessness.

Suchee gave a nod and Karla was escorted out.

She addressed Benjamin again. "You will be punished now." Then, to the officers, "Take him to the operating theatre."

They began moving him away.

"Wait."

They stopped, and all turned to stare at Jason.

"I need him," Jason stated, suddenly forthright.

A stunned silence followed. A slim ray of hope sparked inside Benjamin.

"Why?" Suchee responded dispassionately. "What do you need him for?"

"For the project."

With others in the room, Jason refrained from fully naming it, but the women knew what he meant. A tense pause ensued, then Cynthia turned to the officers still propping up an ashen-faced Ralph at the end of the table.

"Take him away," she ordered.

They half-dragged, half-carried him to the door and departed, Ralph still clutching his midriff.

Cynthia dismissed the officers behind Benjamin, and the guard. "Wait outside the door," she told them.

Secrecy was secured. Any knowledge Benjamin gained would soon be rendered superfluous. She fixed a hard look at Jason. "You've done no tests for the project yet, on him or anyone else."

"That's right," Jason acknowledged, staying cool. "As you know, I've had difficulty finding the right subject."

Cynthia was contemptuous. "I know you've been deliberately delaying it, because of your feelings about the effects on the subject. We've warned you about that."

Jason remained composed, on familiar ground. His technical expertise was still beyond Family control, despite their efforts to make him less indispensable. "For the project to succeed, we need to be sure results are authentic and reliable. I must check the stored memory for distortion or loss in the course of transfer. The subject must be someone with as long a memory as possible of facts and experiences we can easily verify. That's why it's been difficult."

The women watched him closely, searching for a weakness in his explanation.

"What's that to do with him?" Cynthia's eyes flicked towards Benjamin.

"He's the best prospect I've found," Jason replied assuredly. "He's been in Records a long time. He has factual knowledge we can easily check from the records. No one else I know of has so much verifiable memory over such a long period of time."

Cynthia nodded imperceptibly. She turned to Suchee and they whispered for several moments. Cynthia addressed Jason again.

"You will use him for the project. However, he must be punished for inciting subversion and being the father of Karla's baby."

Benjamin's heart sank, his hopes dashed again. A Promart was certain, but would only be part of the punishment! An image in his mind of the fearsome steel hemispheres in the DNA lab brought on a fresh wave of panic, and he gaped at Jason, horrified. Jason's intervention had only worsened his plight.

Jason was unperturbed, shaking his head. "After a Promart, he will be of no use. It will change his characteristics. Test results would not be reliable. I would have to look for another subject. There is no one else this good."

The two women studied Jason at length, their hard faces revealing little. Again they whispered together, but only briefly.

"The three of you will remain as you are," Cynthia ordered, casting a look at the GM Laboratories, Jason and Benjamin in turn. She and Suchee left the room.

The tension eased immediately and an eerie silence descended. Jason and the GM, standing wide apart, looked straight ahead, ignoring Benjamin and each other. Benjamin was intrigued. The GM had contributed nothing. What sort of relationship did they have? Appearances suggested none at all, yet the nature of their work surely necessitated a closeness even the Family would not be privy to. Proof of that was in the cover-up over Karla. The GM had escaped being implicated. Was she just lucky? Benjamin looked at her curiously. Her face was deathly pale, worse than when he last saw her days ago. And she seemed unsteady on her feet.

The door opened. Cynthia and Suchee returned behind the table. They focussed on Benjamin, quietly scrutinising him for some moments, crushing him mentally. Eventually Cynthia spoke to Jason in harsh tones.

"Jason, you will use him for the Memory Storage Project. You will keep him locked up here. I remind you of how important this project is. You will begin in the morning as top priority, now that you have a suitable subject. And you will maintain secrecy."

A fateful silence followed. "I'll keep him locked in the DNA operating room," Jason concurred. "Then no one will see him."

"The General Manager will supervise the project. There will be no more --- delays."

She emphasised the final word, with a sardonic look at Jason. She glanced at the General Manager, who acknowledged her role with a quick nod. Finally, she turned to Benjamin.

"I'm sure Jason's concerns about the effects on a subject are well-founded. It will be suitable punishment for your behaviour."

A cold chill of fear made his skin crawl. What would Jason do to him? Could it be worse than a Promart?

The two women, satisfied, left the Interview room. Straight after, the two officers returned to resume their positions behind Benjamin. The GM Laboratories took control, heading for the door. Benjamin felt a jab from behind, and all followed her in silence, down the corridor to the DNA lab. Jason let them in. With a rough shove from an officer, Benjamin stumbled across the floor then inside the operating room. The door closed behind him. The last sound was the click of a key in the lock. He was alone in the pitch blackness.

He enjoyed a moment of relief as the immediate threat of more torment lapsed. But he knew it would be different in the morning. He bumped into the operating table and lay on it. A chance to rest his weary, aching body.

* * *

A light to his left gave him dim awareness of the room, reminding him of where he was. Instantly alert, he leapt off the operating table. Surely he had not slept till morning!

The light swung randomly then settled on him. A figure moved closer. Benjamin tensed, expecting trouble.

"It's me," a familiar voice sounded. "Jason."

Relieved but surprised, Benjamin peered at Jason's face outlined behind the beam of his torch. Jason swung the torch to indicate the external door in the back wall, open now. Darkness beyond signified that morning was some way off.

"It's best if you escape," Jason stated. "You don't want to be here in the morning."

Benjamin was confused, sensing a different Jason from the hostile one who had callously shifted the burden of guilt from himself. He stared at him, disbelieving.

"Why would you help me?"

"The project will be traumatic for the subject."

Benjamin was unconvinced Jason really cared about that. "I know about the Memory Storage Project. Karla told me what Suchee intends to do. That means pressure on you to advance the project. So why do you want me to escape?"

Jason paused before replying. "I used to be like you in my younger days. Determined to discover things and how to make a difference. I buried myself in research. Now, it's all different." He shook his head slowly in reflection. "Many people have been hurt. Karla says I should help you because you tried to help her. Karla means everything to me. Always my downfall, unable to resist a woman. Now she thinks I've abandoned her. Kelly told me to look after you. I respect her. She's different from the others. She's very lonely and thinks about you a lot."

He fell silent, an air of fateful resignation having replaced the tough image he normally presented. Benjamin studied the dim outline of his face, affected by the strangely profound atmosphere his mood created. He felt a new respect emerging, realising that Jason was hardly better off than other men - a lonely figure gaining solace with Karla, now pushed to the limit by her demise. But one question seemed irreconcilable.

"If Karla means everything to you, why don't you protect her and your baby? Suchee knows you're the father, but she names me to clear the way for her own ambitions. And you said nothing! Karla has good reason to feel you've abandoned her, and your baby. A real baby, not a copied one!"

A moment of bitterness overtook him as he spat out the last words.

Jason shook his head again. "No. Suchee is obsessed with her ambitions, unrealistic as some of them are. And personal revenge. Nothing will sway her. It's best this way. If the Family knows I'm the father, her secret plans will be foiled, sure. But Prohyst punishment will then follow for Karla. Nothing could be worse than a Prohyst. That's why I said nothing when Suchee named you as the father."

"And saved yourself from a Promart," Benjamin retorted, "at my expense."

"They intended punishing you anyway, for inciting subversion in others. And I knew I could give you an escape route."

Jason indicated the door in the back wall again. Benjamin contemplated his words and comprehended that perhaps Jason had attained the least disastrous outcome. Karla's punishment would be repetitive and indefinite, but not immediately destructive like a Prohyst. A small hope was always there that future events might turn and spare her further pain. Termination of her baby was unavoidable in any event. He felt the emerging respect for Jason strengthen.

Then another thought struck him. What if Kelly did what he asked and revealed the truth to her mother? Suchee already had her own solution accepted by others anyway. With little reward likely for the risk, the only consequences would be the worst possible for Karla! Benjamin cursed himself for having misread the situation. Was it already too late? He had to see Kelly!

"What time is it?" he asked Jason anxiously.

"About one o'clock."

Jason played the torch beam over the instrument trolley. He chose a solid, spear-like implement, then scratched marks around the door lock, pushed it in and twisted it until something crunched inside. He tested the handle - the lock was useless. He dropped the instrument on the floor with some others.

"Your escape will upset them. The Family Police will look for you. You'll have to hide."

Benjamin realised he would be an outcast, a fugitive to be hunted down and dealt with mercilessly. "I have nowhere to go, nowhere to hide."

"At least you're free."

They passed through to the outside landing and Jason pulled the door closed. A bag was on the landing. He handed it to Benjamin - a parcel of food. Benjamin departed, relieved to embrace freedom.

At the base of the steps, he hesitated then moved round the side of the building. A lone bike was still in a rack. He retrieved the Family Police shirt from the saddlebag and took a last lingering look at the faithful means of transport that had been a part of him for most of his life. But no longer. Despondent, he turned away.

He retraced his steps to the rear of the Clonesseum and swung down the track leading away. Taking a familiar route, he passed down the fenceline of the Family area, found the narrow road to the effluent processing plant and eventually arrived at his apartment without encountering a patrol.

He gathered some items - extra clothes, binoculars, full drink bottle. With the bag of food Jason had given him, he wrapped all inside two blankets. Then another thought. From the chest of drawers, he extricated a large folder with dark green cover. He had not looked at it for many years, but could hear his father's words vividly now – 'If anything happens to me and your mother, you must look after this book, keep it safe at all times.' Reverently, he dusted off the cover and stared at it, respecting the history preserved within. A priceless account of why he stood here today. He placed it with the other items and tied up the blankets.

He put on the Family Police shirt and his black jacket, the torch still there in a pocket. Sorrowfully, he looked around his apartment for the last time. Many years he had spent here. Although the drab, stark conditions had only worsened over time, it represented the main security in his life, his only haven from the callous, uncaring mentality endemic in all their lives. Now, he would be cast adrift without a firm base to sustain him.

The clock showed just after 2.00am. Benjamin moved to the door, lingered a moment longer then passed outside, the door bumping closed behind him with a sombre note of finality. Returning the way he had come, he reached the Family side gate, dropped the blanket-wrapped bundle on the ground and settled against the fence to wait. He listened anxiously for the gate to click open, visualising Kelly's curly blonde hair and smile, the memory of two nights ago exciting him. Their dedication to each other had never been in doubt.

Time passed slowly. A sinking disappointment gradually overtook him as he realised 3.00 am was well gone, and no sign of Kelly. Had she heard of him being interrogated and locked up? Or was it her mother again? Frustration set in and the disappointment deepened into a dismal depression.

He felt truly isolated now. No longer was he part of the community. Indifferent and uncaring as people were, he at least had been part of something. A feeling of rejection was common, but never as absolute as this. Being part of nothing was the most terrible feeling of all. Why did Kelly not come?

He barely noticed the cold, numbed by a state of desolation. With nowhere to go, he remained there, staring at the faint swaying outline of crops at the edge of darkness. All around was quiet.

Chapter 24

Benjamin struggled with his predicament, continually wiping tears from his eyes. The cold night, the dimly silhouetted crop fields, the gate in the fence he leaned against, all reminded him of why he was here. No Kelly. The depressing confirmation tormented him.

It started faint but easily discernible in the still night air, and grew steadily louder. A high-pitched whine. An electric car? Benjamin held his breath, alarmed. Someone was coming. Soon it pervaded the air all around in a frightening way. Surely too loud for one car! He stood and, with one eye, peered through the thin gap between gate and fence but could see only a narrow strip of road surface.

He had an idea. Grabbing the tied-up blankets, he took off along the fenceline. Soon he rounded the corner to reach the trees. He dropped the blankets, leapt for the lowest branch of a familiar tree and climbed to the branch he had sat on before. As the Family area came slowly into view over the fence, Benjamin was profoundly shocked by what he saw.

Lining up along the main road were many cars, each with a trailer. A bizarre stack of headlights stretched back to the open double gate at the far end, and beyond. More were arriving in the distance. Clones were disembarking and moving forward in regimented columns, forming up along the road from the near double gate. The numbers were far more than at any training

313

exercise. Benjamin's eyes widened in dismay as he noted the heavy clubs each carried.

A few Family Police, their red-padded white shirts standing out, milled around, herding the clones. They gave no instructions. An ominous silence was in place with all cars now stationary, broken only by the occasional smacking of a cane or whip. The operation was highly efficient, an air of controlled inevitability about it. An immensely significant event was under way.

The well-lit area contrasted starkly with the dark night outside, adding to the incongruity of the scene unfolding. Dawn could not be far off. Was the timing deliberate? A dreadful sense of foreboding gripped Benjamin, paralysing him into immobility on the tree branch. With horrifying clarity, he realised what the only purpose could be. Even as he watched, an officer opened the gates and the clones strode forward. The success of their actions was a programmed surety.

A desperate panic suddenly motivated Benjamin, as if releasing him from a trance. In a flash, he was down the tree. He snatched up the blankets and sprinted. Every moment passing was a vital moment lost! His heart raced as the adrenalin drove him down the fenceline.

"Brenda!" he gasped, frantic. "Brenda!"

She was the only one left. How he hated the Family! Every time they took someone from him, a piece of himself was ripped out, a part of his heart died. Natalie was gone, Janine, even Karla and Ralph. Benjamin was beyond tolerance, unable to endure losing someone more. Brenda! He must save her!

He ran hard, as never before. Past the corner of the fence and straight on. Where was the narrow road? His feet hit the hard surface and he flew, fixing his eyes on the distant town lights. The effluent plant was too far. He shot past it. Then the piles of debris, beyond them the apartment blocks. He sprinted through and slammed into an end wall, clawing along it in a frenzy. Gasping for breath, his chest heaving, he peered round the corner.

The main road was deserted. No patrol in sight. No sign of the clones yet either, just an eerie silence emphasising the town's vulnerability. Time was suspended, awaiting the onset of dramatic action. How far away were the clones, clutching their heavy clubs in combat mode?

The seconds ticked by. He had come one block too far. Panting hard, he took off again. Still no clones. At Brenda's apartment, he hammered on the door. The sound crashed through the silence but he ignored it. He threw open the door and rushed inside.

"Brenda!" he shouted, moving to the bed.

Brenda leapt in fright, her privacy invaded.

"Hurry!" he yelled at her, clutching her arm. "The clones are coming!"

"What?!" She scrambled out of bed awkwardly, suddenly wide awake. She had never seen Benjamin this way. "Coming where?"

"Down the road! There's no time. We must get out of here. Hurry!"

Motivated by his alarming urgency, she pulled on her clothes and threw a few items into a bag. Benjamin grabbed her hand and charged to the door. Every moment was precious. They dashed outside. The road was still deserted, but even as he scanned to their left, there was movement at the branch road intersection. The first clones were coming into view.

"Look!"

Brenda caught her breath, horror-struck. In panic, they swung right and ran. At the end of the apartment block, they dived round the corner. Out of sight, but had they been seen? Benjamin plunged ahead but Brenda stumbled and fell.

She cried out, clutching her left leg.

Benjamin stopped. He looked back at the road, fearful. The clones would soon be here! Surely they would overrun the apartments. They had to get away, to hide somewhere. He helped her to her feet.

"Can you still run?" He was frantic. Could he carry her?

She was breathing heavily, clasping her weak leg pushed too hard in a few violent minutes. Wincing with pain, she tried to continue. With his arm around her waist, they began a shuffling run. Mercifully, they passed the rear of the apartments, then between debris piles offering momentary shelter. They paused, both gulping in the air.

Benjamin looked around. No sign of dawn yet, but it must be close. To be out in the open would be suicidal at their slow pace. An image of clones sprinting to round up others flashed through his mind. When daylight broke, they would have no chance.

"This way!"

They resumed their shuffling run, moving behind the piles of debris. Past an apartment block, then the next. Brenda was staggering, exhausted, barely keeping her feet even with his help, but she drove herself. At last no more apartments. The road was in clear view between piles. They paused for breath. Suddenly, they were staring at each other, shocked by the shrill blast of a whistle piercing the air. A dreadful fear stabbed through Benjamin, his mind overwhelmed by the image of clones violently battering dummies.

Desperate now, he lifted Brenda and urged her on, past where the road began curving. They must hide! Would the clones come this far? They cannoned into debris, a hard, immovable object. He grabbed at it - a large drum. Drained, Brenda leaned against it while Benjamin cast around behind it for shelter. Suddenly he was ecstatic. Space was there! In a frenzied burst of energy, he pulled debris away, forming a place of refuge. The drum was the first of several in a line. Soon he had enough space for the two of them. He helped Brenda in and they crouched down, cowering in fright.

A length of twisted steel protruded from the debris. Brenda sat on it, taking the pressure off her leg. She bowed her head, exhausted by the huge effort, her shoulders heaving. Benjamin recovered quickly. Their frantic dash over, he became aware of action down the road.

Sounds of violence were clearly audible - smashing, shouting, screaming. Distant but unmistakable. Brenda heard it too, looking aghast at Benjamin. He peered over the drums cautiously. In the gloomy light, beginning to strengthen as dawn broke, he had a view straight down the road.

Clones were swarming everywhere, attacking the terror-stricken occupants of the apartments. Traumatised men ran aimlessly, no chance of withstanding the merciless onslaught. The emotionless, single-mindedly focussed clones struck them down, wielding their heavy clubs with flashing speed and ferocious intensity. They worked up the road systematically, bashing through doors to enter apartments, dragging out their targets, slaughtering them. Screams filled the air from crazed, defenceless people.

Cringing behind the drums, Benjamin and Brenda watched, horrified. The action came frighteningly close, taking on a shocking realism as terror became visible on people's faces.

"No, no!" Brenda cried in a desperate whisper.

A clone dragged a man from the last apartment. Panic-stricken, the man tried to run. Two clones wielded their bloodstained clubs, smashing at his head and body. His head burst open and he crumpled to the road surface, a pool of blood and brain fluid quickly spreading around him.

Some men made a bid to escape between apartment blocks, but were easily caught by the fleet-footed, well-practised clones. The bloodied light and dark grey figures performed with soulless efficiency, as if crushing a man's head to pulp was part of another training exercise. The road and surrounds became littered with bodies.

The gruesome carnage continued well into the morning, until the screams of terror were fading, finally the last of them dying away. Only the clones were left standing, yet still they assaulted the bodies where they lay, relentlessly following their indoctrination.

Then the signal came - two long blasts on the whistle. Instantaneously, all clones stood rigidly to attention. A sudden end to a hitherto unbroken frenzy. An unreal silence prevailed, accentuating the finality of the outcome.

A small group of red-padded white shirts appeared in the distance. Walking slowly and silently up the road, the officers issued directions by pointing with their batons to the apartments. The clones, clutching their heavy clubs, began moving, and soon all had disappeared, taking up occupancy inside. Satisfied, the officers departed down the branch road. A bizarre conclusion, it was the ultimate irony - clones supplanting the men they replicated.

No signs of life remained. An aura of evil settled over the scene like a cloak of damnation. A dramatic reversion to life had occurred through the actions of a single morning. The air was deathly still. Bodies strewn along the road were the only residual evidence of a town that had died, along with any hope for the future.

Benjamin stared at the sea of corpses, unable to comprehend the senselessness of it. Brenda shivered violently, her shaking hands clasped together over her open mouth, silently screaming with the victims. The raw power of the clones was horrific for her, seeing it for the first time.

Benjamin turned to her and they held each other. They sat on the twisted steel, his arms around her, she resting her head against him. Neither spoke.

Eventually Benjamin stirred. "Are you okay?"

Brenda nodded. Gradually, her body was relaxing. After what seemed a long time, she looked at him fondly.

"Three times you've saved me," she whispered. "I must be very lucky."

Benjamin felt lucky also. To survive was more than others had been allowed. To have Brenda beside him was a victory, fate failing to take from him this time. Mutual dependence, vital for them now, had been growing steadily since the strange encounter that had brought them together.

"It's not luck," he replied, remembering it. "When I fell off my bike, it was the first time anyone cared enough to help."

Brenda smiled, feeling strengthened.

Benjamin untied the blankets he had miraculously held on to in their dash for freedom. Too overwrought by events, neither could eat the food, but each took a long drink from the water bottle. The welcome relief almost transcended the desperateness of their situation.

They looked critically at their hiding-place. The narrow cleft scratched out from dirt and debris, with broken pieces of construction material jutting out in a tangled mess, was not fit to be in. But to them, it represented salvation. Benjamin brushed back a loose strand of her hair from across one eye, then wiped at the dirty marks on her face.

"I feel like part of the rubbish here," she responded.

"How does your leg feel?"

Brenda stood and slipped her trousers down to below the knee, revealing the wound. The flesh was red but healed over, with no signs of lingering infection. An ugly wide, slightly hollowed out scar was forming.

"It's healing well," he noted. "The muscles just need to strengthen."

"It'll carry me wherever we have to go. We can't stay here." She pulled up her trousers. "Oh!" she exclaimed, peering over the drums again.

Benjamin jumped to his feet. Electric cars were appearing from the branch road, stopping, and officers were throwing dead bodies onto the trailers. When full, they returned down the branch road. A cycle soon established as they worked their way methodically up the road. The final act in a gruesome massacre.

Benjamin and Brenda shrank back behind the drums, catching a glimpse of the last few bodies close by being flung on board a trailer, like hunks of meat. Finally, the last cars and trailers left. The road was empty, sullied with gory patterns of blood as the only evidence that life had ever been there. The clones continued to occupy the apartments unobtrusively, programmed to remain inside. A dreadful pall settled over the road.

"What are we going to do?" Brenda muttered, daunted by the terrible finality of it.

Benjamin was contemplating the same question. "We must stay out of town. The Family will think no one has survived, so they won't be looking for us. We must wait until dark."

Brenda nodded. "What about food and water?"

"I'll try to see Jason. I may have been wrong about him. He might help us."

On their makeshift seat, they settled down to rest and wait for darkness.

The first fading of light was not long in coming. They stood and peered over the drums. The road was deserted, the town enshrouded in a deathly quiet, no sign of the clones closeted inside the apartments.

"No one around," Brenda observed, anxious to leave their filthy, cramped hiding-place.

Benjamin wrapped their possessions and tied the blankets. Under cover of dark, they crept out and moved cautiously up the road. After passing the water treatment plant, they were swallowed by the blackness of night. Brenda limped along and they settled into a slow pace, concentrating on negotiating holes in the crumbling road surface.

Benjamin felt in his jacket pocket. He clicked on the torch, keeping his hand hooded over as he played the beam in front. Brenda murmured her approval. Regularly, he swung the beam to their right.

At last, there were no more debris piles. With greater concentration, he followed the road edge. Suddenly he stopped.

"Here it is."

Relieved, he shone the beam down the overgrown road leading off. Brenda was struggling with her leg now. He supported her with his arm and they picked their way unsteadily over the rough surface, which gradually steepened to a sharp decline. Finally, they reached the bottom and stood wearily at the entrance to Bunkertown.

They stepped through the yawning black hole, both in awe as Benjamin played the torch beam around. The steel portal frame, concrete door, rusty opening and closing mechanism - all decayed and useless, but offering a place of safety.

An eerie atmosphere closed around them as they shuffled further inside. Down one rock wall, the openings leading to the rooms beyond showed up. As they approached the far end of the cavern, the beam picked out the empty frames high up that used to be read-out screens. Beneath at floor level was the dais.

"Do you remember this place?"

Brenda smiled grimly. "Vaguely. I was only four at the time. Too young to understand what was happening, why we had to come here."

Vividly, he saw in his mind the image of carefree young children engrossed in a game of table hockey - himself and Kelly, and a little girl pulling at the hand of her older brother. Just a couple of corridors from where they stood now, but as far away as two opposite worlds from different ages.

"I remember seeing you then, with your brother Eric." The image took in another young boy. "Do you remember Omar? I hardly saw you after he made friends with Eric. What happened to your brother?"

Brenda bowed her head, a quivering sigh escaping her lips as bad memories flooded back. They hugged and she wept quietly on his shoulder. Benjamin felt her pain, reminding him of his own. She stepped back and wiped the tears from her eyes.

"Omar." She repeated the name bitterly. "Yes, I remember Omar. He was responsible for Eric's death."

"What!" He stared at her, aghast, as she told him about it. Her horrific experience added to his own bitterness as he reflected on

Omar's rise to success that Kelly had told him about. Thankfully, his attempt for a relationship with Kelly had failed.

Brenda put her hand to his cheek and looked into his eyes. "Eric was very much like you. Strong and positive. But unlike you, he didn't know when to be cautious. He paid the highest price for that. I had no one then. Our parents were killed when the Family first took control."

"I'm sorry." He held her hands and shared her grief. It was part of the bond between them.

"You told me about your mother and father," she went on. "Any brothers or sisters?"

"No, there was only me."

He realised he should tell her about Kelly. But after the events of today, he and Kelly were further apart than ever before. Almost certainly, he would never see her again.

"We both know what it means to be lonely," Brenda added. "But we have each other now. If we look after each other, we can survive."

Benjamin nodded, lifted by her strength and confidence.

He untied the blankets, placed the items on the dais, then spread the blankets with one end abutting, where the floor was driest away from damp rock walls. Conditions were dirty and it was cold, but they had shelter. Brenda stretched out, using her bag as a pillow, relieved to take the pressure off her aching leg.

"I feel tired." She closed her eyes and drifted to sleep without another word.

Benjamin sat on the dais, his mind still active. How ironic they would take refuge in Bunkertown - a place constructed to save people from destructive ambition. Yet those most resentful then, now had ambitions even more extreme. The conditions of terror were far worse this time. Had people, given another chance, learned nothing? Benjamin shook his head in disbelief.

What was it about human nature that drove people towards self-destruction? An ingredient inherently evil in the human psyche? Perhaps a naturally occurring insecurity, people competing for power as over-compensation for the fear of rejection? Power was the ultimate achievement - a negative fear rather than positive triumph? Surely not. It must be more simple. Like the buzz of adrenalin gained through being bad compared to the boring monotony of good.

Was that the all-important ingredient; adrenalin? He had no idea. He only knew it was of such immense influence that not even the near obliteration of humanity had done anything to improve the fundamental driving forces in people. The Family's ruthless quest for ultimate power was proof of that.

Benjamin played the torch beam around the huge cavern, realising how insignificant they were. Despite his efforts, they had no prospects, grateful merely to survive in the most decrepit circumstances imaginable. For how long? The futility of it all!

He shook himself. Brenda was with him – a wonderfully strong, determined woman. He studied her face, for now at peace as she slept soundly. He smiled with affection. No longer did he feel that dreadful loneliness pervading his entire existence. He gave silent thanks to the fate that had spared them.

He switched off the torch and slid off the dais to lie close beside her.

* * *

He woke slowly, aware of the cold, hard surface beneath him. He rolled onto his back. An amused Brenda, already sitting up with her back against the dais, looked down at him.

"At last. I was beginning to think you didn't want to face the day."

Benjamin smiled and eased himself up beside her. He looked around the huge cavern. The morning light, a square block of brightness filtering through the entrance at the other end, was providing a gloomy illumination. He had slept well.

"Would you blame me?" he responded.

In spite of their situation, each felt uplifted by the close presence of the other. The comfort of sleeping side by side, unrestricted, through a full night was an enriching experience.

Benjamin reached for the food parcel Jason had given him. They ate hungrily. Both needed a wash, and their clothes were filthy. He glanced at Brenda with amusement.

"We need water. Especially for your face."

They laughed. Brenda's even smile reached her deep, hazel eyes, lighting up her face despite its grubbiness. She was happy to be alive! The mention of water was a reminder of their circumstances. Benjamin stood and found the torch.

"We must look for anything useful in the rooms."

They started at the kitchen then explored the long communal dormitories, toilets and bathrooms.

"The Rest Cavern," Benjamin murmured as they passed through to the second large cavern.

He shone the beam at the thick glass wall of the laboratory - useless now, just as it largely had been during two years of entombment. They moved on, in and out of every room. The Games and Entertainment Centre brought back memories. And the Education, Medical and Maintenance Centres, the Control Centre still an open grave for corroded machinery too heavy to remove. For Benjamin, a journey of nostalgia. Brenda had vague recollections only, but appreciated the immense undertaking Bunkertown had been. Every room was a clammy crypt, housing no items of use.

Nearly back to the start, they entered the water treatment room. Benjamin flashed the torch at the water supply main, its control valve open, supplying town. Then the branch pipe, empty, its control valve closed. Gleefully, Brenda leapt on top of the pipe and grasped the valve wheel.

"Come on, let's open it!"

Benjamin jumped up and gripped the wheel from the other side. With all the strength they could muster, they tried to turn it. To begin with, it would not budge. Then suddenly, with greater effort, it gave slightly with a deep graunching sound. A splash of water sounded faintly from within.

Brenda danced up and down, waving her arms. "Water, water!"

Benjamin punched the air and they cheered with joy. They put their ears to the pipe, laughing, clapping their hands. A rare, precious moment. Their lives saved once more!

Their euphoria gave them added strength, and they opened the valve further. Water cascaded through, soon in a roar as the branch pipe and reticulation system began filling. Benjamin opened an air valve and they stood with eyes glued to the pipe, grinning and hugging each other. They returned to the cavern.

Excited, Brenda spread their meagre possessions on the dais. "We must work out what we need. This will be our new home!" Like an impressionable young girl, she spread her arms, embracing a place better than her decrepit apartment.

Benjamin laughed. "We need many things." He paused, thinking of more priorities. "I should take a look outside."

Brenda was momentarily concerned then nodded. "Good idea. But don't be long."

Taking the binoculars, he left the cavern. At the top of the slope, he dropped to hands and knees then crawled along the edge of the steep cutting, weaving between scrub tussocks. Keeping low, he passed the top of the vertical rock face and soon reached the highest point, where a low structure protruded above ground. Dome-shaped originally, it had been twisted grotesquely by extreme heat. Benjamin stared at it, the cruel image flashing through his mind of wildly fluctuating then blacked-out read-out screens. He slid away from the structure.

Propped on his elbows, he lifted the binoculars to his eyes. Separating him from the distant town was the treeless, scrubby, gently undulating terrain merging into a low spread-out sea of debris overgrown with tussocks. The line of pushed-up piles denoted where the road snaked towards him. No signs of life. He focussed on a route across country that would later lead him around the debris to the far end of town. With a sweep to his left, he picked up the road, which faded into the distance towards a small dot - the lookout post. He looked up at the diffused sun. Late morning. Keen to return to Brenda, he crawled back and descended the slope to the cavern.

Where was Brenda? The satisfying sound of water was still prominent. He moved towards it, then hesitated as he realised it was coming from a bathroom. Noticing a dull glow of illumination from inside, he passed through the entrance. Immediately, he caught his breath in a shallow gasp. The blood began coursing through his body in a hot flush of excitement. Brenda was standing beneath one of the showers in a strong flow of water, completely naked.

He stood transfixed by the sight of her magnificent body, seductive in the glow of the torch. The water was cascading over her head, plastering her hair back to below the shoulders as she smoothed it with both hands. The water flowed over her full breasts and curvaceous hips, running down her shapely legs to splash into a shallow pool in the sunken floor around her. Her body was firm, well proportioned. Her smooth, lightly browned skin glistened in the water to complete a picture of captivating sensuality.

He watched, in awe of her beauty, his heart pounding. The hot flush deepened to an aching desire, swelling him where the desire was strongest. She saw him then. With an alluring smile, she outstretched an arm towards him, inviting him. He shed his clothes and stepped under the bracing water. His arousal was obvious and she closed her hand around it, stroking it. She looked into his eyes, wildly capturing him with her excitement.

She washed the water over him, through his hair, over his shoulders and back. Her breasts brushed his chest and their thighs pressed together, his hardened desire pushing against her. The water lubricated them. He caressed her body, feeling her sensuous curves. Then she reached up, clasping him around the neck, and they kissed, a long, passionate kiss sending their emotions soaring. She leapt against him, wrapping her legs around his waist and he slipped easily inside her in a sensational moment of joy.

He pressed her to the rock face awash with flowing water, and their bodies were as one as they made love feverishly, giving to each other in a euphoria transcending all else. Higher and higher they climbed. As his fire gathered and burst forth to flood her depths with pulsating pleasure that racked his body, Brenda cried out, ecstatic, passion sending a powerful surge of pleasure sweeping through her body, possessing her. Their hearts beat furiously. Clinched tightly together, their bodies were spent.

Brenda unwrapped her legs and they stood in blissful peace, holding each other as the water engulfed them in their own world. Gradually, their heartbeats returned to normal, their desire fulfilled. Eventually, she released him and turned off the water.

"That was beautiful," she murmured.

They hurried back to the cavern with the torch and their clothes. Before the cold began to bite, they dried off and changed into other clothes each had scrambled from their apartments.

She began organising their dirty garments. Benjamin watched her, enchanted by her every move. Noticing his interest, her face lighted up with a broad smile.

"What did you see above ground?"

He came back to reality. "There's no one in sight. We'll be safe here. The Family are not interested in this place. I must go into town after dark and see Jason."

"Yes," Brenda agreed, but concerned. She moved to him and they hugged. "You must be careful. If they get you, then I die also."

They set about doing what they could to improve their future living conditions. Brenda washed their garments and draped them across the dais. The afternoon hours slipped by. When the light filtering through the entrance began to fade, Benjamin changed into the still damp Family Police shirt and put on his black jacket. They moved to the entrance.

"Please be careful," Brenda whispered anxiously.

They kissed and held each other. He smiled at her reassuringly then departed.

Chapter 25

As he crossed the road, not far from the Family area gate, awareness of change struck Benjamin. He was some way from town, but could feel the morbid atmosphere hanging over it like a pall of damnation. The quiet of the dark night was pervasive, everywhere deserted. He shivered, nerves taut, senses heightened by a weird feeling of being exposed through being alone.

He made his way to the rear of the Clonesseum. The place was quiet. Steeling himself, he climbed the steps and passed quickly to the door he had previously escaped by. The broken lock rattled slightly as he pushed the door open and closed it carefully behind him. A sliver of light showed beneath the door to the DNA lab. He felt his way past the operating table. The door was not locked. He opened it a crack and peered inside.

Jason was alone in the lab, standing at a workbench. He looked up, alarmed, as Benjamin entered.

"Benjamin!" He moved out from behind the bench and surveyed him in a curious but not particularly welcoming way. "What the hell are you doing here?"

Benjamin approached. "I want to talk to you."

They stared at each other for several tense moments, then Jason looked away, relenting. He went to the entrance door and locked it, then beckoned towards the internal corridor. Benjamin followed him past the lighted encasement, heavy coolroom door and hideous steel hemispheres, sobered by the thought of how close he came to being inside one of them. The door just within the corridor was to Jason's office, and soon they were seated on either side of a desk.

"You're taking a big risk coming back here," Jason commented, sitting stiffly in his chair.

He looked tired and worried, weighed down by burdens, responsible for the deeds that isolated him.

Benjamin opened his mouth to reply but instead caught his breath, his eyes widening as he stared past Jason to the far end of the room. A figure was rising from a bed, partly obscured by cabinets. He recognised the plump woman immediately. The GM Laboratories!

Stunned and fearful, Benjamin's first reaction was to jump up and run, but it was already too late as she had seen him. He sat glued to the chair, confused. Why did Jason bring him here, exposing him to her? What sort of relationship did they have? Surely not a physical one! He knew something bonded them, enough for the GM to cover up for Karla's baby.

The GM walked towards the desk, her eyes fixed on Benjamin. She said nothing. She looked different, more alive and healthy than Benjamin had seen her before. Her eyes were focussed, her thin-lipped mouth looked fuller with the usual hard set to it moderated. Most noticeably, there was more colour to her complexion. She glanced away and headed for the door. Jason followed her out, and they talked in a quiet murmur in the corridor.

Bewildered, Benjamin turned his attention to the bed. Next to it was a bench, making the small area seem suitable as living quarters. On the bench was a large glass jar, like those he had seen in the third laboratory, half-full of a red fluid - blood? A box, bunch of tubes and a few medical items were beside the jar. What had Jason done for her?

He turned back to Jason, who resumed his seat. "What's the GM going to do," he asked anxiously, "now that she's seen me?"

"She won't say anything."

Benjamin felt unconvinced, unsure of Jason despite his help two nights ago. He needed to find out where Jason's true allegiance lay. After so many years with the Family, why would it be different now?

"You've got some hold over her," Benjamin observed. "To make her cover up for you and Karla. Is it something to do with why she was here?"

Jason glanced at the set-up by the bed. "She needs me, or what I can do for her. She has ADS."

"What's that?"

"You don't know? Yes, I suppose you were too young. Anaemic Deficit Syndrome is a disease that arose early in the millennium. She told me her family ran a farm then, cultivating genetically modified food. The practice was discredited when ADS and other diseases were linked to structural distortion in some foods, but it was too late for many people. ADS attacks the blood. It's degenerative, taking years even to show up at all."

"Really! So that's what you're doing for her, treating her blood?"

"Not treating it, topping it up. Blood cells are killed off over time, until anaemia becomes critical. When I first knew the GM, it hardly affected her, but now it's at an advanced stage and she needs help regularly."

"I see." Benjamin now comprehended the remarkable change in her, from the unsteady deathly pale figure of two nights ago to the healthy woman he had just seen. "Where do you get the blood from? Surely not from donors?" He eyed the large jar on the bench.

Jason smiled with satisfaction. "No donors at all actually. I produce it from her DNA. I clone blood products by her for her. But I don't know how long she can last. She's hoping I'll perfect the Memory Storage Project before it's too late."

"But that's only for the Family women!"

Jason gave another quick smile, a glint in his eye. "The GM is hopeful."

Benjamin nodded slowly, contemplating her predicament. Her dependency on Jason gave him all the power he needed over her.

"Why did you come back here?" Jason asked after a lengthy silence.

Benjamin was reminded of yesterday's events and the part Jason had surely played, knowingly or otherwise. "Did you know what the clones were going to do?"

Jason turned more sombre. "No. The Family don't tell me everything. Some matters they discuss in closed session. I had an idea this could happen sometime, but there was no warning. How would I know? I'm only a man." He spoke in a resigned, slightly cynical tone but with genuine sincerity. Events were finally forcing him to face the naked reality of what his efforts had led to, pushing him towards crisis point.

Benjamin watched him, trying to assess the complexities of his mind. "You've helped them," he retorted incisively. "I know from Records what's going on. I know about the combat force and sending clones to China. I know about making them self-sufficient using their own DNA, and male-female hybrid clones. I saw it all in the case files, and I've found out what it's all about. You set everything up for them. Without you, none of this would have been possible. You must know what their plans are."

Jason looked impressed with Benjamin's knowledge, but in the end he shook his head. "It's true I wanted to create the combat force. The reasons for that were good, and still are. But I can do nothing about what else the Family wants to use clone production for. Some Family women have learned about the processes and techniques. They believe they're not far off getting rid of me if necessary."

"I understand that," Benjamin conceded. "But I also understand how clone production has made men redundant. So they eliminate us, because we're worthless. That's incredible. I never expected that, not even by the Family."

Jason nodded, genuinely troubled by what had happened. "What you say about self-sufficiency and hybrid clones is true, but a long way off. Women in the community will be needed for some years to come. Not so the men, however."

An image of clones single-mindedly slaughtering men was vivid in Benjamin's mind. "The clones behave the way they've been treated. As though they're not even human. Factory-made animals!"

"That's correct." Jason kept nodding his head slowly. "They're nothing more than human stock."

Benjamin finally realised it was pointless blaming Jason for everything. He was as trapped as himself when it came to taking action over events perpetrated by the Family. Personal loss had further alienated him.

"Did any men survive?" Benjamin asked.

"Not a one. They targeted everyone along the main road, leaving the women's areas untouched. They destroyed the Pro House too, killing everyone attached to it. There's no need for it any more."

Benjamin stared at him, the familiar hollow feeling of loss stabbing through his heart once more. Patty, Ruth and others. All dead, all gone. Could it get any worse?

"How did you survive?" Jason asked him.

Benjamin told him of his arrangement with Kelly, who had not shown, then of seeing the clones congregate inside the Family area, of fleeing from the apartments with Brenda and witnessing the massacre hidden in a pile of debris.

"You saw it?" Jason raised his eyebrows.

"We got out of town last night and found a safe place to stay. We need supplies. Can you help us?"

Jason gestured around the office. "I can give you what you need."

Benjamin glanced at the bed again and wondered if this was where Jason and Karla had carried on their affair.

"I stayed here for a short time," Jason mused, as if reading Benjamin's mind. "When Suchee and I fell out. It caused problems with the Family, so I had to move back."

Benjamin reflected on his own movements. "What did they say when they found me gone from here?"

"They were not pleased," Jason replied with amusement. "But they accepted you must have broken the lock yourself. They'd expect you've now been eliminated with all the men."

A pang of guilt struck Benjamin for a moment. He had saved himself, but not Ralph, Natalie and Janine, punished because of his influence on their behaviour. Perhaps even the disaster imposed by the clones as well! Had the Family reacted to an increase in subversive activity? Undoubtedly, they were planning to do it sometime, but a horrible sense of responsibility still overwhelmed him. He owed a debt. Frustrated, he had no idea what he could do.

"Kelly asked me about you," Jason offered. "She heard of your interrogation and detention, and escape. Last night, she was very upset after what the clones did, thinking you'd been killed. I didn't know what to tell her. She's a very lonely woman, Benjamin."

Benjamin dropped his head in exasperation. "It's better if Kelly thinks I was killed. There's no future for us. But don't tell her about

Brenda. I wouldn't upset her like that." He looked at his hands, as if they were responsible for the death of his friends. "What will happen now?" he murmured soberly.

Jason pondered the question. "The Family has taken a big step. The way ahead is easier for them now."

"The town is as dead as the people that were in it. The clones occupied all the apartments after they finished slaughtering everyone. Maybe the Family want to gloat. Clones taking over from the men they were created from. Disgusting!"

"More clones arrived this morning to join them," Jason added. "Every clone is here now, even the youngest."

"Really? What's the point of that?"

Jason looked away, staring past Benjamin into space. Benjamin was surprised, sensing he was loath to open up about some things. He had to penetrate the barrier, to target what was of irresistible interest before Jason ended their exchange.

"I know about DNA manipulation, replacing characteristics to perfect clones, and the Family's vision of perpetuating themselves using this Memory Storage Project. What other ambitions do they have? What other developments are possible?"

Jason looked at him sharply but said nothing, struggling. He drifted with his thoughts before eventually replying in subdued tones. "It's only the beginning. Anything is possible. As research leads to achievement, new opportunity unfolds. This is the nature of research. No one can know where it will lead. I only know that further awareness will generate further ambition. Nothing is more certain than that."

Benjamin's eyes widened at the clear implications. "This project, exploring the brain, transferring memory. Is this the new opportunity? If manipulation and replacement of DNA now, why not the brain and memory next?" He stared hard at Jason, trying to understand him, wanting to trust him. "This is all departing from how nature intends us to be. It's fundamentally evil!"

"I don't believe the project will work. It's too invasive, destructive to the brain. And I have grave misgivings about infusing a mature memory into a young clone's unprepared brain. I've told the Family this but they don't listen. 'Keep trying and testing until it works,' is their only answer."

"Are they searching for immortality? Repeatedly transferring, soul and all, to a new body, an improved clone, indefinitely? Knowledge and experience accumulating each time over successive lives. Is that what the project will give them? Everlasting life!"

"That is the idea. But I think it's likely a young clone will implode on itself, go haywire with the pressure forced on it. And I don't believe a soul is transferable. I believe a spiritual source assigns souls on a unique basis. I even suspect the source is not assigning souls to clones at all, perhaps treating clone production as alien to humanity."

"That's it!" Benjamin exclaimed. "Clones behave as though they have no soul. They're empty vessels." He shook his head slowly, appalled at his own realisation. The Family regarded the clones with callous detachment in supplying spare body parts, yet the greatest possible attachment for the transfer of memory concept. Clones were merely vehicles of convenience.

"At least if the concept doesn't work," he went on, "the Family will have no reason to produce clones of themselves, other than for spare parts, of course."

Jason looked vacant, his mind turning inwards, his eyes losing focus. "Have you ever known the Family to give up on anything?" he muttered.

"Is there more to it?" Benjamin sensed something in Jason's voice.

Eventually Jason surfaced but spoke quietly, as if to himself. "A subtle change in attitude is taking place in the Family. The senior women control everything, make all the decisions, indoctrinate the younger ones. But the younger ones represent the future, having sons and daughters with Family Police. The senior women are too old for that and wouldn't want the involvement anyway. Most have no family."

"But they're not too old to have a clone? Of course! Anyone can provide DNA and have a clone made, using a young clone mother." He stared at Jason. "Many left their families behind when we entered Bunkertown. Some were embittered, blaming and hating men for what they lost."

"Exactly," Jason replied, more attentive. "As some approach old age, they face the prospect of leaving nothing behind when they die. So they can have a clone. No involvement with a man. They know it'll be female, not a future man. A clone is like leaving themselves behind, perhaps even perfected by manipulating the DNA and replacement. And if the Memory Storage Project does work, they'll be ready to take advantage of that."

"I'm surprised they haven't done it before," Benjamin considered. "If they did it exclusively, they wouldn't need relationships with Family Police at all!"

"Early priorities were to set up systems, establish dominance and ensure perpetuation of the Family. And they've always had an 'I am unique, there is only one of me' mentality, regarding clone production with contempt in terms of status, a means to an end only. That's changing now, new developments bringing on exciting possibilities. Priorities change."

With a shudder, Benjamin realised the manipulation was not only of DNA but of humanity and the fabric of society itself. And for the older Family women, time was running out. "There must be conflict within the Family about this," he suggested, spurred by the possibility of a destabilising split, "with the younger women wanting sons and daughters normally. And the sons and daughters are growing up, too. They'll soon be of age to form relationships themselves and develop their own ideas."

A humourless smile touched Jason's lips briefly, but he made no reply, troubled again by deeper concerns. Benjamin knew the signs, realising there was a lot more to come out. How could he excise the demons from Jason?

"No," Jason replied eventually, with a grim look. "There is no conflict, nor will there ever be. The senior women will enforce their principles, to ensure the future can only be how they want it. The younger ones are just as determined to maintain Family dominance. They understand what they're told to understand."

"I see," Benjamin murmured. Yet he failed to comprehend Jason's unwavering conviction that it could never be different. Was there a deeper agenda? "The indoctrination process must be very effective."

Jason nodded. "It is. But that is nature's way." He drifted again as he said it, as if afraid to face something.

"Nature's way?" Benjamin queried, puzzled. "What do you mean?"

Jason hesitated. When he spoke, he was philosophical. "Indoctrination is a natural process, even when it's deliberate. The effects can be greater than expected, unknowingly so. Any influence exerting pressure over a period of time invariably forces change in favour of that influence. It's a brainwashing effect. Clone production has done this, exploiting the Family's resentment of men. The way the Family women look, dress and behave - they've no interest in being feminine or attractive. The brainwashing destroys sex drive because clone production supersedes sex." Jason gave a quick smirk, indicating what he thought of them on that score.

Benjamin felt awed by the forces at work. "That must be a big factor in changing those priorities, building clone production to be the preferred method. If the younger women can't resist it, what does that mean for the future evolution of humanity?"

"Good question. What does it mean?" Jason paused. "Evolution, like the brainwashing process, is relentless, but only offers evidence of itself over a long period of time. Action and reaction. Clone production, the action, is unnatural. Consequences are therefore unnatural, for us. But in evolutionary terms, any change is natural." He reflected on his words for a few moments, then with a deep sigh continued. "Sex, the most basic of instinctual desires and made pleasurable to ensure we reproduce ourselves, will become obsolete, since the cloning process needs no physical interaction between man and woman. So nature will phase it out through evolution. That's the reaction, all powerful. The human body will change, sexual organs reducing in size and effectiveness until they are useless. Already, after only fifteen years, we see the beginnings of change in the Family women. And in the role of men?" He shrugged his shoulders. "Evolution will always make the final decisions."

"Men are not needed at all!" Benjamin concluded. "Cloning only needs DNA, not male sperm. Female DNA to reproduce females. A world without men!" He stared at Jason, daunted by the trend, one that had accelerated dramatically yesterday!

"Exactly," Jason muttered, intensely preoccupied now.

Benjamin sensed another revelation. "Is there more?"

Jason rubbed his eyes wearily. An ominous silence followed, lasting a considerable time before he finally responded. "Yes, there is more. About the cloning process." He hesitated again. "The first clone, more than thirty years ago, was a sheep. Dolly, they called it. Within two years, tests showed that Dolly was ageing more rapidly than normal sheep. Bernard and I were in Germany then. Our research confirmed that any clone product would seek to attain the age of the DNA cells from which it was cloned. The older the DNA donor, the more accelerated the ageing. Soon after, another research team solved the problem in a group of monkeys, actually reversing the trend to establish the potential for longer life than normal. Everyone was excited about the possibilities then. But when human cloning began later, it wasn't the same. It was like Dolly. The principles applied to the monkeys did not work with humans. No medical reason was found to explain it. Then events moved quickly and the emphasis shifted from research to production. The problem was still unresolved when we left Germany."

"Accelerated ageing!" Benjamin uttered, flabbergasted. Part of what Jason said struck a chord, reminding him of a conversation with Natalie. "No medical reason. Could the reason be non-medical? Spiritual?"

Jason looked at him sharply. "Yes. That's something I've thought about a lot. Nature's way again. Perhaps this is the penalty, the reaction. Perhaps the same reaction is why clones are not assigned souls. Is cloning acceptable for animals but not humans? There are many questions I have no answers for."

"What does it mean? For the future of clone production and the clones alive now? What do the Family women think about it?"

"Every clone is deteriorating, becoming old before its time. A few deaths have occurred recently at the Training Centre, I believe due to this. Growth hormone accelerates it further. The Family don't know. I've never told them. They think the deaths and evidence of ageing are due to the growth hormone or overtraining. They don't care. The number lost is not many so far. But the oldest clones are only fourteen. The problem will worsen rapidly."

"You never told them!" Benjamin exclaimed. "Why not?"

Jason suddenly looked very old, his face drawn. He rubbed his eyes again, leaving them red-rimmed as he re-focussed on Benjamin. "In the beginning, the Family were frantic to start clone production.

Bernard and I were very positive about creating the combat force, too. Problems like this had no impact then. I pushed it to one side, telling myself I could resume research on it later. When later came, it was too late, everything too advanced. So I didn't tell them."

Benjamin shook his head with amazement. There was a weakness and it had come from the Family's own strength. The entire concept of clone production was fatally flawed! "But they'll have to know sometime!"

"There's no time left to research a solution, even if there is a medical reason. That's what happens when implementation proceeds before problem solving. When ambition overrides pragmatism."

"And the Memory Storage Project," Benjamin added, suddenly realising what the Family women were letting themselves in for, especially Suchee.

"Exactly. Everlasting life? What a joke! Even if the project succeeds, which I doubt, a Family woman will use it when she's old. Accelerated ageing in the clone she transfers to will be rapid. And if done repeatedly, the effect will be worse and worse, the original donor age carrying over, older each time. It's like problems with in-breeding, only much worse. The two clones produced from clones' DNA a year ago are only three months old, but already show signs of faster ageing than in other clones. It will be a diminishing, shortening spiral until eventually …." Jason left the obvious conclusion unfinished.

Benjamin continued to stare at him, horrified. "You must tell them! You can't rely on the project failing. And you said the older Family women will establish having children by cloning regardless. If a world without men eventuates, humanity will be doomed! When the diminishing spiral becomes too short, there'll be no way back without men. Don't you see what this means? Men are essential to life after all. If clone production is discredited, a return to normal life will follow. You must tell them!" He became agitated as he spoke, more so with Jason continually shaking his head in rebuttal.

"No point," Jason replied grimly. "It'll make no difference. The Family will force me to research the problem until I develop a solution. Just like transferring the soul, they believe nothing is beyond manipulation. Basically, they're right, given time."

"You're afraid to tell them," Benjamin pursued. "They could give you a Promart and still force you to do the work."

"They could. But ultimately, the result will be the same whether I tell them or not. The Family will only give up if I can't research a solution before the spiral becomes too short, as you say."

"Are you working on it?"

"No."

"Why not?!" Benjamin glared at him, dumbfounded by his callous disregard for the consequences of inaction. But how ludicrous was the circumstance they had reached - now advocating solving a problem that would enhance clone production at the expense of men, because the alternative was even more horrific!

Jason made no reply. He sat studying Benjamin, appraising him once more. Benjamin found it disconcerting. He tried to think positively.

"The Family have taken a big step eliminating men in the community. If we don't destroy the clone production system, it will destroy humanity. What can we do?"

Jason shook his head ruefully. "I could smash the equipment, but it would make no difference. Others know the procedures and would start up again, without me."

"Then we must destroy the Family." It sounded wildly ridiculous even as he said it. "What about the unattached Family Police? Many of them are frustrated and resentful. They could overpower the attached ones and Family women."

"No chance," Jason refuted. "They're not organised for that. They compete for favour. Something monumental would have to happen to unite them for that sort of action. They're afraid, too, after yesterday. I've never known the recreation centre to be as quiet and tense as it was last night."

Reluctantly, Benjamin had to agree. Even the remote chance of a split within the Family seemed inconsequential in the context of what would need to happen. With a sigh of exasperation, he gave up wrestling with it all. He thought of Brenda.

"I'd better go," he murmured. "Can you give us supplies? Food and bedding?"

Jason went to the far end of the office. He rolled up the light mattress and blankets from the bed, wrapped a waterproof sheet around and tied it with light rope. From a larder, he filled a bag with food items, then dropped bag and bedroll on the floor beside Benjamin. Once again, Jason studied him intently, this time making a decision. He moved back to his chair and beckoned Benjamin to remain seated.

"I do have an idea."

Surprised, Benjamin waited expectantly while Jason fell deep into thought for some moments.

"I have to leave here," he said at last.

"What!" Benjamin exclaimed, astonished. "Leave! To go where?"

"I must tell them about the problems with cloning, before it's too late. You're right about that. If I stay, they'll punish me then force me to research a solution. If I leave, I'll still make sure they know, but no one will be here with the necessary expertise. The Family's ambitions for themselves and other exotic developments will no longer be viable. Even basic clone production will have no credibility, although the Family will continue with it for the combat force, to expand domination from their base in China. Anyway, the combat force is good if used to maintain balance against the Germans, who undoubtedly have been developing also."

"Yes," Benjamin agreed solemnly. "And then there must be an acceptance of normal relationships and reproduction via sex. There could no longer be a world without men." He paused, trying to comprehend what Jason had in mind. "But where can you go? How can anyone survive away from here?"

A hint of a smile passed Jason's lips. "It's isolated here. The only contact with another place is by the ship going back and forth to China. Only Suchee and Tylin know what's really going on over there. So the isolation suits them and the pursuit of personal obsessions without interference. In China, factions within the large surviving population cannot be controlled the way the Family controls people here. But eventually, when they do establish domination there like here, they'll transfer to China. That's why I need to get over there. While there's still a chance I can generate a new power base and change the course of events. The Family could become isolated absolutely, with its vision in tatters. Especially if the ship doesn't come back."

Benjamin's mouth dropped open. "To China!" he responded, impressed by the initiative. "But the Family would never let you go.

And the ship must have gone already. The clones were loaded over a week ago. It won't be back for months!"

"No. Suchee was delayed in going there with her final instructions, because of what happened with Karla. The action yesterday further delayed it. But Suchee will go there tomorrow morning. The ship will leave around midday. I know the ship well. The captain and most of the crew are the same as when Bernard and I came on it. I can hide on the ship until it's well out to sea, then it will be too late. There's no communications, of course."

"Tomorrow!"

"Yes, tomorrow. I'll take Karla with me. Termination of her pregnancy would have been yesterday but for the action by the clones. Now it's planned for tomorrow afternoon, after Suchee returns to witness it. By that time, the ship will have left."

He smiled confidently. Then he gave Benjamin a penetrating look. "I'd like you to come as well. You can bring Brenda. Or better still, Kelly. I can arrange for her to sneak away from her mother. With the four of us, we'd have the beginnings of a new life in China."

Benjamin was bewildered by the sensational prospect. For an instant, he wanted to grab it hungrily. Then the dilemma struck him. Jason was making him choose. Brenda or Kelly. Not both.

"You must tell me now," Jason added. "I'll have to see Kelly by herself tonight before she goes home from the clinic."

"I can't leave Kelly behind." The words came out as if someone else was saying them. He felt sick, knowing he could not leave Brenda behind either.

"I'll arrange it," Jason confirmed, as if the choice had been made. "Tomorrow, find your way up the beach by late morning and hide against the bank close to the jetty. I'll do the rest."

Benjamin said nothing, stunned by the notion that fifteen years of hopelessness could suddenly give way to freedom. But despite what Jason expected, he would never betray Brenda. She would come with him and he would handle whatever problem arose with Kelly. He must tell Brenda about her when he returned. The task daunted him and he inwardly castigated himself for his dishonesty in failing to tell her before.

"One more thing," Jason said, as he stood.

He went to a cupboard, soon returning with pins, scissors and a roll of red cloth. He handed them to Benjamin.

"In case you're seen," he explained. "And the ship's crew only recognise red shoulder pads, not black."

Benjamin slipped out of his jacket and Family Police shirt. Soon red shoulder pads were pinned over the black ones. The shirt appeared authentic. Dressed again, he picked up the bag and bedroll. They left Jason's office and passed through the DNA lab to the small operating theatre. Both hesitated as they stood by the open rear door, silently expressing confidence in each other and what they would do tomorrow. Then Benjamin stepped onto the landing. He moved along the back wall of the Clonesseum and descended the steps to return the way he had come.

Chapter 26

Benjamin stopped abruptly, jolted from confused thoughts. He peered out from the trees. The road was deserted. Sounds of men shouting in heightened excitement were coming from beyond the Family Police double gate. He had been with Jason a long while and had no idea of the time, but it felt too early for the recreation centre to be closing.

The disturbance was escalating, the shouting becoming a constant roar as if from many angry men. Further up from the gate, the rapid movement of figures clearly indicated a violent scene running out of control. Alarmed, Benjamin eased his way out then darted across the road to dive into refuge again. At the road to the Family area, he hesitated, keeping behind a tree. The solid double gate had no guard outside.

Although alerted by the sounds of violence, his mind was still on Brenda. By now, she would be anxious for his return. Yet he felt nervous about facing her. The calculating way he had deliberately avoided informing her of Kelly challenged his own belief in himself. As if to delay getting back, he dropped the bag and bedroll behind the tree and moved closer to the gate, looking for a tree from which he could gain a view of the Family Police compound. He paused; it was a crucial moment of indecision.

Without warning, the gate opened. A pair of bright lights pierced through the gloom, catching Benjamin fully in the glare. Mesmerised by the shock of sudden exposure, he froze, as if a clammy hand had clamped him to the spot. A sinking sensation hit him in the pit of his stomach and his heart began racing. To run was futile, declaring guilt. As the lights moved towards him, he had a better idea.

He took off his jacket and tossed it behind, thankful for Jason's foresight which had given him a red-padded shirt. An electric car pulled up alongside. A Family Police officer on the passenger side lowered the window and looked up at Benjamin.

"Doesn't leave ban apply to you?" he challenged, projecting an aloof air.

Benjamin stood tensed, without a sensible answer. The light was poor, but the officer's manner and a glimpse of short, straight black hair reminded Benjamin of someone. Omar! He caught his breath in shock and stepped back a pace. Omar, failing to recognise him in the semi-dark, dismissed him with a patronising gesture. He turned to his driver and they laughed arrogantly. The car moved off down the road.

Benjamin stared after it, stunned by his first sight of Omar for many years. He had every reason to hate him for his effect on the lives of Kelly and Brenda, but he felt only a momentary pang of bitterness. Omar was merely a cog in the Family's wheel of misfortune. He wondered where they were heading. To check on the clones?

Before he had time to feel relieved and move on, he was suddenly startled again. An officer, after opening the gate, had passed through and now confronted him.

"What are you doing?" he demanded to know in a gruff voice, thrusting his face forward aggressively.

Benjamin struggled for a reply, his heart racing again. The officer hardly gave him a chance to respond.

"We're not to leave the area," he admonished. "Why are you out here?"

Benjamin's confidence lifted with the acceptance of his bogus identity. A moment of inspiration came to him. "I was in the other area, at the recreation centre," he replied, returning the officer's penetrating stare. "It got a bit violent, so I left."

The officer looked at him with scorn. "Where have you been? At the Training Centre? We don't socialise with them. You should remember that."

Benjamin said nothing, gladly accepting the rebuke. A reaffirmation of the friction between attached and unattached Family Police. The officer was enjoying the compromising circumstance he had caught Benjamin in, and the opportunity it gave him.

"They'll be interested to know what you've been doing," he gloated, with a gleam of anticipation. "We'll return inside now."

Benjamin was fearful as the officer began ushering him towards the gate. Outside it - freedom. Inside - imprisonment! Panic gripped him. He felt a desperate urge to run, but for some insane reason, he followed the officer, as if a fateful destiny was overriding his better judgement. Soon they were past the gate and the officer was closing and locking it behind them. He was trapped!

With a self-indulgent smirk on his face, the officer led Benjamin along the road, intent on causing him trouble. Many people were milling about, in surprising contrast to the previous occasion Benjamin had been here at a late hour. Family women looked authoritative but sexless in their uninspiring dress. Family Police, without exception, were wearing their red-padded shirts, as if by official decree. All seemed expectant, giving an impression of unusually significant activity in progress. No sons or daughters were in sight.

People were streaming across the road and between parked electric cars to a neatly grassed area opposite the first side road. Reaching the fringes of the crowd, the officer left Benjamin and quickly disappeared. Benjamin felt vulnerable - a stranded impostor. No one took any notice of him, everyone pressing towards a set of steps that accessed a small dais against and near the top of the fence. Two women were on the dais, observing the action inside the Family Police compound.

The crowd buzzed with anticipation, reacting to the still intense sounds of Family Police violence. Instinctively, Benjamin knew something terrible was about to happen.

"Not long now," a voice at his shoulder proclaimed.

He glanced at an officer who was regarding events with enthusiastic approval. The officer moved away, unimpressed by his failure to respond similarly.

Two Family women and the officer who had caught him outside the gate emerged, the officer's outstretched arm pointing directly at him.

"There he is!" He looked pleased with himself, enhancing his standing by reporting Benjamin's waywardness.

Benjamin felt sick as drastic consequences loomed once more. One of the women stepped forward. She was hard-looking, with cold eyes and a thin slit of a mouth that promised no compassion.

"Why were you …," she began.

"Wait," the other woman interrupted. "You're Benjamin!"

Benjamin was stunned. Kelly's mother!

They glared at each other for what seemed an eternity. Stupefied, he could only take in how old she looked. She was almost unrecognisable from the mildly attractive woman she once had been despite her unhappy, insecure nature.

After the initial shock, a sense of loathing began to grow inside him. Knowing her from early childhood gave him insight, overriding his fear. He looked piercingly into her eyes, sending a message that he knew her and what she was answerable for.

Marcia returned his look coldly. Then her eyes flicked away for the briefest of moments and Benjamin knew his message had touched something inside her. Was it a moment of guilt about Kelly? But she would never allow herself to feel responsible for the dismal sadness in her daughter, relying on possessiveness and an over-compensating aggressiveness to hide from her own inadequacies, using Family mentality as a vehicle to assert an otherwise unattainable control, over herself as much as over Kelly.

Her fleeting moment of uncertainty was small satisfaction for Benjamin. He longed to tell her of the precious time he and Kelly had spent together, a wonderful triumph of a bond fundamentally strong and good, unable to be destroyed even by the Family. And to witness her reaction when he took Kelly from her tomorrow. But the prospect suddenly conjured a horrible desperation in him. Had he lost the chance? He had to find a way out! How he detested Kelly's mother.

Marcia wrested back control. "This is the man who escaped from the lab," she stated in a steely tone, glancing at the other woman. "The one Jason wants for the Project."

"I see," the thin-lipped woman responded, her eyebrows lifting in surprise. "He must be returned to Laboratories and locked away securely this time."

With an awful feeling of dread, Benjamin realised this was the end of the line. He could not expect Jason to save him again. And after tomorrow, Jason would be gone, without him. Salvation was so close. The cruellest fate of all!

Marcia spoke to the officer, who moved away. He returned shortly after with two tough-looking officers like those Benjamin had encountered at the Clonesseum.

"Take him to Laboratories," Marcia instructed them. "Lock him in the cell and bring me the key." She paused, looking toward the dais, beyond which the sounds of violence had died away. "You must hurry while there's still time. Through the side gates."

A sinister gleam of satisfaction in her eye was of a woman without the slightest recognition for what Benjamin had meant to her daughter. The officers moved behind him and clamped hold of his arms with vice-like force. Benjamin broke out in a cold sweat as pain shot through his arms. He had no chance.

They pushed him through the crowd. No one showed them any interest. They reached almost to the clinic and began angling across the road. The ground was familiar, although it seemed an age since the night Jason had brought him through this way. His time was running out. He flung a desperate look around, a final sight of a place he expected never to see again. And evil still walked free!

As they approached the line of cars, a figure careered towards them.

"No! No! Benjami-i-in!" Kelly screamed, distressed.

She leapt at one of the officers, beating her fists against his chest in a frenzy. "Leave him alone! Leave him alone!"

The officers fell away in astonishment. Kelly flew into Benjamin's arms, crushing him to her as if to life itself. He held her, shocked by the suddenness, feeling her rigid, shaking body, sharing her agony. For an instant, a false hope flickered, then it died, barely touching the surface of all that was lost. He wanted to tell her of tomorrow, but it was only a hopeless dream. Reality was a choking flood of emotion, uniting them in aching sorrow. An impossible grasp for what they once shared.

For a few cherished moments, time stood still. No one moved. Even Marcia was motionless, paralysed by her worst fears of alternative loyalty in Kelly. For the first time, her face cracked, as if the brittle defence could no longer withstand the pressure of honest examination. Instead, her deep-seated sense of personal insecurity lay exposed as a startled look of vulnerability. But her self-doubt went unchallenged. Kelly and Benjamin were too distraught to notice, and the crucial moments passed. Harbouring a fragile fear of showing detectable weakness, Marcia snapped back to normality and seized the initiative. She rushed forward with aggressive vengefulness.

"Kelly!" she screeched. "Get away from him! Get away!"

She grabbed Kelly by the shoulder and tried to wrench her free.

"No!" Kelly screamed. "Leave us alone!"

Incensed, Marcia signalled to an officer, who stepped forward and grasped Kelly by the arms. The officers behind Benjamin clamped their vice-like grip on him again.

"No-o-o-o!" Kelly shrieked. She clung to him, frantically fighting the forces separating them. But finally, it was too much. The officer prised her arms from around Benjamin's neck and dragged her back. Kelly's legs kicked in furious hysteria as her feet lifted off the ground.

"Benjamin!" Her yell finished in another scream. Her mouth stayed open as a numbing shock took over, her eyes fixed on his, desperate to bridge the gap between them. Her clenched fists shook as she held them to her face, the curly blonde fringe of hair plastered across her forehead. Benjamin felt the full impact then, the horrifying reality of losing Kelly again, this time with devastating finality. His eyes stung, his throat was constricted and an awful hollowness gripped his stomach as if the loss was draining straight from there. He despised Kelly's mother as never before. What chance for Kelly while she was still alive?

Marcia stood by Kelly possessively, a sick look of satisfaction back on her face. "Take him," she snapped at the officers.

"Wait."

Another woman had joined the small group unnoticed, choosing the right moment to make her presence felt. All turned to stare in surprise at Suchee. She stepped forward a pace to ensure she held everyone's attention. She glared at Benjamin with a deadpan expression, but only for a moment, then fixed a steely look at Marcia.

"You and I will accompany them to Laboratories," she announced decisively. "Jason is there. We will instruct him. You will oversee the use of this man by Jason."

In the presence of officers, she was careful not to mention the Memory Storage Project by name. Marcia, always in awe of her, was mindful of an idea she had put to Suchee in private yesterday. Seemingly, it was accepted. The prospect of having an active role in the project that had fired her imagination since its conception thrilled her.

Benjamin detected the same flicker at the corner of Suchee's mouth he had noticed when she delivered her insidious performance two nights ago. Did she have a hidden agenda now as well? The reason she gave for her intervention seemed innocuous and unnecessary. Why would she allow Marcia closer to her own secret intentions? Then suddenly, another thought. Had Kelly told her mother about those intentions, as he had asked her to? If so, what had Marcia done about it? In a flash, Benjamin knew there was more going on in the stirring undercurrents.

Suchee was holding two red-padded white shirts. She handed one to Marcia. With the shirts on, they started towards a gap between the cars. Benjamin had time for one final look at a traumatised Kelly, then contact was broken as the officers shoved him forward. A hopeless despair engulfed him.

At the fence, they passed through the gate, which an officer locked behind them. Slipping by the grandstand and stage, they turned down the road. Officers were on the road in numbers. Their violent expression was over, but a tense atmosphere remained, symptomatic of their resentment, now heightened according to Jason. Suchee and Marcia ignored them as they led the others toward the recreation centre.

Suddenly, the officers behind Benjamin stopped dead in their tracks, jerking him to a halt. The two women in front had stopped also. With a shock, Benjamin saw why.

The clones!

The regimented clones were advancing up the road, led by a lone Family Police officer carrying a box. He brought the front line to attention just short of the recreation centre. Equal numbers of light and dark grey uniforms streamed up behind to form a lengthening grid as each line came to rest. They graduated oldest to youngest from front to rear, every clone from the Training Centre included. Each had the same emotionless expression, and each carried a heavy club.

Family Police near the recreation centre took fright and fled, shouting and gesticulating at each other. One ran to the centre, yelling wildly as he burst in to warn everyone inside. On the opposite side of the road, Suchee moved back from the edge to stand in the shadows of a building. Marcia followed her example. One of the officers holding Benjamin glanced at the other nervously.

"What do we do? Why don't we cross the road and get away?"

Both looked to Suchee for leadership, but she was unperturbed.

"Keep back," the other officer replied uncertainly. "They won't target us. Our shirts have the right insignia."

With a rough push, they manhandled Benjamin away from the road. Tense, Benjamin watched Suchee expectantly, realising she was a leading instigator out of those present. Why did she not wish to pass through and avert pending action while ample opportunity was there? Almost as though she wanted to remain. He had a strange feeling about her. He switched attention to the clones, all clutching their clubs, standing impassively awaiting a signal. Then he caught his breath as he stared at the officer leading them. Omar!

Omar moved to the road edge just a few metres away, placing the box at his feet. He looked at Suchee then fixed a long hard glare at Benjamin. Their eyes met, and Benjamin saw nothing he could relate to. With a smirk of contempt, Omar turned away.

Suchee went over to him. They engaged in an intense dialogue, dominated by her as she instructed him. Benjamin sensed a weird rapport between them, certain it played a part in Suchee's deliberate step-by-step actions. Her composure was unchanged as she returned to Marcia. All was still. A morbid quiet hung over the scene, as if fate had suspended time until all participants were in place.

With sickening clarity, Benjamin understood the reasons for what was to happen. The unattached Family Police were no longer of use to the Family, representing only trouble and hardly needed to control only women left in the community. Their venting of frustration had demonstrated a real fear of redundancy.

Was this the next stage? First men in the community, then unattached Family Police, then what? Attached Family Police? What about their sons? A world without men! Just as he and Jason had agreed could happen. No wonder Jason had been distant, preoccupied with a deeper awareness. He knew what the Family might do! Why else would he insist the older women would perpetrate their future through cloning without conflict with the younger ones? Unaware of the fatal drawbacks in cloning, the Family would eliminate conflict by eliminating men. But it was irreversible, and unfolding now before his eyes!

Blind panic gripped him. A critical moment in time had arrived and there was nothing he could do! Soon they would lock him away. Horrified, he tried to focus, desperate for a last chance to do something.

Suddenly, the stillness was shattered as officers began pouring from the recreation centre, yelling frantically at each other and pointing at the clones. Omar had been waiting for the right moment. He held the whistle to his lips and blew a long, shrill blast, then returned it to the box.

"Ha!" The clones responded instantly. Their disciplined lines broke and they surged forward to attack the Family Police with devastating speed and ferocity. The stream of officers exiting the centre had no hope. Panic-stricken, some tried to run, others to defend themselves, but none could match the swiftness of foot and physical power of the clones. Soon the road was a seething mass of violence, the air filled with screams of terror as the heavy clubs smashed into their targets. Officers began falling to the road surface, vanquished by the crushing blows.

Incredibly, not a hand was laid on the few whose red-padded white shirts afforded natural protection. Omar remained immobile, confident, an unassailable sentinel. Suchee and Marcia were the same, their expectations being fulfilled moment by defining moment. Benjamin, held firm by the officers, watched in disbelief as evil played its hand, altering the course of life. He was powerless to stop it.

A clone chasing an officer passed very close, giving Benjamin a vivid frontal view of the face. A horribly bizarre, empty mask of a face. Branded across the forehead was a name with the number 1 appended. But what shocked him more was the lined, craggy texture of the skin, that of a much older specimen than fourteen. A hideous manifestation of the ageing process Jason had described. It was a fleeting insight only.

The clone, with unfeeling efficiency, as if repeating a training exercise, swung the club with savage force at the screaming officer. The officer toppled to the ground, his head burst open to release a growing pool around his face.

The stark reality of it struck Benjamin to the core. Something snapped inside him. With decisive conviction, he knew he must act. No one else could. The worst scenario was happening, the consequences for men and humanity unthinkable! Fear of doing nothing stabbed through him crazily, overpowering all other fear, focussing him, tensing his body. Silently he pleaded with fate to give him an opportunity. Just one!

His eyes fixed on Omar. He was the key. As if on cue, Omar looked behind, not at him, but at Suchee. Suchee gave him an almost imperceptible nod and he strode across the few metres of ground to join her and Marcia. Then, without warning, he moved behind Marcia and grabbed her arms, pinning them behind her. Marcia shrieked.

"What are you doing?! Get away from me!"

Omar was strong. Grinning with insidious pleasure, he twisted her arms further, forcing her to her knees. Marcia squealed with pain and outrage, uncomprehending. Then Suchee had a knife in her hand. A wicked-looking weapon, its long blade curved to a sharp point. With a vile glint in her eye, she hovered over a petrified Marcia, brandishing the knife an inch from her face.

"Now you will pay for discovering my secret. I do not care how you found out. And I do not need a partner in the project, so your idea yesterday is worthless. You will tell no one because you will no longer be a threat."

A strangled plea escaped Marcia's throat, her eyes bulging, lips trembling with fear. Unmoved, Suchee grasped her by the shirt and deftly severed the red pad from one shoulder, then the other. She returned the knife to its hidden pouch behind her back and stepped away.

"No! You can't do that to me!" Marcia screamed, terror-stricken.

Omar lifted her, then shoved her out from the shadows of the building towards the road. His hate for her was obvious. Marcia stood no chance. Without the protective insignia, she barely had time to regain her balance before a clone swooped on her. The club pulverised her skull with one blow and her body flopped like a jelly to the ground. The clone landed several more decisive blows before moving off to seek another victim.

Benjamin gaped at her prone body. There lay Kelly's mother, insecure and downtrodden in early years, artificially confident later, now gone - her frailties finally winning out to cause her downfall. The irony of it - he and Kelly had unwittingly set it in train for her. He was stunned by the shocking termination of a part of his own history.

Then he saw Omar, the image of him uncommunicative as a boy, how Kelly had described him, and now - arrogant and triumphant. And the evil of Suchee, indomitable. But even more vivid was the action raging around them, officers fleeing from the centre, caught in the clones' single-minded onslaught, blood-splattered bodies strewn about.

It snapped him back to reality. Frantic to act, he re-focussed. Then he saw it. The opportunity was there, a few metres away. The officers behind him, mesmerised by the events unfolding, had loosened their hold. Benjamin leapt forward, breaking from them easily. He pounced on the unattended box, scooping it into his arms, then sprinted across the road, taking his chances with the clones. The red shoulder pads carved a path of immunity and he reached the other side without being touched.

He opened the box, grabbed the whistle and blew two blasts. All clones stood rigidly to attention. Benjamin stared at them in startled amazement. Even though he had seen it before, the effect was far more definitive than he had dared imagine. Passive compliance had replaced violent fury instantaneously.

Only the cries of traumatised Family Police survivors fleeing up the road could be heard now. An eerie stillness presided, as if time was suspended once more, the next action pending. Benjamin and, on the other side, Omar and Suchee, all stood spellbound. Then the spell broke. The aftermath unfolded swiftly, as though with prearranged inevitability. Having given the Family Police a lifeline, Benjamin turned to run. A sudden urgency gripped him as escape via the side gate behind the centre beckoned. He must deprive anyone of the whistle. Then he stopped abruptly. The hand of fate was clamping him to the spot. The task was incomplete. The means to complete it was offering itself from inside the box. A crucial moment had arrived.

As if guided by a higher command, Benjamin lifted the klaxon from the box. He pushed the button in its centre and a shrill wail rang out. In the same instant, Omar shook himself from paralysis and, with an angry shout, started across the road towards him.

"Ha!" Every clone flew into action again. But this time, it was combat with each other, light greys versus dark greys, as commanded by the instinctively recognised signal.

The clones tore into each other, knowing only one way. Mindlessly oblivious of using heavy clubs this time, not the thin rods, oldest to youngest alike embarked on another exercise, a destructive one unstoppable except by the klaxon Benjamin held.

Omar was part way across the road when they started. He reached no further. Unlucky or fated, he crossed the path of a swinging club, which struck him across the forehead. A spray of blood shot from his skull and he thudded, lifeless, to the road.

Benjamin watched his sorry end without pity. The cause of justice had been served. The two officers and Suchee, for the first time not in control, took fright and ran. They disappeared up the road. Benjamin was alone with the clones. He dropped the whistle in a pocket and, with the klaxon in his hand, headed for the gate, leaving the scene to play itself out.

He approached the Pro House. He hesitated. Compelled to witness what Jason had told him, he moved cautiously inside. The place was deserted. In the dull glow from surviving light bulbs, he saw broken tables and chairs, a sea of broken glass, dried pools of blood on the floor and splattered down walls. He bowed his head and cried for those he had known and cared about; gone, dead. He felt the pain deeply as he shuffled through the debris. In the stillness, he could almost hear the sounds of people he had gravitated to in his own desperate loneliness. Their courage in the face of despicable degradation had not been rewarded. He had followed his vow to repay them, but it was too late, there was no reward here.

Benjamin wiped the tears from his eyes, stepped back through the door and hurried away. The Family Police would surely be moving to intercept him, to regain the whistle and klaxon. He must hide. No one was in the vicinity yet. He slid down the bank to the beach. Wheeling to his right, he put distance between himself and where he had been, stopping only when well beyond the glow of the town lights. Blackness was all around. Welcoming it, he lay against the bank to rest; to think and to cry some more.

* * *

He opened his eyes at the first light of dawn. For a brief moment, he thought it had all been a ghastly dream. But the klaxon on the sand next to him was very real. With caution, he returned to town. There was no one about. The all-pervasive quiet told him something was terribly wrong.

As the morning light strengthened, he stood motionless by the open gate, shocked by what lay ahead. The bodies of clones were strewn on the ground. Not a single sign of life. He crept forward, passing the recreation centre, picking his way between broken, lifeless forms. At the road, he saw the full gruesome reality. Light and dark grey uniforms were littered up and down, sprawled over each other, lying in pools of blood. Nothing moved. It was a sea of mass slaughter.

Many of the clones still gripped their heavy, bloodstained clubs, slain while in the throes of violent combat. Interspersed amongst them, the white shirts of Family Police officers stood out, a legacy of the clones' first action.

A lone shirt had red shoulder pads. Omar. Benjamin stared at his body, feeling no remorse. Another figure a few metres away caught his eye. He stood over the twisted body of Kelly's mother, her upturned face fixed in an awful grimace. He felt nothing for her, no hate, only a sense that fate had dealt its own justice in the end.

He turned away and began weaving along the road, awestruck by the enormity of the massacre. He looked up quickly, fearful, as a movement caught his eye. Two blood-splattered light grey clones were staggering towards him, their knees buckling, near collapse. Yet with unrelenting single-mindedness, they were trying to swing their clubs at bodies. Despite how pathetically inept the effort was, however, their feeble blows were still aimed at dark grey uniforms. Programmed machines switched on by a signal and yet to be switched off. But only two of them.

Why had no one found other means to stop them? Then he realised he still had the means. He held up the klaxon and sounded it, twice. With a whimpering cry of "Ha", the two clones dropped their clubs and tried to stand to attention. They wobbled weakly, their haggard, ageing faces pointed straight ahead. Benjamin swung his arm in a wide sweep. Freed at last, they crumpled to the ground.

He continued on. Where were the surviving unattached Family Police? Many had not been attending the recreation centre, others had been lucky, the whistle having sounded in time to save them. All around was deathly quiet. An awful feeling of dread squirmed inside him. He reached the grandstand and stage, halting abruptly to stare down at a body. Red shoulder pads. Matted straight black hair partly covered the face. The eyes, bulging and wide-open this time, were those of Suchee. Two officers, also with red pads, were lying not far from her. Benjamin gazed at each body, uncomprehending. The protective red insignia had not saved them. He knew the clones had not done it. Then he saw the gate in the fence hanging off its hinges, forcibly wrenched open. He stepped around the gate and entered the Family area. A scene unfolded that shocked him more than anything he had seen before.

Family women and Family Police officers were lying everywhere, as broken and lifeless as the clones. The silence and stillness in the air were ominous signs of further evil. As he passed between electric cars to the road, he saw it all. Slowly he moved through, passing the bloodied, twisted bodies of women, officers with red and black shoulder pads, even the children dragged from their homes. The devastating carnage, evidence of hate-driven insanity raging in a desperate battle to the bitter end, had left no one standing.

Instruments of battle were littered amongst the bodies. Inflamed beyond endurance, the unattached Family Police had brought to bear every available implement as a weapon. Axes, tools, knives, and many clubs gleaned from fallen clones. The women and attached officers had responded with equal fury. But their means had been no better, never having needed to be.

Benjamin was numb. He thought of Jason's words - in a bizarre twist, a prophecy! 'Something monumental would have to happen to unite them for that kind of action', he had said. And it had! Driven over the edge by the clones' first attack, the unattached Family Police had taken vengeance, over even the clones by engaging everyone capable of finding other means to stop them self-destructing. Benjamin felt the whistle in his pocket and looked at the klaxon in his hand. Had fate, or the forces of nature, finally run out of patience, conspiring to make it happen by giving him the means?

A terrible thought occurred to him. "Kelly," he murmured, feeling sick.

He focussed more closely on the bodies, fearful of encountering her. As he shuffled between them, stepping over pools of blood, the pain of loss again welled inside him.

He reached the intersection without finding Kelly. He paused. Opposite the side road was the open ground leading to the dais against the fence. A movement there caught his eye and he jumped in fright. A small group of Family Police officers was walking slowly towards him. Each carried a heavy club and each had black shoulder pads on his shirt. Although not approaching aggressively, they represented the murderous victors in this terrible slaughter. Benjamin, horribly aware his shirt had red pads, ran.

Down the side road he went, past more broken, bloodied bodies. They thinned out further on, conjuring a picture of people chased and cut down as they headed along a natural escape route. He was doing the same, fleeing anywhere to get away. The last building loomed up, beyond it the fence. For an instant, he felt trapped. Then he saw the open gate. He rushed towards it and through to the outside.

He stood for a moment at the spot where he and Kelly had lain together. A precious memory. He looked at the gently swaying crop fields then up and down the fenceline. No signs of life. Yet people had reached the gate and escaped. Who had the lucky ones been? Was Kelly one of them? He moved away, soon coming to the far corner of the Family area. Continuing on, he passed where the narrow road turned off, retracing the path he had taken to arrive last evening. Further along, he left the road, skirting the debris as he headed across country. The flat countryside stretched beyond sight. He saw no one.

Benjamin realised he should feel elated at having emerged victorious from the terrible evil perpetrated by the Family. He should feel satisfaction at having set the clones against each other, and the train of events that had followed, eliminating the threat to real, natural life. He should feel hope for the future, for a new start and the chance for survivors to have another try at life. Instead, he felt only an overwhelming sadness that so many people had died, so many had suffered. All due to selfish ambition. He'd search for Kelly and Jason later. If they still lived, he'd find them. Benjamin thought of the ship and remembered Jason's promise. Would they be there, waiting for him? The sun felt a little warmer as he walked through the scrubby land.

He understood the irony of where he was heading - to take refuge in Bunkertown again, then re-emerge a second time, perhaps to join other survivors, perhaps to go with Jason and Karla and Kelly. But for now, there was someone he knew would be there for him. Benjamin quickened his pace.

As he left the town further behind, he wondered if people would learn more this time than from the first Re-emergence. What would the next attempt at society produce? Certainly, they would start better off in terms of materialistic development, but in human terms they were more destitute than ever. What chance did that suggest for the re-establishment of a viable society? Had the suffering been enough? Or would the same driving forces prevail? How far would another group advance before excessive ambition again overreached the tolerance of nature?

Benjamin saw a lone figure standing beside the low, twisted structure above Bunkertown. As he approached, he watched the shoulder-length hair blowing gently in the light breeze. Brenda lowered the binoculars and ran to him. Her face lit up with a broad smile as she flew into his arms.

"It's over," Benjamin murmured wearily. "It's over."

END

Vaughan Whitlock

Vaughan was born in New Zealand, attended Takapuna Grammar School and graduated with a civil engineering degree from Auckland University. During the 1970s and '80s, Vaughan worked on large dam and water supply projects, was Resident Engineer on hydroelectric construction and spent two-and-a-half years in Papua New Guinea as Chief Engineer for the National Housing Commission. In 1987 he migrated to Australia. Vaughan was part of an aid group to Swaziland in 1989, developing a water resources computer model. On return to Australia in 1992 he left civil engineering to own and run a squash centre in Mackay, Queensland with his wife, Bernadetha. In 2006 they moved to Brisbane, running management rights unit and townhouse complexes until 2018.

Now semi-retired, Vaughan has drawn on his experience in developing countries and indulged his love for writing to present his unique novel *Human Stock*.

In a bleak, dry world unable to recover from total war 20 years before, a crazed megalomaniac uses his computer genius to control an army of indestructible combat machines and lord power over surviving communities. In southern China, an ambitious research doctor studies the human brain. The clash of technologies drives Artificial Intelligence across the threshold, and the machines take over. One man, attaining special powers of insight from a near-death experience and motivated within a euphoric but abuse-founded love triangle, leads a small resistance group. Can he succeed? What does he ultimately discover!?

Vaughan Whitlock in his latest book Consequences challenges the political climate on a path of revolutionary change versus corrupt sameness, and the reader on social issues such as discrimination, political correctness, equality, privacy. This book is an exciting read for those who love to look over the horizon at profound consequences.

www.ingramcontent.com/pod-product-compliance
Lightning Source LLC
Chambersburg PA
CBHW072002180726

48291CB00002BA/317